THE
AWAKENING
FIRE

THE

AWAKENING

FIRE

CASSIDY FALINE

THE AWAKENING FIRE

Cover design: Jeffbrown Graphics
Illustrations: www.shutterstock.com
Editing: Enchanted Ink Publishing
Book Design and Typesetting: Enchanted Ink Publishing

ISBN: 978-1-958852-01-9 (E-book)
ISBN: 978-1-958852-00-2 (Paperback)
ISBN: 978-1-958852-02-6 (Hardcover)

Printed in the United States of America

Dedicated to my dear sister, Rachel.

May you always keep writing.

1

THE MEETING

AIRSHIPS FLOATED ABOVE the shining steel city like giant bloated fish. Hieronymus Purvis stretched out his hands to touch the vision. This was it. This was what he had been looking for. The city stretched out before him, farther than he could see, fading away to blue and gray at the edges. Hiero felt the wind lifting up behind him, pushing him gently toward the edge. Hiero took another small step closer. He couldn't rush down the mountain into the city, even though every fiber in his body ached to be there. If he got too close, he knew the vision would disappear.

The wind pushed at him again, more insistently, and Hiero stepped back from the edge. He knew it wasn't real. He could feel the assuring stiffness of his mattress against his back, even with the image still lingering in front of him. He sighed and forced himself to close his eyes. If he kept breathing in this mirage, he would only be more discontent during the day.

The feeling of weightlessness faded from his limbs slowly. His eyes opened, and he was in his bedroom. Gray light cut through the threadbare curtain over the one window.

So, it was morning then. How disappointing.

Hiero rolled over and grabbed the book that still rested beside his head, thumbing it open to the pages he had been reading the night before. He had to squint to read in the dim light.

"The dead hulls of the ships stuck out of the ground below us at abnormal angles, their connecting cloth having rotted away hundreds of years ago. The great steel spires could still be seen from the wall's edge, eliciting simultaneous worship and terror from my men."

Hiero's voice was low and reverent. He shut the book with a satisfying snap and a deep sigh. If given the chance—and enough candles—he could've read about the Ancients all night. That vision of the perfect society still danced before his eyes.

Hiero wanted to walk the land of waste on the other side of the Adamantine Wall, to see what was left of the old land. Nobody had been over the wall to explore the old cities since humanity had fled them about eight hundred years ago. Even the writer of this book, a famous Jasberanian noble, had not gone more than a mile out of sight of the wall before his men had grown afraid, forcing him to turn back.

Hiero threw his covers to one side of the bed and stepped out on the bare wood floor. It was nearing the end of summer, and Hiero was glad that the heat had lasted. The floorboards felt comfortable under his feet. He stepped up to the far wall of his bedroom, where two bookshelves were filled with so many books that their shelves sagged from the weight. The book in his hand slid easily into its place, and Hiero lifted a smaller leather-bound volume from the top of a stack of books beside him on the floor. This book was not machine-bound like the many others that Hiero owned. This book had been sewn by hand.

In Hiero's mind, there was only one way to achieve that perfect society: humanity needed to return to the Ancients' laws. Hiero thumbed the book open to the front page, stepped closer to his window, and prepared himself for the recitation. He closed his eyes and held his breath, stifling the yawn that threatened to break out.

"There is to be no murder. Man is not to raise his hand against another man. There is to be no war. Man is not to raise funds or armies to attack other men. There is to be no strife. Man is to elect his leaders without intimidation or coercion. There is to be no classism. Man is to be judged on his merits alone and not on the circumstances of his birth. . ."

Hiero kept reciting, but his mind wandered. The Ancients' laws were considered absolute, not just by those who tried to observe them today, but by those who'd lived under them over eight hundred years ago, in the time of the Ancients. It was said that in those days, the smallest infraction of the law would earn the penalty of death. Scoffers called the Ancients' law the Law of Blood, and they called the Ancients tyrants.

"There is to be no filth. Man is to wash himself daily and dispose of his filth outside of city limits, away from supplies of water and food. There is to be no thievery—"

Hiero's voice failed him. He breathed out. He swallowed, but he couldn't continue. He glanced down at his hands. They shook so badly he couldn't read the page. A fat, heavy tear rolled off his chin, splashing onto his bare foot. He needed the Ancients' law to be enforced today. He needed those who stole and those who judged to be dealt with now.

Tap, tap, tap.

"Hiero? Are you awake?"

The voice was soft, but it jerked Hiero out of his thoughts. Quickly, he closed the book, placing it back on top of the stack.

"I'm awake, yes! Just a moment." Hiero shut his eyes just a moment more, breathing out a quick prayer for protection and peace in the day to come. Then he crossed the room and pulled his door open.

Joanna stood outside, leaning over the table in the common room. A large carrying basket was set up beside her. The common room had a high ceiling, where one could see the dark ebony rafters in stark contrast to the whitewashed walls. A table and several comfortable chairs were all the decorations this room held. Joanna whirled around at the sound of the door.

"Ah, Hiero! I'm sorry for waking you, but I have to go. Do you remember Felan, the baker? Something happened to his family. I don't know the details yet."

If one did not know the two of them very well, one might easily have assumed that Hiero and Joanna were mother and son. She was a middle-aged woman with the same blue eyes and orange-red hair. Hiero had never been able to locate his real mother, the prostitute who had brought him into the world. He had searched the city of Reta for his mother, but to no avail. Finding his mother didn't appeal to him anymore. He had bigger ambitions.

Hiero had no problem with the city folk thinking that Joanna was his mother. It kept them from asking any more serious questions.

Hiero rubbed his eyes. "It's not even the sixth hour yet! What could have happened?"

Joanna looked pained. "Fritz sent me a message. It's the city guard."

Hiero's warm, happy sleepiness evaporated like a summer cloud. Felan wasn't just a baker; he was a calligrapher, one of the few they had left. He stumbled the rest of the way out of his room and put his hand down on Joanna's basket before she could pick it up.

"You can't go! They'll take you too!"

Joanna's right eyebrow rose dramatically, and she glared up at him. He towered over her by a foot and a half, yet Joanna's look always made him feel small.

"Hiero, they won't know who I am. Felan knows to hide all his manuscripts in the rag bag if anything happens." She fastened a shawl over her hair and under her chin and tossed the excess cloth over her shoulder. The color was a pale blue brightened with an interspersing of white threads. She grabbed the handles on her basket and gave them a yank. "And I'm the rag lady."

Hiero relinquished the basket. She would never listen to him, and she had a plan. That was better than nothing. "Ancients be with you," he whispered.

"They are with me, Hiero. Always." She slung the handles over her shoulders and jumped, settling the basket on her back. "If I'm not back before you leave, please lock the back door. Not that anyone would try to come in, but just to take the weight off my mind."

Hiero nodded. "Of course."

Joanna gave him one last smile before slipping down the stairs and out of sight. He heard the door to the outside open, the sound of early morning winds, and then it closed. The house was still and quiet behind her.

Hiero vocalized a deep sigh to cut through the silence. If Felan had been arrested for worshiping the Ancients, it meant that the city guard had some way of knowing who they were. The thought was understandably terrifying.

Hiero's mind kept whirring—too full to get back into his recitation, too full to spend time reading. He retreated to a wooden bar suspended across the rafters and pulled his chin up over the bar again and again until every muscle in his arms and back burned. His chest heaved from the exertion.

It wasn't just the Ancient worshipers who had to fear in the city of Reta. Hiero didn't have a personal hatred for Lord Reta, but he knew many who did. Lord Reta, the current reigning monarch, had alienated many different groups of people in his quest to subjugate the country under his rule.

Lord Reta had made it clear that any escaped criminals who made their way to the capital would be sent back. Lord Reta had allowed the borders of the city's slums to grow, to the detriment of decent families below the city. He did not enforce any particular discipline in his city guard, allowing for numerous abuses on the common people in the city. Lord Reta had gutted funding for the city council. He had raised taxes on imported fish, Stentillian stone, watch parts, etc. The list could continue into infinity.

Finally, Hiero released the bar and collapsed into a chair. Lord Reta would continue to be a horrible ruler as long as he tried to remove any remaining culture of the

Ancients' laws from the people of Retall. Hiero didn't know who would make a better king because it seemed like every noble family in Retall had the same apathy toward curbing humanity's natural behavior. To the contrary, they seemed to relish their own vileness. Not even Lord Teris, the most lawful of them all, really believed that the Ancients were still worthy of worship. Hiero growled. It made him so angry.

He needed to get ready for work. The blacksmith would be expecting him to come in before the shop opened, as he did every day. It allowed Hiero to slip away early in the afternoon for other pursuits.

Hiero washed himself from the rainwater bucket outside the back door, his skin prickling from the cold. The sun was just peeking through the alleyway between two businesses, covering the whole back side of Joanna's building in bright yellow light. He needed to hurry.

Quickly, Hiero walked from room to room, emptying each chamber pot into a small wooden barrel. This would be Joanna's task normally, but Hiero knew she'd give him an earful if he didn't take over today. He knocked on Fritz's door out of sheer habit before he entered. Fritz barely slept in his own room anymore. The bed was made, and Fritz's chamber pot was empty. Hiero shrugged. Better to check and be right than not to check and be wrong.

Hiero locked the back door as he left and set the barrel to the side, making sure the lid was on tight. The filth cart didn't make its way through their street until midday, and Hiero couldn't stand the smell when the neighbors forgot and left theirs open.

As Hiero turned and started to walk away, he heard a tapping, almost like a woodpecker. It stopped, and then it started again. Hiero craned his neck to look all the way up the house, but he didn't see anything. Woodpeckers were a menace to any building. They would peck through resin-protected wood, leaving a building open to rot or insect infestation. Hiero groaned. He'd better find the thing before it got any farther.

Sucking in his chest, he slipped into the tight alleyway on the side of the house and stared up the wall. He didn't see anything there either. Maybe the woodpecker wasn't attached to their house at all. He stared up the side of the neighbor's house, listening. The tapping came again, closer. He was on the right track. Hiero forged through the small space, headed for the front.

He squeezed out of the alleyway into the main street, blinking. The city was already stretching its limbs, preparing for a new day. Across the street, the printer had his curtains open as he cleaned fingerprints off his large front window. Farther down the street, a bookseller's front door squeaked as his young daughter swung back and forth, hanging from its handles and singing to herself. The shawl around her head had come undone, and a corner of it dragged in the street behind her.

The tapping yanked Hiero out of his distraction. He jerked his head to the left. It wasn't a bird at all. Someone stood at their front door. Hiero's brow furrowed. The visitor wore a cloak with the hood pulled over their head, and the shape underneath looked like a man. He wasn't even knocking properly, just tapping with a single knuckle like he meant to test the door's thickness.

"Hey, you!"

Hiero strode toward the door, determined to send the fellow packing. He didn't have time for this, and Joanna probably wouldn't be home for hours. She didn't need a line forming at the front door while she was away.

"The rag lady is out collecting her daily donations." Hiero started talking before he'd even reached the man. "She won't be back for a while. I suggest you move on."

The man recoiled from the sound of his voice, hunched as if he were scared. Hiero sighed. It wasn't the first time someone had reacted poorly to him. Having a solid six inches of height on every other man he met was intimidating. The man peered at him from under the hood, but Hiero couldn't make out his face.

"Did you hear me, sir? The rag lady isn't here. You're knocking at an empty building."

"Hiero?"

Hiero's grin faded. Only people who knew him well were allowed to call him Hiero.

"Who—"

"It is you! Hiero Reynard." The man reached up and lifted his hood just enough to shed some light on his face. "It's me! Gannon!"

It felt like the ground under Hiero's feet had suddenly plunged at a sharp angle. He was dizzy. The face looking up at him from under the hood was one he hadn't seen in six or seven years.

"What are you doing here? You—" Hiero's head whirled around. They stood in the open street. He couldn't think of a worse place to be right now. "You have to get out of sight. Come with me. Quickly!"

He led Gannon through the alley and inside the back door. Gannon shed his cloak immediately. He was dressed in a bright red coat with silver trim and a matching tricorn hat. Hiero shook his head.

"Gannon, are you mad? What if the wind had blown your cloak open? What if someone had caught a glimpse of your face? You'd be arrested on sight!"

Gannon didn't look the least bit apologetic for Hiero's concern. A smug smile crept across his face as he looked around the small dining and kitchen area. Finally, he met Hiero's eyes.

"Hiero, I found you, all by myself, without any help from my father."

"You're trying to prove something? Here? In the most dangerous place possible? Gannon, what is going on?"

Gannon puffed out his chest. "I've run away from school, Hiero. I've come to Theras to kill the king and take the throne."

Hiero felt his mouth hanging open, and he shut it with a snap. His hands clasped around Gannon's upper arms, and he gave him a good hard shake. "What in Isle's name are you talking about? You can't be king! The Reta family sits on the throne now!"

The fear in Hiero's voice seemed wasted on Gannon. His eyes sparkled like he'd been offered a challenge.

"Hiero, you know as well as I do that the throne belongs to the Teris family. That was the deal the nine sons of Brandon made with one another when Therys was founded. Each one of them would become a lord over their own territory, except for the eldest. Teris was to be the ruler of all the territories combined, and his capital would be Theras!" Gannon had slowly become more intense until his hands shook like he wanted to throttle the air. "Lord Reta murdered my grandfather, and Lord Reta will die for it!"

Hiero felt a headache starting to form between his eyes,

and he rubbed at it absently, knowing nothing would help. Nothing took away a headache that was firmly rooted.

"Gannon . . ." He sighed. "It's not Therys anymore, and the capital isn't Theras. It's *Reta*. We live in the country of *Retall*. The lords of Retall made that change before either of us were even born."

Gannon shook his head, and Hiero could see the anger slowly transferring from the situation to him. Gannon was unstable in a way that Hiero had never seen before. Of course, Gannon had only been a boy of fifteen or so when Hiero had seen him last, before he'd left Retall to go to school in Jasberan. What had happened in that time to make him so volatile?

"No! Don't you dare side with them, Hiero! They changed that name only two years after our throne was usurped, and our family had ruled for hundreds and hundreds of years!"

"Our family?" Hiero crossed his arms over his chest. "So, this is your father's work? What schemes has he been breathing into your head?"

Gannon glared. "He's always wanted our family back on the throne. You can't spend an hour with him and not know that."

"I agree, but Renald Teris is the one who should be here. It's his revenge. He actually saw his father die. Why are you here? And why are you angry? He's stirred you up to do his dirty work, hasn't he?"

Gannon deflated. "No." He sounded almost sullen. "You're wrong. I'm here because I want the throne. It will be mine eventually . . . somehow. Father will see to it, but I don't want to be his puppet any longer."

"Puppet?"

Gannon stumbled back a step, ripping his hat from his head and crumpling it in his hands. "It was terrible, Hiero! The letters he sent me at school made me feel like there were actual chains around my neck. He wants to marry Shelia to Lord Sita. He wants me married to some daughter of Lord Yus. I don't even know her name! He's planning to put every lord of Reta under his thumb and then force a takeover!"

Hiero felt the need to look over both his shoulders, even though there wasn't anyone else in the house. This was a dangerous conversation to be having anywhere in Retall, much less in the capital itself.

"Yes, Gannon, that's who your father is." Hiero spit out the words like they were poison. "He has a different face for every day of the week. You should know him better than that."

"What are you accusing me of? I've told you my intentions here with complete transparency! I intend to kill the king with my own hands and take back my family's throne."

"How?" Was Gannon really this pampered and naive? He couldn't just march through the palace gates and right up to the king. He'd be killed a hundred times before he ever made it inside. "Gannon, how do you, all by yourself, intend to get within sword range of the king of Retall?"

"That's why I came looking for you, Hiero. You've been living in the city this whole time! I'm sure you can help me." He leaned in, his look conspiratorial. "And just think, once I'm the king, I can order my father to let Shelia marry you. We'll both get exactly what we want!"

There was a ball lodged in the back of Hiero's throat. He couldn't even swallow. Sound rushed past his ears like a wave—so close but impossible to grasp. Hiero swung around and marched off, through the kitchen into the storefront. He needed air, and Gannon wasn't giving him any.

"Hiero? Hiero, what did I say?"

How could Gannon do this to him? What gave him the right to waltz in and try to shatter all of Hiero's well-laid plans? He didn't know how close Hiero was to getting what he wanted—without anyone else's help.

Gannon jogged after him, his arms stretched wide. "Hiero, you have to talk to me. What is it? You wanted to marry Shelia; I know you did! And I wanted to call you brother!" Gannon had to run around in front of Hiero to get him to stop walking. "I want to help you!"

Hiero glared. Yes, they all wanted to help the poor, helpless bastard. A bastard couldn't do anything to change his circumstances. A bastard wasn't allowed to rise without someone else's help. Even in Gannon's eyes, Hiero was nothing but a useless bastard. He was a dog to be ordered around as Gannon saw fit and then given a treat. Was Shelia just an object to him too?

"Gannon, get out."

"What?"

"I don't want you here. For your information, my name isn't Hiero Reynard anymore. It's Hieronymus Purvis, and I'm thriving on my own, without anyone's help. I don't want to be part of anyone's power games. Not yours, and not Renald's. Just leave."

Silence covered the room for several seconds. Finally, Hiero had the strength to look Gannon in the face again. Gannon looked shocked. He kept shaking his head, over and over.

"B-b-but, I don't have anywhere to go."

This was just another face, just like his father. It wasn't real. "Oh, the great Gannon Teris, future king of Retall, can't reach into his wide pockets and buy himself a room for one night?"

Gannon was completely deflated now. "I don't have any gold left. I couldn't bring very much with me lest I arouse suspicion in my warden. It wasn't a school so much as a prison!" Gannon's face contorted, and for a second Hiero thought he might cry.

Something resonated in Hiero, a need to reach out and comfort. Despite time and distance and everything that had happened to him, Gannon still felt like a brother. Hiero grabbed Gannon's shoulder and pulled him into a hug. After a few seconds, he pulled back.

"Gannon, you can stay here today. But no more talk of plans or thrones. Agreed?"

Gannon smiled shyly. "I am grateful."

That was more like the boy Hiero had known. He clapped Gannon on the back. "You should be safe here, provided you keep your face away from any windows." He breathed out and let all his frustration go with it. "It is nice to see you again." He smiled. "You've gotten tall!"

"Me?" Gannon chuckled. "You're the one who's doubled in height! And when did your arms become as thick as tree trunks? I don't remember that!"

Hiero shook his head. "It didn't come easy. I've been training them every day. Come see!"

They were halfway up the stairs before Hiero could no longer hold in his questions. "Gannon, is Shelia—"

"She isn't promised yet. Father is only planning the match with Lord Sita. He hasn't finalized anything."

Hiero felt the tenseness around his heart start to dissipate. "Do you have any idea how long—"

Gannon set his hand on Hiero's shoulder. "I don't. I've been locked up at school on the other side of the Middle Sea, remember? I haven't seen her myself since . . ." He sighed. "Blessed Isle, that would have been before your father died."

Hiero nodded, trudging the rest of the way up the stairs. He could feel the burning in the back of his throat, an anger he could barely control. He had to control it. He couldn't let Gannon see.

"That was the last time I saw her too. I thought—" He had to swallow to get anything through his tight throat. "I thought things would be different. Renald seemed so welcoming, and then—"

"I know I'm not my father, but I apologize on his behalf. He shouldn't have led you on like that. I don't know why he did."

Hiero frowned, collapsing into the nearest chair. Renald had treated him with respect, as long as he was useful to have around. Lord Teris had told him he had a mind for both machines and books, as well as a strength that rivaled that of almost all his men. But the moment Hiero wasn't useful anymore, Renald seemed to forget that classicism was against the Ancients' laws.

The silence felt awkward. Gannon strode around the common room like he owned it, greeting every fault in the walls with a humph.

"Do you see your half brother at all, living here? He works at the palace, does he not?"

Hiero frowned. What did Gannon know about Lamont? He didn't have the strength to talk about this right now. "He does."

Gannon's eyes narrowed. "Shelia sent me letters at school. She told me everything."

"Everything? Truly?" Hiero didn't know how he felt about that. Who else had she told? Was his misery on display to everyone at the Teris manor? Hiero shrugged. "It wouldn't matter, though, even if my half brother decided to give me back my title and land today. Renald would never give me Shelia. I'm not important enough."

Gannon had the good sense to look sheepish. "I would never do that to you, and I can tell from just these brief moments together that you still love my sister. I know you said no talk of thrones or plans, but, Hiero, I want to see the two of you married! If I were king—"

"Gannon, stop. I don't want to discuss Shelia or my brother. It's exhausting."

Hiero could hear the eighth bell tolling from the capital's council hall clock. Hiero had always been punctual. The blacksmith would most likely assume he was ill. Hiero frowned. And he couldn't leave Gannon alone in this house, not when his presence could get Hiero and the rest of its inhabitants sent straight to prison.

Hiero yanked a second chair over and set his feet on the seat, leaning back with a sigh. "Pull up a chair and tell me everything that's happened to you since we said goodbye six years ago. And don't leave a single detail out."

2

HIDDEN WORDS

JOANNA MARCHED DOWN Reta's streets like she owned them. She could not erase her fear, but she could mask it so deeply that no one else could see it. The capital guards were like rabid dogs. If one showed strength, they would slink off in defeat. But if one betrayed weakness—

Joanna shook the thought from her mind. She had faced down city guards before. There was nothing to worry about.

Felan's house, being a bakery, was a short walk away from Trader's Square, the main thoroughfare by which all merchants entered the capital. Like all establishments that served food in the city, they had to buy their ingredients weekly, if not daily. Cyro, the miller, already had his wheel turning, filling the street with the sound of heavy grinding.

Joanna shook her head. Cyro had a small mill. He probably only provided flour to a few bakers in the city.

With Felan gone, whom would Cyro sell this flour to now? From whom would the people on this street buy bread? It was madness.

Half of the street was blocked by two empty wagons, set up on their sides. Traffic seemed to spill around the area as if nothing were amiss. Joanna had no issue getting in front of the wagons without being stopped. She took a deep breath. This was where she had to step out of the crowd.

There was a city guard at each corner of the small square building and one more standing inside the front door. They were easily recognizable in their black uniforms with gold sashes. The one standing in the door was the captain. She didn't want to get into a conversation with him. He would know better.

Joanna rehearsed a few possible lines in her head as she watched the captain sigh, turn his eyes to the sky, shift from one foot to the other, and finally turn to take a few steps inside. She still hadn't decided exactly what to say. The most influential words were always impromptu. She knew what she needed to do, just exactly as she would do on a rag bag pickup that didn't involve city guards.

Joanna strode forward the moment the captain disappeared into the shadows, aiming for the small side alley she knew led to the bakery's back door. The guard lounging against that corner looked bored. He picked at a string at the bottom of his sash and barely noticed as she breezed right past him.

"Huh? Wha—hey!" Joanna kept going, head down, shoulders square, until a hand grabbed her. Joanna was spun roughly around. This city guard had the same appearance as every one of them. He was young, clean-shaven, and wore the most imperious look.

When he made out her face, his expression changed to contempt. He sighed out loud. "This building is under watch right now. No one is allowed inside." The words sounded like something he'd been forced to say too many times already today. Joanna didn't even let him finish.

"I've got to get inside! You're going to let me in!"

"What? Goodmother, don't be foolish. Come back to the street before you get yourself in real trouble."

Joanna reached out and smacked the hand that held her. "You disrespect an old woman? I told you to let me in! I have property in there that I intend to retrieve!"

The guard suddenly looked suspicious. "You don't live at this residence, do you?"

"Of course not! I'm a rag lady. I have bought and paid for a monthly bag of rags from this residence." She lowered her brows. "Maybe I should talk to your captain, let him know that the city guard is now robbing me of my livelihood too."

The young man shook his head and quickly looked over his shoulder. His voice dropped. "No, no, none of that. We don't need a scene. Show me where this bag of rags is and then be on your way."

She led the guard to the back door and opened it. Just inside the doorway was a thick sack so full that many multicolored rags spilled from its mouth. Joanna frowned. How many manuscripts were hidden at the bottom of that sack?

"Oh, well, that's not going to fit in my basket. I'll just have to take the sack with me."

"Fine, fine." The guard fidgeted nervously. "Are you even going to be able to carry it?"

Joanna chuckled. "I'm stronger than I look, boy. I'll be fine."

"Good! Go that way so no one sees you."

Joanna followed his waving down another small alley and onto an entirely different street. She jostled another guard on her way out into traffic, and he sneered at her. Joanna let out a sigh of relief. She'd done it. And she hadn't gotten arrested.

Joanna resettled the sack on her shoulder. Despite her boasting, this sack was too heavy for her to go very far, and she couldn't risk anyone watching her strangely. She ducked into the next quiet corner she saw and pulled the sack open, letting the rags spill out as she dug inside.

There they were, Felan's beautiful calligraphed pages of the Ancients' laws. They stared up at her like lost children, some half-finished, some crumpled as if they'd been tossed together quickly. Suddenly tears blinded her. His whole family— his wife, his two young daughters, his son—must've been so scared. It didn't matter if the city guard found no evidence of Ancient worship; they would find some other charge to convict them of, and within a week they would be sent north to Lord Kiad's prisons. Very few got out of the system once their names were on his ledger.

Joanna tried to breathe. She needed to move. These pages needed to get to their binder, Laise, before she looked at someone wrong and got arrested herself. She shoveled the pages into the bottom of her basket as carefully as she could and covered them with rags. Thankfully, Laise didn't live too far away.

It wasn't until midafternoon that Joanna returned home from her rounds, her back aching and her basket full. She reached for the key on her belt but didn't even get it in the lock.

Her back door was open. Joanna's heart leaped into her throat. The door was barely open, just a crack, but that meant Hiero had never locked the door. Or perhaps he had and someone had broken in. Perhaps that person was still here.

Joanna's mind scrambled for a solution. She couldn't call the city guard for help. There was too much incriminating evidence in her home to risk it. Perhaps she could run to the blacksmith's shop and retrieve Hiero. He would be able to deal with any robbers.

Joanna reached for the doorknob, trembling. Maybe the robber had long since escaped. She wouldn't know until she was inside.

Joanna pushed the door open as fast as she dared and ran inside, her eyes scanning the kitchen. No one. She was about to run into the next room when a voice made her jump in place.

"Joanna?"

"Fritz!" Joanna wanted to strangle the man as he stepped out from behind the door. He still wore his black-and-gold uniform. He must have just gotten home. "You left the door open? You know how frightening—"

"No." Fritz's voice stayed low. His deep brown eyes looked hollow and sleep-deprived. His long auburn ponytail was a mess of tangles, and his chin was shadowed by stubble. He was only about an inch taller than she was, and he was built thick from all his years working in a smithy. "I didn't. It was open when I got here. I've been waiting for someone to come down."

Joanna's breath caught in her throat. She cursed how loud she'd been just a second ago. "Do you know who?" She moved in closer. "Did you see?"

Fritz looked about as serious as she had ever seen him. He shook his head. "I haven't seen anyone. I heard them moving upstairs. There are at least two of them."

Joanna closed her mouth and her eyes. She could just make out the thump of slow footsteps upstairs. She sighed.

"Should I call the guards? With you here, we might be safe—"

"No. With the city guards around, no one is ever safe." Fritz sighed. His hand tightened around his sword hilt. "We'll go confront them. Grab a pot, a broom, anything, and block the stairs. I'll engage, and we'll try to convince them to leave peacefully."

Joanna wanted to groan. Why did Fritz always assume she wanted a part in whatever he was planning?

"Fine." She grabbed her old broom from the kitchen wall. The handle would probably crack the moment she hit anything with it, but the robbers didn't need to know that. "But if this goes wrong, I'll—"

"You'll beat me within an inch of my life, I know." Fritz smiled. "Let's not kill me three times in one day, all right?"

Joanna gave him a look as he started up the stairs in front of her. He'd need to explain that comment to her later.

Unfortunately, Joanna's stairs were squeaky, so they didn't linger on them. Fritz took the stairs two at a time, and Joanna hurried up after him. He practically jumped onto the landing, his sword drawn.

"You! Stand still! Hands where I can see them!"

Joanna reached him a moment later. The room was empty but for a single man dressed in a loud red-and-silver coat. He threw his arms out immediately.

"Whoa! Hold your sword, guard! I will not fight you."

Fritz started to circle the room, staying away from the bedroom doors. "Good to hear. You're intruding on this goodwoman's property. Where's your companion?"

The man nodded with his chin toward Hiero's bedroom door. Joanna winced. Hiero always left his copy of the Ancients' laws right out in the open. He was going to get them all in deep trouble.

The young man looked her in the eyes, and Joanna could have sworn she'd seen that face before. Besides, who had the power to walk freely in Retall wearing the colors of the Teris family? He should have already been arrested—

"I think there's been a misunderstanding, goodmother. I was invited to stay here tonight by my friend. He's just inside that room, resting."

Joanna felt like her mind was grinding away at something, something she should've remembered. His face was so familiar! Where had she seen it?

Fritz had almost made it to the man's side, but he kept the wall at his back. "And I'm sure you'll want me to go up to the door so that my back is turned. Not for a moment! You are going to walk from here to the stairs, your hands over your head, and—"

"Fritz, wait!" Joanna had found it, the memory that had eluded her. She'd been just a young girl, wading through the crowds at the king's birthday to catch a glimpse of him on his raised platform. She swallowed. Their faces were the same. "You're a Teris! You have to be!" She felt like she was looking at a ghost. "You have the exact face of the late Arran Teris."

The man's face changed from something innocent and humble to something feral. "He—" The man swallowed and grimaced. "He was my grandfather."

Fritz looked confused. "Gannon Teris? Truthfully?" He looked back and forth from Joanna to him. "We've heard so much about you."

He looked a little smug. "Yes, fame has its drawbacks. Hiero—" The Teris caught himself. "Hieronymus invited me to stay. This city isn't the safest for me."

Fritz's eyes narrowed, and Joanna could see he was thinking along the same line as she was. He frowned. "No, it isn't." It also wasn't safe for them to be near him. At any moment the city guards could come knock their door down. "Why would you choose to visit a city where the leader would like to see you and your whole family dead?"

Joanna winced. She wasn't needed here. Fritz would see to it that Hiero and his friend received a thorough tongue-lashing.

She took a step back from the common room. "Sorry, men, but I have to go. There's work to be done, and day-light is disappearing. Please excuse me." She didn't wait for Fritz to nod before she turned and went rushing down the stairs. The day was wasting, and now the Faithful were one calligrapher short of what they needed.

3

PAPER PLANS

FRITZ DIDN'T LIKE Gannon Teris from the first moment he saw him, but now that he knew he was a lordling, it all made sense. His sword hand dropped limply to his side, and he shot an obvious glare at the man.

"Well, you didn't answer my question. Why would you come here?"

Fritz felt like he knew Hiero better than anyone else, and he didn't need to ask him to know that Hiero would not have wanted to see Gannon here—or now, for that matter. Fritz shook his head. The timing was too coincidental.

Gannon straightened his spine and seemed to loom over Fritz. His arrogant smile made Fritz despise him more. "Isn't it obvious, guard?" He made the word sound like a slur. "I've come to kill the usurper and take back my grandfather's throne."

Fritz couldn't keep his eyebrow from twitching. His mouth opened and closed. "How—" His voice started too high, and he had to cough. "How is that obvious?"

Gannon looked down on Fritz, right down the end of his nose. "I'm Gannon Teris. The throne belongs to my family. I've broken into the usurper's stronghold, arrayed in the ceremonial colors of my family." He patted the saber hilt at his side. "I even carry a sword handed down from father to son for centuries. There is no better time for you to abandon loyalty to your lord and join me." His grin still looked unfriendly. "When I am king, you'll be well rewarded."

It took all of Fritz's self-control not to say something snide. "Well, that is certainly an offer I've never received before." He coughed and swallowed. "I hope you won't think me rude for stepping out, but I need to talk to Hieronymus. Good day."

Gannon's smile wavered for just a moment. "You aren't going to arrest me?"

Fritz stopped midstep. Oh, right. He was a city guard now. Gannon couldn't know that Fritz used to live here or that he was Hiero's friend.

"No, I'm off duty. Carry on. Good day."

The man looked flabbergasted. "B-but, you aren't going to join me?"

"No." Fritz's mind scrambled for something to say that wasn't rude. "Neither of those appeals to me. I'm just going to ignore your presence here. You're welcome."

"Probably the first time anyone has had the gumption to ignore you," he muttered to himself as he opened Hiero's door.

Hiero's bed was empty. Fritz shot a look to the side, and there he was, hiding in the corner, a book across his knees. He looked frustrated, his brow wrinkling as he met Fritz's eyes. Silently, he motioned him in, and Fritz shut the door.

"I met him, Gannon Teris. You never told me he was that arrogant."

Hiero sighed. "He wasn't that bad when I knew him. We were good friends." His eyes were sad. "I would even have called him a brother."

Fritz went over and sat across from him. "And now?"

Hiero shrugged. "I still care for him. And more than him, I love his sister. I would never want to hurt her family. I had to keep him safe."

"I know. Joanna will expect me to reprimand you. She will say that you are being reckless again, endangering us all."

Hiero smiled without his eyes and thrust his arms out, wrists up. "I will always be reckless. The Faithful can't hide in silence forever. Go ahead, do your worst."

Fritz shook his head. "Just fasten your sleeves down. She won't ask." There was silence for a few moments. Fritz felt the awkwardness in the air. "Look, I have good news for you. That's why I came home at all. I'm finally getting my posting."

Hiero's expression shifted immediately. "Yes? Is it as we hoped?"

"It is. I've been stationed in the palace."

Hiero laughed. He threw his head back and his arms into the air. "Praise the Ancients! We did it!" he whispered.

"We haven't done it yet, mind you. We still need to figure out—"

"Ah, yes, but now we're so close! Closer than we've ever been before! We should talk through this, plan it out!"

Fritz's stomach twisted uncomfortably. "Not here. That lordling could be listening at the door."

Hiero was already standing, offering him a hand. "Be serious, man! Gannon is trapped inside these four walls. He leaves, and he's caught. Who would he tell?"

Fritz took the offered hand. "Anyone. Anyone at all, and we would be doomed."

"Where is all this pessimism coming from?" Hiero closed his hands around Fritz's shoulders and squeezed. "Fritz, I am sworn to help you get your sisters out of bondage, and I will do it. Gannon may be an arrogant child, but I trust him. He's on my side." He gave Fritz a soft shake. "Come, let's help Joanna boil the rags. We can talk easier down there."

Fritz shuffled through the common room, with his head down. He didn't want to engage with the peacock. Hiero stopped for a moment to tell Gannon that they would be busy and that he could read his books if he so desired. The two were talking again before they even reached the bottom of the stairs.

"He may be on your side, but are you on his?" He'd muttered the question, but Hiero had good hearing.

He gave Fritz the eyebrow. "Am I on Gannon's side? What does that mean?"

They took a turn into the kitchen, where Joanna already had two enormous cauldrons filled to the brim with boiling liquid and rags. She saw them coming and vacated her post, leaving them with a stirring stick for each pot. The sound of the boiling would drown out their voices from anyone who wished to overhear.

Fritz sucked in a deep breath of the harsh steam. He missed this smell. The barracks only ever smelled like unwashed men.

"He seems to think that anyone he meets is going to just drop whatever life they have to join his cause because he is the 'rightful heir.' " Fritz gave Hiero the side-eye. "What does he believe? You told me Lord Teris claims to worship the Ancients. Is Gannon one of the Faithful?"

Hiero shook his head. "I don't know. I don't think Lord Teris worships anything, except perhaps his revenge. And Gannon used to be different. We would pray together, Shelia, Gannon, and I. He doesn't seem like the kind of person who prays anymore."

Fritz caught Hiero looking at him and stared into his pot. That was a shame. The Faithful could have used one of their own on the throne.

Hiero sighed. "You know there's an element of truth to what he says. The sons of Brandon struck the deal to keep one another satisfied. But the deal they made wasn't lawful according to the Ancients' laws. If we are going strictly by the law, Lord Reta is a murderer. He should die. But should Gannon become king in his place? No, because the Ancients wanted man to elect their rulers."

Fritz stirred his pot in silence for a few moments, fishing out the rag fibers that had come apart. "So, you won't be joining him?"

"No, though he does tempt me. It would be nice to have the king of Retall be my personal friend." Hiero shook his head again. "No, I can earn Shelia by myself. I don't need or want his help."

"We need to figure out how we're going to lure Lamont away from his protection. I'll be working in the palace, but I don't think I'll be able to convince him to just take a walk with me outside the palace gate."

Hiero's pan of fibers was starting to fill up. He jerked his chin toward the other room, and Fritz followed him, taking his own pan with him. It was quiet by comparison in the next room. A large table held at least fifty paper molds. Joanna brought her mallet down again and again on the denatured rag fibers pressed tightly in a mold.

"Set them right here. I'll get them in a moment."

"We'll take over here." Hiero picked up a mold and started to spread the fibers within. "This is harder work."

Joanna nodded without a word and ran back into the kitchen, her feet smacking the floor with the weight of each tread. Hiero waited until the sounds disappeared.

"I guess I had always assumed you would help me sneak into the palace and we could ambush him there together."

"I don't know how feasible that is either." Fritz brought his mallet down with a heavy grunt. The noise helped take away the sting that traveled up to his elbow. "There's only one entrance into and out of the palace. Someone is bound to stop you and ask who you are."

Hiero shook his head. "No, there's a way. Renald and Beni Teris were smuggled out by their nurse. Do you think she was able to carry them right out the gates? There has to be another way in and out."

"Where? How would I find it?"

Hiero shrugged. "I don't know! Start pressing wall panels, maybe?"

"Hiero!" He was being too flippant about this. If they weren't careful, they would end up in a wagon rolling north to a Kiad prison.

"Well, if you can get me inside, I can start pressing wall panels for you."

"That's not—" Fritz squeezed the bridge of his nose until the pain in his temples disappeared. He sighed.

"Hiero, we need a real plan. How can I get you inside the gates? Food supply wagon?"

"You don't think they check underneath wagons?"

"I don't know. I suppose I'll find out when I get there."

"Where in the palace did they post you?"

"Not sure. No specifics yet."

"Fritz."

Finally, he turned and looked Hiero in the eyes. Hiero smiled.

"You're getting all worked up over an issue that we don't even know will be an issue. Calm yourself. We'll figure it out, and by next week we could be on horseback riding to free your sisters."

Fritz nodded. "First your justice, and then mine. Thank you, Hiero."

Hiero grabbed Fritz's shoulder in a tight grip. "We made a vow, didn't we? I won't abandon you. Never."

Fritz had never been able to handle much physical intimacy, but Hiero exuded kindness like a sunray. There wasn't a moment that Fritz didn't trust him. He was a natural leader.

"Hiero?" Gannon had materialized in the doorway behind them. He looked back into the kitchen. "Any idea where a famished man might find some food?"

Hiero set his mallet down and turned to go. "I can find you something small, but we usually eat together once all the work is done."

Gannon walked into the room, his gaze dismissive. "What sort of work? What have you been up to these past few years?"

"It's, uh—"

"Paper!" Gannon walked right past Hiero and up to

the table. "I've never seen it made before." He looked genuinely interested for a few moments. "This is wonderful!"

Hiero shot Fritz a confused look. "Have you become a book enthusiast after all those years in Jasberan?"

"No, Hiero, don't you see? This is how I'll get into the palace!" He spun around. "Oh, you have to help me now. This is fated."

"All right." Hiero put his hands down on the table and leaned in. "I'm confused. How is paper going to get you through the palace gates?"

Gannon rested his hands on the table and leaned in too, leaving Fritz feeling for a moment like an eavesdropper. "You asked me, Hiero, how I intended to get into the palace and get near the king with no army or backup. This is your answer." He leaned in farther, like he had a magnificent secret to tell, his voice dropping to a whisper. "Rebellion. Unrest. Use this paper to spread hatred for Lord Reta across the city. Rile up the common folk to want a return of Teris rule, and then I can lead them en masse to the palace. We will beat down the gates and drag the usurper out into the daylight to face his crime!"

Gannon looked positively gleeful. He could barely control himself. Fritz shot a look at Hiero. Gannon's plan fulfilled the requirements of the Ancients' law. If the people clamored for him to be their king, that would make him elected. Hiero's face was blank.

"Gannon, that is–" He blinked. "That is a wonderful idea."

"Then you'll join me? You and your companions?"

Hiero glanced over. Fritz narrowed his eyes. He had better not think he was okay with this.

"Actually, Gannon, give us some time to talk it over.

We'll have dinner together, and I can give you an answer then."

"Of course!" Gannon's eyes were bright. He clearly believed that Hiero would agree. He turned and sauntered into the kitchen, chin high.

Fritz gave Hiero a dangerous look. "I won't—"

"I know. Neither would I, if I could think of a better idea. Gannon's idea is perfect, Fritz! The Faithful in Reta would certainly want to see Lord Reta pay for his crimes, and Lord Reta has enough animosity against him that I can see the common people siding with us. This is how we'll get inside the palace gates! This is how we'll get to Lamont!"

Fritz frowned. "He'll kill the king. The whole country will be on high alert. What if we can't get to my sisters after that?"

"That's not a known issue. We don't know what the fallout will look like. It could be a very peaceful transition. Fritz"—Hiero leaned forward and grabbed his arm—"think about it. Not only can I take revenge on my half brother freely, but by helping Gannon take his family's revenge, I indebt the new rulership to us. Renald will owe us respect."

Fritz crossed his arms over his chest. "I don't want anything to do with these lordly families. They have caused us nothing but trouble. Hiero, we should find our own way. It's as you told me before: they'll never see you as anything more than a bastard dog to be ordered around." He swallowed. "And I'll never be anything more than a workhorse."

"Maybe things can change." Hiero's eyes were fixed on the floor. "Perhaps that is wishful thinking, but perhaps not. I want to believe that change is possible." He sighed. "And I think Gannon can be convinced to allow worshiping of the Ancients again. We could do a lot of good for a lot of people."

Fritz didn't like the way this conversation was going. Soon he'd have to agree with Hiero, and that he did not want to do. "And what of my sisters then? If you stay here to advise the new king, when will we free them?"

"Fritz, you are imagining a situation that does not exist. Gannon would still have to go to the lords' council and be recognized as king before he could start to rule!" The upset on his face vanished suddenly. "Sorry, I just realized you wouldn't know anything about the process. The point is that there would be a gap of time right after Lord Reta's death where we can steal two horses from the palace stable and go wherever we need to go. Is that not a good plan?"

Fritz chewed the inside of his lip. If he said no, Hiero would be upset, but he wouldn't go against him. They were in this together. Slowly, Fritz forced himself to smile.

"It's a good plan. With this plan, I might even see my sisters before the month ends."

Hiero's face betrayed his relief. He threw both arms around Fritz in a bear hug. "Yes! Think like that."

Fritz closed his eyes. The faces of his sisters, Seran and Leah, were still clear in his memory, even after all these years. He had been a young man when they were taken, and now he was older than any of the guard recruits that had joined with him. He was older than Hiero, older than many of his officers. His sisters would be changed, but he didn't want to think about that now.

He melted into Hiero's arms and let himself believe for just a moment that he would soon see their faces just as they'd been, with youth still in their cheeks and innocence in their eyes.

4

LONELY NIGHTS

GANNON STOOD IN front of the monstrosity of wheels, rollers, and gears and swallowed nervously. The thing was alive. Bits and pieces moved inside it, and the corrugated metal stamp directly in front of him came down with a thunk. Gannon's heart jumped. This would be impossible.

"Stop standing there gawking, lordling. The printer only gave us until the morning to get this done." That city guard was still hanging around, throwing him dirty looks. He strode over and stuck his hand into the machine, cranking until the stamp was in its previous position. "Am I going to have to do it for you every time?"

"Did it work?" Hiero came around the edge of the machine with a crank in his hand. "Ah, see, just like last time!" He whistled. "Look at that, Gannon!" He grabbed the edge of the paper and yanked it out, lifting it up. "See how each letter is distinct? That's how much ink should be used!"

"Except he's not the one who did it. He's done nothing but stand here while I do everything for him."

"Fritz, please." Hiero's positivity evaporated. "Gannon, what's wrong?"

Gannon felt surly. Why did they need him to do anything, especially with something so dangerous? "I'm really not good with machines, Hiero. Aren't you afraid of being smashed?"

Hiero shrugged. "It isn't likely to happen if you understand how things work." He gave Fritz a smack on the arm. "You take over, and I'll try to get him acclimated."

Hiero grabbed Gannon's arm and led him to the middle of the printer. "There is no reason for you to ever touch this area unless you are cleaning or repairing. The gears here can hurt you." He moved to the back of the machine. "The only things you need to keep track of here are the release lever and the back crank, which should fit in here and crank the stamp back up. It doesn't work back here, so we have to do it manually in the front." Hiero shrugged. "Ferrold doesn't have the money to get this thing fully repaired, so we do what we have to." He slapped his hands on his breeches. "It's hard, dirty work, Gannon, but we can get what we need done by morning if we try."

The stamp came down with a heavy thud, and Gannon's heart leaped into his throat. It wasn't natural for something not alive to move so. It made him uneasy. Hiero chuckled when Gannon grimaced at him.

"It isn't as though being dirty will kill you. Come on!" He rubbed his hands together and pulled him back to the front of the machine. Gannon sighed. Now there were black fingerprints on his shirt. Fritz saw them coming and moved aside, still giving Gannon a look. That was something he'd have to deal with the moment he became king. Couldn't let an attitude like that remain unpunished.

Hiero barely seemed to notice the tension between the two of them. "You already know that all the work happens up here, so let's go through it. Once the stamp falls, you crank it up with this. Click this to release the paper, then pull it to the edge like so, and click it back." The paper sheet instantly separated from the roll. "Now the press is set for the next printing. You take this thing"—he pulled a stick wrapped in ink-soaked bunting from a pan beneath the paper—"and you rub the ink into the entire stamp. All that is left is to pull the lever and begin all over again."

The stamp fell again with a heavy thud. Gannon felt ill. He could just imagine his hand getting trapped in there and crushed to pieces. Hiero clipped the sheet off and held it out to Fritz, but Gannon snagged it in midair.

"Now why should I be the one dripping in ink while he sets the leaflets out to dry? I'll do his job."

Hiero looked back and forth between the two of them and sighed. He finally looked defeated. "Fine with me. Fritz?"

"Let's just get to work already. I have to report to the palace before dawn."

Gannon skimmed the paper between his fingers. "A treatise on the need for Lord Reta's crime to face justice? This is well written, Hiero. You have a talent." He cracked a grin. "How would you like a position in my court?"

Hiero shook his head as he walked to the back of the machine. Gannon crossed the room and laid the sheet down on the table. Hiero had to raise his voice to be heard over the stamp falling. "If everything goes as planned, Gannon, I plan to be a sir!"

The stamp came down, and Fritz cranked it back up. Gannon took the paper from his hands and walked it back to the table. "Do you think your half brother will give up his inheritance so easily?"

Hiero glanced around the edge of the machine. He looked upset. "I don't intend to give him the choice."

Gannon ignored the rising tension in the air. "There's no need to get upset, Hiero. I have no issue with you taking revenge. If I am receiving my satisfaction, so should you."

Hiero sighed loudly. "It was an idiotic situation. I intend to have what was mine. And I'm prepared to do quite a few things to get it."

Gannon turned to set the paper down, only to find an imprint of his thumb in the top line of text. He growled. "Personally, I've resigned myself to killing. Lord Reta needs to die, or my family will never walk freely again." He paused for a moment. "I don't know if that's a good thing or a very bad one."

Hiero gave him a curious look, but Gannon ignored it. How much remorse could he possibly feel after avenging his grandfather's murder? He assured himself he would regret nothing.

Time passed, and the papers Gannon set out on the table turned into stacks. Gannon's hands were sticky and gray with ink he hadn't intended to pick up. The world outside was brightening. The stamp came down one last time, and even Hiero looked relieved. He wiped his arm across his forehead. "Last one! We need to be out of here before Ferrold gets up to work."

Gannon grimaced at his hands. "I need to wash up."

No one seemed to hear him. Fritz had deep dark circles under his eyes. His hands were stained fully back, with tendrils creeping up his arms. He wiped his hands on his handkerchief and grimaced. "Sorry, but I can't stay to help clean up. I need to eat before I leave. I don't know how well they will feed me at the palace."

Hiero nodded. "Of course, go! We'll be all right here." He lifted the type cast out of the printer and then stopped. "Wait, Fritz, take Gannon back to the house with you."

Gannon shook his head. "What?"

"You need to get back inside before the sun comes up and people are able to recognize you. Sleep in my bed. I know how Ferrold likes all his letters cleaned, and I'm the one who is distributing the leaflets. You should get your rest."

Gannon followed Fritz back to the house and collapsed into Hiero's bed, his boots in the corner of the room. His body ached from sleeping in hard beds, and his head ached from little sleep, but it was a good ache. It felt good to be out from under his father's thumb. It felt good to be this close to avenging his family. Gannon rolled over on his side. Hiero had looked so excited to distribute the papers. He was almost a little too excited.

Gannon wasn't an idiot. He knew that relations were strained between them. Hiero hadn't been happy to have Gannon barge back into his life. He did seem suddenly eager to see him on the throne though.

Gannon rolled back. It was Shelia for sure. Gannon smiled smugly at his powers of manipulation. He had pegged Hiero perfectly. Even that city guard, Fritz-something, had fallen right into line to get what he wanted. Gannon was surprised that the guard had joined them so easily. Perhaps there were many more discontent guards just waiting for a reason to rebel.

Gannon rolled over again. There was no denying it; he was restless. He stood and paced softly, one hand on his hip, the other over his heart. He massaged the muscle beneath his shirt, feeling his heart beat faster.

Why did he feel so anxious in this house? It felt as though he had done something wrong.

Gannon glanced at the window and strode over to it. The sunrise was a deep red. Hiero's curtains didn't block out enough light to calm Gannon down. He slumped at Hiero's desk and watched the traffic passing below the window before he felt tired enough to finally fall asleep.

The room was black as ink when Gannon woke up, wondering why he had. The door of the room creaked open, and Hiero's figure was silhouetted in the doorway.

Gannon leaped out of his chair, suddenly awake. "Hiero! You're back!"

Hiero nodded. He couldn't seem to lift his eyes from the floor. "Need to sleep. Are you using the bed?"

Gannon's back was a carnival of pain from sleeping at the desk, but he wasn't tired anymore. "No, I couldn't get comfortable. Hiero?"

Hiero grabbed the blanket from the bed and rolled up into it. Gannon swallowed. "Were you able to distribute the leaflets? What happened?"

Hiero groaned something unintelligible, and a second later he started to snore. Gannon sighed. He had to know what was going on. Where was the guard? The woman? Someone had to know what was happening.

He hurried out of the room, pulling his jacket around himself. He felt chilled to the bone after sleeping that long, and his stomach growled at him. He found the goodwoman sitting at the rag table, her hands around a bowl. Her hair was unbound, falling around her shoulders in a wave of orange.

Gannon couldn't tell if she was asleep or not. He wavered in the kitchen doorway, and the floor creaked under his boots. Her head came up, and her eyes met his. They looked red, like she'd been crying. The half second of silence was too much for Gannon. He stumbled into the room, thinking only of the possibility of food and company.

"Madam, are you well?"

Maybe she had been asleep. She certainly looked weary. She shrank away as he got closer. "No, not really."

Her tone was cold. Gannon stopped with his hands on a chair. Was she angry with him too? What was wrong with all the people in this house? He ignored her coldness and sat down.

"What ails you?"

She studied him. "Every time I look at you, it's like seeing a ghost. I feel a shudder deep in my chest."

Gannon frowned. How old was this woman? She didn't look old enough to remember his grandfather in any detail. And he wasn't going to get any food at this rate. "It wasn't my intention to scare you, goodwoman. I can go if that's what you want."

She smiled, an emotionless gesture. "No, you'll do whatever you want to, regardless of what I say."

Gannon felt his mouth hanging open. Where did she get the gall to disrespect him like that? He hadn't done anything to her!

"So, I have offended you then? Please accept my apology."

She looked down on him as though he were a child, shaking her head. "It's Hiero you should be apologizing to. He's doing this for you. All of the Faithful are risking their lives because you decided to drop in out of nowhere. Does that mean anything to you? We might all be slaughtered in our beds by the morning!"

Gannon shook his head. He couldn't get his mouth to work properly. Did that mean Hiero had been unsuccessful? What was going on out there?

The back door opening was loud enough to make them nearly jerk out of their seats. Gannon glanced over. Her eyes were as wide as his.

"It's me." The guard's voice came drifting in from the kitchen. "Is anyone yet awake?"

"We're in here, Fritz." She excelled at the whispered shout. When Gannon turned to look, Fritz was striding in. He looked almost as tired as Hiero had. His arms hung limply at his sides. He didn't give Gannon more than a glance as he walked over and gave the goodwoman a kiss on her forehead.

Gannon couldn't hold himself in any longer. "Do you have news? What's going on out there?"

Fritz's coldness had melted away with his energy. He fell into a chair. "Things are moving faster than expected. Hiero's leaflets made a lot of people angry, not just the Faithful. I don't think people really thought about what their leader had done and is doing until they saw it all written out in front of them." He yawned so wide that his jaw popped. "We had peasants standing in front of the palace gates shouting, trying to throw things through the bars." He shook his head. "This is madness."

The woman put her hand on Fritz's arm. "Do you think the guards know who distributed them? Are we safe?"

Fritz shook his head again. "If they knew who it was, they would already be here. The talk among the guards is that the king is furious. He's ready to start taking heads tomorrow."

"You're joking. Over a few thrown rocks?"

"Joanna, the man is a deviant. A murderer. He sees betrayal in his evening soup. There's no predicting how far he'll go."

Gannon's fingernails dug into the table. "Then we don't have time to sit around! Those who want a change should be marching on the palace now, before they are picked off!"

Fritz's signature glare returned. "Don't you look well rested, lordling. Did you enjoy sleeping all day?"

The house shook from a violent pounding on the front door. Gannon's head snapped up, and the goodwoman gasped. Fritz brought his hand down on her arm.

"Don't move. I'll take care of it."

Gannon's butt felt frozen to his seat. Were they looking for Hiero? What if they had come for him? Maybe someone had seen him through Hiero's window!

Fritz disappeared into the front room, and Gannon heard the bolt being drawn. "I'm opening up! One moment!"

Gannon yanked himself out of the chair. Maybe he needed to escape out the back. He didn't trust that these two wouldn't hand him over to save their own necks. He paced toward the kitchen just far enough to peek through the other doorway into the main room.

Fritz finally got the door open. "I had just taken my boots off! What is the racket for?"

Three city guards stood outside, just as grumpy as Fritz was. "There's unrest near the barracks," the senior officer stated. "They're calling every guard from every quarter. We are needed."

Fritz grumbled, "Lead the way," and pulled the door shut behind him.

Gannon fell back against the wall and took a deep breath. His heart was skipping. Unrest already? How could things be changing so fast? How long would it be before he had the throne?

He glanced over, and the goodwoman had both hands held over her mouth.

Slowly, she shook her head. "This can't be happening."

"You're speaking what I'm thinking." He tried to calm his heart. He massaged his chest to no effect. A grin covered his face from ear to ear. "The city must have been at its boiling point already! That's the only reason this is working the way it is!"

She shook her head. "Someday we will regret this. It's not the way the Ancients would have wanted it done." She sighed. "I can only hope they forgive us."

The next day passed in an orderly manner, except that Gannon felt trapped inside. He might have stood by the window all day, waiting for each news crier to walk by, but he knew how that would affect his heart. Instead, he chose to read, he paced, he lay motionless on Hiero's bed, and he finally grabbed a blank sheet of paper and sat down to write out his first official orders as king. There was nothing as terrible as waiting. Gannon berated himself, but he could not stop his impatience.

Not one of the three inhabitants of the house came home the second day. Gannon took his meal alone and finally forced himself to bed.

In the middle of the night, Gannon was flung from sleep by the sound of a bell. He leaped from the bed and pulled the window open. The news crier's voice was clear, loud, and young. He beat the bell like a gong as he marched up the street, and his words nailed Gannon to the floor.

"Hear ye! Hear ye! The palace is closed! The vile oppressor has taken refuge inside! The barracks have been burned! Hear ye! Hear ye! Tomorrow the people of Reta will petition the king for a change of governance! The people's champion, Hieronymus Purvis, will lead the way!"

Gannon looked to the south, stretching out of his window to see. It was true. The lower end of the city burned. It sounded like Hiero was in charge of the whole thing. What was he thinking, styling himself the "Champion of the People?" It made it sound like he intended to face Lord Reta. Gannon shook his head. Well, at least he hadn't been throwing Gannon's name around. He could only imagine how quickly Lord Reta would have had Father and Shelia assassinated.

Gannon covered his heart protectively. What had happened to Fritz? To Joanna? Why had they not come home?

Gannon could not sleep for the rest of the night. Every third hour a crier would pass by, updating the news. The next day passed by uneventfully. The city was frighteningly quiet. No businesses opened, no foot traffic filled the street below. Only the town criers came by, once every hour. Gannon spent the whole time by the window, wondering if it was time to join Hiero yet. Wouldn't Hiero come to retrieve him? When?

He couldn't stand the waiting. The more news he heard, the more he could not stand the waiting. Hieronymus was riding through the city. Hieronymus was overseeing the burned barracks. Hieronymus would be speaking in Trader's Square at the eighth hour of the evening.

Gannon stood up suddenly. He couldn't stay in this house anymore. He would find Hiero at his speech and join him there. He could not wait another moment.

Gannon pulled his red coat from the back of the chair and gave it a good hard shake. This was the symbol of his house. The Teris blood had run red and silver since the very first flag had been raised on Therysan shores. Looking at it, Gannon felt confident and powerful. This was his night; he could feel it. Tonight, his family would be avenged. Lord Reta would be destroyed.

Gannon slipped the coat on, feeling the fabric's thickness, experiencing its richness again. This time putting it on was different. There was meaning to its weight on his shoulders. Gannon took a deep breath and let it out. He wasn't just Gannon Teris, the grandson; he held the spirit of his father and his grandfather within him. He held the spirit of every proud Teris who had ever dared to raise his head. Gannon held all that expectation on his shoulders for just a moment. It felt good. He was ready.

Gannon still didn't feel safe walking out openly in the Teris colors. What if the king had a spy hiding among the rebels? Gannon pulled his plain brown cloak out from under Hiero's bed and secured it around himself again. The cloak was just as baggy as when he'd bought it. The edges trailed the ground like a cape. It was perfect.

Gannon locked the back door of the house behind him and looked out over the city of Reta. Reta was built on what one historian had called a "rising plateau." The southern edge of Reta flowed easily into the surrounding farmland, where the width of the city was several miles across, but as one moved north up the city, it inclined, growing sharper until one reached the palace at its pinnacle, four hundred feet above the Great Forest.

Hiero's house was not very far up Reta, and Gannon could still see the place where the city wall cut the city off from the surrounding farms. The peaked roofs shrank away from him, and the traffic on the Great Highway looked like an invasion of ants. People were leaving in droves. Those must've been the families who didn't want anything to do with the rising conflict. Gannon knew it would only take three days for the whole of Retall to know what had transpired in the city and another two weeks for the whole of Stentil and Jasberan to hear.

Trader's Square was the largest square in Reta and was located directly behind the main gate. This was the place where traders brought their carts and wagons to sell wares every day of the week. Reta was a city of thin streets, so the traders had been regulated to Trader's Square exclusively. This made the traffic in and out of the square congested during certain times of the day. But traffic to the square was more immense now than seemed normal. People were going to the square, but none were coming back.

Gannon stepped out into the street and followed the crowds until they led him into the square. There were people everywhere. He could see a few women, but the majority of the tightly packed bodies were men. Gannon felt lost and self-conscious. Where should he stand? Was there a commoner protocol for waiting? He looked for Hiero but could not find him. Slowly, more and more people pressed in until Gannon couldn't move freely anymore.

There was Hiero. He rode a horse into the square through the crowd, waving. The people shouted for him. He made it all the way into the middle of the crowd, and the people pressed in on him.

"My people!" Hiero's voice echoed in the square, and it was suddenly silent. "Today is the day our circumstances change! Today the king will hear our grievances! We will march to the palace as one, and our voices will fill this place! Will he hear us?"

The overwhelming consensus was no. Gannon looked at the faces near him. These people were ready to kill the king with their own hands. He could already see himself on the throne.

"My people!" Hiero's voice rang out again. "Why are we so angry? Why do our hearts burn? Because our king has betrayed us! He has a duty, as our leader, to provide us law and order, but we have been served with corruption! He has ignored and suppressed the laws of the Ancients to the detriment of every single one of us! The laws of the Ancients are not only good; they are just! And without them, there will be no peace! If our king will not repair the damage in his government, if he will not allow us to worship in peace, new leadership is needed!"

The cry rang out from every corner of the square, so that one could not tell where it had started, until it had become a roar. "Hiero the King! Hiero the King! Hiero the King!"

Hiero stretched out his hands. "My people—" He couldn't even be heard above the roar. He waved his hands in the air and shook his head, but no one could hear him.

Gannon had the air yanked right out of his lungs. This could be no accident. He had been betrayed.

5

BURNING VISIONS

LAMONT LET HIS eyes close for just a moment. The night and the day had been very long. He still smelled of smoke from the burning of the barracks, and his face was grim. His shoulders sagged with the weight of the water he had hurled ineffectively on the flames for hours. His neck sagged with the weight of the child that had clung to him as he rode like a madman up the city and into the safety of the palace. Both of her parents had been trapped in the barracks fire. The palace was shut now, and he, along with anyone of power in the capital, was trapped inside.

Lamont's head drooped with exhaustion and then snapped back up before he could fall over. He was still leaning against the wall. Lamont sighed, shook his head, and ran his fingers through his shaggy silver-brown hair. He needed to either sleep or wake up fully. He was wasting time in this in-between state.

Lamont's ribbon had been lost many hours ago, and his hair waved freely about his face. He ran his fingers through his hair again, smoothing it back. He needed to have it cut, but the feeling of it sliding through his fingers was addictive.

For the thousandth time that day, Lamont wondered how this could have happened and how no one had seen it coming. Weren't there signs when a town was about to go into open revolt? Lamont had no idea what those signs could have been. This was the first time he'd seen open revolt.

The king had been deathly calm throughout the entire day, barely reacting as Lamont paced holes in the carpet. His eyes bored into the same map they had been staring at for hours. Softly, Lamont pushed off from the atrium wall and went to stand beside him. The king breathed in sharply, and his eyes fluttered. He was tired too. His black robe and dark gray hair made him look older and more worn than he really was.

Lamont reached out and placed his hand on the king's shoulder. "Your Majesty, you should rest."

The king shook his head furiously. "What good will it do to sleep now? The crowd will not rest."

Lamont sighed. "They are human. They will have to."

Lord Reta shook his head, ignoring Lamont's words entirely. He ran his hand down the map, stabbing his fingers into the fist-size dark green block that represented the Great Forest. "The Teris family is behind this, Lamont. I know it!" He growled, and his fingers dug into the map, threatening to tear it. "If there were any way I could, I'd have their throats cut in the night—tonight!"

Lamont glanced down at the map. If the king was right, then a Teris would eventually show himself. As of now, the people were hailing the name of some Hieronymus Purvis, a peasant with a large set of lungs. There wasn't yet any indication of foul play by a lord.

A soft knock came at the door.

"Come," the king said without raising his head. The door opened softly, and a trio of servant girls came in carrying the evening meal, bowing their heads as they entered. Lamont pinched the bridge of his nose between his fingers. How could it already be this late? The day had flown by.

The girls shuffled across the soft golden carpet wordlessly and laid their trays on the table beside the map. Lamont nodded his thanks, but the king did not even acknowledge them. He was utterly absorbed.

"We need to get a rider out, Lamont."

Lamont looked up from the tureen lid he had just lifted. "Hmm?"

"Lord Kiad must know of this treachery!"

Lamont sighed. Lord Kiad was Reta's strongest ally and had been since the founding. It was said that during the days of Brandon's life, Reta and Kiad had been the closest of the nine brothers, but Lamont wondered if that was just a modern legend.

The door clicked shut behind the girls, and Lamont set the lid back down. "Your Majesty, Lord Kiad will know within a day. There isn't a rider in all of Retall who wouldn't want the reward he will pay for this news. They are likely racing one another to death on the Great Road right now."

Lord Reta shook his head. "It is something else that bothers me! I need to let him know that the Teris family is responsible so he can arrest them straightaway!"

"I would like it if he stabilized the city first."

The king shook his head again. "That will give them the chance to escape into Jasberan or Stentil! He has to strike them first!"

Lamont felt a ringing in the cavity behind his eyes. He needed to sleep, but first he needed to eat. He set his hand on the king's shoulder.

"Uncle, you should eat."

It was the familial address that brought Lord Reta out of his thoughts. He gave the tureen a suspicious glare. "Yes, I suppose I should."

Lamont knew that look. He set the king in his chair and carefully ladled some soup into a bowl. A sip was all it took. "It's not poisoned, Uncle."

The suspicion in the king's eyes dissipated. "Very well then. Serve me."

Lamont served the king soup and bread before he got his own. But even while he ate, the king seemed preoccupied with the map. He continued to glance over at it, almost obsessively.

Lamont swallowed before asking, "Is there something besides the Teris family that is bothering you?"

The king nodded. "Many things. Lamont, what do you think would happen if the crowds were to get into the palace?"

Lamont's eyes narrowed. "You mean through the gate?"

"Yes, let's say the gates fell."

Lamont ran his thumb across the shadow on his chin. "There would be fighting. Soldiers would die. Ultimately, they would overwhelm us. They outnumber the palace staff by almost a hundred to one."

"You don't expect the peasants to run away screaming when faced with trained soldiers?"

Lamont shook his head. "No. Perhaps if there were fewer peasants, or if we had more soldiers, but even if those at the front wished to turn around, the press of the crowd behind them would keep them moving forward. I expect soldiers and peasants would get trampled."

"And after that? What would you expect to happen?"

Lamont shrugged. "We might be captured, held in some stinking cell until Lord Kiad's forces arrive." He reached across the table. "But, my king, they will not break through the gate. It is solid iron. It has stood strong for over two hundred years! They might climb it, but they would be shot down."

The king's eyes were faraway, distracted. "I don't know why, Lamont, but all of today I have felt watched, like a hateful gaze is driving into my back. I believe the people want me dead."

Lamont's face was serious. "Have you seen—"

"No, no." The king waved the question away. "It is just a feeling, but perhaps a vision is coming. All of this is vitally important somehow."

Lamont nodded. He knew better than to take the king's feelings lightly. "You should sleep. We should both sleep. If you are too tired to understand what is coming to you, it becomes useless."

The king sighed. "I won't be able to sleep with my mind so full."

"You will sleep if you try. Eat more. The food will help."

It was not long before a soft knock came again at the door. The three girls entered with candles and lit all the lamps in preparation for sunset, taking the empty dishes with them.

Another several minutes and Lamont was alone in the atrium. The king slept in his bedchamber, the room beyond. He had fallen asleep almost the moment he'd lain down.

Lamont smiled to himself. Uncle was always the same, getting wrapped up in his work and forgetting to take care of himself. Lamont pulled his chair out from the table and sat in it. Mother had been just like that. And he hadn't been there to care for her. Lamont frowned. It was such a difficult thing for him to think about, even after all these years. He still felt guilty.

Now he was a man, but then he had been a boy. Maturity had replaced foolishness. Knowledge had replaced ignorance. Still, there was a fear, a gnawing, painful fear of losing another that he loved. Every time Lamont saw his uncle eating well and sleeping well, the fear would hide itself, but it was always there. He couldn't let anything happen to his king. He was bound to him both by blood and by love.

Lamont put his hand to his head and let his fingers play in his hair. Why was he allowing himself to get so worked up over this? The king wasn't even in danger! The crowd could beat all it wanted against the gate, but it would not get in. As long as he was here, nothing could harm the king.

Lamont slouched in his chair and closed his eyes. The food was working for him. He thought to himself that perhaps he should go find a bed, and that was when his mind succumbed to weariness, and he slept.

He did not know how long he slept. Deep inside his mind, curled up in the blackness, he heard a voice calling him. Whose voice was that? Then there was a crack like thunder that shook the palace and sent Lamont flying out of his chair, wide-awake. The king was calling his name.

Lamont's hand was on the hilt of his sword, and he

flew across the room, yanked a door to the bedchamber open, and forged inside. "My king!" he shouted.

The room was darker than it had been before. He had to have been asleep for longer than an hour, perhaps two. The light was fading, and the room was a deep purple. He couldn't make out a shape in the bed. Lamont turned back, grabbed a lamp from the atrium, and lit one of the lamps in the bedchamber.

The king lay in his bed. His eyes were open, but he was not awake. Lamont stopped dead in his tracks. The king's irises, normally the same dark brown as his, shone a brilliant bright blue as they stared right through him.

"Lamont!" The king's voice was haunting. "Lamont! Why have you betrayed me?"

Lamont released the hilt of his sword and knelt slowly, bowing his head to the king. He swallowed. "I have not betrayed you, my king. I swear."

The king did not appear to hear him and gasped in fear. "Fire! Lamont, I see the man of fire! He will wake her! No!"

Lamont jumped forward. "My king! Your Majesty, wake up!"

The king shrank away from his touch, and then his eyes cleared, returning to brown. His body slumped back onto the sheets, and he breathed.

Lamont stayed on the ground, his hand on the king's knee until he had caught his breath. The king shuddered and sat up. His clothes were drenched in sweat. His eyes met Lamont's, and he looked away.

"That was terrible."

Lamont leaned in. "Will you tell me what you saw?"

The king looked lost. "So many terrible things. I can't explain what I saw." He took a deep breath and then let it out. "Except I know for sure now that I will die."

Lamont felt his head go light and his face go hot. He laid his forehead on the king's knee, trying to fight the nausea. "It can't be true."

There was a terrible pause, and every bone in Lamont's body willed him to say that it was just an interpretation. Every vision had multiple interpretations. This one was just difficult to read.

The king's voice was low and fatherly. "Lamont, I am going to die tonight."

"No!" Lamont pulled away from the king and strode to the other side of the room, facing away from him. It couldn't be true. Just because it was a vision didn't mean that it was set in stone. It couldn't make something certain.

Lamont had a horrible thought. Slowly, he turned around. "You said that I had betrayed you. I heard you. Am I the one who kills you?"

Like a moment from a terrible story, the clouds broke suddenly, and Lamont could hear the rain as it poured on the roof. The king looked away from his gaze. "No, Lamont, no. The vision came in two pieces. In the first piece, I was still alive. I stood out in the courtyard as a man on fire walked toward me. There was no making out his face in the inferno that surrounded him. As he got closer to me, the fire licked off his body and swirled around me, killing me instantly.

"In the second part of the vision, I opened my eyes, and I flew above the city, looking down. The man was no longer on fire, and he looked like a statue carved from pure ruby. You stood at his side, and what he commanded, you did. I saw a knife flashing in your hand, a tool to kill for him. Then the man drew his sword and stabbed the ground; Reta cracked open, and it crumbled into dust." The king paused, and his face looked pained by the telling.

"You believe he is the one who will kill you?"

"I died by fire. I don't know who will kill me."

Lamont ignored that detail. The fire had come from the man; that was all he needed to know. If Lamont wanted to stop the king's death, he would need to stop the man of fire. A plan revolved in Lamont's mind. There was no such thing as fate. He had a choice, and this man of fire was still just a man.

"You say he made the city crumble?"

The king nodded. "And what lies underneath was revealed to the whole world."

The implications of that were even more terrifying to Lamont than the king's death. "What will he do with the sleeper? Did you see her? Do you have any idea?"

"I didn't see her, Lamont, but there was one more scene. I saw an Ancient girl."

Lamont's eyes narrowed. "What? Are you certain?"

"Her hair was darker than night, Lamont. She could be nothing else. The city of Reta disappeared from under me, and I flew above her. The moment my shadow covered her face, her eyes opened. They shone blue."

Lamont's face had gone stone-cold. "She has the seeing eyes."

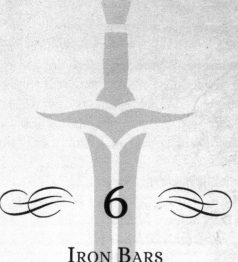

6

IRON BARS

HIERO FELT WIND rushing past his ears. For a moment, he couldn't hear, couldn't even breathe.

The people shouted his name. They wanted him as their king.

Hiero tried to shout above the crowd to tell them to stop. He waved his arms, but nothing could be heard above the din. Hiero's left leg started to quiver in the saddle. This wasn't his fault. He hadn't planned this. What would Gannon think of him? Hiero's blood froze in his veins. What would Renald think of this?

Hiero could just see the doors in front of him crashing shut. If Renald heard that Hiero was taking the throne from Gannon, Isle would have no fury like that man.

Hiero swung around in his saddle, searching the ground below him. He screamed at the first news crier he saw. "You there! Come here! Quickly!"

It was a youth, probably around sixteen summers old. The boy had his crier bell strapped to his belt. He loped forward, both arms swinging a path through the crowd. He came up to the horse, grabbed the bridle, and looked up into Hiero's face. Even in the gray light of dusk, Hiero could see the light in his eyes.

"Boy!" Hiero could barely hear himself. "Can you ring your bell? I need them to stop yelling my name!"

The boy's hand flew to the bell at his belt. "Yes, sir, but why, sir?"

Hiero felt panicked. His leg bobbed like it had a mind of its own. Every moment he delayed made him look like an opportunist.

He shook his head. "It's not my name they should be yelling! The Teris family, they are the true heirs to the throne!"

The light in the boy's eyes seemed to dim. "No, sir! The Ancients said we can choose our own rulers! We don't want no corrupt lordly houses anymore! We want you!"

The young boy's straightforwardness ripped Hiero's panic away and tossed it like a grain of dust in the wind. What was he thinking?

Hiero looked out on the crowd still shouting his name, their fists thrust into the air. For two days and a night he'd been preaching the importance of the Ancients' laws. He had reiterated over and over how powerful and just they were, how they were the only way to build and maintain a perfect society.

Yet he, in his first moment of fear, had forgotten them. Hiero swallowed on a dry throat. This was not his place to intervene. If the laws of the Ancients were to apply to all men, that included him and the Teris family.

Hiero put a hand to his head. Was this really happening?

He felt like he stood on a precipice. On one hand was the life of ignominy he had accepted all this time. On the other was some glorious, bright future he couldn't even clearly make out yet. It felt like he was standing on that cliffside in his dream again, wondering if everything in front of him would vanish if he took a step forward.

Hiero shook his head. No, none of this would vanish. These people were not grumblers and dissenters; these were true believers in the power of the Ancients. He could bring back the laws of the Ancients. There would be peace. There would be prosperity. Finally, corruption would be broken.

Hiero looked down at the boy, still holding on to his bridle, and smiled. "Thank you. I needed to hear that. Ring your bell! We will march on the palace!"

Hiero turned his horse's head toward the north. It was time. He would lead these people to the palace and give them the society they wanted. The main plan would stay the same. Fritz was inside the palace right now, doing his share.

The people's shout changed to a chant as Hiero kicked his horse forward. As they marched out of the square, they began to sing the song of the Ancients. Hiero wanted to cry. It was beautiful. Hands reached out to touch his horse's flanks as he passed by them. The song started low, but it grew as more and more caught the power of the song.

The price of war,
The plague of death,
Was Ancients' curse
Of final breath.
The sea, it carried us,

ANCIENT'S BLOOD

Time passed over us,
But we did not repent.

Faithful people!
Lift your eyes!
For future's sake,
We must rise!
Faithful people,
Take your stand!
Bring the Ancients back
To our holy land.

At the opening of the square, the people moved aside, pressing against the storefronts and housefronts as if they had practiced it, leaving Hiero a channel through which to pass. Hiero kicked his horse softly, and it trotted down the channel to the front of the procession. It felt like a parade for a conquering king.

The people moved in behind him. Hiero's throat tickled and his eyes watered as he felt the mass of people behind him, lifting him up. Hiero felt like he couldn't turn around. His spine was straight and stiff. With their eyes on him, he felt compelled to be rigid.

He walked his horse to the pace of those behind him. Every moment was its own century. As they passed houses, people came out in mass to join their number. The music was so loud now, Hiero wondered if the king could hear it all the way at the top of Reta.

The procession passed Joanna's house, and Hiero remembered Gannon. He watched the front door to see if he would emerge, but he did not. Hiero raised an eyebrow. Was Gannon asleep? He should have joined the procession. That was how Hiero had imagined it.

Hiero shook his head. There was no way Gannon could sleep through this. The man was likely rushing into his clothes at that moment and would join the procession farther back. Hiero held his leg in place to keep it from tapping. It would not matter if Gannon joined. Hiero had been chosen by the people, and Gannon alone would not tip the vote. Hiero didn't wish any ill will on him; he just didn't want to deal with him. He knew all that guilt would come rushing back the moment he saw him.

Today Hiero was the hero. Today he was important without a powerful name. The thought of what he did now made him shiver. For his whole life, he had been a problem, a mistake, a secret. He had no inherent claim, even to his father's name. But the crowd did not judge him by his manner of birth, nor by the years he had been hidden away as a ward in the Teris mansion. They judged him by his passion and his beliefs, where he could be judged without bias.

Hiero closed his eyes for just a moment and let passion fill him. He was breaking the tradition of man and renewing the ways of the Ancients. It was the Ancient way that leaders be chosen by the people, and it was man's way that gave the lords that power. He was giving it back to whom it belonged.

Hiero felt warm, a chest-filled, chin-raised warmth. He, a bastard, had done this! He had to succeed. The time for change had come.

The incline of Reta's streets increased, and the road curved to the east to make it passable for horses and carts. They were traveling up a set of ramps built around homes and shops to conserve space. The sky rumbled, and soon rain began to wash over him, quickly soaking him through.

Above the ramps stood the palace, powerful in its stillness. There was a thin square before the palace, and Hiero rode straight through it, up to the gates. The people did not slow either. There was focus in their movement.

It had taken three hours to walk the height of the city from Trader's Square. For Hiero, his ride was far from over. He rode back and forth in front of the gates twice. The guardsmen were all lined up on the other side of the metalwork, watching him intently. Hiero tried to look commanding. He was already tall, but the height of the horse increased his confidence even more. He was not a dog but a conquering king.

He rode the length of the gates two more times. Finally, he threw out his arm. "Men of Reta! Men of Retall! Men of Theras! This is your land as much as it is mine! How can I live peacefully knowing that my brothers suffer under Lord Reta, who has hidden himself away without explanation? Only a tyrant would ignore his people's cries!"

Hiero knew the pain of being ignored, of being cast aside. It filled his chest. It was his pain just as much as the people's. He had to make them see it.

Hiero met the guards' eyes one by one, sending his pain through that connection. "This is the moment you choose whether you will be men or slaves! Open these gates, join us, and embrace the future of Retall!"

It was a tense moment. Hiero couldn't tell if his plea had been heard at all. The guardsmen stood perfectly still, watching him. No one offered a challenge. No one drew his sword.

Hiero was soaked to the skin, and he shivered under his clothes. How long were they going to make him wait? The sky rumbled, once, twice. Hiero clenched his jaw to keep it from chattering.

"Guardsmen of Reta! What do you say?"

Suddenly a voice rang out over the rain and thunder.

"Hurry up, you lazy dogs! The mayors of Reta have commanded you! Open the gates!"

The guards stumbled back from the gates like they'd been stabbed. Hiero's gaze traveled the length of the courtyard. Through the haze, he could just make out the shape of a giant man at the doorway of the palace.

"Did you hear me? The mayors of Reta have chosen to surrender the palace! Let the people in!"

The courtyard was thrown into chaos. Swords were drawn on every side. Archers reached for the arrows on their backs. Every man of the city guard found himself on unsure footing. Hiero backed his horse up from the gates.

The battle was over within seconds of beginning. Men began to shout out their loyalties, and those standing for the king quickly realized they were outnumbered. The guardsmen for the mayors saw that the other side was disarmed, their weapons thrown into a large pile. A few minutes later the hinges squealed their disapproval as the palace gates creaked inward.

Hiero couldn't hold it in. A great laugh bubbled out of him. "Come, my people! The palace is ours!"

The horse's hooves seemed to ring differently once he had passed through the gate. The people moved more excitedly, and the guards cheered him on, even in the pouring rain.

Hiero rode right up to the palace steps and dismounted. Two guards opened the double doors to the palace for him, and he strode in, letting his rain-sodden cloak fall from his shoulders. He had done it! Law and order had won!

The interior of the palace was black and gold, the colors of Reta. Hiero noticed them, but he had little time to let them affect him. The man who had given the order to open the gates sidled up on his right side.

Hiero took a step back. The man had to be a foot taller than him! Hiero had never met someone inside Reta who was taller than him. He smiled and extended a hand.

"Hello, I am Hieronymus Purvis. You are the man who got the gates open for me, yes? I am grateful to have found such strong support in the palace."

The man gave Hiero a crooked grin and ignored the hand. "I'm Hollis Larkon, the king's bodyguard. The palace knew your crowd was coming. The mayors are waiting for you in the throne room."

Hiero raised an eyebrow. "The mayors of Reta are waiting for me? What do they know about me? And what of the king?"

Hollis shook his head and began to walk forward, prompting Hiero to follow him. "The king has gone missing. Escaped in the confusion, most likely. The mayors have gathered to surrender the palace to—" He shrugged. "Well, to whoever was leading that crowd. Which happens to be you."

Hiero nodded. "In the absence of their king, they would barter to save their skins? That makes sense."

Hollis stepped in front of the throne room's double doors. He still looked down at Hiero like he was a piece of fresh meat, but Hiero did not acknowledge it. The man had no reason to respect him yet. He would have to give him a reason to. A man like that would be a great asset.

"This is the throne room, my king." The title smacked of sarcasm.

Hiero felt a small victorious fire light in his breast. "Thank you, Hollis. Please announce me."

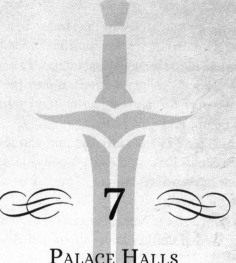

7

Palace Halls

I T WAS ALL so clear now. Of course Hiero would not join his cause when the hatred was so clear between them. Gannon spit on the ground by his feet. Accursed bastard. Father had taught him well—perhaps too well. Gannon nervously fingered his sword hilt under his cloak. Hiero had never known the true fury of a Teris, and he could not know what his declaration would cost him.

The crowd began to move. Gannon fell into pace with the others. The people around him still shouted for Hiero the King, and Gannon felt his rage building.

How could Hiero betray him? He had no claim to the throne whatsoever. Gannon's grip tightened on the hidden sword. Hiero would have to die. He had once been a brother, but now he was an enemy. The sky was heavy with clouds, and thunder punctuated the cries of the people.

Gannon had completely lost sight of Hiero. He would be at the front, but where was that? Gannon felt as though he were surrounded by every man in Reta. He pushed against the people in front of him, trying to walk faster, and the looks he received were so suspicious that he immediately fell back into step. There was no getting to Hiero in this mob.

Gannon chafed at the very thought of such a fiercely loyal crowd. It was his name they should've been shouting. It was the colors of his house that would adorn the streets once he had killed the king.

How could Gannon have forgotten the king? Of course Hiero would want to kill him himself. In the eyes of the people, that would make him their champion. Once he had crossed that edge, there would be no return.

Gannon had to get to the king first. If he could kill him, the eyes of the mob would move to him, and he could explain himself and his claim to the throne.

Or he could go home. Gannon's brow ruffled. The lords would never accept Hiero as a contender for the throne, not even if they bore only daughters. Hiero was the bastard son of a minor house, making him less than the dirt Gannon walked on. Even if Hiero did kill the king, it would mean nothing once the soldiers of a lord—any lord—stepped into Reta. Gannon could turn around right now and go home, and all of it would still be his.

Gannon's hands tightened into fists. He could not do it. He could not stomach the thought of being his father's puppet once again. He must grasp the throne for himself. He wanted to see the king's blood spill from his sword. Gannon's jaw tightened. And Hiero's blood would be next.

The crowd was winding their way up the streets of Reta, shouting Hiero's name and singing songs about the Ancients. They were such fools. Did they believe that the Ancients were truly so grand? Such was the lot of the unlearned and the ignorant, praying to their oppressors. Was there not some way that he could stamp out these dangerous beliefs? If one king could be destroyed by the Ancients' spirit, then so might another. Simply banning prayer to the Ancients was not enough. The people did not need shrines to pray. They could pray in every private house as long as they did so silently. He would need to demonize the Ancients themselves.

Gannon glanced over his shoulder. They were already so high. Through a break in the buildings, he could see the valley below Reta, a sickly gray green in the shallow light. A shiver went up his spine. His gaze darted back to the palace just as a lance of light struck across the sky and shattered against one of the towers. Gannon swallowed. Only a fool would believe that the Ancients had any power in the world now. It was simply a late summer storm, nothing more.

He pulled his cloak tighter as the wind picked up. He couldn't let his rich clothes be revealed. Was he the only one who felt this wind? The people around him marched on without reaction. The palace grew closer, more imposing, and Gannon's heart felt more uneasy. He could already see the massive black iron gates from where he stood in the crowd.

And then the crowd stopped. The front of the procession must have reached the gates. He wasn't as far behind as he had thought. This was a chance to get ahead. Gannon reached for the shoulder of the man in front of him, and a drop fell on his hand. Gannon's eyes turned upward, and a drop hit him in the eye. Quickly, he grabbed the edge of his hood and secured it tightly around his face.

Moments later, rain pelted the crowds without mercy. His heart beat urgently. He needed to catch up to Hiero. Gannon forced his way through the two men in front of him and began pushing through the crowd. The rain had a disorganizing effect on the people. They moved uneasily. A man's sudden jerk shoved his hip into Gannon, knocking him onto his hands and knees. Another man's misstep brought his heel down on Gannon's hand, and Gannon's scream was lost in the shrill cry of the black iron gates as they opened.

Gannon yanked his hand back and pulled it against his chest as he stood, holding it tight with the other. His mind shouted curses, but his mouth stayed firmly shut as he shuffled along with the rest of the crowd. It was his right hand, his sword hand. He wriggled his fingers experimentally, wincing at the pain and the stiffness. It wasn't even broken. How could he have screamed like that? If it were not for rusty hinges, nothing would have kept the whole of Reta from hearing him.

Gannon passed through the black gates and into the courtyard, barely noticing that he had. This was not his home yet. All that mattered was the king.

The courtyard allowed more freedom than the thin streets of the city, and the crowd spread out. Gannon walked faster, weaving through the new spaces toward Hiero. And there he was. Through the sheeting rain, Gannon could see a horse standing on the palace steps and Hiero dismounting and striding for the double doors of the palace as they opened for him.

Gannon pushed forward more vehemently, but now the crowd was bottlenecking at the colonnade entrance. Hiero slipped inside and disappeared.

The time seemed painfully long until Gannon stood under the colonnade and shook the water from his hair. Even though his teeth chattered, he fought the urge to pull off his dripping cloak. Someone would recognize him.

Around the palace doors was a warm puddle of light from the lamps within. Gannon pulled his cloak tighter as he stepped in. It was much warmer inside.

Gannon realized for a moment how strange this was that the whole of Reta was walking about freely in the palace, singing and shouting. How was anyone going to protect the palace's valuables? Who would take responsibility for his family's artifacts if they were stolen?

It was at that moment Gannon got a good look at the interior of the palace, and a fire filled him that he had never known before.

Everything was gone. The red carpet that Father had spoken so fondly of was gone, replaced by a deep black one with gold rimming. The busts of Teris kings stretching back to the founding had disappeared from the walls. The Teris tapestries—beautiful ageless works of art—had been blackened by torch smoke. He could still make out the designs, but they had been ruined.

Gannon looked down, and his hands were shaking. How dare he. How dare Lord Reta do this to his home. He clawed at his heart, feeling it burn. He wanted to rip the man's heart out with his bare hands. He had to get to the king before this rage burned through him and left him exhausted. Perhaps he could show his uniform just enough that the crowd would let him pass through. He could even shout, "Messenger!" and they would step aside. The king could not harm his family with the whole city against him.

Gannon ground his teeth together. But Hiero was his enemy now, and if he saw him coming, he might order him to be held.

Gannon turned to the man walking beside him. "Sir, do you have any idea where we're heading?"

The man's eyebrow arched. "Where are we going? To see the king pay for his crimes! Why else did you think we marched through the city shouting for it?"

"That isn't what he asked, Paule!" An older man on the other side of Paule elbowed him. "I think we're headed to the throne room, son. I've heard the city mayors are gathered there."

Gannon's eyes narrowed. Now he had a clue. He turned quickly and cut through the crowd behind them. He ignored the dirty looks and slipped silently into a small hallway.

It was here he paused and took a deep breath. He could breathe outside of the crowd. The hallway was in shadow, and Gannon pulled off his soaked cloak and threw it down. Light flashed off the silver and red of his coat. A Teris had finally come home.

Gannon drew his sword, testing the grip. His hand was well enough. He could beat one old man in combat. Tonight he would be the bringer of death.

He closed his eyes, pulling up images from his childhood. He knew the way to the throne room. His father had drilled the palace diagrams into his head many years ago. His eyes snapped open. If this was the second hallway, then the throne room would be down another smaller hallway to the left, then another left. Of course, Hiero would already be there; he had a straight shot to it.

But there was a second story Gannon knew of. The cleaning crew used it to get to the chandeliers. He ran down the hallway, looking for the secret door he knew would be there. He didn't mind looking frantic to a degree, running back and forth from one side to the other, pushing on the wall panels for one to click. He had to ignore the horrid black-and-gold design that now covered them.

He had just finished giving one panel a good push when he heard a slight click behind him. He turned slowly.

A servant girl stood in the open space behind a panel, one foot in and one out, staring at him with the widest eyes. Ice-blond ringlets spilled out from under a tight-fitting cap. Her face befitted a child more than someone with her mature shape. Gannon straightened and curled his fingers around the hilt of his sword.

With a cock of his head, he took a jaunty step toward her. "Were you spying?" It did not seem possible, but her eyes grew wider, and her head shook like she was shivering. Gannon cocked his head the other way and stepped again. "It sure looks like you were spying."

The girl's eyes shot to the right, toward the throne room. "Please forgive me, sir. I was cleaning."

Gannon stepped right up to her, curling his fingers around her chin. "How old are you, child?"

Her eyes darted to his face, fearful. "I am eighteen summers old, my lord."

Gannon shook his head. Older than he'd expected. "Too young to remember. Do you know what happened to me in that room just over there?"

The girl looked confused. "Were you promoted, sir?"

Gannon was amused. "You call me lord, then sir." His lips brushed the small hairs around her ear. "I am neither."

The girl clutched at her robes beneath her collarbone and at her hip. She was old enough to fear nobles who got too close. "Please, my lord, forgive me! I will not do it again!"

Gannon's grip tightened on her chin. "I told you, I am not a lord!" The girl was on the verge of tears. Gannon kept their eyes locked together. "I am your king!"

The whimpering stopped with a sudden snap. She watched him with new wide-eyed wariness. Gannon smiled. Her allegiance was so obvious it was almost funny. His fingers lost their cruel grip.

"I am the ghost of Arran Teris! I was murdered in cold blood in that throne room by the vile usurper. For thirty-two years I have wandered these halls, waiting for the moment of my revenge." His smile widened. "It is today. Today my murderer will fall!"

The girl had started to back up. Gannon grasped her arm and wrenched her to his side. She pulled back, trying to rip his fingers from her arm. "Let me go! You are mad!"

"I am not mad." Gannon's voice was flat and colorless. "Why would I release you? So that you might inform your master of a vengeful spirit haunting the palace halls?"

The girl shot him a venomous look. "Spirits cannot walk or grasp, nor can they speak!"

Gannon's smile was dour. "Then I must cause a true spiritual crisis in you." His grip tightened, and the girl whimpered in pain. "I know who you are, little whisperer, and I know your master. Your hair and your face betray you. A generation or two cannot change a Kiad from what he is, and I know the look of his little nieces. You know where the usurper is. You will tell me. Now."

The girl blinked. "I do not know where the king is hiding."

Gannon raised an eyebrow. "So, he is hiding? Curious that he did not choose to flee. Where did you say he was hiding?"

The girl gritted her teeth in frustration. "I will tell you nothing."

Gannon could not help himself. His head rolled back on his shoulders, and he laughed. "Do you think I will be

73

angry with your stubbornness, little whisperer? That I will be so enraged as to give you a swift death?" He wound an arm around her waist and pulled her in until she was pressed tight against him. "I have many hours left to find the usurper while the foolish rebels get lost in the palace's maze." He felt her shiver. "You know they won't find him, and the usurper must be certain he can't be found, or else he would have fled."

Gannon ran his other hand down her back. "You are a very well-built woman; do you know this? I wonder what young swain out in the city holds your heart." His hand pulled her with him as he stepped toward the dark doorway in the wall. "I wonder if you will cry his name in your moment."

Her arms were locked against him, and she struggled fruitlessly. "Let me go, or I'll scream!" she threatened.

Gannon's foot pushed the panel open wider, and they slipped inside. "Ah, of course you will, and bring down the swarm of rebels who also want to know exactly where the usurper is." Gannon tapped her nose with a finger. "No, I think you'll stay very, very quiet."

He let the wall click softly behind them. The room was only a few feet wide, and the steps began directly beside the door. With one arm under her knees, he laid her down on the steps. A pitiful whimper vibrated in her throat.

"No. Hush." Gannon leaned over her. "These stairs lead directly to the throne room. The sound will travel easily." He looked up the stairs. "I can hear the rumbling from here."

The light in the hallway was dim, but it glittered off a tear that slipped out the side of her eye and tumbled into her hair. Gannon could feel her heart pounding rapidly beneath him.

"Do you have anything you want to tell me?"

Her eyes snapped open, and her mouth formed a stubborn line.

"I see then." Gannon ran his fingers through the stray hairs on her forehead. "You leave me with little choice." His hand went down, down, and ran along the curve of her leg. "So, this man who holds your heart, is he handsome?" Gannon chuckled at his own question. "He cannot be more handsome than a pureblood Teris, can he?"

Her eyes closed tightly, and her mouth was shut. Gannon paused. At this rate, he wasn't going to get any information out of her. He needed her to truly dread what he could do. He lay down on top of her, splaying his limbs out to either side, and breathed slowly, his mouth beside her ear.

"You are not that kind of woman." It was a statement. He felt her breath change. "If you were, you would be living at the bottom of this rock rather than up here. What binds you to the usurper if you do not share his bed?" His words were meant to bite. "Do you know what is done to impure women in this city? Have you ever been to the slums?" She was going to cry; he could feel it. Slowly, he rubbed his chest against hers. "I'm feeling warm, little whisperer. Perhaps I will make you a child. Would you like that? A little bastard prince to take home to your lover?"

A choked sob cracked the silence. Gannon's voice changed again, from silk over knives to knives over harp strings. "Tell me," he begged. "Tell me where he is, and I will leave you. I will not touch you again."

The girl's eyes finally opened. "He is hidden in the royal bedchamber."

"Alone?"

She shook her head. "The grand general guards him."

Gannon sat up. "I have no quarrel with Reynard. Thank you, little whisperer." He found his footing and stood. "Remember me to your lover."

Minutes later, Gannon was shooting down the hallway, his eyes alight with vengeance and excitement. He had him! There was no way Hiero could reach the king before him.

8

HANDED TITLES

LAMONT'S THROAT HAD gone dry, the tickling, annoying kind of dry that made him growl deep to get it out. "I thought—" He coughed. "I thought that it wasn't possible for two with seeing eyes to be alive at the same time."

The king nodded. "It isn't possible. But my eyes saw the future. That girl is likely the one who will replace me."

Lamont felt flattened. After all the work they had done together, the gift would still find its way back to the Ancients. It was frustrating. "Can anything be done about it?"

"I don't know." The king looked as shocked as he was, but Lamont wondered how much more the king had seen that he was not willing to tell. He lowered himself into a chair. If Lamont could stop this man of fire, he could stop everything the king had seen—even this. He would kill the man of fire before he could get anywhere near his king.

Silence took over the room, and Lamont listened to the rain striking the roof. The silence was not awkward. Lamont was so wrapped up in his thoughts that he did not notice the passing of time until the king lifted his covers and stepped out onto the floor. His black robe fell to his ankles. He motioned softly with his hand.

"Lamont, come here. Kneel."

Lamont stood and stepped over to the king, kneeling at his feet. The marble was hard on his knees. He felt the king's hands on his head, running through his hair, and it was comforting. He felt just like a child again. In fact, this was exactly like the moment he had first met his uncle. He had been distracted, a little sad, and confused by the big man putting his hands on his head. He felt that way now.

The king cupped his hand under Lamont's chin and lifted his head up. The nostalgia was powerful. Lamont felt like he could cry if he let himself. The king smoothed Lamont's hair back from his face, and their eyes met. He stroked Lamont's cheekbones and studied his face.

"Lamont, you may be my nephew, but I have always thought of you as my own son. You look so much like your mother." The king's voice failed, and Lamont knew he was struggling. He felt the wrinkled hands shaking against his face.

The king's face hardened as he composed himself. "I remember hearing of your birth only hours after I took power from the Terises, and I thought to myself, it is a sign." The king's eyes were soft. "All those years ago, you were a boy. Where did the time go?" He paused again and ran his fingers across Lamont's eyebrows. "You are so similar." Then he sighed and released his face, turning away.

Lamont got to his feet, still feeling like an awkward boy who had missed the point in the adults' conversation. The king sat back on his bed with a huff.

"Will you sit with me?"

Lamont felt guilty that he even had to ask that. "Of course I will." He sat down beside him and felt the mattress conform to his frame.

The king stared silently at his hands for a while. "It is a frustrating thing having reached the end of my life and having to think hard to remember what I did with it."

Lamont bit his lip. The king truly believed that he was about to die, and he couldn't contradict him. It would be cruel to toss his feelings away with a simple, "That isn't going to happen."

"My king, if it weren't for your choice, the kingdom would still be gripped by sinister superstition, praying to the tyrants of humanity. If not for our work, the Ancients may have already returned to Retall. That is invaluable."

The king chuckled and patted Lamont's leg. "I know, I know, I've done many things, but nothing seems very important right now, does it?"

Lamont wanted to grab the king's hand and swear to him on his life that he wouldn't let him die tonight, but he couldn't. He was rooted to the bed.

"Uncle, you've said many times that my birth was a sign. A sign of what?"

The king smiled wide. "A sign that you were meant to be my heir."

Lamont's mind went blank for just a moment, and when it came back to him, he turned his body to face the king, looking him right in the eyes. "Your Majesty, you have a son."

It was amazing how quickly the king's demeanor changed, and it was not the first time Lamont had seen it happen. His eyes sparked as he glared at Lamont.

"I have told you before never to mention him to me! I do not want to talk about it!"

Lamont's face was determined. "We have to talk about it!"

The king jumped to his feet and stormed away from the bed. Lamont slapped his hands on the mattress and followed him, grabbing him by the shoulder. "If you are truly going to die tonight, we must talk about your son!"

The king jerked his shoulder away from Lamont. "I have no son!"

"You do. I remember him as a child, and I remember you sent him away. Why?"

The king did not meet Lamont's eyes. "He was not my son. I could not allow him to reign after me."

The candid way in which he spoke those words caught Lamont off guard. "The queen betrayed you? But with whom?"

The queen had died not long after the prince's disappearance, and Lamont could count on his fingers the number of times he had spoken to her. The king's eyes flashed at Lamont's words.

"No, not like that! He was my blood, I am sure of it, but—" The king glared sullenly at the wall. "He found out about our work, what we were doing with the experiments. I don't know how." The king shook his head. "He confronted me about it."

The king held out his hand. "Just a boy, just that tall, stamping his foot and waving his finger at me. I was almost proud of his spirit until he told me that he had prayed to the Ancients. He'd prayed for their return." The king gritted his teeth. "My own son! While I stood there, shocked, he lifted his voice and started praying that I would be forgiven for my crimes, right there as I watched!" The king's voice broke. "I hurled him into the wall until he was silent." He snapped his fingers. "He was gone the next day, shipped off on some boat to Jasberan. I will never see him again."

Lamont swallowed. He hadn't realized how much had happened in those few days so many years ago or why the king's demeanor had so suddenly changed. "It makes sense now. I understand. Do you not fear that the lords will try to seek him out?"

The king shook his head. "No, I had all the documents pertaining to him burned. Officially, I have no son." The king placed his hands on Lamont's shoulders. "I want you as my heir, Lamont. When I am dead, I want you to take the throne and continue the work we started. Can you promise me that you will do that?"

Lamont had so many other thoughts running through his head, but he nodded dutifully. "I will continue your work, of course."

The king pulled him into his arms and held him tightly for a moment. "Thank you, Lamont. Thank you. I can die peacefully now."

Lamont squeezed his eyes shut. He could not handle much more of this. The king speaking of his own death was painful enough, but Lamont needed space to think and process all the new information. Lamont pulled away.

"Uncle, you should sleep. I'll be guarding the door, so you have no need to fear. Just sleep."

The king's hand traveled to the clasp of his robe and reached inside, pulling out a silver strand and the ring that dangled on it. "Wait, you will need this."

"Your signet ring? But—"

"You are the heir to my family, and thus, by definition, you have a claim to the throne." Lord Reta put up a finger. "But not all the lords are going to recognize that claim. Some, like Teris, are going to try to eliminate you. Stay as far away from him as possible, and go to Lord Kiad." The king let his ring fall into Lamont's hand. "He will support your claim in my name."

Lamont was suddenly suspicious. "How long have you been planning this?"

The king smiled sadly. "Since the day I lost my son, I have been guiding you. You are the man I want on the throne." His hands rested on Lamont's shoulders again, forcing him back into the present.

Lamont pushed his frustration away and met the king's eyes.

"I know you, Lamont, and I know you don't believe that I will die. You don't believe in visions or fate, and you never have. But I don't want you to think that you can do something to save me and be caught up in my future. What is important is your survival. When the moment comes, and you will know it, I want you to surrender me." Lamont looked away from his eyes, and the king pulled his face back. "Do you understand me? I want you to leave me!"

Lamont looked into the king's eyes and blinked hard to keep the tears from welling up. "Uncle, please don't make me."

"Leave, Lamont. Go."

Lamont pulled away from the king, ran out of the bedchamber, and closed the door behind him. How could he leave his king? It wasn't just wrong; it was impossible. The gates were shut tight!

Lamont crossed the room and collapsed into a chair. The king's signet ring was hard and heavy in his hand. He opened his hand and studied it. Was he able to be king of Retall? He had never considered the possibility. Because of the context, the idea felt terrible and evil. Lamont shook his head. What was he supposed to do now?

There was a knock on the door, not the soft knock of a serving girl, but a frantic pounding. Lamont leaped out of his chair and lunged for the door, pulling his sword with one hand and holding it to the side as his hand curled around the door handle. Was it the man of fire? Was this his chance?

He yanked the door open, and there stood a city guard, breathing heavily, holding a spear with a torn and trailing flag. Lamont lowered his sword. He had almost attacked his own ally. What was wrong with him? This was the palace. He was safe. Why was he acting so afraid?

Lamont nodded to the soldier. "What is it?"

The man looked nervously over his shoulder. "May I come in? I have some news from the gates."

Lamont stepped aside. "Come in." He shut the door behind the man and sheathed his sword. "You look like you've seen a spirit, soldier. Why?"

Lamont had never seen this guard in the palace before and could only assume he was a refugee from the city barracks. The man acted terribly afraid, looking all around the room with wide eyes. His voice was hushed when he spoke. "Is the king safe? Is he here?"

Lamont's eyes narrowed. "He is safe, yes. What has happened?"

The man shook his head. "You won't believe it, General. I wouldn't even think it possible, except I saw it with my own eyes. The city guard has opened the gates to the crowd!"

Lamont's eyes went wide. "You are lying!"

The man bowed his head. "I am telling the truth, General, I swear! The people should be inside the palace by now! The palace has proclaimed its loyalty for Hieronymus Purvis!"

For the second time that night, Lamont felt flattened. The world seemed to phase in and out, and his knees buckled. Lamont grabbed hold of the table with one hand.

"What did this man look like, the leader? What did you see?"

"He was tall, General, with a strong, confident look about him. His hair looked like fire under the torchlight."

Lamont sat down hard. "It's him. He is the man of fire."

Adrenaline flooded his system, a familiar feeling, and Lamont could not keep his fingers out of his hair. He wanted to fight, but there was no one here for him to fight. Lamont couldn't just sit down while energy coursed through him. He would end up feeling sick. Slowly, he stood back up.

"The man of fire, General? What do you mean?"

Lamont shook his head. "It's not important right now. Do you know how far behind you the crowd was?"

The man shook his head. "I don't know. It is more likely that I was not followed and the people will have to search the palace for the king."

Lamont circled the table, running his fingers through his hair. "Of course, they don't know the palace. That will give us some time."

The man turned his head curiously. "What do you intend to do?"

"I'm going to try to get the king out if I can." He put up a hand. "I will only be a moment." Lamont sucked in a deep breath and knocked on the door as he opened it. He stepped in and leaned back until the door clicked shut. The king lay in his bed, and his eyes were open. He sighed when he saw Lamont and slowly sat up.

"Lamont, what are you doing?"

Lamont held his hands up in an appeasing motion. "I thought you would want to hear the news. The gates have just been opened. The guard has surrendered the palace."

The king closed his eyes. "Then my end is close. I would like to sleep a little more before my time is up."

Lamont took a step forward as the king rolled over. "I have a better idea. Why don't we leave the palace?"

"If the guard has turned against me, I will be captured on sight."

Lamont nodded. "If we choose to leave by the front gate, yes."

The king rolled back over. "What are you referring to?"

Lamont crossed his arms over his chest. "We should escape through the chamber of the sleeper. The passages are all secret. No one would have any idea where we went."

The king's eyes flashed with anger. "You fool! And lead the man of fire right to her power? I will die in this bed by my own hand before I will allow such a thing!" The king pointed at Lamont. "And I forbid you to leave by the tunnels either. The risk is too great."

Lamont bowed respectfully. "I understand." He had turned to the door when he felt he should turn back. "Uncle, I think I know who the man of fire is."

The king's head popped back up. "Oh?"

"Yes, the leader of the people, Hieronymus Purvis. He convinced the guard to side with him."

"I do not believe it is him."

Lamont's eyes narrowed. "Then who do you believe it is?"

The king's eyes were cold as steel. "I believe it is Teris. His vengeance toward me has always burned hot, just like a fire."

Lamont turned around fully. "Did you see any physical attributes of this person in your vision that would give us a clue?"

"Simply what I said before. He was a man of fire. A man made of fire."

Lamont nodded. That didn't help at all. "Yes, my king."

"Wait!" The king put up a hand. "Lamont, I don't know if Lord Kiad will see the use of attacking the Teris family, so I will leave that responsibility with you." The king's eyes bored into Lamont. "This is my final order to you. I want you to destroy the Teris family. Kill them all."

Lamont sighed. What good would that do him? The execution of an entire lordly family was an extreme move. Uncle hadn't even had the power to do it when he became king. Lamont wanted to reach out, sling his uncle over his shoulder, and start running, but instead, he bowed his head. His king's word was law.

"As you command, my king."

9

Scripted Lines

THE DOOR TO the throne room opened, and Hollis stepped in. His clear voice echoed down the room. "Announcing Hieronymus Purvis, the champion of the people!" He stepped aside for Hiero and leaned down to whisper in his ear. "You are not afraid?"

Hiero's eyes turned toward him. "I have no reason to be afraid."

Hollis grinned sharply. "You do now." He shoved his knee into Hiero's back, causing him to stumble through the door into the throne room.

Hiero's heart rate spiked. He windmilled his arms, trying desperately to grab his sword hilt. He yanked himself upright, his eyes roaming to the left and right. That had felt like an ambush, but it wasn't. The only people in the room were gathered behind a large table at the other end of the hall. Hiero straightened his clothes and started to walk.

Ah, the throne room! It was rich, so much more than he had imagined, yet he felt nostalgic seeing it. Yes, Hiero could see the Teris mansion in all of this—the pillars, the arches, the marble, the tapestries. It was as if Lord Teris had drawn up the plans for his mansion, saying, "Even in exile, we remember."

Hiero strode down the long gold carpet in the center of the hall and took in the way it muffled his boots. The carpet was as thick as the sole of his foot. It had been so long since he had experienced richness.

At the far end of the throne room, clustered around a long table, was a group of men watching him with sharp, suspicious gazes. Each of them wore a sash designating their position. An old man leaning heavily on his staff hobbled around the table right up to Hiero and glared at him from under thick white eyebrows. The sash across his chest designated him the mayor of trade.

"You don't look like a Teris!" he snapped.

Hiero stopped short, and his eyes moved from face to face. Each man wore a similar calculating look. A tall, thin man stood up and placed his hand in the middle of the table. Hiero raised an eyebrow. This man was only an apprentice.

"He is not the Teris, Father. He is only the forward party. Where is the Teris, son?"

Hiero felt all the little bolts of lightning strike one another inside his head. Slowly, carefully, he let out his breath. This was not the time to let out the rage that bubbled inside of him. He was enough, all by himself.

"There is no Teris. I am the champion of the people."

The looks quickly turned darker. The mayor in charge of health tripped up to him and pushed the elder aside, lowering his voice. "We were informed that Gannon Teris was here!" he hissed. "Where is he?"

Hiero set his jaw. That would have been Fritz's doing, unfortunately. Hollis was right. It was a fearful thing, facing down the mayors of Reta. But these were not lords; most were not even sirs, only common people just like him. The king had given them their positions, and not one could stand in his way. Hiero filled his chest to the bursting point and widened his eyes.

"I am Hieronymus Purvis, and I am taking the throne, not Gannon Teris."

The reaction was instant. The mayors were horrified.

"Who are you?" the mayor of water sputtered. "What gives you any right to the throne?"

Hiero's head turned to meet the eyes of every man. He needed to exude more confidence than he ever had.

"Mayors of Reta, I believe in the Ancients' laws. I believe they still have the power they had hundreds of years ago. Lord Reta does not believe in those laws. He does not believe in any law. Under his reign, Retall is falling into chaos and corruption. The people of Reta are done with the chaos and corruption. They want a return to the Ancients' laws."

He looked back up at the mayors. Their faces had changed. They were not angry anymore, but hard and serious. They were listening to him.

"I am already king. In accordance with the Ancients' laws, the people have chosen me. It is time the power of the lords was broken and given to the people as it was back in the time of the Ancients. I am the voice and the hands of that change. Will you stand with me and see Retall change?"

The pause was tense. Many of the men looked at one another in bewilderment. The mayor of trade stared at Hiero intently.

"You want to be king, boy?"

Hiero blinked at the man. He did. He understood that now. "Yes, I do."

The mayor tapped Hiero's chest with his staff. "Then you will be king!" He grabbed Hiero's wrist and pulled him in front of the table. He was surprisingly strong. "Mayors of Reta, I've chosen this man as my king!"

The apprentice looked absolutely horrified. "Father, what are you doing? This man has no claim to the throne! We don't have any idea who his family is!"

The old man gave his son a look. "I remember three kings. I remember that harvests were better under one and trade was better under another. And I remember the change that came over this place when Lord Reta took command. It is time for another change." He turned to the rest of the mayors. "I have read this man's writing, and I believe he would make a good king!"

The silence felt malevolent. The apprentice put his hands up. "This is all well and good, but we can't choose the next king." He shot Hiero a dark glare. "All we can do is surrender the palace. We will call you the people's representative. Is that acceptable?"

Hiero nodded. "It is."

"Then you will be held responsible for whatever damages these peasants cause while they are rampaging. This also accounts for any missing valuables." The apprentice marched stiffly around the table and lined up a stack of papers before handing them to Hiero. "The mayors of Reta have agreed to these terms of surrender."

Hiero took the papers and flipped through them. It was all fairly standard, damage reparation and the like. Hiero skimmed through it, and his eyes came back up.

"What of the king? This says nothing about him."

The apprentice shrugged. "The king is not an issue. He isn't anywhere to be found, and we can only assume he has escaped."

Hiero felt a new spark ignite in the back of his head. "What?"

The ice in Hiero's voice froze the apprentice. Only his eyes moved, darting back and forth. "We don't know where he has gone. He's been missing for hours!"

Hiero let his eyes close while he composed himself. The king needed to pay for his crimes, but there could be no justice until he was found.

Hiero looked back at the papers in his hand. Ah, paperwork. Not something he had missed while being a peasant. He laid the papers down on the table, leaned over it, and began to read. It didn't cross his mind until he was halfway through the second page that he had impressed the mayors. The contract wasn't printed; it was scripted. Never mind that he was reading at all. Peasants often were not taught how to write and read script because it was simply not needed. He was acting like a sir's son without even realizing it.

Hiero finished reading the terms and flattened the last page with an open palm. "Do you have a quill, gentlemen?"

A head nodded, and an inkwell was pushed across the table at him. Carefully, he tapped the extra ink from the quill and brought it to the paper.

"Effective immediately, I am taking control of the city of Reta, as well as the palace. This has been added."

He dipped the quill and brought it back. There was only silence as he signed his name. Hiero lifted his head. "I will expect all of you to sign as well, giving over your powers until there is a king in Reta."

The mayor of health snatched the paper from Hiero's hand. He glared as he read Hiero's addition. Finally, he sighed, and his hand fell to his side. "We would be giving you the standard power of a king within the city of Reta. Traditionally, it is protocol for the mayors to take on that extra power until the new king is crowned."

Hiero shook his head. "That protocol was not followed when the current king took over the palace. He took control immediately, and it was at least a month before the lords elected him. Since this protocol has proven optional, I am disbanding it."

The mayor of health sighed. "You truly intend to be king? Even though you know the lords will never allow it?"

Hiero hardened his gaze. "I do."

Frustration filled the mayor's face. "You will bring ruin to Reta! The rest of the lords will kill all the people who aided you! You are putting our names to a death warrant!"

"The people of Reta want change. They are willing to die for that change." Hiero turned to the entire council. "I won't lie, gentlemen. I fully expect the lords to go to war with us."

The mayor of industry, wearing a dark blue sash, slapped his hand on the table. "That's preposterous! The lords would never do such a thing!"

Hiero flung out his arm. "And what moral code will stop them? The rest of the Ancients' laws have been abandoned multiple times! What will stop man from once again using war?"

The mayor of trade leaned on his staff and shook his head sorrowfully. "How far our world has fallen. The Ancients would be so disappointed in us."

Hiero's eyes pleaded with them. "Please, mayors, join me. You have a say in this election as well. Can't you see that if man continues as he is, we will soon face punishment from the Ancients again? Can you imagine another great plague?"

"I agree." The mayor of trade put his hand on Hiero's shoulder. "I choose to elect Hieronymus."

The mayor of industry looked disgruntled. "Then I will as well!"

Another man stood, followed by another and another. "I stand with him."

"I will as well."

"As will I."

The apprentice watched in silence as the entire council stood to side with his father. Finally, he took the terms with a sigh and signed them. Then he straightened.

"You have power over Reta; however, you will not be styled as king in our paperwork until the lords have bent the knee to you. Do you understand? We must have some way to defend our actions here."

Hiero nodded. "I understand. And you will see it happen."

They lapsed into silence as the terms were passed around from hand to hand and signed. The old man was the last to sign, and he winked as he handed the papers over.

"Now you are the lord of Reta."

Hiero bowed to the city council. "Thank you, gentlemen. I will inform the people."

Hiero had turned and was walking toward the throne

room doors when they banged open, and a guard pulled a young woman into the room by her arm. He dragged her up the carpet and stopped short before the table. His eyes darted from Hiero to the mayors before he stepped up to Hiero.

"This serving girl was caught trying to leave the palace with a horse stolen from our stable."

Hiero gave the girl a sideways look. "And why would she do that?"

She shrank back. "Who are you?"

"I am Hieronymus Purvis. I am currently overseeing Reta and the palace. What is your name?"

The girl swallowed. "Ani Kiad."

Hiero smiled. "Ah, well, that makes sense. Lord Kiad certainly wants to hear about this." He stepped closer to her and lowered his voice. "Do you know where the king is?"

The girl's mouth shut tight. Her eyes glinted with spirit. "I won't tell you anything."

Hiero looked curious. "Why is that?"

"You want to kill him!"

Hiero sighed. "I want him to face justice. He is a murderer, after all."

The girl watched his face for a moment. "It is a better reason than the one I heard before."

"From who?"

"There was a man who forced me to tell him where the king was. He said that he was the spirit of the dead Teris, but I could feel his warmth and his heart beating. He said he wanted revenge on the king for murdering him."

Hiero sucked in a breath and tried to control his face, but the girl reacted to his fear. Gannon was here, and Gannon knew where the king was. His flair for the dramatic had not disappeared with age. This was very bad. The victories of the day could still be lost if the mayors found out Gannon was here, and Hiero could see himself executed alongside the king.

"He's a bad man, isn't he? I sent a bad man to the king."

Hiero swallowed. "Please, Ani, you have to tell me where the king is. I have to stop this man!"

The girl studied his eyes for a moment. "You are going to stop him? Truthfully?"

"If I can, yes."

The girl looked down. "The king is in the royal bedchamber. The grand general guards the door."

"Thank you!" Hiero clapped her on the shoulder and ran around her.

"Wait!" The apprentice's voice shattered the silence. "Where are you going? What are you going to do?"

Hiero looked back over his shoulder for just a moment. "I am going to see that justice is done."

10

DEADLY MOTIONS

THE KING'S BEDCHAMBER, the one that had been built in the palace's expansion two hundred years ago, was located on the north edge of the palace and overlooked a prosperous valley and the outskirts of the Great Forest from its spacious balcony. It was one of the few rooms in the palace that had no secret entrance. It made it defensible, but it also made it a trap. There was only one door in and one door out.

If Lamont Reynard was guarding the king, Gannon had no desire to enter by the door, and that left only the balcony. There was no room above it that he might drop in from, and the balcony stretched out far from the floor below, likely to deter any climbers. But Gannon was utterly consumed with his revenge, and he would find a way.

Gannon ran up a short stairway to the second level and sped across the open walkway on the east side of the palace.

He followed the edge of the palace until he reached the northern side. Rich bedrooms were here, their impressive views raising their value.

Gannon marveled at the lack of servants. They had either fled or joined the mob. Gannon ran into one bedroom and pulled open the shuttered doors, leaning out to see where the king's balcony lay. It was above him, far to the right.

He grasped the door's wood frame and pulled himself up and out onto the ledge. A short railing ran along the edge, offering a paltry protection were he to slip, and the possibility was quite likely. The wind raged around him, whipping at his clothes. The stone was slick from the rain. The downpour was now huge pelting drops.

Gannon tightened his coat, wishing for his cloak. This would not be a simple feat. The king's balcony was only about ten feet above him but about twice that to his left. He tested his fingers against the stone beside the shutter, and they slid off, completely without resistance.

Quickly he climbed back into the room. Just a few moments in that terrible weather had sapped his motivation. There had to be another way in. Gannon stepped to the wall and rapped his fist against it. The hollow sound of wood answered him back. He knew the floors of each level were crafted stone and there was no way through that, but if he could find a wood or a plaster wall adjoining the bedroom, perhaps he could break in.

Gannon placed his hand across his chin, a thoughtful habit he had inherited from his father. His brow knit as he remembered the thin lines of the palace diagrams. The smell and sound of the old study came to him in a flash, and Gannon opened his eyes. This was not the time for nostalgia.

The king's apartment was alone on the north wall, but there were two old towers on the east wall—the queen's twins. What of the roof? If he could get into the towers, could he not walk across the roof and drop onto the balcony? The thought was enticing.

Gannon closed the shutters before running back out into the hall. He followed it to the east to search for the stairs up to the twins. On the inner ring of the east wing, he found them. The stairs were set apart in their own chamber that rose the full height of the palace. They were circular stairs, shooting away from each other and back together like two golden dancers. The bright shine of their wood turned the whole chamber to gold.

Gannon swallowed. It had been many years since Retall had had a queen. Lord Reta's wife had been dead since Gannon was a child. He reflected that he must choose a woman so beautiful that she would deserve this glory.

Gannon had to shake his head to break out of the thought. The king was waiting. *Hiero must not reach him first.* Gannon leaped up the stairs two at a time until he reached a landing with double doors. This was as high as the stairs went. As Gannon stepped up to the doors, his face hardened. The doors were locked fast. Chains were threaded back and forth through the handles and locked with a padlock.

Gannon looked over his shoulder before drawing his sword. May his father have mercy if he ever found out what Gannon had done to such a valuable door. Carefully, Gannon inserted the tip of his sword around the chains and into one of the screws holding the handle to the door. He twisted, and the screw rolled slowly out of its place, fell to the floor, and disappeared under the door. Gannon winced and went on with the next.

As all four screws were removed, the handle grew less stable, and it knocked back and forth as he screwed. Finally, it slipped down in its casing and hung limp. Gannon set his sword down and wiggled the handle. It was still attached to the knob on the other side by a small clip. Gannon twisted it apart with his fingers, and the handle fell into his hand.

Gannon couldn't help but smile at the perfectness of it. The handle wasn't damaged at all. He laid the handle on the ground, and the chains followed. Gannon's fingers curled softly around the hilt of his sword, and he pressed his palm against the door. It swung in, too easily, and Gannon was frozen for a moment, breathless. There shouldn't have been anyone here. Why did he feel the need to be hushed?

Gannon stood and stepped into the queen's northern twin. His boots left their signs of passage in the thick dust that covered the carpet. No one had been in here for many years. Gannon felt like he was not allowed to be in here. An unfamiliar trickle of fear tripped down his spine. The curtains were slashed. Bookshelves were overturned, and their books littered the ground. A vase was broken to pieces in the center of the room. Gannon's eyes darted around, taking in each new destruction.

There was no blood. Whatever had taken place here had not involved killing. The light peach carpet would have been stained irreparably. The second of the queen's twins was to Gannon's right, across a gorgeously carved walkway. There was a strong smell of mold in the room, and Gannon could see why. The doors to the outside had glass broken out of several panes, and the carpet beneath them was stained dark with mold. Still, Gannon saw no blood.

Quickly, he stepped out onto the walkway, eager to close the door behind him. The room scared him in a way he had never experienced before. Outside, the night was utter blackness. The sky rumbled dangerously overhead, and Gannon remembered the bolt of lightning he had seen strike the palace.

Gannon stepped up to the railing. At least it had stopped raining for the moment. The sky only spat at him. Down below, he could see the roof of the second floor, and beyond that, the great domed roof of the throne room scattered light like a prism. It was not a long drop to the second floor, so Gannon sheathed his sword and leaped over the railing with one hand.

The wind tugged his hair away from his face, and the small of his back became weightless for a moment, traveling into his chest, and then *clu-clunk*! He landed solidly on heels and hands.

The roof was longer than it had looked from above. The dome stretched away from him across the tiled wasteland, and off to the north was a great dark lump that could be nothing else but the king's bedchamber. Gannon ran.

The land that had looked so flat from above was alive with hills and ridges. As his boot came down on one tile, it shifted and shot off with the weight of his momentum, dropping him flat and scattering sparks as it shot down the roof. Gannon lay on his stomach for just a moment, breathing, watching the sparks fade.

He was running out of time. It still felt like the small of his back was roaming around inside his body, and it was getting heavier. He struggled to his feet. There was the king's bedchamber, a darker black than the sky around it. It was as if the edifice glowed softly.

Picking his footing carefully, Gannon made his way around it. It was slow going, and Gannon felt like he was truly struggling. He sat back against the stone and allowed himself a moment to breathe. His hand found the space inside his coat where he could feel his heart. It beat against his hand like an animal trying to escape.

So that was it then. He was afraid? Gannon shook his head. He could not be such a fool. He could not let himself be frightened by a trashed bedroom or a simple fall. He was Gannon Teris! He was the heir to the throne! He had a destiny to fulfill!

But perhaps it was fear. Gannon stroked the cloth above his heart. Was he afraid to kill the king?

He had heard his father speak of Lord Reta in pure rage, and the story he'd told over and over was terrifying: a young Teris forced to watch his father's murder, followed by the murder of his elder brother and then his nephew. If Gannon failed, that evil man would not hesitate to take his head too.

Gannon's hand tightened on the hilt of his sword. He was a Teris. There would be no failing.

The rally spurred his heart to a steadier beat, and Gannon pushed himself off the stone wall with a resolution. He would win.

The glow turned to flickering as Gannon reached the edge of the roof. The roof began to fall steeply, and Gannon approached the balcony on his hands and knees, his body braced up against the stone. The roof ended suddenly, and a yawning blackness blew up into Gannon's face. His palms went cold.

He could see the balcony. It was only four or five feet from him, but there was no climbing to it. He would have to jump. Gannon crawled tentatively from the wall, trying to gain a better angle. The slope of the roof made him nervous. Gently, he stood and bent his knees for the jump.

Something slipped. Gannon slid right off the roof, and his hands scrabbled on the metal for purchase, catching the edge at the last moment. It bit. Gannon winced. His legs flapped uselessly in the darkness, hundreds of feet above a swift death.

Somewhere in his fear-addled brain, Gannon remembered the balcony. It was there to the right, just above his waist. He flung out his leg desperately, and the metal bit harder into his hand. His leg was over the rail. Gannon gritted his teeth together in an effort not to scream. He released his right hand, moved it a foot to the right, and grabbed the metal again. He was there. His left hand came away wet with blood. He pulled it next to the other. He was there. He was there!

He could feel the balcony floor with the tip of his boot. He flung out his right hand and grabbed a crevice in the stone. With a mighty jerk, he fell onto the balcony in a heap. Thankfully, his hilt did not clang. Gannon lay still for just a moment, listening. His heart was pounding like it wanted to wake the whole world. There was no sound from the bedchamber.

Silently, Gannon shifted into a crouch. He was alive, but he raised no thanks to any deity. He felt a calm settle over him, a deathly, heart-pounding calm. He had survived that. There was nothing else that could go wrong.

A bloody handprint remained when he lifted his left hand. The cool wet marble felt good against it. His right hand was uncut, but the stiffness had not fully faded. Gannon flexed it. He pulled a handkerchief from inside his coat and knotted it around the bleeding hand.

The lamp inside the bedchamber was lit, but Gannon could not see any movement. Staying low, he moved to the doors. They were latched from the inside. Gannon slid his sword between the doors and pushed the latch up until it fell to the other side. With a soft pop, the door was levered free.

This time, Gannon's sword stayed in his hand. His breath slowed to silence as he squeezed through the space in the doors. The inside was much warmer, almost comforting, but Gannon's back was arched, and his eyes were wide. Only after looking back and forth across the room for several moments did Gannon feel comfortable to stand. This room was empty. Lamont and the king must've been in the atrium.

His boots padded softly as he strode to the door. His hand was on the knob when he heard a sound from behind him. He whirled around, his sword ready. The covers on the king's bed shifted, and an old man sat up, blinking at Gannon.

"Lamont?" His face changed as he took Gannon in. "Arran? It can't be!" He wiped a hand across his eyes. "No." The fear in his eyes faded. "You must be Gannon. You resemble your grandfather mightily, boy. Has no one told you?"

Gannon's mind was frozen. Was this Lord Reta? Slowly, he lowered his sword. Gannon had imagined a giant man with a wicked face and hair as thick and shaggy as a dog's. He had not imagined a frail old man.

Lord Reta looked him up and down. "You are young. Younger than I was when I first killed. It should be your father here. It is his revenge." His eyes burned into Gannon's. "I would have you understand something, boy. I did not spare your father because he was a child. I did not spare him for any sympathy that I had. I had none. I was young, and regret meant nothing to me."

Gannon's body was shaking. There was ice at the base

of his spine. He felt like he might be ill. Reta's gaze had turned him to stone.

"I tell you truthfully, boy, you will feel regret. It will lie awake with you at night. It will eat you alive like a rat does, tearing away piece by piece." He paused again, as if he expected Gannon to answer.

"I remember the day you were born. I remember the rider, twenty-one years ago, his eyes wide as he ran to me. 'The lady Teris has given birth to twins!' he shouted to me. 'A boy and a girl!' I should not have been surprised. The Teris family always produces twins at some point. I admit, I feared you. I thought to have you killed and chose against it. It would have been simple. Just a signature on a piece of paper."

Gannon felt a spark of anger ignite in the small of his back, and it shot into his arm. His hand tightened on his sword, and he stepped toward the king. "How long do you intend to babble?"

Reta's face was impassive. "Do you intend to be king?"

"I do."

"You will never be king. I have seen this."

Gannon stopped short. "You have seen it? How?"

The king's face was as serious as a stone. "I have seeing eyes."

Gannon's burning rage exploded. "How stupid do you think I am? Do you think I am such a child that you can spin Ancient tales and I will believe you? You are a fool!"

The king raised an eyebrow. "Your pretty little Jasberanian school is showing, boy. Make no mistake; they are not legends. I can see the future. You will never be king, though you will fight for it again and again. The one who will be king is close at hand." The king's eyes changed. The brown inside them drained out to be replaced by brilliant blue.

He took a deep, shaky breath. "His name is Hieronymus Purvis."

"No!" Gannon screamed and drove his sword through the king's chest. The king's eyes still burned blue, and it brightened, heading toward white.

"You fool!" Blood came out with Reta's breath. "You have not killed a king; you have crowned an emperor! An emperor of the Ancients . . ." His breath failed, and his body slumped back, his blue eyes still wide, staring at something unseen.

Gannon pulled his sword from the king's chest. His breath came in gasps. He had done it. His hand hovered protectively over his heart. So much for Ancient omens and idiotic legends. All that stood in his way now was Hiero. Gannon wiped his sword robotically on the king's sheets. One more to go.

11

CHOSEN DUTIES

THE SOLDIER JUMPED to attention as Lamont entered the atrium. "The king will not be leaving, and so neither will I. If you fear death, soldier, I advise you to join the crowd."

The man shook his head. "I can stay with you."

"This is not going to be a pleasant experience, I want you to understand. It is only us against an entire mob."

"But this is my place, guarding my king."

The man's words cheered him. Lamont smiled. There were yet those with some honor in the world. "Thank you. I could use the backup. What is your name?"

The man lifted his chin. "Fritzgerald Damian, sir. City guard."

Lamont nodded. "Lamont Reynard, grand general." He chuckled softly. "I am relieved to have you by my side. I apologize if I don't seem grateful."

Fritzgerald shook his head. "I feel it as well. What this event might set in motion is terrifying. It is easy to see the appeal of a new young leader and much harder for people to see its negative effects."

Lamont raised an eyebrow. "You speak well, soldier. Are you a sir's son?"

A shadow of something crossed Fritzgerald's face. Sadness? Anger? Lamont could not make it out.

"I was once, many years ago. No more."

Lamont did not feel a desire to pry. There was too much hidden behind his words. "So, what do men call you? Fritzgerald seems rather long."

Fritzgerald chuckled. "It is, isn't it? My comrades call me Fritz, and I like it. I am the only Fritz in the guard."

Lamont nodded as he leaned back against the wall. "Makes it simple." He sighed. "I can't think like this. I need to do something. Isn't that strange? I was patient for hours and hours as the people rioted, and now I can't stand still!" He started to pace again. "I wish there were something I could do."

Fritz coughed. "Pardon me if I am too familiar, but if you could do something, what would it be?"

Lamont sighed as his fingers ran through his hair. "I would stop this rebellion. I would stop the man who leads it. If he were to die, his followers would likely scatter."

Fritz cocked his head. "You seem confused by your own desire."

"No, it isn't confusing. I was ordered to leave."

"Ordered to leave?" Fritz echoed his words incredulously.

"Yes, the king believes he has no choice but to die, that the future has already been decided. I do not. I still have confidence that he might live."

Fritz and Lamont fell into silence. Lamont felt as though his mind were working hard enough for Fritz to hear. He watched as the man rubbed his finger across his stubble. It wasn't kind to judge. Likely every guard in their force had stubble after these sleepless nights of rebellion.

"So, you feel torn between obedience and duty?"

"Not exactly. There is an aspect of duty in my leaving, and it is more love that holds me to his side. I don't want to lose him."

"Lose him? He is precious to you?"

Lamont nodded. "He is my uncle. He raised me since my mother's death seventeen years ago. I remember coming to the palace to enter his care and begin work in the guard at the same time."

"Your uncle? Why is this not well-known?"

Lamont shrugged. "It is known among the people I interact with. I think it displays a certain favoritism that people tend to look down on."

"You don't seem old enough to start work seventeen years ago."

Lamont chuckled. "I don't? Well, that is nice. I will reach thirty-two years soon. I was born on the day the king took the palace."

Fritz's eyes went wide. "Really? That is amazing!"

"Yes, the king thought so too. He believes in signs and prophecies and all that." Lamont paused. "You surely knew that though."

Fritz shook his head. "I didn't. Most common people have no idea who their king really is, and that might have contributed to the problem. I just assumed, because I heard no different, that the king despised all things that could not be proven as fact." Fritz looked almost frustrated. "Why do you love the king? Because he is your uncle only?"

Lamont shook his head. "No, of course not! He is—" Lamont paused. "Kind. I have many happy memories with him."

Fritz watched his face for a moment. "You fear what you do not know, and you do not know a life without someone you can call family." Fritz swallowed. "You will have to learn to live without one."

Lamont knew pain when he heard it. Fritz had shown a crack. "As you have?"

"As I have." Fritz smiled sadly. He seemed to be making a decision behind those eyes. "You should go. Fulfill your duty to your king."

"I feel guilty for even considering it!"

"You must let him go. You were given an order. It is no longer in your hands."

Lamont ran his fingers through his hair. What was he thinking? If he didn't do something, the king would die. He couldn't let that happen. He had to. He was going to be the next king, wasn't he? And this was his first decision. Lamont sighed. His heart felt heavy, like a stone in the center of his chest.

Lamont walked over to the map. It would be a three-day ride north from here. He would need a horse and either provisions or money. Money would be easier to carry. On the map it was only three handbreadths long, but Lamont knew it was full of forest and farmland. He couldn't just ride north. Lord Kiad's territory was vast. Lamont needed a road that would take him directly there.

As Lamont leaned over the map, Fritz came around beside him. "Do you know where you're going?"

Lamont tapped the map with his finger. "To the only lord I can trust: Lord Kiad."

Fritz started coughing, and it took him a moment to

settle himself. "Ah, of course. He's Lord Reta's strongest ally."

Lamont put up a finger. "Wait. Do you hear that?" He listened for a few moments. There was a rumbling, low, almost from the ground. "What is that?"

Fritz grabbed his shoulder. "It has to be the mob. They're coming!"

Lamont ran to the door and yanked it open. The room outside the atrium was the staircase and the king's sitting room. The staircase spread down below him like a rich black cloth lined with gold. Lamont took a few tentative steps onto the landing. The rumbling was louder outside the room, and Lamont could make out words in it. They were shouting the name of Hieronymus.

Lamont tried to remember where the passageway was. Could he still get to it, or was he already cut off? If he met the crowd coming, the consequence could be deadly. The king did not want him to leave by the underground, but he was cut off from the courtyard.

The noise was becoming distinct. Lamont turned and rushed back into the atrium, shutting the door and sliding the bolt across it.

Fritz looked concerned. "What is it? Have they found us already?"

Lamont ran his fingers through his hair, calming himself. "Yes, I'm trapped now. And they're coming."

12

FIERY ENGAGEMENT

HIERO STRODE DOWN the wide hallway, followed by the people. The king's bedchamber was on the third floor, and the people doggedly followed him up halls and staircases, cheering loud enough to shake the whole palace. If Gannon was somewhere in front of them, he knew they were coming.

Hiero's mind was a rolling sea of thoughts. The king was up there, Gannon would be up there, and Lamont would be there too. Hiero winced. He couldn't forget Fritz. Hiero had told him to follow the king in case he somehow got out of the palace. How would Fritz react if Hiero had to attack Gannon?

This was all going sour fast. If Gannon was heading for the king's bedchamber, he would likely be the first one Hiero had to face. Hiero pulled his sword. Gannon could be in any of these shadowy hallways, waiting to pounce on him.

The furnishings around them had grown visibly finer. There was a short hallway of servant bedrooms and then a parlor-type room with bookshelves lining the wall. A staircase lifted out of the center of this room, leading to a set of double doors. This was the king's parlor. Hiero didn't see Gannon anywhere, so he must've been inside.

Hiero ran up the stairs and was halfway up them before he thought to look over his shoulder. The people filed into the area, filling it and the hallway behind it. They raised their arms as one and shouted, "Long live King Hiero!" Then there was silence, and they watched him. He lifted his sword in silent salute and ran up the rest of the staircase.

The double doors were closed. Hiero turned the knob and pushed softly on one door. It didn't budge. It must've been barricaded from the other side. Hiero knocked. After a short silence, someone answered, his voice muffled by the thick wood.

"Yes, who is it?"

Hiero let out a breath to calm himself. That was not the voice of one who had just battled. Perhaps Gannon was not here at all.

"I am Hieronymus Purvis. I am the champion of the people. I am here to negotiate the king's surrender."

There was silence, and then the voice said, "The king is not here. He has fled."

Hiero knew that voice. Rage surged through him. This was the moment for his vengeance.

But there was a crowd behind him. Hiero froze. If he was to be king, the upholder of the Ancient laws, could he still justify killing his half brother?

Hiero's mind scrambled inside his head. Ancient historians said that the death penalty had been applied to every crime, but was that true? Murder should certainly be punished by death, but what about stealing? He tried to control himself, but his sword hand shook with anger.

"I have the palace. I have the city. No help is coming for you. You will either negotiate with me or with the crowd."

Silence returned, and there was scratching on the other side of the door as the barricade was lifted. The door opened only a crack.

"You will enter alone."

"Yes, I will."

The door swung inward, and Hiero saw Lamont Reynard, the man who had stolen his life away, standing on the other side of a large table in the center of the room. There was no way of knowing how many more men were in there. Hiero's grip tightened on his sword, and he walked in. He glanced to the left and relaxed. Fritz held the door. He met Hiero's eyes for a brief moment before glancing away.

The door closed behind him. Hiero scanned the rest of the room, but it was only the three of them inside the atrium. The king must've been farther in.

Hiero glanced back at Lamont. His sword was not in his hand. Did he not intend to fight? Hiero stepped up to the table and met Lamont's eyes. In all truth, he did not know this man. The Lamont he'd known was a boy of twelve leaving home for military school. This heartless villain had no relationship with him. There was no recognition in Lamont's eyes either. His stare was cold.

Not that his half brother would have looked at him lovingly even if he had recognized him. At the insistence of his father, Hiero had spent most of his young life working for the Teris manor, out of contact with him. And that may have contributed to Lamont's betrayal two years ago, even though he had all the wealth he could need. Hiero could feel his anger and bruised pride just below the surface, threatening to leak out. He couldn't allow himself to give in to vengeance anymore—not if he was to stand for justice.

Hiero gave Lamont a curt nod. "You do not remember me?"

Lamont's eyes narrowed. "I have only learned of you and your rebellion these past two days."

Hiero shook his head. "No, you knew me before this. We have seen each other many times. You have betrayed me, and you have stolen something very dear to me."

Lamont's eyes narrowed even more. "I knew your face seemed familiar to me, but I do not walk around this city berating peasants or stealing from them. Why would you accuse me of such a thing?"

Rage spiked through the back of Hiero's head. Logic sped away. The future he had spent so long building had been stripped away with this man's one foolish action, and he did not remember?

"I'm not a peasant!" he spat. "I was born Hiero Reynard, son of Sir Reynard and a prostitute!"

Lamont's mouth fell open, and his eyes widened. "You!"

Hiero gritted his teeth. "Yes, me. My life was left in ruins by you, but no more. I intend to have everything you cost me!"

Lamont grabbed the hilt of his sword and drew it. "Don't threaten me. You don't have any power here."

Hiero's eyes burned. "Why did you do it, Lamont? Why did you revoke our father's will? He left the Reynard land to me!"

Lamont looked disgusted by the suggestion. "Have you lost your mind? You're a bastard! Don't you know your place? Father should never have pampered you the way he did; it let you think too highly of yourself."

Hiero closed his eyes. He needed to calm down. At this rate, he would kill his brother. "All I need from you is the Reynard signet ring. With that, I will have my land and title, and I will be able to marry the woman I desire. Give it to me, and I will let you leave here in peace."

Lamont's expression shifted for a moment. His hand went to his chest and tightened around something inside his shirt. His eyes grew thoughtful, and then they snapped back up to Hiero, angry and dangerous again.

"Do you intend to take it by force?"

Hiero sighed in exasperation. "If you give me no other choice!"

Lamont stepped away from the table and into the center of the room, putting himself between Hiero and the double doors into the king's bedchamber. "I'm not a fool, Hiero. I know you came here to kill the king. I don't intend to let you! Fritz?"

Hiero wanted to scream in frustration, but he let his feet slide apart into the ready position. He heard Fritz drawing his sword behind him. Hiero wanted to jab a thousand holes in Lamont for what he had done, but he had to rein himself in. This was two against one. His own life was in no danger. Hiero reminded himself that he only needed to get Lamont out of his way, but the fire burned hot in his chest. Lamont had called him a bastard.

Lamont's limbs trembled. "Fritz! Get him!" His eyes looked wild as Fritz did not obey.

Hiero cast a glance over his shoulder. Fritz still stood by the door, his sword in his hand. He nodded. "I can take care of this, Fritz. Only intervene if it becomes necessary."

The apple in Lamont's throat bobbed. His wide eyes

spoke of resignation. He had decided to die with his king. Hiero stoked the fire in his chest just a little, and it blazed up. What else could Hiero do but oblige him?

Hiero made the first move. From a young age, Hiero had worked to wield a blade with either hand. Most swordsmen only knew how to fight with their right hand. As they faced each other, Hiero's sword was in his left hand, and he intended to use that to his advantage.

Quickly, he feinted to the left, and Lamont jumped to the side to block. His blade connected with thin air, and Hiero spun around him. He held his sword with both hands and brought the flat of his blade down hard against the back of Lamont's head. Lamont crumpled to the floor. Hiero grinned. The battle was over already. Good riddance.

Hiero turned and made for the bedchamber doors. He would get to the king before Gannon had any chance to.

Out of nowhere, Lamont's left elbow struck him square in the jaw. Hiero was shoved to the side into the wall, and his right shoulder crunched as it hit. Hiero whirled around to block Lamont's blade from burying itself in his back. The tip of Lamont's blade sliced into the wall, but Hiero's sword was in its way, and the blade stayed. That had been close. Hiero hadn't even seen him coming. How had he recovered from that blow so quickly?

Lamont's eyes had a new confident gaze in them. "I have the training and the experience. You are no match for me!"

Hiero shoved Lamont back with his hip and stood tall while he steadied himself. He was at least a head taller than Lamont. "You are foolish to think you can win. You might have the training, but I am stronger, and you will lose. I will give you one more chance. Give me the Reynard signet ring and leave. You will not be hurt."

Lamont stepped back and raised his blade. "Do you think that scares me? That I am afraid of being hurt? I am here to protect the king!" He pointed his sword at Hiero. "You are nothing but a self-absorbed bastard! I'm the trueborn son! I will always deserve Father's inheritance, no matter who he chose to leave it to!"

That was it. Hiero could see nothing but fire inside his own eyes. The voice of reason was drowned out by the pounding of blood in his ears.

Hiero flew forward, forgetting that he had a sword in his hand, and smashed his shoulder into Lamont, bowling him into the table and knocking it over. The crash was terrific. Hiero's and Lamont's bodies came down hard on the bottom of the table.

In the tangle of limbs, Hiero's knee landed on top of Lamont's right wrist. Bones cracked. Lamont screamed. Hiero saw his chance and jerked the sword from Lamont's useless fingers. He tossed it, and the metal slid away across the floor.

Hiero stood. His heart pounded, and his chest burned. Lamont lay at the bottom of the table, dazed. The table legs stood in the air like empty flagpoles. Fritz stood on the other side of the table, ready to assist, his face wrinkled with concern.

Seeing Lamont subdued wasn't enough. Hiero wanted more.

He sheathed his sword and knelt in front of Lamont's body. There was a particularly cruel punishment that he had run through his mind many times just after Lamont's betrayal, always with a tantalizing amount of fear for even considering such a thing. He considered it now. His half brother was here, under his control, and completely helpless. There was no greater revenge.

Hiero unbuttoned Lamont's uniform and pulled it open. Under his black-and-gold uniform, he wore a white buttoned shirt tucked into his drawstring pants. Hiero pulled the shirt completely out and untied the knot with a quick tug. Immediately, Lamont's head jerked up. He grabbed at Hiero's hair with his left hand, got a good handful, and yanked. With a growl, Hiero took hold of Lamont's head and smashed it into the hard wood of the table once, twice. Lamont's fingers relaxed.

Hiero gave his face a quick glance. He was still alive. His eyes were closed, and he groaned under his breath. Hiero grabbed the band of Lamont's pants with one hand.

"No!" Lamont's voice was weak. "What are you doing?"

"Isn't it obvious?" Hiero hissed. "I'm doing to you what you did to me!"

"What? What are you talking about?" Lamont's left hand curled around the hand that held his pants. "I would never do this to anyone!"

"You misunderstand me. It was you who took away my ability to be married. Now I will do the same to you."

Lamont's eyes grew huge. "You wouldn't dare!"

"I would. I have imagined this moment many times in the darkest part of my heart for the past two years, getting to see Lamont Reynard stripped of his manhood."

"No!" Lamont tried to move his broken wrist and wheezed in pain. "Please let me go! I'll give you anything you want! The Reynard title is yours!"

Hiero felt the bitter taste of a comeback rise in his throat, and then Fritz's hand was on his shoulder. "Hiero, it is enough. You said you would let him leave."

Hiero let out a deep breath and released Lamont. He had been so close. If Fritz hadn't been there—

Hiero couldn't take his gaze off Lamont's face. All he could do was breathe. Slowly. "Thank you, Fritz. I had lost myself." He stood. "Thank you."

His chest still heaved, and his heart still pounded with anger, but he was calm. Hiero drew his sword and let the tip of it rest against Lamont's abdomen.

"The ring?"

Lamont's hand shook as he reached inside his shirt, pulling out a chain from which the signet ring dangled. He snapped the chain off and tossed it at Hiero's feet.

Hiero's eyes narrowed. Finally, it was his. "I want you gone. Get out of Reta. Get out of Retall. I never want to see your face again. If I do, I cannot guarantee my ability to control myself. Do you understand?"

Lamont nodded. "Yes, yes, I do."

Hiero turned to Fritz. "See him safely out of the palace. No one should be allowed to harm him in your company."

"Right." Fritz sheathed his sword and knelt to help Lamont to his feet. He shot Hiero a sad smile as he stood with Lamont's arm across his shoulders. "You conquered your anger, Hiero. Well done."

Hiero turned to the king's bedchamber, his eyes dark. "We will see."

13

FALLING-OUT

ANNON HAD ONLY to crack open the door to the atrium to hear the full-blown battle going on outside. Wisely, he shut the door and stepped away from it.

Hiero had found the king's hiding place too, it seemed.

He turned back to the king's body. Had he not searched every inch of it, he would not believe it to be so, but it was. The king's signet ring was gone, and Hiero could not have gotten to it first. Gannon felt the fear in the small of his back again. The king's eyes were closed, but Gannon could feel him watching.

"You did it, didn't you? You named an heir before I could reach you!"

Gannon massaged the flesh above his own heart, but he couldn't shake the feeling that something was terribly wrong. He turned back to the door. Perhaps in joining the fight he could catch Hiero off guard and end this terrible night.

Gannon turned to the door, and his hand hovered over the handle. Why did he hesitate? His hand trembled. He swallowed back his sudden fear. He had decided this already. Hiero had to die. He pushed the handle down, and the door swung outward with no resistance.

Hiero's hand was on the outside handle. His face jerked back from the moving door, only a foot away. There was a moment of silence, of shock. Hiero's eyes widened, and Gannon felt the ball drop in his back again.

Gannon tossed his sword aside and yanked the door shut. He pulled desperately on the handle, trying to keep it shut, but Hiero was stronger. The door jerked open an inch, then another inch.

"Gannon, let me in!"

Gannon could see the wild look in Hiero's eyes, and he released the door, scrambling back from it. His fingers scraped his sword from the ground, and he whirled around. Hiero stood in the doorway, his eyes scanning the bedchamber.

"You've killed him." His face betrayed no negative emotion, and his eyes were blank when they met him. "Well done." Hiero's deadpan voice sent a shiver up Gannon's spine. Gannon tightened his grip, and he brought his sword point up.

"Hiero, I can't trust you. You declared yourself a king to that crowd. I need you to stand down. Sheathe your sword and leave the palace."

Hiero stepped into the room and closed the door behind him. His sword split the air as he brandished it. "I expected nothing less from you, Gannon. I am proud of my little brother."

Gannon swallowed. Now he wanted to call him brother? What was Hiero playing at? Was he on his side or not?

Hiero's gaze was condescending as he looked down the length of his sword. "But I am already the king. You cannot make me leave."

Gannon's eyes narrowed. He was already the king? Had he already gotten the king's signet ring? "So, you do have it then. I thought it wasn't possible."

Hiero's eyes narrowed next. "What are you referring to?"

"You have the king's signet ring."

"I do not."

Gannon pointed at the king's body with his sword. "He doesn't have it. Where is it?"

Hiero's face flushed. "Don't try to incite me, Gannon. You were the only person in here with the king."

Gannon's cockiness returned in a rush. So, the ring was gone then. Hiero had no legal right to claim the throne. "Don't look so worried, Hiero. The lords would never have chosen you, even if the king had picked you with his own hand."

Hiero's smile looked sad. "I don't need any ring to be king, Gannon. I will not be elected by the lords."

Gannon's face was incredulous. "Even the usurping Reta was elected by the lords. What gives you the right to circumvent that?"

Hiero's wild gaze glinted in the light of the lamps. "Exactly. The lords cannot be trusted to choose the best leader for Retall. They operate completely for their own interests." His gaze turned sharp. "What favors will you promise them, Gannon, to gain their votes?"

Gannon glared back in return. "For hundreds of years the lords have elected who will sit the throne of Retall after the monarch dies. For years it was nothing more than formality! Making that one wrong choice should not remove them from their oldest, most ingrained task." His words tumbled out in a rush, toppling over one another. "Of course they would choose me! I'm the only male heir of the Teris family!"

The moment the words left his throat, Gannon knew Hiero would not listen to him. He heard him laugh, long and loud.

"The time of lords is over! Like the Ancients' laws demand, the people have chosen me!" He brandished his sword again and crouched into the ready position. "I won't disappoint them by dying now!"

Gannon felt sick to his stomach. "Hiero, please don't do this. I am the rightful king, and you know it. Please just walk away."

Hiero shook his head. "No, Gannon, I can't. But you are my brother. I can at least offer you the same courtesy. Walk away now, and I won't be forced to hurt you."

Gannon's gaze fell to the floor. He was confused, angry, frustrated, and sad. He looked over at the body of the king. Lord Reta had given up his very humanity for power, and Gannon didn't even understand why. Did he have that kind of strength?

His body ached all over. Blood seeped through the cloth around his left hand. He could not defeat Hiero like this. He didn't even feel a desire to try. It was strange. Where had his pride gone? He could only feel the edge of it left, like a sharp thorn in his heart. At that moment in time, all Gannon wished for was a warm bed to collapse into, where he could forget the dead king's shining blue eyes.

Slowly, he lifted his sword and slid it into its sheath. He would go to Father, Father would take him to the lords, and the lords would elect him, just as they had previously elected the Teris sons for over six hundred years.

Gannon forced himself to smile at Hiero. "I cannot fight you, my brother, no matter how hard I try. Shelia would never forgive me." He stepped toward the door, moving to the side to bypass Hiero. Hiero's sword flashed out and smacked Gannon's chest with the flat. Gannon's heart spiked with fear again. His eyes darted to Hiero. Hiero leaned in.

"Not that way."

"What?"

Hiero had the grace to look sheepish. "The crowd has filled up the chamber below the stairs, waiting for me. If you go that way, they will see you."

Gannon gave him a look of pure hatred. "And they will know that I have killed the king."

Hiero looked away. "Yes."

"I see." Gannon turned away from Hiero's blade and walked out to the balcony. "I got in this way. I can get back out." Gannon stepped out onto the balcony, into the dark. The doors clicked shut behind him. The clouds had cleared, and the sky no longer spat down rain. Gannon looked for the moon before he remembered that it was the night of no moon.

He walked out to the very edge of the balcony and stared into the blackness. Cool night breezes fanned his face from below. He could see the farmland surrounding Reta, dotted with small homestead lights.

It was beautiful. It was still his. Gannon didn't want to think of how angry Father would be. He was still a child messing up things for his father to fix.

Gannon shivered. His wounds made him cold. He had no desire to go stomping across the palace roof again. Perhaps Hiero could be convinced to let him stay hidden until the crowd had dispersed.

Gannon glanced over his shoulder into the king's bedchamber. Hiero stood by the king's bed. Gannon's teeth clenched as he realized that Hiero was coating his sword in the king's blood. He turned away from the sight, disgusted and angry. His victory, his family's victory, was going to Hiero, a bastard!

Suddenly, the fire ignited in his breast again. A warmth filled his body from the heart outward. His right hand tingled, and he clenched the hilt of his sword to abate it. Yes, it was his victory, and he would have it no other way.

With a refreshing, powerful *shing*, he drew his sword from its sheath and held it before his face. He was the only son of House Teris. This vengeance was his.

He whirled around and ran across the balcony, kicking the balcony doors open as he reached them. A broken doorknob flew across the room and clattered at Hiero's feet.

Hiero stopped, his hand on the atrium door, and turned around. His eyes were cold. "Well, that is the way it will be then."

Hiero's coolness hit a nerve in Gannon. An audible growl shook his throat.

"Hiero!" he screamed and ran at him, alive in his anger. His sword swung in a vicious arc at Hiero's head, and the crash as Hiero's sword swept up to meet it was painfully sharp. Gannon's teeth vibrated as though they had been biting the bare metal. He gritted them as he stumbled back.

The vibration rumbled through his heart and forced him back to Hiero. Their swords crashed together, and Gannon was pushed back again, breathing heavily. Hiero was clearly stronger, and that made Gannon angry enough to fly at him again.

Their swords met with more and more ferocity each time. It wasn't fair! Gannon had all the training, yet Hiero had the advantage. Another crashing blow sent Gannon reeling. He didn't have time to lose his focus. He needed to think. If he couldn't match Hiero's strength, he had to use strategy. But what could he use? He was being driven back faster and faster now.

Gannon dodged and stepped out onto the balcony. He was running out of places to run. Gannon jerked to the left, hoping to skirt Hiero and get back inside. But Hiero moved with him, shoving his sword up against Gannon's.

The stone railing was hard against Gannon's back. The wind from below whirled his hair crazily about his face. Gannon's eyes darted to the yawning blackness behind him and back to Hiero. There was no sign of mercy in that face. Hiero's eyes burned with his passion. His blade pushed Gannon nearly parallel to the stone. Gannon heard his back pop.

"Hiero!"

Hiero's eyes narrowed. "Gannon, do you concede? Do you concede the throne to me?"

Gannon couldn't feel his heart anymore. He couldn't feel the ball in the small of his back. He was as hard as stone. He glared right back at Hiero, pushing with all his strength to keep Hiero's blade from his chest.

"I will not concede! I am Gannon Teris! I am the true king! I will never allow a sir's bastard to rise higher than me!"

The strength in his words hardened him, but it did nothing to relieve the pressure on his body. Hiero pushed even harder. The glare of torchlight in his eyes burned wild.

"All my life you have made me small," Hiero hissed. "And it does not matter what accomplishments I have gained; you will always stand over me!" Hiero pulled his head back. "Goodbye, Gannon. The time of the Teris family is long over. Today I am the fire that burns the world."

"Hiero! Ugh—" Gannon's shout was caught in his throat as the world spun suddenly around him.

Hiero had swept his leg under Gannon's and shoved him from the balcony. Gannon tumbled into the darkness. His mind scattered into a thousand seconds. He struck out with his sword, hoping to catch it on something and slow his descent. It struck something hard and glanced off. The cliff would be slightly inclined by the time he reached its base, but by that time he would be dead.

Gannon lunged with his sword again. It caught on a fissure in the rock, stopping him for a brief second, and snapped. Gannon felt the jar in his neck and metal shrapnel spike through his clothes. He shoved his broken hilt into the rock face again and flattened himself against it. Pain was everywhere, in every pore. His skin was being peeled away. But he was slowing down. He wasn't falling; he was sliding now, and with a jarring thump in his spine, Gannon landed on his feet and fell back onto his tailbone.

He rolled onto his back, fighting the scream that was still caught in his throat. Everything everywhere was on fire. But he had not screamed for the entire fall. Had he really fallen from way up there? Gannon stared up at the palace in shock. The four hundred feet looked like a mile from here. Had his fight with Hiero been real? Perhaps he had just been lying here the whole time, dreaming.

Gannon ran his fingers through the grass on either side of him. He was alive. He had fallen from the palace, yet he was alive.

Slowly, Gannon inspected himself, testing his muscles one by one. His feet were fine, protected by heavy boots, but his legs screamed curses at him. His fancy coat was entirely gone. Only a few strings remained around his shoulders, and the skin on his chest was rubbed raw. His back was lit up with a different kind of pain, deep and drumming. Something was greatly injured there. His neck was jarred, but Gannon had lived through that once before. Blood trickled from a thousand small cuts up and down his arms.

Yes, his muscles were sore, and his hands were skinned, and he was likely a patchwork of bruises, but his eyes still followed his lead, and his ears still heard the wind whistle beside them. He was alive. Nothing else seemed to matter.

Gannon closed his eyes. He didn't intend to sleep, but he did anyway, and he woke up with a start. There were voices nearby. He heard stealthy movement through the grass.

He was fully awake now. It had to be Hiero, back to finish the job. He rolled onto his stomach, wheezing from the pain, and started to crawl away. Suddenly, there was light around him, and two strong arms hooked around his shoulders, pulling him roughly to his feet.

Gannon wheezed in pain before a cloth was shoved into his mouth and pulled tight. The men spoke in hushed tones. The lantern light bobbed softly until it came in front of Gannon. This was not Hiero. The man was old and gaunt, his face pockmarked. Gannon held his breath from the man's smell.

The man grunted softly as he took in Gannon's face. "Ah, he's a pretty one. Let's go."

Gannon could not resist as he was hauled off into the darkness.

14

TREACHEROUS ROAD

Fritz had Lamont's good arm strung across his shoulder as he weaved through the mob.

"Hieronymus has shown us mercy!" he shouted again. "We have surrendered our posts!"

He ignored the dark stares and continued forging forward until the crowd parted to reveal an empty space. They were a good hundred feet down the hallway. He couldn't even see the king's atrium from here.

They walked on a little farther, passed every now and then by a straggler trying to rejoin the main crowd. Lamont moaned under his breath with every step.

Finally, he wheezed. "Fritz, please. Can we stop just a moment? Let me catch my breath?"

Fritz frowned. The sooner he was done with Hiero's half brother, the sooner the two of them could be on their way north, off to find his sisters. He didn't want to waste any time.

He tried to stifle a sigh as he helped prop Lamont up against the wall. Lamont moaned under his breath again. Fritz tried to calm himself. That sound was so annoying.

He felt Lamont studying him, and his gaze burned into the wall. How long were they going to stand here? They were wasting time.

"Fritz, he knew your name."

Fritz froze. He ground his teeth together. *Say nothing. Don't give him any reason to think we had a connection.*

Lamont huffed, a sound almost like a laugh. "After hearing you talk about loyalty, you know, I really believed you. You must have been working for him from the beginning. Why? Why did you betray your king?"

Fritz sighed. If they were going to have this conversation, he had better make it quick. Finally, he met Lamont's eyes.

"I didn't betray my king, thank you. I never joined the guard to serve him. I joined the guard to help my friend, Hieronymus, in his quest to retrieve his inheritance from you." Fritz paused for a moment to let that sink in. "Neither Hieronymus nor I have anything personal against your uncle, except—"

Fritz stopped. Maybe he did have something personal against the king. Notwithstanding, he was one of the Faithful who had been forced to hide their praying, but the king was allied with Lord Kiad. Was it not reasonable to think that Lord Kiad might have been operating this whole time under his protection?

Lamont watched his eyes carefully. "Hiero could have killed me, but you didn't let him. Why did you stop him?"

Fritz felt like a scolded child. "The Ancients' laws prohibit murder. I know Hieronymus would regret his actions later, even if he doesn't believe it." He glared. "You're going to Lord Kiad, aren't you?"

Lamont nodded. "Yes. I'll be safe there. I doubt your friend is the only one who will seek action against me. Especially as—" He sighed, and his face grew cold. "Ah, never mind. By now Uncle is dead. I should get out of the palace."

Fritz felt suspicion creep up his back like a ghost. "You were about to say something and stopped yourself. What was it? Why would anyone else have a grudge against you?"

Lamont shook his head. "Are you sure that your friend only entered the palace to seek action against me? The whole mob seems to be ready to crown him on the spot. They expect him to kill the king. Do you?"

Fritz's face screwed up at the thought. "No! We talked about this before we chose to take any action. This rebellion isn't for him!"

Lamont's eyes burned into him. "Then who, Fritz? Who?"

Fritz glared. Lamont kept using his nickname, and it grated on his ears. He pulled his arm away from Lamont and stabbed his finger into the center of his chest.

"We aren't friends! Get up! I don't have time for this."

Lamont's good hand snapped around his wrist faster than Fritz had thought possible. His instincts kicked in for a half moment, and his other hand went to his blade.

Lamont looked just as startled as he did. "We have enough time. Put the sword away. Tell me about your family."

Fritz tried to pull his wrist away only to find that Lamont was about as strong as he was fast. "I have no family. I told you that already."

"But you did. What happened to them?"

Another Retallian denizen shuffled past them in silence, heading for the main crowd. Fritz felt exposed. "Since you insist, they were sent to Lord Kiad, just as I was. I had the good fortune to escape. They did not."

"Ah." Lamont released him. His face hardened. "And that makes us enemies."

"Your uncle shielded him, didn't he? He let Kiad operate however he wanted."

Lamont sighed. "It's not like that. Lord Kiad wields incredible influence, even here. Uncle didn't dare cross him." He looked away. "I know it's hard to believe, but not every lord or sir has a desire to oppress their people."

He didn't look sorry enough. He didn't care that Fritz's family was still in chains with no end in sight.

"If you cared, you would have done something to stop it."

Lamont grimaced. "It may be hard to believe, but there are more perils threatening mankind than a single lord farming out a few criminal peasants. You are right, it shouldn't be happening, but the king has—" He swallowed. "Had more pressing issues to deal with."

Lamont winced. "Fritz, you seem more compassionate than my brother. For saving me, I'm willing to trust you. Uncle named me his heir." Lamont placed a hand over his chest. "He gave me his signet ring to prove it to the lords. If I become king, I can repair some of the breaks in our society that have caused the people of Reta so much anger. But I need to know who is against me. Who were you and Hieronymus working for?"

Fritz's eyes widened before he could catch them. This man was the king's heir, and Fritz had almost let him walk right out the gates! He placed his hand on Lamont's chest, keeping him against the wall.

"I'm afraid you aren't leaving the palace tonight, General."

Lamont shook his head. "Ah, so I misread you. I thought you had loyalty only for your friend. The person you're working for must be a far better man than I am." He pushed off the wall, defying Fritz's pressure. "You are taking me back now, yes?"

As Lamont came forward, Fritz found himself off-balance. Gannon was a better man than Lamont? No! He was a horrible, arrogant lordling who believed the country existed only to serve him. It was at that moment Fritz realized he didn't want Gannon Teris as his king.

"It's Gannon Teris," he whispered. "Hieronymus inflamed the city to usher in Gannon Teris as the new king."

Everything about Lamont's demeanor changed in an instant. His defiance drained away in a snap. His eyes flickered with fear. "You aren't lying."

Fritz furrowed his brow. "No."

"The king was right. Somehow, he knew!" Lamont grabbed Fritz's shoulder with his good arm. "Look, I must get out of here! If Gannon Teris is the man of fire, his father can't be far behind, and he will kill me, heir or not."

Fritz nodded. "I'll help you." He strung Lamont's arm across his shoulders again, and they started to move, urgently this time. Lamont seemed steadier on his feet, certainly feeling the pressure of not being fully safe.

They met citizens on their way, and most of them watched blankly or ignored them altogether. Perhaps injuries were common in the palace tonight.

The courtyard had more people milling about than the inside of the palace. In the gray light of morning, they seemed faceless, but they shifted to let them through. Fritz glimpsed a flurry of activity in the eastern courtyard, beside the stable, and made a mental note to pass that way as soon as he was done.

A citizen guard of three men stood in the gap between the palace gates.

"Stand!" The nearest guard stepped forward, raising his lantern. "What is your purpose?"

Fritz answered. "To get this wounded man home."

The citizen took in Lamont's pallor and stepped aside. "Go on, quickly! Retall thanks you for your surrender today. Ancients bless!"

The farewell, spoken so loudly, smacked Fritz hard in the chest. His heart pounded, and he wanted to duck his head and hide. But there was no one left to arrest them. "Thank you," he whispered back. "Ancients bless."

A few steps beyond the gate, Lamont started to pull away. "I will be fine from here, thank you."

Fritz watched Lamont stumble a little and shook his head. "No, I can't just leave you in this state. How will you get away? You'll be captured!"

Lamont reached a wall and used it as a prop. "No! I'll be fine! Go back. You and Hiero had a mission, didn't you? I can do this on my own, I promise."

Fritz shut his mouth and watched until Lamont disappeared around a corner. He sighed and released a brief prayer to the Ancients. Lamont would make a much better king than Gannon—if he survived.

Fritz turned and trudged back to the gates, trying to come up with a good lie that would get him two horses from the palace stable. Then he'd have to come up with an excuse to get near Hiero and whisk him away.

The same citizen saluted him on his way back in. "What happened to your friend? He—"

"He knew the way. He felt ashamed of being wounded

and having to go home." Fritz glanced at the other two men. "Who set up a guard detail?"

The man seemed to stand a little taller. "Ah, sir, we made that choice ourselves. And already as we have stood here, looters have come with packs of palace silver and gold, and we have caught them. There are three of them in the dungeons already."

Fritz's jaw clenched. "The fools. This is a night to celebrate freedom, and they sully it."

The guard nodded. "My exact thoughts, sir."

"You are doing good work. I'm sure Hieronymus would be pleased."

"Aye!" The man shot his fist into the air. "Long live King Hiero! Long live King Hiero!" The other two guards joined in, along with everyone standing nearby.

Fritz looked around at them all, massively confused. "Hiero? Hieronymus is king?"

The man slapped Fritz on the back. "We've only just heard the news ourselves! He defeated the king! The old king is dead!"

Fritz found himself feeling faint. What was going on? Had something happened to Gannon? He swallowed. "And where is Hieronymus now?"

"The king?" The man laughed. "I wouldn't know a thing like that!"

Fritz stumbled away from the man as he continued to laugh. He had to find out what was going on. In his peripheral vision, he saw a bonfire flair to life in the center of the eastern courtyard. He moved toward it, feeling lost. Where would Hiero be now that they were making him king? He bumped into a man much taller than he was, and the man gave him a curt shove.

"Watch where you're walking, soldier."

Fritz mumbled an apology and had turned to go when he heard his name.

"Fritz!"

"Hiero!"

Hiero stood beside the tall man and put out an arm to stop him. "Hollis, this man is one of my closest friends. He'll be under your protection as well. Fritz, come." Hiero grabbed Fritz's arm and pulled him away from Hollis, just out of earshot. "Fritz, Lamont tricked us. We have to get him back. Which way did he go?"

Fritz jerked his arm away immediately. "Hiero, why are they trying to make you king? What happened after I left?"

"Gannon tried to kill me."

Fritz's mouth hung open. "What?"

Hiero shook his head furiously. "It's a tale for a different time! Fritz, Lamont has the king's signet ring!"

Fritz felt flattened. If Hiero knew that he had sided with Lamont, even for a moment, he would be hurt. "I know where he is, Hiero. He can't have gotten very far. We'll find him!"

"Let's go. Hollis! With me!"

They ran through the crowd, Hollis making a path for them. Fritz's chest burned with the pressure. He didn't want Gannon as king—he knew that much—and Hiero couldn't be king, as far as Fritz understood. Lamont might stop the slave trade, and that slim chance was enough.

They ran through the gates and into the street. Fritz led them to the other side of the square, opposite from the side Lamont had disappeared into.

"That way! Down that alley!"

They ran down it, looking to the right and the left, and then they split to run down each point of the intersection. Fritz could see no one in the distance. He turned in a full circle. "I-I don't understand, Hiero! He was limping!" Fritz cupped his hands around his mouth and shouted, "We'll get you, Lamont! There's no escape!"

Lamont heard Fritz's shout and clutched at his broken wrist, wedging himself tighter into his hiding place.

"Thank you, Fritz," he whispered. "I won't forget this."

Lamont was wedged between the angled roof and a chimney, where he had a clear view of the square and streets below. He saw another man run up to Fritz, attracted by his shout. Lamont gritted his teeth. It wouldn't be long before there was a search. The Teris boy was already looking for the king's signet ring, and when he couldn't find it, fire would break loose.

Lamont shoved his body even tighter into the area. The king had been right about the Teris family all along, and Lamont had simply brushed him off. Lamont shook his head. If only he could apologize for his foolishness.

He had felt himself growing weaker inside the palace, but he hadn't known how serious it was until he had felt his legs failing. Apparently, his body was taking his injuries seriously. Using two fingers and biting down hard on his shirt, Lamont straightened out the bones in his wrist until he could take no more pain, and then he relaxed, letting his head roll back against the chimney.

The night still had a few hours left, and a few hours of sleep was all it would take. His cuts would be healed, his wrist would be knit, and the horrible pounding in his head would subside. Hiero might believe that Lamont had faked the stumbling, but he knew that the injuries were not fake and would expect Lamont to still be weak by the time the sun rose. Lamont lay back and shut his eyes. *They could never be more wrong.*

A few hours later, Lamont felt the first rays of the sun peeking over the horizon. He stretched out his wrist to feel the bones fall back into place. His wrist was completely healed.

Lamont needed to get out of the city. By now the king was dead, and this place was a death trap for anyone who loved him. Lamont gripped the side of the wall and lowered himself down to the abandoned alley. His best bet would be to take the mountain road down to the slums. From there he could rent or buy a horse, and then he would ride to Lord Kiad.

Carefully, Lamont stood in a thin alley between houses, listening until he was certain no one was nearby. For the time being, no one was looking for him here. He stuck his head out first, into the street, and then he squeezed himself out.

Lamont walked away from the palace. It had to be the middle of the sixth hour. In another hour or so, stores would begin to open. Until that time, he would look out of place. But by the twelfth hour, Lamont intended to be out of Reta. He knew the Teris family would send an alert after him across Reta as soon as possible, if they had not done so already.

The need for urgency fought hard against Lamont's desire to look casual, and he began to walk faster, eventually breaking into a jog. Every dark window and closed door seemed to be a threat of recognition. How many of Reta's citizens knew his face? He feared the answer.

It was not long before he reached the eastern edge of the city. There was a wall built here, against the edge, to keep people from unwittingly falling off the cliffside.

Through the barred view holes, Lamont could see that the sun had just barely cleared the horizon, and it hung there like a gigantic orange. The city of Reta had been built on a plateau rising in altitude from south to north. The slums were against the bare cliffs on the eastern and western sides of Reta. They were not on the plateau because the original city edict had not allowed brothels or businesses of ill repute to be built on city property.

In order to get to them from the city, one had to either go out through the city gates and around Reta or traverse the cliffside trail. The cliffside trail, or Slum Road, had had a terrible reputation in the time of the Teris rule. It was a continuous staircase, a little more than a yard wide, from the top of the cliff to the ground. The steps were cut straight from the rock, and there was an overhang that kept off the elements, but none of this was the reason for its reputation.

In the time before its renovation, there had not been gates to keep people off the road at night. There had not been guards at the top and bottom to check that inebriated people were not using the road, and there had been no guardrail to keep people from falling to their death at the slightest slip.

Lamont had heard that in the days of Teris it had been common to hear of at least one death a night from Slum Road. Nobody had cared about the danger because the people who died on the road were "fools" and "reprobates." Lamont did not disagree with the sentiment, but he had read that since the installment of security precautions, fewer people traveled the road due to its much more public nature. People seemed to have an innate desire to keep their visits to the slums quiet, and the presence of two guards, one at the top and one at the bottom, didn't allow for that.

After traveling down the eastern edge of Reta for another half hour, Lamont reached the slum gate. It was a rickety little thing, seven feet tall and two feet wide, strapped between two official-looking posts. A guard was not present, and the gate was locked. Lamont sighed. He had expected this. All the guards had been holed up in the palace since the barracks had been burned.

Lamont glanced around, running his fingers through his hair as he searched the street. No housefronts faced the slum gate, and Lamont did not see anyone hanging out of a window watching him.

In one swift motion, Lamont ran forward, jumped up against the gate, and shimmied up to the top. He regretted his decision immediately. The gate felt extremely unstable, and Lamont was four feet away from a sheer drop-off. He swallowed his fear and swung his legs over the top, landing on his feet at the bottom. He grasped the guardrail behind him.

Lamont had never been on Slum Road before, and he wondered why anyone would ever want to be. It was terrifying. Even with both his hands wrapped securely around the guardrail, the stones were slippery, and the wind struggled mightily to blow him off. Lamont could see that the description of the overhang had been greatly exaggerated. If it had been raining, only half of him would've been dry.

He remembered the few times he had been to the slums, always on business. Men seemed to go down there and then mysteriously forget they had sworn oaths to the city. He remembered it being bright and garish, full of activity and noise.

Down Lamont went, about a mile of stairs, reconsidering his fear of heights. After some time, it was not as frightening, with the ground steadily growing closer.

Lamont shook the thoughts from his head. He had never been afraid of heights. He wasn't going to start now.

As he descended, Lamont reached the place that the slums called "the point of night." As the cliffs rose to the west, they blocked the sun from the slums for the majority of the day. It was considered "high time" for the slums. Lamont had seen it once, and he wanted to be out before it began. In the prime portion of the slums, right up against the cliff face, there was only daylight for about six hours, giving it an almost never-ending nightlife. But right now, the sun was in the sky, and Lamont found himself staring down at a ghost town. He came off the stairs into a street that had once been festive and was now abandoned.

Lamont swallowed. This place didn't feel right. Where was everyone? Everything was closed, and some places were even boarded up. Lamont turned and headed toward the only open door he saw. The sign over the entry advertised free ale for those who bought the dart package. Lamont ducked his head to keep from smacking it. The inside was lit with lamps, but it still felt dark. As he entered, five men stood suddenly.

"Hey, you! Are you from the city?"

"Yes." Lamont found himself swarmed with questions as the men surrounded him.

"Are the gates open?"

"Is the city still standing?"

"Is the king dead? He's probably dead."

"How many people are dead?"

"Was there any starvation?"

Lamont put up his hands. "Gentlemen, please! I can't quite understand when you're all talking at once. Could you let a man sit first?"

The men looked frantic, but Lamont took a chair and waited patiently as they poured him a drink. He took a swallow and looked around the table.

"All right, I will tell you what I know, and you will tell me what you know. First of all, the palace has fallen, and the king is dead." The men nodded, and there was the slightest sound of a chuckle. Lamont's eyes narrowed. "Do you find this funny?"

The man at whom he directed his gaze shrugged. "It's more of a good riddance thing, sir, if you get my meaning. I didn't mean to offend."

"No, apparently not." Lamont took another sip from his glass. He'd had better ale. "So, a leader has appeared, a Hieronymus Purvis, and the crowds want him to be king. As to the condition of the city, I can't tell you that. You asked if the gates were closed?"

The men looked at their glasses. "Aye, sir. The city has been totally shut up today and yesterday. We've had no communication. We're just trapped out here."

Lamont's brow furrowed. "I didn't know."

"Well, that was after we saw the fire."

Lamont nodded. "The barracks of the city guard were burned, yes. We tried our best to get the families out."

"We, sir?"

"I-I tried to get the families out. I knew some of them personally."

"Perhaps you wouldn't mind me asking you a personal question, sir?"

Lamont raised his head. "No. What is it?" The look on every man's face was dead cold. Lamont glanced from face to face nervously. "What seems to be the matter, gentlemen?"

Their eyes burned into him. "Tell me," the largest man began, "how in the name of Isle did you manage to escape the palace?"

Lamont chuckled and leaned back in his chair. "What are you talking about, man? The citizens have won!"

The man shook his head. "No, don't try to play me false, sir. I know what spoiled palace fool smells like." His glare froze the base of Lamont's spine. "And you reek!"

At that moment, there was the sound of a bell, hoof-beats, and a deep, bellowing voice hammering out the news.

"Alert! The palace has been taken! The old king is dead, and Hieronymus Purvis has been declared lord of Reta! Alert! Grand General Lamont Reynard escaped during palace raid! Hieronymus offers reward for live capture! City is to remain closed until he's captured! Alert! The palace . . ."

Lamont took another sip from his glass and relished its bitter aftertaste. "So, gentlemen, I'll just be on my way."

"Oh, I don't think so." The men rose one by one from their chairs. "We intend to take you in."

Lamont nodded with a sigh. "Of course you do." He jerked, tossing the ale in the nearest man's face, and then fell to the ground, rolling under the table as they lunged for him. In the next second he had shoved the table up, knocking one over, and swung the table around to knock another man out. The big man lunged at him with a knife, and Lamont backpedaled, nearly tripping over the man he had just knocked out. He fumbled and sat down hard, avoiding a wide swipe. He shuffled back as fast as he could and stood up.

"Hold! I thought you were going to take me alive!"

"Maybe." The man brandished his knife. "And maybe I just want to see a palace rat bleed."

Lamont sighed. The wall was behind him, and unless

he planned on going through that, he had to go through them. Lamont looked to his left. The bar. He could use that.

He sped for it and leaped over the counter. The man ran after him. Lamont grabbed two bottles out of the rack by their necks and held them ready below the counter, where they couldn't be seen. The man ran all out for him, his knife held out in front of him like a spear, not noticing or not caring about the counter directly in front of him.

Just before the man reached him, Lamont jumped to the side, brought both bottles up, and smashed the man's head between them. The man released his knife. Lamont felt its impact like a dull thud, like an extra weight in his belly. He pulled two more bottles from the rack and quickly incapacitated the other two men.

Then he looked down, and his heart stopped beating for a half second. His head felt light on his body. Lamont brought a hand down on the counter to keep from falling over. He thought he'd only been grazed, but it was inside him, almost up to the hilt, about five inches of steel.

Lamont grabbed a rag from the counter and yanked the knife out before shoving the rag into the hole. He grabbed another towel and tied it tightly around his waist to hold it in place. There was no more time to waste. He would be dead if he stayed here any longer. He had to get to Lord Kiad.

Lamont crawled over the counter, feeling his wound with every movement. He could not help being terrified. He had never healed from an injury like this, and he did not have the time to sleep right now. He didn't remember what organs were there, what could possibly have been damaged. He feared those possibilities. Lamont staggered out of the tavern.

He heard the bell again. The crier had made his rounds through the slums and was heading out toward the Great Forest. "Sir! Excuse me, sir!" Lamont tried not to stumble as he flagged the crier down. The man stopped his horse at his word.

"Good morning, sir! Have you a question?"

Lamont hobbled over. "I do! I do! Where did you get such a fine horse?"

The man looked flattered. He smiled. "She was a gift from the company for five years of excellent service."

Lamont reached up and patted her neck. "She looks strong on her feet."

"She is. We're always on the move together!" He followed Lamont's motion and patted his horse's neck, leaning over in the saddle.

Quicker than he could blink twice, Lamont had grabbed his wrist and twisted around, flinging the young man from his saddle and into the dirt. In another moment, Lamont was up in the saddle and riding away, leaving the crier to cough in the dirt. Lamont winced at the pain in his side and the blood he could already feel soaking through the cloth. His heart's own steady thrum was slowly sending him to his death. There was no time to waste. He turned the horse's head north and rode hard.

15

Innocent Wind

SHELIA SHIVERED AS a cool wet wind blew through the stable. She pulled her feet up under her nightgown and drew her robe tighter around her knees. She could have chosen to perch on the crossbar closer to doors and been better protected, but then she wouldn't have been able to see the whole length of the yard.

Lord Teris saddled his horse in the flickering lamplight. He looked deadly serious. All the men did. He fastened his saddlebags and stepped up into his saddle. Rigel, the bannerman, followed his lead, settling himself in the saddle before he took the heavy banner from Mich. Lanus and Mich mounted a few moments later. Lord Teris looked them all in the eyes before he spoke.

"All right, most of you already know why I've mustered you from your beds in the middle of the night. The city of

Reta has been taken by anarchy. You all know that a rider was just here. He told me that the palace has just been overrun. The rioters are being led by Hieronymus Purvis. Some of you may remember him as Hiero Reynard, the bastard who was under my care. He was Gannon's close friend. Since I have received word from his school in Jasberan that he has gone missing, I can only assume that Gannon has something to do with these events. Being my son, he is likely their catalyst."

Lord Teris cleared his throat loudly. "Now, I know what all of you are thinking, but we are officially going to Reta to see that Gannon is well and that his transition to power is expedient. Any punishment that needs to be exacted will be exacted by me. You have all grown up together, and perhaps you don't take him seriously, but Gannon is about to become the heir to Retall. Remember that."

With a twist of the reins, he turned his horse's head toward the gates, and the two gatemen made a mad scramble to get them open. He raised a closed fist to the sky.

"In the return of the Teris name to its rightful seat of power, may the Ancients defend us!"

All who could thrust their fists into the air with him. "Ancients defend us!"

From where she hid in the stable ceiling, Shelia saluted with them and raised a silent prayer of her own. "Please protect Hiero."

Rigel maneuvered his horse to the front of the formation and waited as the gates were opened fully. There was a moment of silence, and then Father brought his hand down. "Riders of Teris, onward!"

Loose dirt and clods of grass were flung about as they galloped out the gates and into the night. Shelia waited until the gates had been shut tight before she crawled back along the crossbar and climbed down a set of shelves built into the wall to the ground. Her nightgown was white, and she knew how visible that would be even with no moon, so she pulled her dark robe completely around herself and tied it tightly.

The stable was a large open building with three entrances and a wide expanse of stalls, most of them empty. Shelia had been told that at one time all the stalls had been needed and there were so many stable hands that it was difficult to walk from one entrance to another without breaking stride. But that was many years ago, before she had been born.

As she made her way out of the stable, Shelia paused to pat her horse on the nose. "Hello, Beya. Were you sleeping well? I haven't really slept at all. Things are too exciting, you know? I hope Hiero and Gannon are both safe. Maybe Father will let us go and visit them at Reta! Would you like that?" Shelia giggled as Beya tossed her head. She ran her hand down the soft nose one more time. "I'll let you get back to sleep."

At the stable's back entrance, Shelia crouched and squeezed easily through the large crack at the bottom of the door. She held her hair with one hand to keep it from catching on the jagged wood. She knew exactly how to twist herself so that nothing would snag. She'd been sneaking in and out since she was little.

The ground outside was bitterly cold compared to the packed dirt inside the stable. Shelia's toes curled against it. She stood slowly.

The stable was between the manor and the servants' quarters, and Shelia faced the servants' quarters now. No one should've been awake at this time, but Shelia still moved stealthily, sliding from shadow to shadow. Once she was around the edge of the stable, Shelia ran for the manor. The ground was soft, and she ran on her toes to avoid footprints.

A few moments later, she was crouched next to the manor's front door, breathless and giggling. Her heart pounded with mischief, and she grinned from ear to ear. They hadn't seen her. No one had caught her out of bed. It was such a wonderful rush! The servants would never know. If the servants didn't find out, then her father never would.

Shelia glanced through the porch rails at the gatehouse before standing, grabbing a handle of the double doors, and yanking the door open. She slid inside, letting it click shut on its own behind her. Shelia threw her arms out and spun in a circle. Victory! Gannon was going to be king! He would let her marry Hiero! Everything was going to work out now.

Shelia skipped toward the stairs, and as her foot touched the first step, she heard a creak from the door beside the stairs.

"Shelia, what are you doing awake at this hour?"

Shelia turned to see two feet push open the swinging door, followed by a wheeled chair.

"Uncle Beni!" Shelia dropped from the stair and slid to her knees beside his chair, throwing her arms around him in a giant hug.

"Shelia! Shelia!" Uncle's voice was strangled by her embrace. "What has gotten you so excited?"

Shelia pulled back to give him a wide grin. "It's Hiero, Uncle!"

"Ah!" Uncle's head rolled back, and his eyes rolled with it. "It must have been a wonderful dream. What did he do this time?"

Shelia's mouth became a stubborn line. "No, Uncle, it wasn't a dream!"

Uncle's forehead crinkled. "What do you mean?"

Shelia lowered her voice and leaned in, setting her elbows on the chair's armrest. "Did you notice how strange Father was acting today?"

Uncle ran his fingers through his beard. "Come to think of it, I did. He was so quiet at breakfast, and then he took dinner in his room. You think he acted strange because of something Hiero did?"

Shelia smiled with her eyes. "It was because he was receiving secret messages all day, and just now he went riding out the gate with Rigel and Lanus and Mich!"

Uncle brought his hand down on her arm. "Shelia, please tell me what you know from the beginning, otherwise it's confusing. What secret messages has Renald been receiving?"

Shelia thought for a moment. "Well, there was a slip of paper caught in the kitchen door this morning. It said, 'Barracks burned. Gates are closed.' I think things got worse sometime in the evening because he wouldn't talk to me at all, but he was having a hushed conversation with Mich. I know they were talking about Reta and the king."

Uncle's hand tightened on her arm. "The barracks at Reta have been burned? The gates are closed? That sounds like plague, Shelia!"

"No, no, Father addressed his riders before they left. He said Reta has been taken over by anarchy and Hiero is running the city!"

"Our Hiero? How is that possible? What happened to the king?"

"Father said the king is dead."

Uncle sucked in a deep breath. "Of course. That explains why he went." Uncle smiled. "He must be so excited."

"Excited for Gannon to become king?"

Uncle chuckled. "Well, I'm sure he is excited about that as well, but the palace was his home. He hasn't gotten to see it for thirty-two years. He is finally going home!"

Shelia tossed her head. "What about you, Uncle? Don't you miss the palace?"

"I was just a baby, Shelia. I don't remember it at all."

Shelia put her chin in her hands. "I wonder what it will be like, living there."

Uncle gave her the sly eye. "Don't you want to marry Hiero?"

Shelia's eyes went wide. "Of course I do!"

Uncle shrugged. "Hiero might not want to live in the palace."

Shelia shrugged back. "Well, that's fine, as long as we visit!"

Uncle reached out and brushed stray hairs out of her face. "Shelia, you look just like your mother. In look, in spirit, in action. Sometimes I can only see you as Lisanna."

Shelia watched his face curiously. "Do you miss her?"

"I do. She was like a mother to me."

Shelia looked away. "I wonder if my children will look like me."

"Who can tell? Perhaps they will all look like Hiero."

Shelia giggled. "I'm going back to bed, Uncle. I'm tired, and all the excitement left with Father."

Uncle ruffled her hair with a laugh. "You do that. I'm sure we will hear the whole story in the morning."

Shelia wrapped her arms around him in another hug and kissed him on the cheek. "In the morning, Uncle."

"In the morning, Shelia."

Shelia stood and ran up the stairs to her bedroom. She couldn't wait to see what the morning would bring.

16

CAPTIVE PRINCE

GANNON OPENED HIS eyes. A gag was tied around his face, and he was bound spread-eagle to a bed. A thin, cruel-looking man with a cloth hat shoved over long tangled brown hair sat in a chair against the door.

Gannon's eyes rolled back into his head. His arms strained against his bonds. As if ants had been set loose on it, his bare chest itched and burned like fire. He wanted to scratch it so badly!

Gannon had a sudden realization that derailed his discomfort. His bonds weren't chafing his wrists. He turned his head to look. It wasn't rope. Soft cloth, probably silk, was wrapped around his wrists and tied to the bed. And that wasn't the only interesting development. Gannon saw dried blood under his fingernails. Surprise overcame panic, and Gannon strained to look at his chest.

It was awful. His chest was a mass of oozing scabs, and he could see where his fingers had scratched in his sleep, ripping off scabs and leaving a bloody trail. His captors wanted him to heal. Gannon studied the man at the door. He might've been dirty, but the gag in Gannon's mouth was clean. Clearly, he wasn't the person in charge.

Gannon looked to the roof. Whoever held him captive had money. Gannon could think of a million more things surprising about this situation, but those things weren't important. He was being held. He had a gag around his mouth, bonds on his wrists, and a guard at the door. However nice this captor may have been, Gannon had to get away. It was important that his father hear about Hiero's treachery as soon as possible.

Gannon strained against his bonds and shouted into the gag. The guard's head jerked up. His eyes were dazed. He knocked on the door behind him, then stood and moved his chair out of the door's path. A few seconds passed, and the door opened from the other side. A boy stepped in, dressed like a man. He wore brown leather breeches, and his hair was red brown, like an autumn leaf. He looked just younger than Gannon was.

He stepped in softly and dropped a coin in the guard's open hand as he passed him. The guard turned and bolted out the door the moment the metal touched his skin. The door creaked shut before the boy stepped forward.

"Good morning. My name is Anias Kaiden."

Gannon glared. He had to be a sir's son. His accent was distinctly northern. His leather breeches were stained and spoke of a life in the saddle. His hands were expressive, fluid.

"I understand that you are hurt. I understand that you

might be afraid or in pain. I want to assure you that I have no ill will toward you. You are safe in my care. I will see that you are fed, that your wounds are treated, and that you always have a clean place to sleep. There is no need to worry about such things. Whatever harsh life you held previously does not exist. You are now in the service of Lord Kiad."

Gannon felt the hard ball drop in the small of his back. That was fear—living, cold fear—wrapped around his spine. He was in the service of Lord Kiad? Gannon had heard about this, this underground slave harvesting.

Slavery was illegal in Retall and always had been, but since Lord Reta had wrestled power from Teris, secret slavery had begun, and it had begun with Lord Kiad. Lord Kiad's ancestral seat of power had always been over the execution of justice. Over the hundreds of years since Retall's founding, all prisons had operated out of Kiad territory and under the family's guidance. It was simple: you broke the law, and you were shipped north, sometimes to return, and sometimes not. But once Lord Reta became king, things changed.

It began with accusations of twisted justice. A peasant family filed a petition for the release of their eldest son, whom they claimed had been arrested without warning and without a crime. Their petition never received a reply.

Slowly, such incidents became more and more frequent, and the king released a statement to silence the rumors that the justice system was corrupt. The only explanation was Kiad money funneled to the throne.

Then the news came that shocked every man in Retall: Lord Kiad had been outsourcing prisoners. No one knew for how long exactly. He claimed that the recent increases in crime were taxing the justice system beyond what it was able to handle and that there were not enough facilities on Kiad land to house them, so Lord Kiad advertised his prisoners to the other lords of Retall as "labor." For a minimal fee, a prisoner would serve their sentence as part of that lord's labor force. Despite the ranting of the young Lord Teris, the outsourcing became common practice, and the flow of humans to and from Kiad land increased by hundreds.

And now Gannon found himself on the receiving end of this human trade. Fear ran a dozen different thoughts through his head, but he latched on to only one solution: he had to let this slaver know who he was. Lord Kiad could not be fool enough to put himself at odds with another lord. Even in this unstable time, that was political suicide. Once this man knew who he was, he would release him.

Gannon flailed his arms and banged his head back against the sheets while trying to form clear words through the cloth, but his voice came out as nothing but a garble.

Kaiden gave him a stern look. "Please refrain from struggling with me or my associates. You will only cause yourself more damage."

There was a creak as the door opened, and a portly man in rough clothing stuck his head in. "Kaiden, sir?"

"You're awake!" Kaiden slapped the man on his shoulder. His whole tone and demeanor had changed completely. He was the boss now. "Blessed Isle, man! What happened to you? I had to hire some miscreant to watch the door for me!"

The man rubbed his head sheepishly. "There was a fight."

Kaiden's hands rested on his hips. "I gathered that. I told all of you not to have more than two drinks!"

"It wasn't us, sir, I swear!" The man put his hands up protectively. "The boys and I, we would never fight like that! Not even if we were drunk."

"Are you trying to convince me that you weren't drunk? Every one of you smelled like a brewery when I found you!"

"Let me explain, sir. There was a man. From the way he spoke, we could tell he was a sir or some other palace rat, and my first thought was that he was snooping around for information. Then a crier rode by, saying that the grand general was a fugitive and that there was a reward for him. I realized that if he could be captured, he would bring Lord Kiad good coin."

"One man beat all of you alone?"

The man's head pumped up and down. "Yes, sir! He was so fast! I barely remember most of the fight!"

Kaiden turned and looked over his shoulder at Gannon. He looked worried. "Why would the grand general be a fugitive?"

"He told us that the rebels had taken the palace."

Kaiden's head snapped back. "That can't be true! The palace gates are impenetrable!"

The man shrugged. "He also said that the king was dead."

Kaiden looked shocked to his core. He slumped against the wall. "We need to get moving. We need to get away from Reta now!"

The man took a step toward him. "Why so suddenly? What's the problem?"

Kaiden shook his head and righted himself without help. "If the king is dead, there will be a lords' council to elect another one. I can only think of one man with the strength of claim and influence to be a contender, and that is Lord Teris." Kaiden held up a finger. "Lord Teris has tried to shut down our work more than once, and he has nearly succeeded. When he becomes king, he will have all our heads displayed on the palace gates. Do you understand?"

The man nodded. "We will be ready to leave within the day. I'll go get the carts prepped and ready now."

"Good. Oh, also, when one of the others wakes up, send them up to take care of him." He tossed his head at Gannon. "I am almost certain he has to relieve himself by now."

The door shut solidly behind the man, and Gannon was left alone with Kaiden. It was ironic. They were afraid of his family on the throne, yet it was their fear that kept him from becoming king.

Kaiden pulled the chair over and sat in it, watching him. This man was a fool to think he could do such things and walk away clean. When Lord Teris heard of this, he really would have all their heads on spikes.

Kaiden's eyes met his, and then he looked away guiltily. "I'm glad it is over." He glanced at Gannon and away again. "I can't handle the guilt of this work forever." He sighed. "You are the last, and perhaps with you Lord Kiad will be satisfied. Maybe he will finally set me free."

He spent the time after that in silence. Gannon felt indecisive. If he were given the chance to speak now, would it be wise to reveal his identity? Lord Kiad would almost certainly use him as leverage against his father, and this Kaiden was a slave himself and bound to bring him back to his master. What a terrible situation.

How had things gotten so difficult? Hadn't he defeated the enemy of his family? Hadn't he by his own wits survived a fall from the palace? Where was his reward? What was he supposed to do now? The only logical action Gannon could take was to wait and be silent. Once the lords' council started looking for him, it would already be too late for Kiad to use him against his father. Lord Kiad would be ruined.

Gannon was eventually taken out to relieve himself, but his gag stayed in, and his arms were bound behind his back. The men holding him had cuts on their faces, and they were not gentle. Shame was not an issue for Gannon right now. If he had a chance to escape, he would take it. But there was never a chance. From the outhouse, the men led him toward the carts, where Kaiden was mounted, watching the area around them with his hand held up to shade his eyes.

"Get him inside quickly!" he shouted. "We might have trouble!" He pointed to the horizon, and Gannon followed his arm. He could see a company of horses on the Great Road, and the man riding before them held a banner.

Gannon strained his eyes. Could that be? That was his banner! That was the banner of the house of Teris! Father was coming for him! Gannon found the strength to fight. He jerked his body one way and then the next to loosen their grips. He smashed the hardest part of his head into one man's face, and the man dropped like a stone. The other Gannon kneed in the groin, and he went down cursing.

And then he was running. His arms were still bound, but he cycled with his shoulders. He heard Kaiden's shout behind him, but all he saw were those Teris horsemen and their red banner.

Suddenly, the horizon wobbled and flew out of his vision, and Gannon lay coughing in the dirt. The largest of the men had tackled him. His scabs were open, and he could feel them bleeding. Two more men ran up to surround him, and the three of them restrained him and lifted him up like a sack of flour.

Gannon twisted in their arms. He could still see the horsemen! They were so close! Gannon screamed through his gag, hoping desperately that they would hear him and hurry to assist. Then the Great Road curved. They continued on.

His father's horsemen and the horizon melded together as Gannon's eyes filled with water, and he wept.

17

DAY DREAMS

LAMONT'S STOMACH SLOSHED. That wasn't a good sign. His left arm had been wrapped protectively around his abdomen for hours, and he felt it slowly growing more wet inside. Something inside was still bleeding, but Lamont had no way of knowing what. The outside bleeding appeared to have been stemmed from the pressure he had kept on it.

Lamont had tried to sleep on the road with mild success, but for only short periods of time. His body was already taxed to its limit of wakefulness. He needed to sleep, and if he did not, it was highly likely he would simply slip off his horse in the middle of the night.

He had made it through the open land and into the Great Forest while the sun was at its highest. The sun was heading down now, and Lamont had no idea how much of the forest was left. He couldn't ride hard anymore. The way his belly moved frightened him.

Lamont slowed the horse to a trot and leaned down in the saddle to try sleeping again. This time was not like the others. The deepening evening and his own utter exhaustion threw him into a new kind of waking sleep.

He slept, yet he remembered seeing the sun set. He remembered the nighttime forest and someone shouting just before his horse bolted into a gallop. The forest whirled crazily in his vision, and he felt himself slowly sliding out of the saddle, yet he could not wake up to slow the horse.

The wild ride continued on and on for infinity. The wind was cool and comfortable in his hair. Lamont thought that perhaps he was already dead and that was why his body would not answer him. Suddenly, his horse grew two wings and jumped into the sky. Lamont jumped too, but he did not have wings, and he fell into the dirt.

As he lay there looking up, the stars came alive and danced all around his head. One of them had a face, and it was the face of a little girl. Lamont slept.

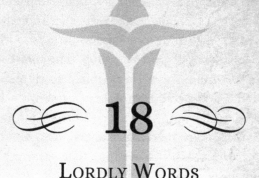

18

Lordly Words

Hiero felt like he had just closed his eyes when there was a knock on the bedroom door. He opened his eyes and sat bolt upright. Where was he? How long had he been asleep? A deep-throated chuckle pulled his attention to the door. "Hollis!"

Hollis stood just inside the door, chuckling. "Would you like me to let your friend in, Your Majesty?"

Hiero put a hand against his heart and laughed at his own fear. "Yes, Hollis, please let him in."

The door opened, and Fritz strode in. "Ah, you're awake! Good. So much has happened! First, Lamont has disappeared. He isn't in the city, he isn't outside the city, and we can't even find someone who claims to have seen him."

Hiero sighed. "So, no chance of finding the king's signet ring." He gave Fritz a pained look. "Have you found Gannon?"

Fritz's mouth snapped shut, and he shook his head. "I'm sorry, Hiero, no. If it is any consolation, we haven't found a body yet."

Hiero's eyes drifted to the floor. "It's all my fault. I failed to diffuse his anger."

Fritz scratched behind his ear and shifted uncomfortably. "You should know, the king's body has already been burned according to the law, and we are taking care of the other bodies the same way. If we do find Gannon. . ."

Hiero refused to answer that. "How many casualties?"

"Less than a hundred. More may be discovered as the day wears on."

Hiero looked blankly out his bright window. "What time is it?"

Fritz coughed into his hand, trying to hide a smile. "Just after the thirteenth bell, Hiero."

Hiero leaped out of his chair. "The thirteenth bell! Fritz, I've got work to do!"

Fritz put his hand up. "Hiero, the people are still shouting for you."

Hiero put a hand to his head. "Still? It's been two days!"

Fritz nodded. "And if you don't want to be forcibly conscripted into the throne, I suggest you stay hidden."

Hiero flopped into the chair. "Is there any way I can take care of my administrative duties here? I have a city to run, Fritz!"

Fritz crossed his arms. "Yes, that bothers me, Hiero. We should already be sneaking out of the city and on the road to Kiad's territory. Why did you make the mayors turn their power over to you? It doesn't make any sense.

That has been their duty for hundreds of years! No wonder Gannon got the wrong idea!"

Hiero shook his head. "I can't trust them with their own duty! The law has no meaning to people like them. They betrayed the Teris family before, bending the rules for the usurper before he became king. They are crooked old men who only care about growing their own power. Gannon isn't here, and I am not going to leave everything in anyone's hands I can't trust!" Hiero came to an abrupt halt.

Fritz gave him a cold stare. "There is more, isn't there?"

"I am worried about Lamont." Hiero rubbed his chin. "I am almost certain he has the king's signet ring. If you are right and he is heading for Lord Kiad, I am certain that Lord Kiad will support his claim to the throne. And if Gannon is dead, that will make Lamont virtually unchallenged." Hiero's eyes went blank as they met Fritz's. "In that event, I will have to become king."

Fritz rubbed the bridge of his nose wearily. "Not this again. Hiero, it's madness! You can't be king without being elected by the lords."

"I can be elected, Fritz. The people have already elected me."

Fritz looked exasperated. "Let's not discuss the inconvenience that we are still in the palace after two days or that most of the city is so riled up they won't settle for anyone but you on the throne. Let's focus on things that will definitely lead to death. The lords will have your head!"

Hiero stood and paced to the wall. "I'm not going to lie to you, Fritz. This is selfish, but if Gannon is dead and Lamont becomes king, my head is going to roll anyway. I highly doubt that our encounter has been forgotten."

"He did not strike me as a vengeful person."

"Possibly not, but he can be unspeakably cruel. He has no empathy for those below his station," Hiero said. Fritz sighed, and Hiero put up a hand. "No, no, don't shake your head at me. There is more. Even if Lamont, in a single act of mercy, lets me live, will he sign an order letting me marry Shelia?"

Fritz's eyes closed, and he sighed again. "Oh, Hiero. You promised me. My sisters—"

"I know, Fritz. I know. But remember that Lamont and Lord Kiad are intertwined. He won't free your sisters either. Maybe on the throne I can do something."

Light dimmed behind Fritz's eyes. "So, if Gannon is dead, you intend to take the throne?"

Hiero nodded. "And I will fight to keep it with everything I have."

"And if he's alive?"

Hiero put his hand over his heart. "Fritz, if Gannon were alive, you and I would already be in Lord Kiad's territory."

Fritz shook his head. His deep frown was permanent now. "Something feels wrong about this, Hiero. You saw him fall, but he wasn't down there. It must have been a trick. What if he's hiding, waiting to see what you do next?"

Hiero chuckled, but he understood Fritz's caution. "This is Gannon we're talking about. He's not like his father. He can't comprehend that anyone would ever betray a true-blooded son of the Teris family. What purpose would hiding serve him? He has won. The throne is his! Where is he? He should be here." Hiero sighed. "I'll give him one week to surface before I make a move. If he is alive, it won't take him even that long."

"I don't like declaring a man dead when the body is nowhere to be found."

"We don't have to—not yet. If he is alive, he will come for his throne. That's the one thing he has always wanted." Hiero shook his head. "I truly believe he is gone."

Fritz nodded. "Very well." He turned to the door. "I'll see that you get breakfast and that council paperwork is brought up to you."

Hollis opened the door, and Fritz stepped out. The door shut behind him. Fritz allowed himself to sigh. He felt guilty for this. If he hadn't inserted himself into the situation, Hiero would have killed Lamont right there, and the signet ring would not be missing. Everything would be at peace.

Fritz shook his head. He didn't even believe that. Lamont wasn't the problem; he was simply the scapegoat. Hiero wanted to be king, and he would have wanted it even if Lamont were dead and Gannon alive. But would Hiero make a good king?

Fritz ran down the stairs from the king's bedchamber and jumped the last two stairs, landing with a thump. Fritz had to admit that Gannon's death was likely. There had never been a man to fall from the peak of Reta and survive before.

But the light in Hiero's eyes had been different. He would certainly be impatient this coming week, waiting until the moment when he could become king. Fritz's eyebrows twisted together. What reason did he have? Was it all for the law of the Ancients? Did Hiero really believe that the Ancients could come back?

Fritz had to admit that the thought of his best friend sitting on the throne was nice. And if Hiero were an elected king, he could simply order Kiad to let his sisters go. But it wasn't going to be like that. Once Hiero declared himself king, he would be a criminal. The lords wouldn't rest until he was out of the palace and whomever they chose was in.

Fritz capered through the palace, greeting those he knew as he passed them. This place was already becoming familiar to him, even though he had only been here a few days.

Fritz informed the kitchen of Hiero's need, and stopped in to say good afternoon to Joanna. She'd taken up residence in the servants wing after the palace opened, treating the wounded and debating the ideology of the Faithful with any palace staff who would listen. He kissed her head, as he always did, and told her that Hiero was well.

A few minutes later in another hall, he directed the tall sarcastic mayor to the king's bedchamber so that they could start the day's work. Another short jog and he was outside the palace, reassuring the citizens still camping in the courtyard that Hiero was well, just resting, and trying to convince them to go home. They hadn't listened to him yet, but it didn't hurt to try.

Fritz turned to go back inside just as a horseman carrying the banner of Lord Teris rode into the square outside the palace gates. A moment later, three more horsemen rode up and reined in behind him. Fritz felt a shiver go down his spine. So, the lords were already reaching out. This was not going to end well.

Fritz hurried past the citizen guard standing at the palace gates and jogged up to the horsemen as they dismounted. He tried to look friendly.

"Good morning! I trust you are a delegation from Lord Teris?"

A tall, gaunt man with short graying hair fixed him with a harsh glare. "I am Lord Teris, soldier. Show me to Gannon Teris immediately."

Fritz's smile froze. He saw the resemblance a moment after Lord Teris spoke. Slowly, he bowed. The ground beneath his feet had never looked so interesting. What were they going to tell Lord Teris? "My lord, please follow me inside. Someone there will be able to answer your questions."

He hoped that had been sufficiently vague. It seemed to work. Lord Teris and two of his men followed him through the gates and inside while the bannerman stayed with the horses.

As they entered the palace, Lord Teris sucked in a sharp breath. "Look at it, men! This is the palace of Teris! Look what the usurper did to it!"

Fritz caught the hint of rage in his voice, and his spine stiffened all the way up to his neck. This was going to be painful, and Hiero would have to deal with it. He couldn't imagine that Lord Teris would let them stay another day in this place. At least they would finally be able to get on the road.

Fritz led the men into the throne room, his back so rigid he thought it might snap. Lord Teris sucked in another sharp breath when he saw it.

"More change. This room used to be regal, and now it looks like a crypt." His gaze focused on something in the distance, and finally his face lightened. "My father's throne! It hasn't aged a day." He strode down the throne room, stopping in the center to turn in a full circle. For a moment, his voice caught in his throat. "I did not think that I would see this room again."

Fritz coughed. "My lord, I would have you wait here,

in the throne room, while I fetch someone who can help you."

Lord Teris grabbed his shoulder, clearly becoming impatient. "I want to see my son. Who are you going to fetch?"

"The man currently in control of Reta's affairs."

Lord Teris nodded. "Go."

Fritz left them in the throne room, shut the door, and ran. That was the second time he had ever been face-to-face with a lord of Retall. The first time he had not been so brave. There was a power there that threatened to turn his knees to putty. Fritz had felt like a sniffling child standing in front of him. Hiero was used to it; Hiero would know how to handle it.

He sped through the palace and up the stairs and banged on the bedchamber door, ignoring Hollis's look of interest. Fritz stuck his head in before the door was fully opened. "Hiero! Lord Teris is here!"

Hiero and the mayor stood up at the same time. "What?"

"He's here! He's in the throne room right now!"

Hiero slipped past the table, looking back over his shoulder as he moved for the door. "Keep going. I'll be back."

"But if Lord Teris—"

Hiero looked back over his shoulder, pointing at the mayor. "No. Nothing changes just because he's here. We'll talk later."

And then they were running for the throne room. It added to Fritz's adrenaline, and he felt his heart rate triple. What would Lord Teris do to them when he learned about Gannon? Fritz could only imagine.

Hiero stopped just before the door and straightened

himself. He wore a red brocade vest over a puffed-sleeve shirt and his best breeches. They were the finest clothes he owned. Fritz had gotten his own vest on the same day, in blue. Had it already been a year since then?

"Do I look together?"

Fritz nodded. Hiero hadn't aged a day. It was Fritz who suddenly felt like an old man. "Yes!"

Hiero took a deep breath and let it out. "A lot happens in two years, Fritz. I can't know how much he's changed." He looked nervous. "The last time I saw him, our interaction was unpleasant."

"You have to tell him what happened."

Hiero nodded. "All right! I will! I will!" He grabbed the handle and pushed the door open.

Lord Teris stood beside the throne, and he turned when the door opened. Hiero strode toward him. Lord Teris's mouth turned down so far that Hiero wondered if it would ever turn back.

When he got close enough, Hiero bowed. Lanus and Mich gave him polite nods.

"Lord Teris, it is a pleasure to see you again. I am afraid I have some troubling news."

Lord Teris stepped down from the throne's dais. "Where is my son?"

Hiero sighed. His fingers twisted together against his chest. "That is precisely what I was about to tell you, my lord. He was here. He arrived in Reta about five days ago and came to me first, asking me for aid. He wanted to gain the throne by his own hand and convinced me to join him. He knew that to show his face or spread his name would mean death to his family, so I became the face of this rebellion. It started with greater force than I could have imagined. The people were ready for change."

Hiero paused. Lord Teris had begun to pace.

"Yes, yes, continue!" he shouted, waving his hand at Hiero.

Hiero gritted his teeth. "At some point in our campaign, Gannon disappeared."

"Is that so?"

"Yes, my lord, I asked him to stay inside my home, but he left it, and now he cannot be found anywhere!"

Lord Teris loomed up in front of Hiero, made taller by Hiero's fear. "I know how you speak when you're lying to me, boy. You speak far too fast. Tell me the truth!"

It was as if Hiero were a guilty child once again. His mind took him back to a day in the lord's stables when he had wandered away from his work to play with Shelia and Gannon. Shelia had torn her dress that day. Gannon had skinned his knees. Lord Teris was shorter than him now, but in his memory, he towered over the three of them, a giant.

Hiero closed his eyes. "Gannon is dead."

"And you know this?"

"Yes."

"How?"

"I saw him fall."

"Fall?"

"From the peak of Reta, my lord. From the king's own balcony."

Lord Teris took a step back. "An accident? Or murder?"

Hiero swallowed. "When I stirred up the city, Gannon began to believe that the crowd would break loose and trample the king to death. Gannon wanted that vengeance for his family. He chose to circumvent us by climbing down from the palace roof onto the king's balcony." Hiero shook his head. "It was a wet night, my lord. Pouring rain. The stone was slick—"

"Stop, please!" Lord Teris looked ill. "I don't know if my heart can believe it. This changes everything."

"Yes, my lord, you will need someone to marry Shelia and take his place."

Lord Teris's mind was clearly far away. He tapped his chin absentmindedly. "Yes, I will."

"Me."

"What?" The edge of annoyance cut sharply across the throne room. Lanus's and Mich's heads popped up, and they moved in behind Lord Teris.

Hiero swallowed his uncertainty. "Me! I will marry Shelia, and continue the Teris family name. She already loves me. I know my name is not important, but I would simply be a consort for her. The Teris family would be on the throne again!"

Lord Teris blinked at him in silence as the gears in his mind turned. "Have you lost your mind? There has never been a woman on the throne of Retall. The lords would never agree. And you? The rest of the lords would never vote for you!"

Hiero stood a little taller. It felt like he was pulling a secret card out of a hidden pocket. "I don't need them to vote for me. I intend to do things as the Ancients did them. I will be elected by the people! Law and order will reign in Retall again, and I will pursue the technology of the Ancients until I can see humanity rise into the sky as they did!"

Lord Teris's face turned fatherly. He smirked. "*Myths and Fables of the Ancients, Book Two.* 'The Ancients left clues so that humanity could follow them into the sky.' I read you that book before you ever knew letters. Hiero, I thought you had more sense than to believe such extravagant theories!"

The light in his eyes shifted to sadness and then anger, and his voice rose. "You may have been raised beside a son of Teris, but that does not make you equal to one. You will never have the fire of a trueborn son of Brandon. It is high time you learned your place, Hiero Reynard. It does not matter how you change your name, how great you believe your achievements to be, or how high you set your goals. You will always be a bastard!" His voice dropped to a hiss. "I will not have my daughter married to a bastard. Get out of my family's palace before I am forced to have you arrested!"

At the word "bastard," fire ignited in Hiero's breast, but he held it back, shrugging his shoulders. "And who will arrest me? My people? This isn't your palace, Teris. It is mine."

Lord Teris's head whirled to the many armed men around the room's perimeter. "Guards! I am Lord Teris, rightful heir to this palace! Arrest this man!"

From all sides of the room, men stepped forward. Some wore the uniform of Reta city guards, but most were dressed in common clothes. They glared across the room at Lord Teris as he turned in a circle, shocked. Lord Teris, Mich, and Lanus were quickly restrained.

Lord Teris's eyes widened. "Release me! I am Lord Teris!"

Hiero took a step toward him as he was held. "The people are tired of lords, Renald. I want you to recognize that the time of the lords is over. You can take this message back to the rest of them. The people are in control now." He leaned in. "Get out."

19

Cold Dread

ANIAS KAIDEN LOOKED out at the darkness that was the Great Forest. The lamp attached to the horn of his saddle only lit a small area in front of his horse. Kaiden held up a fist, and the three-cart column behind him came to a stop.

"We are camping here, men. I don't trust the forest at night."

At his words, the men maneuvered the carts into a semicircle. Gatlin jumped from his wagon and started to unhook his horse. Kaiden rode up behind him and cleared his throat. The man's head turned. "See that the prisoner is cleaned and fed inside the wagon tonight."

Gatlin nodded. "As you wish."

Kaiden didn't want to see the prisoner. He wanted to forget he was even there. Kaiden tied his horse up with the others and collapsed in a heap on the ground inside the circle, letting his head fall forward into his hands. He couldn't stand to think of it. The man was exactly what Lord Kiad had asked him to find. Kaiden already knew his fate. It was the same fate Kaiden had been subjected to for many years.

Kaiden leaped to his feet. He couldn't stand this! How could he ever justify what he was doing? Kaiden stormed away from the camp into the darkness. His body shook with simultaneous fear and anger. He watched his hands tremble in the dark. Why did he have to be so afraid? He wanted to stand up to Lord Kiad. He wanted to say no.

Kaiden smashed his fist into a tree and howled, immediately curling up from the pain. He couldn't stand up to Lord Kiad. The memories of what had happened the last time he'd tried haunted him. He remembered the shackles Kiad had mounted to the wall of his office and a large box full of shiny steel implements.

Kaiden curled up into a ball at the base of the tree. He had been much younger than that man when he was taken, perhaps six or seven summers old. He didn't know how long it had been since then. Maybe ten years? Maybe more? He'd lost count. The man looked like he was Kaiden's age now.

The story was common in Kiad's circle. Every year Lord Kiad held a winter hunting festival for all the sirs in his territory. Kaiden's family had been well-off and close to the lord's line in lineage. At the festival, Lord Kiad noticed him and found him beautiful.

Kaiden was the second son. His parents were not particularly attached to him. Everyone knew what Lord Kiad did to young boys, so his parents knew to bargain well. It had been easy for Lord Kiad to line their pockets with wealth and benefits and take young Kaiden in as his "ward."

Kaiden closed his eyes and tried to breathe. He would do himself no favors by losing consciousness out here. His men might not even find him until the morning. Kaiden forced himself to sit up and then to stand. He walked slowly back the way he'd come, as if there were a rock on his back. In another day, two if he slowed their progress, he would be forced to face Lord Kiad again. It had been a blissful two months of freedom, but it was coming to an end.

Kaiden could hope all he wanted, but he knew deep in his heart that Lord Kiad would never release him from his service. Torturing him gave Lord Kiad intense pleasure, and that was unlikely to change.

Kaiden stumbled back into camp. The men had set up a campfire, and they sat around it, talking back and forth. Kaiden needed to eat something, and then he needed to sleep. Curling up in his bunk in his private wagon sounded amazing. It was more than simply being tired; Kaiden's heart was weary.

The men gave him a place around the fire and served him his portion of food. But with him there, the conversation ended. He was their boss, and they did not see him as their equal. Kaiden chuckled softly, but he wanted to cry. It was ironic. They were the freemen, able to leave the lord's employment as they chose, and he was the slave.

Kaiden finished with his food quickly and left the circle without a word. He was moody and erratic, after all. He had no delusions about his emotionalism. No sane person would desire his friendship.

His wagon was his shelter, a place to escape from the eyes, from the gossip. Lord Kiad had seen to that. He had insisted that Kaiden sleep separately. Only a few moments after he closed his eyes, Kaiden was fast asleep.

The next day, they traveled. The forest was a sticky, humid place compared to the flat, peaceful farmland around the capital. Kaiden did not enjoy it. The Great Road was well smoothed, though, and they made good time. Kaiden did not know if his dread could get any worse. The late summer weather was perfect. He had no excuse to delay the company. That night they camped inside Kiad land, and Kaiden was tortured by nightmares. Lord Kiad was waiting for him. There was nothing he could do.

In the morning, Lord Kiad's honor guard was stationed around the camp. They'd snuck up in the night while everyone was sleeping. The next day, they had a protected escort all the way back to Lord Kiad's castle.

Lord Kiad didn't have a manor; he had a castle. The original Lord Kiad had been the only one of Brandon's sons to make his home an impregnable fortress, and each of his descendants had made it a little more their own. It was built of imposing dark stone mined only miles away, and it looked as inhospitable as the city around it. It didn't matter that this was late summer; the north was the north, and every building had a dark, craggy feel to it.

Kaiden tried to block out the world around him; he even closed his eyes. The horse knew the way better than he did. He needed to curb his fear. It would only arouse Lord Kiad.

At the base of the castle, the honor guard surrounded his horse, and the wagons broke off from the group, rolling into a lower courtyard while Kaiden's horse mounted the stairs. Two guards rode in front of him, and two rode behind.

The stairs ended at the upper courtyard, and they dismounted. The honor guard still loosely surrounded him, and the captain nodded to the castle.

"The lord requires your presence immediately."

Kaiden's face was impassive, but he felt like crumbling inside. He took deep steady breaths to keep tears from springing to his eyes. "I expected nothing else after you came this far. Will you escort me the rest of the way?"

"Of course, sir."

The bare stone walls, the unnatural cold, the armed guards—it all made his flesh crawl. He knew this castle stone by stone. He needed no one to lead him. The guards were there to see that he did not run. Kaiden wanted to laugh at himself. There was no point in running now. He had to face Lord Kiad like a man.

Once they reached the interior of the castle, the bare stone was insulated by tapestries and carpets. Kaiden only felt colder.

They followed him to Lord Kiad's personal study. There was no room in the castle that Kaiden knew better. The captain opened the door for him and stepped back. There was no way out of that room, not even a window. Kaiden walked through the door, and it shut behind him.

Lord Kiad was huge, a monster of a man, and stronger than a bear. His hair was blond, streaked with the gray of age. His dark eyes were terrifying. The book in his hand snapped shut, and he slid it back into place on the bookshelf. "Kaiden, welcome back." Lord Kiad turned around slowly. "How was the campaign? Did you bring me what I asked for?"

Kaiden swallowed. "My lord, the king is dead. I thought it best we abandon our mission."

Kiad's eyes studied Kaiden's body, not his face. His finger tapped the bookshelf distractedly. "I heard that the king had died. So many little whisperers have come flying home this past week. Sad that there is no new toy for me. You will attend to me then."

Kaiden's heart shook in his chest like a butterfly flapping its wings. "Yes, my lord."

I'm not a good person, Kaiden repeated to himself. He wouldn't tell Kiad about the man he'd brought back. But it was only to spare his own guilty conscience.

Lord Kiad stepped toward him. He was more than a head taller. Kaiden grabbed two handfuls of his cloak, but his hands still shook. Lord Kiad glanced down at his hands, and the light turned on behind them.

"Kaiden, are you cold? And I thought the fire in here was too warm. Come."

Kaiden flinched as Kiad's fingers came near his face. Lord Kiad waited a few moments for him to respond, then wrapped his hand around Kaiden's shoulder.

"I said come!" He yanked Kaiden across the room and threw him down on the carpet in front of the fireplace. Slowly, he leaned down and grabbed a poker to stoke the fire. "Are you warmer now, Kaiden?"

Kaiden could feel the warmth. A drop of sweat ran down his forehead, yet his body still shook. The glee in Kiad's eyes was unmistakable.

"Look at how cold you are, Kaiden. It must be all those clothes keeping the cold in." Kaiden couldn't move. Lord Kiad's eyes had frozen him to the ground. He reached for him. "You should take them off."

"No!" Kaiden's voice came out as a panicked, feverish scream. He bit his lip instantly. What had he done?

The light in Kiad's eyes went cold. He grabbed Kaiden's shirt in his fist. "No? You intend to tell me no?"

Kaiden wanted to look away, but he could not make himself. "Please, my lord! Please forgive me!"

Lord Kiad's fist relaxed, and Kaiden's butt fell to the floor. Kiad reached forward and placed his hand on the back of Kaiden's neck while his other hand slipped under him and lifted him into his lap. Lord Kiad embraced him.

"Shh, yes, that's right. I'm your lord." His embrace tightened. "I'm your master."

Kaiden's body kept shaking, and he couldn't stop it. Kiad's breath tickled the hair on the back of his neck.

"The next time I ask you to undress, you will do it without question. Now, we are going to undress, and I am going to take all that cold away from you." He kissed Kaiden's neck. "Relax, and I will make you warm."

When the wagon rumbled to a stop, Gannon expected it to be the usual respite. Then the door was flung open, and two men in blue and gray jumped into the wagon and unshackled him, carrying him out of the wagon between them. Gannon blinked in the sunlight at three more men in the blue-and-gray uniform, one with a silver pin on his shoulder.

Silver Pin frowned at him. "Why is he still gagged? There's no need for that here."

The gag was taken out immediately. Gannon worked his stiff jaw before trying to speak. "Where am I?"

Silver Pin raised his arm, and Gannon looked where it pointed. "You are at the castle of your lord and master, Lord Kiad. We will show you to your new quarters. If you resist, you will be punished."

Gannon had expected something similar, but to be housed at Kiad's own castle was a surprise. He would likely be moved to another location later. He glared. Father would see that Lord Kiad got what he deserved for this. He'd like to see that castle dismantled stone by stone.

The men began to move, leading Gannon between them. They walked up a set of stone stairs longer than

Gannon had ever seen. His legs ached by the time he reached the upper courtyard, and then there were more stairs to get into the castle.

They led him through a long open hall and down a hallway into a room. The room was a normal size but richly furnished. An old lady and man bowed as they entered. The men released him, and Silver Pin gave the elders a polite nod before turning back to him.

"These two will get you ready for your inspection. Lord Kiad will be with you shortly afterward."

Gannon nodded. That was why he was at the castle. Lord Kiad must've taken careful care with whom he enslaved. Gannon wondered what happened to those who didn't pass inspection.

"I'll be right outside the door if I am needed." Silver pin finished with another nod and shut the door behind him.

A floor below Gannon, Kaiden screamed again. He felt like he was being torn open. Lord Kiad slapped his back with an open hand.

"You're too tight! Loosen up!"

There was a knock at the door. Lord Kiad growled, dropped Kaiden, and stood. Kaiden's chest hit the floor immediately. He didn't have the strength to rise.

Lord Kiad yanked the door open. "What is the meaning of this disturbance?"

The guard took a frightened step back and averted his eyes. "Um, sir, your newest acquisition has been prepared for inspection."

Lord Kiad's whole demeanor shifted. "My newest acquisition?" He turned and squatted down by Kaiden's head, lifting his chin up. "Kaiden! Why did you not tell me? Did you miss my warmth so badly?" Lord Kiad stood and threw his robe across his shoulders. "Don't you fear, Kaiden. I have the strength to satisfy you both tonight." He tied the sash at his waist. "Wait right there. I will be back."

Gannon was in shackles again, and these were not nicely padded. He lay faceup and naked on the room's large bed. His arms were stretched up over his head. There had been a bath. Gannon remembered and shuddered. He had not been forcibly bathed since he was an infant.

But now there was a more important thought on his mind. What sort of inspection required that he be like this? The foot of the bed faced away from the door, so when Gannon heard the door open, he twisted his head up to see who it was. What he saw was an enormous man standing over him.

Gannon swallowed. "Are you Lord Kiad?"

Kiad sat softly on the bed beside him. "Yes, I am." His hand stroked Gannon's chest. It was a much softer hand than Gannon had expected, and a shiver went up his spine, filling him with a terrible fear.

20

GUILTY FLIGHT

L AMONT WAS A prisoner to a very strange dream. There was a light, and he walked toward it, mesmerized. It pulsed in different colors: red, then blue, then green. With each pulse, Lamont felt like he was on the verge of learning or remembering something, only to lose the thought when the light grew dim again. He continued to step toward it even though each step became heavier and heavier, and his feet became stone. He woke when the light exploded outward, filling his head with terrible pain.

Lamont groaned and opened his eyes. A little girl looked back at him with giant eyes. She could not have been more than a few inches from his face. She immediately screamed.

"Mother, he's awake!"

Lamont reeled back from the shrill sound. There was a clatter and a crash from outside the room, and a young woman came barreling through the doorframe, a wooden spoon in her hand. She looked terrified. She grabbed her little girl by the arm and dragged her away from him, lifting the spoon over her head.

"Whoa! Whoa!" Lamont raised his arms to prepare for the blow, but it didn't come. He peeked through his fingers.

"You aren't going to hurt us?"

Lamont shook his head. "I don't know you. What reason would I have to hurt you?"

Slowly, the woman smiled. It looked nervous and strained. "Well, thank the Ancients! You're awake!"

Lamont struggled to sit up. The pain in his head was enormous. As he sat up, a cloth fluttered off his brow. The woman jumped forward.

"Sorry, we've been trying to get your fever down. You were burning up terribly when you got here."

Lamont's hand shifted down to his belly. It was bandaged securely, but that did not stop it from aching or itching. Lamont closed his eyes. It was healing. His blood had done its work. He was out of the danger zone now. Lamont met the woman's eyes.

"Who brought me here?"

"My brothers, sir. You fell off your horse while riding through our field. When I saw your wound, I did not think that you would live."

Lamont smiled. "I am a lot harder to kill than that, madam."

The woman looked surprised. "Oh, someone tried to kill you?"

"Yes, but they will not have followed me. How long have I been here?"

"Nearly a day, sir."

Lamont looked out the cloth-covered window beside the bed. The sun was going down on the horizon. Lamont turned back.

"I need to leave tomorrow morning, by dawn."

The woman's face was suddenly afraid. "Sir, you haven't eaten or drunk anything since you were brought here. You can't ride yet. You need to take time to heal and recover."

Lamont ran his fingers through his hair. "I'm not taking your advice lightly, madam; I just don't have the time to rest properly right now. Once I've reached my destination, I will." Lamont's stomach rumbled audibly, and he grinned sheepishly. "If you are offering food, though, I will gladly take it."

The woman smiled again. "Give me just a moment."

Lamont leaned back in the bed and sighed. This was the part of Retall he loved, the honest and kind common people. No other country could claim the same kind of hospitality.

Lamont ate, and later he slept. In the middle of the night, he woke up suddenly. There were voices and the sound of horses outside. Lamont pushed himself up and shifted the cloth just enough to see out. In the flickering light of lamps, he could make out the uniform of a Reta city guard.

Lamont held his breath. He had been here too long, and now he had been found. He needed to leave immediately. Lamont pulled the covers off and placed his feet carefully on the floor. The doorframe was as dark as pitch, and he could not see if someone was there watching him. He felt that if someone were there, they would have already made a noise. Lamont stood very slowly to keep the floorboards from creaking, but they creaked anyway. Lamont froze, and a face appeared in the doorframe. Lamont swallowed.

"What are you doing up so early, sir?" The woman looked totally different in the darkness. The shadows deepening under her eyes gave her the look of a corpse.

"I need to leave," he whispered. "Do you know where my horse is?"

There was a knock at the door of the house, and the woman's head turned. "Of course I do. My husband is using it." She turned to the door. "That would be him now."

Lamont jumped forward and grabbed her shoulder. "No, it isn't him! The people out there are here to arrest me!"

The woman smiled. "Yes, I know. Did you truly think you were safe once you were out of Reta, Lamont Reynard? The oppressor is dead! The people of Retall know who their king is, and he is Hieronymus Purvis!"

Lamont reeled away from her, back through the door, and fell flat on his butt. She was opening the door. He would be captured. The image of Hiero's eyes glinting with glee was burned into his mind.

Lamont jumped to his feet and dove out the window. His hands hit soft grass, and he rolled. A shout rang out, and Lamont's gaze jerked to the right. A rider posted at the corner of the house spurred his horse toward Lamont. Lamont crawled to his feet and ran.

He had only gotten a couple of yards when the horse was upon him. He jumped to the right, and the horse thundered past. Lamont kept running. Where were the other riders? Why didn't they pursue him too?

The horse came up beside him on the left, cantering at exactly the speed he was running. Lamont was out of breath. He jerked to the right again, but this time the horse turned with him.

Lamont bit his lip. He was being herded back. This was a common tactic for catching a prisoner. Lamont tried to remember if he had been taught the way to get out of it.

Lamont stopped, and the horse kept going, and then he ran to the left. A moment later, the rider turned around and rode past Lamont. Lamont knew he would stop short, and that was just what he was waiting for.

The rider performed the maneuver just as Lamont had been trained to do all those years ago. He stopped his horse short and reared it into a sudden turn, creating a wall of flesh that the prisoner was supposed to run into.

Lamont leaped into it. His left foot used the man's foot as a step, and his left hand latched on to the man's sleeve. As Lamont jumped, he brought the heel of his hand up under the man's chin and snapped his head back. The crack was sickening. The man's body went limp. Lamont shoved it out of the saddle and took the seat, then paused.

He needed to find the road again. He didn't even have an idea which way was north. He heard horses coming and started riding. A few minutes later, he found a landmark he could use. A patch of yellow flowers all closed for the night pointed in the same direction: the direction in which the sun had set. Lamont turned the horse north and rode hard.

A day and half passed before Lamont looked up at Lord Kiad's castle. When he announced himself at the lower gate, his ragged clothes and unkempt appearance received raised eyebrows from the guards, but they rode up to ask the lord anyway. They returned with a serious group of men in uniform.

The captain dismounted and gave him a quick bow. "Lord Kiad wishes to confirm your identity for himself. Please come with us."

Lamont nodded. "Yes, of course."

The gates were opened, and Lamont rode up the stone stairs between the horsemen. He looked out over the gray valley and realized that he felt nothing. He wasn't sad. The king was dead, and he wasn't falling apart. He was out of Reta for the first time in years and had been chased with his life on the line, yet he wasn't panicked. Could he have made that statement about himself a year ago?

Even a few months ago, Lamont would have said that serving his king was his life's purpose. Lamont looked up at Lord Kiad's castle. Was it wrong of him not to be grieved? Perhaps he did not believe the king was dead.

The men led him into the castle and past many halls. Kiad's castle was cold compared to the palace, and it wasn't just the temperature. It felt lifeless somehow. They led him into a parlor. A fire crackled in the corner fireplace. Lamont sat in the first chair he saw. In a moment, he was asleep.

Lamont did not wake until the parlor door clanged shut. Lord Kiad was sitting in the chair across from him, staring at him. He smiled.

"Lamont Reynard. You're all grown-up now."

Lamont noticed that Lord Kiad's face was lined, and gray streaked throughout his hair. He nodded. "It is good to see you as well, Lord Kiad. I have some terrible news."

Lord Kiad shifted in his chair. "I have been informed. The king is dead. Were you present? Did you see it done? There is a price on your head."

Lamont closed his eyes. "I was not there when the king died. I had already escaped the palace."

He could see the harsh change in Lord Kiad's eyes. "You abandoned the king?"

Lamont swallowed. "No, I was obeying his order. He told me to leave him so that his work might continue."

Lord Kiad's eyes narrowed. "His work? What did he tell you?"

Lamont was starting to take offense at Lord Kiad's tone. "I have been part of my uncle's work since I entered the palace. I helped him track each colony. He even included me in his experiments."

Lamont remembered many long nights under the palace, mixing and remixing vials in an attempt to get a reaction. He remembered the feeling, like fire crawling up his veins, as the king made a small incision and placed some of the liquid inside, only for Lamont to do the same to him a few minutes later.

"Ah, I see." Kiad's look turned hungry. "Did you notice any changes?"

Lamont pulled back. He didn't know how much Lord Kiad knew, and he didn't know how much the king had wanted him to know. "This is not something we should be discussing now. There are more pressing issues."

Lord Kiad's smile held a hint of scheming, and he raised an eyebrow. "You need protection from this peasant king in Reta. I grant it. No one will touch you here."

Lamont smiled. "I am grateful for the courtesy, Lord Kiad, but I am in need of your support, not your protection. Before he sent me away, the king named me his heir and charged me to go to you." Lamont reached inside his tattered jacket. "I have only this to prove it to you." He held out the king's signet ring so that Lord Kiad could see the design. Kiad's face went blank from shock.

"You? But the king's son—"

"The king wishes the lost prince to remain lost. The boy was a worshiper of the Ancients. He chose me so that his work might continue."

Lord Kiad stared at Lamont for several moments. Lamont could see in his eyes the careful balances weighing out as he decided whether backing him for king would bring him suitable gain. Lamont waited for the indecision to clear.

"I trust that with you as the king's successor, I will retain all of my current privileges?"

Lamont knew what he was referring to. That fervent conversation in the palace hall came back to him suddenly, vividly. Fritz had let him go in the hope that he would make a change. But this was not the time to enact change. He needed a strong ally.

Lamont cleared his throat. "The current system will be retained."

Lord Kiad nodded. "Then I will support you." He lifted himself out of his chair with his left hand and knelt in front of Lamont, his eyes flashing, and his mouth curled into a cruel grin. "I will support you, my king.

21

BROKEN TRUST

FRITZ FELT THE strong muscles of the horse beneath him bunch up as he leaped a fallen log in his path. He had missed this so much. He hadn't ridden a horse since moving to Reta. It was a wonderful, freeing feeling that masked how he felt inside. He couldn't help but think about his sisters. Hiero had promised to free his sisters, but Fritz had never been more uneasy about their safety. He wished he could just keep riding, past the Great Forest and farther north.

Gannon had the power of the Teris family behind him to make the necessary changes, and now he was dead. Hiero had nothing. He had insulted Lord Teris to his face and claimed that he did not need the lords' election to become king. Of course, like any Faithful, Fritz hoped that the Ancients' laws would someday be revered again, but that wasn't the world he lived in. What man could become king with only the will of the people?

In his left breast pocket, Fritz held two letters written by Hiero's hand. The first Fritz had seen Hiero write, and he knew exactly what it said. It was addressed to Lord Teris, an invitation to Hiero's coronation. He had given it a date that would allow the time needed for the invitations to reach the lords and for them to comfortably travel to Reta. If nothing happened before then, in two weeks Hiero would be crowned king in Reta. There was no doubt in Fritz's mind that the invitations were a sham meant to infuriate the lords. The consequences could be dire. Why was Hiero pursuing this so recklessly?

Fritz had a special mission for the second letter, and he rehearsed it again as his horse galloped through the Great Forest. He was deep in his thoughts when a horse leaped out of the brush a hundred yards in front of him and the rider put out a hand.

"Halt!" he ordered. "This is the private property of the Teris family! The main road is back there."

Fritz nodded. "I know where I am. I have an official message for Lord Teris from the current leadership of Reta."

The man turned away from Fritz and let out a sharp whistle that shattered the woods and left an eerie silence behind it. He looked back at Fritz. "Please follow me."

He led Fritz through a small break in the trees, and the Teris mansion was suddenly before them. Fritz was taken aback. He'd had no idea how close he was. It was cleverly masked. No wonder the rider had looked nervous.

The gates were already half-open when they reached them, and they closed behind them. Fritz glanced up at the second story as he dismounted. The window on the corner—that was the one Hiero had specified. Fritz looked for a movement in the curtain and smiled when he saw it. Yes, she was here.

He followed the rider up to the porch and waited while he knocked on the door. A butler answered, and Fritz was led into the foyer to wait while the butler informed Lord Teris. The butler walked across the foyer to the parlor doors, and Fritz was left alone for just a moment. He glanced toward the stairs.

There was the tiniest creak, and Fritz could just make out the curve of a face behind the topmost banister. He reached into his pocket, checked that he held the second letter, and slipped it into a space between two bricks against the doorframe, right where Hiero had specified. The letter slipped in easily and vanished. Fritz pulled his hand back just in time to see Lord Teris pounding toward him, anger on his face. Clearly, he had not forgotten Fritz.

"You have a message for me? Hand it over."

Fritz grabbed at his jacket in a panic. "Ah, yes, of course!" Let Lord Teris believe he was absentminded, and he would not suspect. Hiero had stressed that, above all else, Lord Teris could not get his hands on the second letter. Fritz pulled the invitation from his coat. "Here."

Lord Teris ripped off the wax seal and pulled out the invitation. His eyes sparked with anger. "What is the meaning of this?" He crumpled it in one hand and threw it away. "You can let Hiero know that his pitiful attempt at humor is not missed." He turned back to the parlor doors. "See that this gentleman is escorted off my property immediately!"

Fritz had to hold in his satisfaction until he was back on the main road. He understood Hiero a little better now. It was kind of funny, watching a lord squirm. He wished he could have seen Lord Kiad's reaction too, but that was another rider's task.

Shelia stayed at the top of the stairs, barely breathing, until the foyer had cleared. Slowly, she approached the doorway, looking both ways before she grabbed the letter from the crack and sped back upstairs. Hiero remembered her! Hiero had contacted her!

So many questions had been burning through her mind in the days since her father had returned from Reta, but he refused to answer any of them. Now he was holed up in the parlor with Lord Sita, mumbling about something. Perhaps Hiero would answer her questions.

There was no wax seal on the envelope. The letter unfolded easily in her hand.

My dearest Shelia, I have missed you so. I can hardly bear to think about you because of the pain it causes me. I want you by my side as soon as possible. I hope you want the same.

Oh, Shelia, I pray to the Ancients that you will forgive me for what I must tell you. I will begin at the point where we parted. For the past two years, I have been living and working in the city of Reta. I don't know if you knew. I did write to you, but I suspect my letters were intercepted. My half brother was here in Reta. That is part of the reason I chose to live here. I will admit that revenge filled my heart more than once, but there was never a time or a place where I could approach him.

I saved all my money, hoping wealth would bring your father's favor, even though I knew it would not. I spent days in despair until I came up with a plan to infiltrate the palace and steal back my father's signet ring from Reynard, forcing him to return my inheritance to me. The plan was proceeding well when Gannon appeared.

It was only a week ago Gannon came to Reta, but it feels like a month, so much has happened. He wanted the throne, and he wanted to earn it with his own hands. I agreed to help him, thinking this was an opportunity to enter the palace and attack Reynard. Now I wish I had not.

I should have paid better attention to your father's lessons while I was under his tutelage. I should have known that to go against the king would bring great sacrifice.

Shelia, I don't know where Gannon is. I saw him fall from the king's balcony, off the cliff of Reta. It was my fault. Gannon could not find the king's signet ring and believed that I had stolen it. He attacked me and slipped off the stone in the rain.

I truly thought he was dead, and I told your father that. But when the group I sent out to find the body returned, they said there was no body. It isn't uncommon for a suicide victim's body to be picked up by guard patrols, but there hadn't been any patrols with the king barricaded inside the palace. I believe Gannon must have been taken by someone else, alive. The only people who make it their business to forcibly take people are Kiad's slavers, and there has been movement by the slavers in the past week. If he was taken by them, he is in Lord Kiad's territory by now.

Shelia, I don't know what I should do. If you tell your father my suspicions, he might attack Lord Kiad, and people will die. And what if I am wrong about Gannon? If I do not tell him, he will continue to believe that I am responsible for Gannon's death, attack Reta, and have me executed. Lord Teris needs no new reason to hate me. It is all I can do to maintain order in Reta as it is. The people want a king, but Gannon is not here. If I do not take the throne, someone else will, and I will be dead.

It is my belief that the king's missing signet ring is with my scheming half brother, and that would mean the king named him heir to the throne. He cannot be allowed to take the throne—not while there is a slim chance that Gannon lives. Even if Gannon is dead, Reynard should not be king. It would only continue the abuses that Lord Reta put the Faithful under.

Please, Shelia, pray to the Ancients that I will make the right decision. I will pray for us to come together soon. I love you more than anything else. Ancients bless, Hiero.

Shelia sucked in a breath. Had she been holding her breath this whole time?

She leaped to her feet. Father must know that Gannon was alive! She couldn't let him attack Reta or execute Hiero!

Shelia grabbed the letter from her bed before flying out the door. She would need proof, or she wouldn't be able to convince Father. She darted down the stairs, tripping over herself in her haste and sliding down half a dozen stairs on her butt. Shelia was so focused she barely even noticed. She yanked herself back up and ran down the rest of the stairs. She jumped the last stairs with a boom and ran across the foyer to the parlor doors, coming to a sudden stop.

Her hair flew everywhere, and her dress was rumpled. Shelia repaired herself, knowing Lord Sita was behind those doors with her father. She breathed out and reached for the doorknob, and then she heard something that stopped her cold.

"Your daughter is a tempting prize, Lord Teris." It was Lord Sita's voice. "And you know I've been so lonely since Amari died."

Shelia swallowed. Something must've been caught in her throat. She couldn't breathe. Her knees wobbled, and she slid down onto them. It couldn't be. Father would give her to Lord Sita? But he knew she loved Hiero!

"With Gannon gone, she is the only child I have. With her by your side, you will have a definitive claim on the throne."

Shelia took a deep breath. That was it. They needed Gannon back. She only had to assure Father that Gannon was alive, and he would forget this silly idea at once. Shelia was reaching for the doorknob to pull herself back to her feet when Lord Teris spoke again.

"Gannon was a fool. I can't believe I had such a stupid son. What was he thinking, climbing the palace in pouring rain? He wasn't fit to be king of Retall."

Lord Sita laughed. "Such is the folly of youth. They believe they are invincible."

Shelia felt a pain in her throat. Father wasn't sad about Gannon. How could he dare to say such cruel things about him to someone outside their family?

Pain filled up two little spaces deep under her jaw. Tears sprung into her eyes. Shelia wanted to choke, but she knew they would hear her if she did. She pushed away from the door and stumbled to her feet.

She mounted the stairs to her room. Father didn't care about Gannon. Father hated Gannon. How could he hate his own son? Shelia leaned back against her door until it clicked shut. What would happen to Gannon if there was no one to rescue him? What would Lord Kiad do to him? Shelia couldn't sit around and do nothing, but it was clear she couldn't rely on her father to help. What could she do by herself?

Shelia wrapped her arms around herself and sank to the floor. Her forehead rested against her knees. How could Father be so cruel? How could he marry her off to Lord Sita when he knew she loved someone else?

Shelia's fingernails left deep red divots in her arms. She grimaced at her own anger. Father was wrong. He was wrong about everything. Shelia felt a strange warmness in her chest, right over her heart. She wouldn't stay here and marry Sita; she'd find a way to save Gannon.

Shelia's eyes narrowed. She would go to Lord Kiad herself. Lord Kiad wouldn't know that Father didn't want Gannon back. She could threaten him with promises of force, and he would believe her.

She breathed in, and her heart beat faster. Could she really do this? She had never left the Teris compound before. If she let anyone know what she planned, they would stop her.

The fire in her breast disappeared. If she was caught, Father would surely be told, and if Father was told, she might be married to Lord Sita tomorrow, tonight even! She had to get out now.

Shelia looked around her room, a little dazed. Where should she even begin? What did she need? She pulled herself to her feet. She would need food and a horse and to get them both without anyone suspecting anything. She could tell them she was going on a picnic. Father had allowed her to eat outside with Gannon when they were younger. She had never had a picnic outside the compound though. She would just have to try it.

Shelia stepped over and pulled a cloak from her wardrobe. She didn't know how cold the forest would get at night. She pulled a small satchel from under her bed. Inside were notes that she and Hiero had exchanged years ago and a stash of coins she had managed to scavenge over the years. Shelia hung the satchel over her shoulder and pulled the cloak over that. She suddenly felt a little taller and a little braver.

Shelia made her way down the stairs quickly. The parlor doors were still closed. Father should have no reason to suspect what she knew. She slipped through the dining room into the kitchen. The cook greeted her warmly, and when Shelia revealed she was going on a picnic, the lady packed her a nice lunch with no question.

A few moments later, Shelia was in the stable. When she asked that Beya be saddled, the hostler, Idris, looked at her in surprise but pulled the saddle from the wall.

"Are you going for a ride around the compound, lady?"

Shelia smiled. "I'm going on a picnic, just like old times."

Idris returned her smile. "Ah, sounds like fun."

Shelia could barely contain her glee. She was almost out. She placed her hand on her satchel, and a thought crossed her mind. Where was Hiero's letter? A cold shiver went down her spine. Had she left it inside?

Shelia told Idris she would be right back and ran to the manor, back up to her room. She pulled her wardrobe open and frantically looked around the floor, but the letter was gone. Fear felt like a cold spike in her chest. She had to leave right now.

Back down the stairs she ran, foot over foot, her heart pounding in her ears. As her feet touched the foyer floor, she heard Uncle's door creak open from beside the stairs.

"Shelia, what's with all the crashing around this morning?"

Shelia turned around, and as her uncle pushed his chair out of his room, she saw the letter sitting on his lap. Suddenly, she couldn't breathe. Uncle's face was hard.

"Please," she wheezed, "Uncle—"

"Shelia, I want you to go back to your room immediately. I will discuss this letter with Renald."

Shelia felt tears slide down her cheeks as she shook her head. "No, Uncle, no. Don't do this."

Uncle reached out a hand, wanting her to take it. "Shelia, I don't know what you intend to do, but I want you to stay out of this. Renald will handle it."

"No!" Shelia wouldn't stay. She wouldn't let Father abandon Gannon, and she wouldn't marry Lord Sita. She had to go.

Shelia jumped for her uncle's lap, ripping the letter out of his hand. His hand curled around her wrist and jerked her back from escaping.

"Shelia, go upstairs!"

Shelia yanked away, but her uncle held on, and his chair toppled over, throwing him to the floor. His hand released, and Shelia ran out the front door, down the steps, and across the yard to Idris, who was holding Beya's reins for her. The gate was already opening, and Idris looked at her strangely as she swung her leg completely over the saddle and grabbed the reins with her hand full of paper.

"My lady? Are you all right?"

Shelia had tears running down her face, and she sent Idris a cold glare. "Where is my basket?"

"Oh!" He reached down and picked it up from the ground, tying it onto her saddle. "There you are, my lady. Stay safe—"

Shelia kicked Beya's sides before Idris could finish speaking and thundered out of the gate before it was fully open, scaring both gate guards as she did so.

A moment after the dust had cleared, Lord Teris ran out of the house, Lord Sita right behind him. "Stop her!" His voice rose in fearful pitch to vibrate across the entire courtyard. "Get my daughter back now!"

22

PENNING LETTERS

GANNON FELT SICK. It had been a whole night since Lord Kiad had visited him, but the ache deep in his body had not gone away. Gannon was afraid. He didn't want to say it, didn't want to think about it, but it squeezed around his heart like an ice-cold hand. What if he had been permanently damaged? What if he was dying?

There was no sleep for Gannon. His heart throbbed dully, and his ears were fully alert to every groan and creak outside the door. When would Lord Kiad be back? What would he do to him next?

Gannon's heart leaped into his chest when he heard steps outside the door. A key clunked into the lock and crunched as it turned. Gannon felt every microsecond of sound in his spine, and his body shook with fear.

The door opened, and the guard captain stepped in.

He took in Gannon's shaking curled-up form with an emotionless face.

"Get up. Your lord needs you."

Gannon couldn't make himself move. The man reached down and grabbed Gannon's shoulder, yanking him to his feet and pulling him out the door. Two more guards fell into step behind them as they came out of the room.

The man lowered his voice. "I understand that you are terrified, boy, but if you ever ignore an order from Lord Kiad like that, he will cause you pain that you can't even imagine. Never disobey Lord Kiad."

The captain's warning echoed in Gannon's mind as he was pulled through the castle. He had to obey Lord Kiad, or he would die. That was the implication. Somehow, it brought Gannon back to himself. He could think.

Gannon took a deep breath and let it out. He was going back to Lord Kiad. Blocking the situation out would not help him escape. He needed to keep a clear mind in case a chance for escape presented itself.

Gannon grimaced as the memories of the first night resurfaced. He had been violated over and over, until it felt like it would never end. He would escape, no matter what, and when he returned with his father's might behind him, he would kill Lord Kiad himself.

A door was opened in front of Gannon, and he walked into a warm parlor. The two occupants looked up when he entered. The first was Lord Kiad, and Gannon stifled the terror that crept up his spine when their eyes met. The other man looked strangely familiar, and Gannon chose to stare at him as he was led to Lord Kiad. The man's face was right at the edge of his memory. Where had he seen it?

The man's eyes dropped to Gannon's waist and looked away quickly. He wasn't wearing anything but a loincloth. Gannon was pushed to the floor beside Lord Kiad's chair, and a heavy shackle snapped around his ankle. The guard bowed to Lord Kiad and left the room as quickly as he could manage. The door banged shut behind him.

Gannon felt his face grow hot. He had not noticed that he was barely dressed. Despite the embarrassment, he was grateful that another level of his consciousness had come back to him. Soon the daze would disappear completely, and he would be himself again.

The man glared at Lord Kiad. "What is the meaning of this?"

Gannon refused to look at Lord Kiad's face again, but he could hear the sarcasm drip off his voice. "Oh, this? Just my most recent acquisition." He leaned forward in his chair, curling his fingers in Gannon's hair. "You did say that the laws would stand as they did before."

Disgust was written all over the man's face. "I was under the assumption that we were working here."

Lord Kiad laughed loudly, his head thrown back. "You need to loosen your collar a bit, Reynard. You'll find you get a lot more done if you allow yourself the simple pleasures of life."

Gannon could not keep his eyes from narrowing. This was Lamont Reynard? Of course, he had only seen his face for a moment in the palace. He couldn't expect himself to remember.

"I try not to indulge myself, Lord Kiad. My father fell into the trap of pleasure, and it consumed him."

"How honorable. You will have to change your views quickly if you are going to produce an heir to your throne."

Lord Kiad shifted in his chair. "Yes, I should find you a suitable wife as soon as possible. A lord's daughter would do nicely."

Lamont sighed loudly. "You are far older than I am and not yet married. Are you not worried about producing an heir?"

Lord Kiad's voice changed again, this time sending a dangerous vibe to Gannon. He felt the fingers tighten on his skull. "I have the strength to satisfy a thousand women. I have no fear of leaving without an heir." Gannon could feel the look he gave Lamont now. "Thank you for your concern."

Lamont shivered. "Please can we return to the task at hand? We were drafting a letter."

Kiad looked back at the paper in his lap. "You may have the king's ring and my power behind you, but I can tell you right now, there will be those that do not attend. Lord Teris, for example."

Lamont's eyes popped back up. "What? Would he not present his own son before the council?"

Lord Kiad seemed genuinely surprised. "Gannon Teris is dead! Apparently, he took a tumble off our good king's balcony sometime during the palace takeover. The entire country must be talking about it."

Gannon swallowed. The whole country believed he was dead? Father wouldn't be looking for him now. It was the worst thing that could've possibly happened. Gannon glanced down at his hands, which shook in his lap. There was no hope for a rescue.

Lamont put a hand to his head, and for just a moment, fatigue showed in the corners of his eyes. "How convenient. And I thought my path to the throne would be difficult."

Lord Kiad chuckled. "That's what I've been trying to say. It will be difficult. If enough lords do not attend, we cannot legally make a vote."

Lamont's eyes narrowed. "We only need the majority, correct?" He pulled a plain sheet of paper from the bottom of the stack. "Which of the lords do you believe will not attend? If we can draft the invitation in such a way that they are lured into thinking they are a contender—"

Kiad's face became thoughtful. "Lord Teris will not. He has no reason to, and Lord Sita will certainly side with him. I received a report that he is with Lord Teris now. I do not believe that Lord Privit will attempt the journey. He is not in the best health."

Lord Kiad's hand moved down Gannon's neck to his shoulder. He lifted Gannon's arm and placed his hand between his thighs. Gannon froze. It was as hard as a rock down there.

Lamont looked relieved. "Is that all? That still leaves us enough lords to vote!"

Lord Kiad looked down into Gannon's eyes and smiled, freezing him to his core. "Take care of this, will you?" he whispered.

Gannon felt his consciousness stripping away again. His mind drifted away from his body as his hand moved mechanically. Lord Kiad let out a sigh.

"Yes, yes, perhaps, but there are more lords, some who are so power hungry they can't think clearly. I've heard that Lord Fieman was incensed by what took place in the capital, by a bastard peasant taking control without the approval of the lords' council. He is the most volatile of the lords. If he reacts how I expect, he will march on Reta to take it back by force. He may succeed."

Gannon could still see the conversation below him as he drifted free of his body and up to the ceiling. He should've gone back. He should've told his body to stop obeying and fight back instead. But he didn't have the strength to get back inside. He was dead, wasn't he? Without his father's help, what chance did he have of getting out of here?

"Lord Fieman? His jurisdiction is over agriculture. I can't see him putting together a force large enough to do anything to Reta."

Lord Kiad shrugged. "The point I'm making is that without a clear line of succession from Lord Reta, most will naturally see the throne as an open field. There's no need to pen it with that implication. Lord Yus is the last of the three large houses now that Lord Reta is dead and Teris has no heir. He will most likely put up one of his sons for consideration.

"If Lord Fieman marches on Reta, I could see Lord Yus being gravely offended, so much so that he might take action against him." Lord Kiad shrugged his tension away. "In the end, we can only send the invitations and hope that this situation will bind us together rather than divide us."

Gannon was not an orator, but he could hear the lack of passion in Kiad's final statement. He knew that the lords were divided far beyond land boundaries even now. Gannon drifted lazily against the ceiling and closed his eyes. Lord Kiad was not saying all he could. Retall was on the brink of crumbling apart.

23

LOFTY CAMPAIGN

IN HIS EXTRAVAGANT mansion in Fietha, Lord Fieman hurled a wineglass against the wall, where it shattered in a beautiful purple cloud.

"What?" His voice was livid to the point of screaming. "We have been humiliated, insulted by this bastard king, and he wants me to wait!" Lord Fieman crumpled the letter from Lord Yus and threw it across the room with the former wineglass. "You and Kiad can keep your precious council, Yus, but Reta will fall to me, and I will see that bastard whipped through the streets before I take off his head!"

Across the room, a man in the Fieman colors of gold and purple cleared his throat. "My lord, what are your orders?"

Fieman rounded on him like a rabid dog. "I'd like you to find me one loyal soldier who didn't die in that thrice-cursed fiasco! Now!"

The man scurried from the room with Fieman's glare hot on his back. Fieman sneered as the door slammed shut behind him. "Damned fool. How am I to kill an upstart without any officers?"

He dug his fingers therapeutically into his armrest. So, Hiero thought he had the people on his side, did he? He'd learn. The only thing those muddy, illiterate peasants cared about was whether they had food in their bellies, and when they didn't, well, the closest person available would feel their wrath. Fieman smiled smugly to himself.

Reta was a city built on a rock. The soil was thin, and it gave them little ability to grow food. Most raw foodstuff was imported from the surrounding farmland and processed inside the city.

Oh, it was so simple! A Reta surrounded by an army would get no food from the outside. Fieman could see the starving citizens of Reta bringing Hieronymus out in chains. So much for loyalty. And the best part was no one would have to die if they cooperated. Except Hieronymus. Hieronymus would have to die.

Fieman shook in anger as he imagined all the horrible things he could do to Hieronymus once he had his hands on him. He would enjoy it very, very much.

A knock on the door spurred him from his sanguine thoughts, and Lord Fieman stood. "Come in."

The frightened man kept his eyes riveted on the floor. "My lord, your remaining soldiers, as you requested."

Lord Fieman's eyes narrowed. "Send them in."

The man backed quickly out of the room to make room for the men in Reta's and Fieman's liveries. It was only a small group. Fieman waited until the doors had shut behind them.

"So, this is it? Form up!" The men jumped into a line. Fieman smiled. They were well trained. "Twelve, fourteen, fifteen men? Is that all that remains?" He shook his head. "The facts remain. Hieronymus Purvis has unlawfully taken control of the throne and shed royal blood. Men that you knew have died or done the unthinkable by joining with him. I don't intend to let this peasant get away with it. As of today, you are all captains in a new army. I know that many might feel lost with such new responsibility, but I trust you will rise to the occasion. Today we begin a muster of troops to march on the capital in seven days. I know time is short. I would like our goal to be a thousand men, an unprecedented force." He grinned. "Reta will never see us coming."

Fieman took a deep breath. "I understand that weapons will be an issue. Get all the smiths in my province alerted to the numbers we will need. Does anyone have a question? No? Then go."

The men almost flew out of the room. They had their orders, and they knew his temper. Lord Fieman settled comfortably back in his chair. He had been clear and concise. His father would have been proud.

Time creaked forward, and the seventh day arrived. Fieman watched the advance guard take off, his banners flapping in the wind as they sailed up the hill. Fieman's stallion snorted and tossed his head. He wanted to run. It was a glorious day. The sun was shining, the wind was whipping, and Lord Fieman had his army, all one thousand men. It was almost too much to ask for. No man had ever felt this good before; Fieman was certain of that. Nothing—not even his wife's company the night before—had the thrill of this moment.

The second trumpet sounded, close enough to be heard this time, and far in front, Fieman could see the second rank pushing forward into a march. His stallion pawed the ground anxiously.

Fieman patted his neck. "All in good time, old boy. It isn't like you to want to run."

The third horn sounded, and Fieman's thoughts turned to his son. He was still young, but even at the age of eleven, the boy had learned the swagger of the Fieman name. He'd gotten a cane for his birthday. The original purpose of the implement had been to keep him in fashion, but last week he'd rapped it across a serving boy's legs for not paying him proper respect. In public, Lord Fieman had praised his son and fired the servant, but he couldn't get it out of his mind for some reason. Was his son ready to be a prince of Retall? And there was another thought, even more worrying, in the back of his mind. Was Retall ready to accept the rule of the Fieman name?

They had never been one of the high houses, like Reta or Yus, and they'd certainly never been as powerful as Teris. Fieman had originally been one of Brandon's middle sons, but in terms of prestige, they were the lower end of the nobility. It was time for the connotation to change. As his son Naises had said, watching the beaten youth flee from the manor, *"If you never show them who has the power, they are never going to know."* Such wisdom in one so young.

The fifth horn blew, and Fieman kicked his horse into a walk, then a trot. He was on his way.

Fieman had realized quickly that he was not as used to the saddle as he had been in his youth, and dismounting for the evening was awkward. His legs were stiff and cold.

His column had reached a town of sorts, and while his captain bickered with an innkeeper over accommodations, Lord Fieman stood by his horse. The evening wind was cool and pleasant, and from where he stood, he could watch the lights twinkling all over town. A boy came up to him, no older than eight or nine, dressed in plain clothes.

"My lord, do you want your horse stabled?"

"Hmm?" Lord Fieman gave the boy a disinterested stare. "You've finally gotten it settled then? Took you far too long. One would think you had rocks for brains!" He handed the boy his reins. "Don't tug on him like that! If you don't treat him properly, I'll have you flogged, boy!"

The boy dropped his head. "Please forgive me, my lord. Are you going to attack the capital, my lord?"

Lord Fieman's eyes narrowed. "I'll do whatever I please. Now move!"

The boy scurried off with his horse in tow. Fieman sneered. "I'm not tipping him!"

His captain came up beside him. "We have our rooms, and dinner is being prepared, along with a bath. Please follow me."

Several hours later, they relaxed over two mugs of beer.

"How far do you think we got today?" Lord Fieman asked across the table.

"Perhaps a third of the way, my lord. It's difficult to tell."

"We should arrive on the third day for certain though?"

The captain shrugged. "Perhaps. Most likely. Was it your intention to make good time?"

Fieman growled. "This is a sneak attack!" He took one last noisy slurp from his mug and stood. "I'm heading to bed now. Remember, we should be marching at dawn."

But Fieman was fast asleep in his bed when the frantic knocking on his door hauled him out of his dream.

"My lord! We've been attacked!"

Lord Fieman struggled out of bed and yanked his shirt over his head before pulling back the bar on his door. "Captain, who was it? Soldiers from the capital?"

The captain shook his head. "No, my lord, we have no idea. They seem to have vanished."

"How many dead?" Fieman asked as he wrestled his boots on.

"Twenty men at least. We have lost all the men on guard duty. It was discovered when no one returned to change shifts."

"Wait." Fieman stopped just before walking out the door. "What time would that make it now?"

"Just after the third bell, my lord."

Fieman's body fell back against the doorframe. No wonder he felt so tired. "Captain, tell all columns to break camp immediately. We march as soon as possible."

The second day's march was uneventful, but uneasiness blew like a sharp wind through the camp. When all the bodies had been totaled, they had lost fifty-three men. Fieman couldn't stop himself from looking over his shoulder now and then. The manner of death had been the same in all instances: a blow to the head and the neck cut open.

Fieman shook his head. What sort of demon army killed only the guards and did not attack the camp? It was uncanny. It felt like a story meant to frighten children.

They stopped in a larger town that night. Fieman had the column camp outside the town, as before, while he and the captain sought accommodation inside. As they rode up the street in full armor, people's eyes grew wide, and they stared with open mouths. It was hilarious. Peasantry were so stupid.

He slammed the door of the inn open and barged in. No way was he letting his captain bicker for hours like last night. "Innkeeper! Lord Fieman demands your presence!" Every eye in the common room was on him now. He casually leaned against the counter.

The man of the house ran in a moment later, his face pale. "My lord, what a surprise! How may—"

"Two rooms, man, and be quick about it! Our horses will also need to be stabled."

The man leaned under his counter to grab a sheet of paper. "Yes, lord, I'll send my—oh! There he goes!" A young boy blew out of the back room and shot out into the yard. "He will take care of your horses, my lord. There is no need to fear. Here are two keys. Will you be dining in our common room tonight?"

Lord Fieman snatched the keys up from the desk and tried to look both bored and upset. He sighed. "Well, if we must."

The man nodded. "Very good, my lord. I will have a table set for you."

It was a good meal, and Lord Fieman enjoyed it down to the last bite. He was so full and happy when he waddled up the stairs to bed that he never noticed the look of pure poison on the face of the barmaid behind the counter. Once he had disappeared, she turned angrily to the innkeeper.

"Father, tell me you at least put ants in his bed!"

"Hush, child!" The innkeeper glanced quickly to the table where the captain was finishing off his mug. "You know there's nothing I can do. He's a guest!"

The girl threw her dishrag on the floor and stormed out through the back room. Under the night sky, she fled to the stables.

"Daric!" she called softly. "Are you there?" The answer came from behind her, making her gasp and whirl around.

The tall stable hand, her betrothed, stepped out of the shadows. "Mirza, are your chores done already?"

She shook her head furiously. "No, I couldn't keep playing a face. Ancients bless, Daric! He's so arrogant!"

Daric slid a conciliatory arm around her shoulders. "Don't let him bother you, Mirza. He won't last many more days like this. Maybe he won't even reach the capital!"

Mirza sighed. "Can I come with you and the boys to-night? I promise I won't cause you any trouble. I just want to see."

"Don't be silly, Mirza. You haven't got a sword, and you don't know how to fight. What if you were seen?" He shuddered. "They would know exactly who we were and where we had come from. Soldiers don't travel with women." He let his hand linger on her shoulder. "Hey, maybe you could cause some trouble on your own bat-tlefield. You could sabotage the lord's handle or put soap outside his door or something."

Mirza nodded slowly. "I'll think of something. I need to go back now."

Daric let his arm drop from her shoulder. "Ancients bless. Long live King Hiero!"

"Long live King Hiero," she whispered back.

At the first bell, a group of boys and men from the town gathered at the town's edge and snuck toward the encampment. As they had been trained, they began taking the guards down silently. The plan was to strike fear into hearts. They knew they could not take the whole army themselves.

Security had been increased from the night before. A single soldier, terrified silly on his shift, raised the alarm when he saw a movement in the shadows. It wasn't even the men he saw, but a stray dog. It woke the soldiers all the same.

The group had taken out all the guards on one side of the camp and were inside the camp, going into tents and killing one man out of four. When the alarm went up, soldiers jumped from their blankets and grabbed their swords to find hooded figures in their tent.

There were shouts of fear, and the townspeople found themselves in battle with terrified men, slashing wildly. In a few moments, the men inside the tent were dead. One boy was wounded, a cut to the leg, and they fled with him held up between them. They ran away from the town into the darkness. They knew the terrain and headed toward a small stream to care for the wounded boy. He had bled much, and Daric sacrificed his sleeve to bind him.

As they finished, they heard shouts from the nearest hill, and they ran again, using the river to hide their footprints and disappearing around another hill.

Minutes later, the pursuing party found their resting place on the riverbank but could find no trail to follow. The men were even more afraid.

Lord Fieman rubbed his bruised back and glared at the soldiers trying to sink into the ground. "And?"

"And we lost them, my lord. The trail ended there."

Fieman growled at the pain in his back, feeding his anger at his incompetent soldiers. "How many dead?"

The men swallowed in unison. "Sixty-eight, my lord."

"Curse it all!"

"A-are you well, my lord? You seem—"

"In pain? Yes, the inn I stayed at was run by idiots. They have no idea how much polish to use on a floor! I took one step outside my door and fell flat on my back!"

The soldier winced. "My apologies."

"Noted, soldier. We can't let this mysterious army keep attacking us. We've lost a tenth of our men already! Do we know anything about them?"

"They cannot be more than twenty men, my lord. The tracks we followed were few. They didn't come on horses."

Lord Fieman gave him an incredulous stare. "Then how, pray tell, did they follow us here?"

The man looked nervous. He shifted from foot to foot. "Um, my lord, we don't think they did. We think it was the townspeople at each place we stopped. They could be Purvis supporters."

Lord Fieman raised an eyebrow. "Armed and trained townspeople?"

The man shrugged. "If they wanted swords, it would not be hard to get them. I am a blacksmith myself, my lord."

Fieman shook his head. "This is impossible! If I didn't have a locked door of solid oak between me and these phantoms, I'd be shaking in my boots! How are the rest of the men?"

"There is a lot of talk, my lord. They want to go home."

"Of course they do, but to turn back now would be mad! We're almost there!" He motioned his captain over with a hand. "We've got a morale problem among the men. It may give us a late start, but I want each officer to go through his column and bolster their courage. Make a speech if you must. I am going to accomplish what I came here to do. All right?"

"Yes, my lord!"

It was just before noon when the camp got moving. Fieman was glad that he had not had to ride any earlier. His back was purple with bruises. His captain rode up beside him once they had reached the road.

"My lord, our break off point is not far. Column five will take the south road."

Fieman nodded. It was all part of the plan. In splitting up the ranks, they could surround the entire Reta plateau and prevent any supplies from reaching it.

"Will we reach the capital by tonight?"

The man looked pained. "No, my lord."

"Curses! Keep the men alert. I doubt the peasants closer to the capital like us any more than those behind.

He nodded. "Understood."

The separation of the ranks at the Great Road fork was not noticeable to Fieman. They were so spread out that column four had taken the north half an hour before column five reached it. Soon the army would surround the entire city, and there would be no escape for Hieronymus Purvis. Fieman would see his head roll.

One week later, Lord Fieman found himself in an intimate dance with despair and terror. The devils must've been everywhere. Every day there were more incidents, each more bizarre than the last. Five men reported their armor missing. Another five found theirs crushed flat. One day the camp was nearly destroyed by a rampaging pack of half-wild dogs, and the next they were attacked by swarming ants. They had suffered a flash flood, a fire, collapsing tents, and multiple disappearances. Over a hundred men were either dead or had disappeared, and the other columns reported similar circumstances. Fieman's army was falling apart at the seams.

He did not sleep anymore and instead sat up in bed with his armor on, waiting for the next disaster. Fieman feared rebellion. No, at this point, he expected it. Would they simply stand still and be killed down to the last man?

That night, Lord Fieman had a nightmare. A fire in the shape of a woman had its hands around his throat.

"More!" it hissed. "Give me more blood! I will feed on all the carcasses of Theras!"

Fieman could not breathe. He was being strangled. Finally, he coughed himself awake only to find his tent on fire and full of smoke.

Lord Fieman, the fifteenth of that name, fled from his first and last military campaign on a horse that wasn't even his, leaving his soldiers to fend for themselves. He did not stop riding for hours. He could still hear that terrible laughter and feel the flames on his skin. When he reached home, thinking himself to be safe, he was immediately taken into custody by Lord Yus's men without getting to see his family again.

Lord Yus's men retrieved Fieman, and escorted him to his manor. There Lord Fieman was tried and executed. He was charged with raising an army without Lord Yus's consent. From that day the name Naris Fieman became an example to all those who thought to act impulsively, regardless of status.

So it was that Lord Naris Fieman was executed during his fortieth year of life and succeeded in lordship by his son, Naises Fieman, all privileges and responsibilities to become his at the age of sixteen. And the city of Reta rejoiced.

24

BLOODY SECRETS

THE ARMY OF Fieman is coming, Fritz! There's no stopping it!"

Hiero's shout echoed down the shadowy hallway, weaving in and out until it eventually disappeared. It was the middle of the night, and they had been trying not to wake anyone. Fritz's shoulders were hunched just like Hiero's.

"Sorry," Hiero whispered.

Fritz shook his head. "Let's hope that goes unnoticed."

They were in the old palace, the original structure built by Brandon Terys hundreds of years ago. The current palace had been built around it, bigger and larger, until the old palace had disappeared inside, unentered and untouched.

"I'm not belittling your opinion, Hiero. I know he's coming. But holing up inside the city and waiting for him to smoke us out is not the best plan. We should be negotiating with him now."

Hiero whirled around, lifting his torch high. "I won't negotiate with a lord, especially not one who treats his people as badly as Fieman does. It would be a betrayal to my people if I honored that man with an audience." His torch flame caught cobweb wisps as they floated gently on the air, and they sparked immediately, going up in smoke. Hiero sucked in a sharp breath.

The old palace gave his spine the shivers. Together for the past three nights, Hiero and Fritz had been quietly exploring the old palace in hopes of finding those rumored secret passageways. If they had a secret passage in and out of Reta, they could survive any siege, no matter how long.

"Those cobwebs were broken." Hiero straightened. "Have we been down this hallway before?"

Fritz shook his head. "I don't think so."

"Someone has been, and recently." He lifted his torch higher. "Feel the walls. See if you can find anything!"

The old palace was the one place that had survived Reta's attempt to scratch out the Teris family's influence. The original tapestries and red carpets were still here. Hiero stepped in front of one and examined it. How many hundreds of years old were they? They were priceless by now!

The tapestry rippled, and Hiero's eyes narrowed. It rippled outward. He swallowed. He believed that all spirits went to the Isle after death, but just in case . . .

"Fritz, come here." He nodded. "Is this tapestry moving?"

"It's moving, Hiero." He sounded as nervous as Hiero was.

"Should I—"

"You go right ahead. I-I'll keep my sword ready."

Fritz pulled his sword and looked expectantly at Hiero.

Hiero bit his tongue. Why had he said anything at all? Carefully, he reached out and grasped the edge of the tapestry, yanking it back. A black space yawned wide behind it. Hiero felt a cool draft tickle the hair on his head.

"Well, that's a passageway." He held his torch out as Fritz came up behind him. "A staircase! Perfect! We have to see where it goes."

For a moment, they were as eager as children, running down the stairs two at a time until they landed in a wide chamber. Hiero was breathing heavily, and he raised his torch over his head.

There were three things he noticed first about the chamber: the air smelled of rot; there were fresh torches in sconces, waiting to be lit; and the floor looked red.

The shiver crawled right back up Hiero's spine, slung its cold arm around his shoulders, and refused to leave. Fritz lit the torches without being asked, and the room flared to life. Hiero couldn't breathe.

The room was much longer than it was wide. Every five feet or so, there was a set of two pillars. Each pillar had three or four sets of shackles drilled into the stone. The floor of the room was not flat. It inclined in a circle, just enough so that any liquid would run to the very center of the room, where there was an obvious drain.

Hiero felt ill. Down every pillar, across every inch surrounding the drain, ran red rivers of dried blood.

Fritz turned around, and his voice caught in his throat. "Blessed Ancients! What happened here?"

Hiero shook his head. He couldn't even think. "I don't know. Maybe this was used for torture? Execution?"

"Hiero." Fritz got his attention and pointed to the floor. "There's no dust on the floor. This room has been in use."

Hiero didn't want to hear that. He didn't want to imagine that. But the smell of rot in the air made it clear. In the past few weeks, someone had died down here.

There was a giant set of double doors at the end of the hall, and Hiero began to walk toward them. Every ring of his boots on the stone made him jerk. He drew his sword and held it out just to soothe the frantic pounding in his chest. A few more steps and the doors came into clear view.

The doors were made of dark stone etched with intricate letters and pictures, delicate, priceless work. Hiero's throat was dry. The doors depicted a fiery ball falling from the sky, burning cities in its wake. People ran in terror as their cities burned. A little farther down, a woman emerged from the burning rock, wreathed in flames, and began to destroy everyone and everything that stood in her path. A little farther down, the fiery woman was held in chains, and the people placed her into a crystal-shaped prison.

"Fritz, you must see this," Hiero said, and Fritz joined him a moment later. "Do you know what this is?"

Fritz's brow wrinkled, and he shook his head. "It looks vaguely familiar, but I'm not sure."

"If I am correct, this is the legend of the Goddess, etched into the stone. I wonder if—"

He glanced behind his back to check that no one was there. "Fritz, I've read that the cult of the Goddess still exists today. They have a hatred for all things having to do with the Ancients and"—he closed his eyes—"some speculate they practice blood sacrifices."

"Hiero, the legend of the Goddess is a myth. It's a story told to frighten children into obedience. And who would dare practice human sacrifice in this day and age?"

Hiero shook his head. "Then who built and used this room? And what did they use it for?"

They were silent for what felt like an eternity, trying to process it. They pressed against the door to no avail. Hiero believed it to be barricaded from the other side. Then Fritz pointed with the end of his torch.

"Hiero, there's a room over there. Can you see it?"

There was a doorway behind one of the pillars, cut through solid rock. The room on the other side was carved the same way. Hiero stepped inside, and his eyes widened.

"Fritz! Look at all the books!"

The room felt about ten feet by ten feet. It was crowded with bookshelves, desks, tables, and chairs, and every surface seemed to be covered with paper. Hiero didn't know where to begin. He set his torch in a sconce and leaned down to read.

"This has Lord Reta's signature."

Fritz nodded. "Over here too. It looks like a daily log of some sort of experiment. I don't understand it."

There was a book sitting open in the center of the largest desk, and Hiero felt drawn to it immediately. His eyes caught sight of diagrams, and he snatched it up.

"Fritz! Machines! The king was working on machines!" He thumbed through the pages eagerly. "I think some of this is in Ancient! Look here. I can't read it, but it looks familiar. Do you think this could be actual Ancient technology?"

Fritz frowned over his shoulder. "Not all of it. That there looks simple enough. The Ancient machines were higher than the understanding of man."

Hiero glared. "People have seen beyond the wall, Fritz. They've seen the skeletons of their flying machines. It's not that different from machines we operate today." Hiero closed the book and set it down with a thump. "In fact, I've read theories from the Faithful that we should strive to reach their level of technology to impress them and bring them back to our world."

Fritz shook his head. "Now that sounds like propaganda."

Hiero shrugged. "Perhaps. I want to study this place more, but there's no time right now. We still have to find a passage out."

About a fortnight later, the city of Reta was shut up tight. Every entry point had the army of Fieman lined up in ranks outside it. They had been here for two days, and Hiero still had no plan to get them to leave. Their food stores would be gone in a week, and after that, well . . .

Hiero couldn't sleep. He kept pacing the halls of the palace, hour after hour. He and Fritz had discovered that dungeon, but it wasn't the passage they needed. He had heard from many sources over the two years he lived in the city that there were passages in and out of the palace and in and out of Reta. Well, they needed a passage out now. He didn't have a choice. He had to keep looking.

Hiero couldn't let his people starve. If there wasn't another option he'd have to give himself up. A bubble of sadness welled up inside his chest. He'd been down this hall already, and that one. He'd been in every room in the old palace, tapping on every wall like a madman.

Hiero set his torch in a sconce and slowly slid down the wall onto his butt. What was he going to do? He didn't want to die, but he knew none of the lords would let him live, and he didn't want to give his people that difficult decision.

All he could do was conserve the food they had and keep praying to the Ancients until there was nothing left. And then he would walk out of Reta's gates.

A sob rose out of his throat and was quickly muffled by his hand. He'd failed them. They needed him to be their king and protect them, but he was helpless.

Perhaps this was his punishment for what he'd done to Gannon. The Ancients had seen him break the law, and now his reign would be cursed. Hiero wanted to claw out the feeling of guilt that pierced through his heart. Was there no way to clean away this infraction?

"Oh, Gannon!" His whisper was so high-pitched it sounded like a squeal. "If you're out there, forgive me! Please! Forgive me!"

"Hiero?"

Hiero jerked away from the sound. His heart leaped into his chest. His sword was in his hand when Joanna stepped out of the darkness.

"Calm down!" She put her hands out. "It's me, full flesh and blood."

"Thank goodness." Hiero couldn't calm his heart. "This place has me looking for spirits over both shoulders."

"I get that feeling too." Joanna sat down beside him and sighed. "Hiero, why are you still down here? Fritz told me you've already gone over every inch of this place. He's worried about you. He says you don't sleep anymore."

Hiero sighed. "I can't. I've tried. The whole city is depending on me, Joanna. I can't let the lords win."

They sat in silence for a few moments. After all that talk, Hiero thought maybe he would fall asleep. The carpet wavered back and forth in his vision.

"Hiero, what do you need Gannon to forgive you for?"

Hiero stiffened. She'd heard.

"You sounded heartbroken."

Hiero shook his head. "It's not important. He's passed on. He will not be able to hear me from there."

"Hiero . . ." Joanna used a motherly tone when she didn't believe him.

Hiero sighed. She was the closest thing he had to a mother. He needed someone's advice.

"Joanna, did I tell you how Gannon died?"

"Yes, you told us he fell from above the balcony while trying to climb down."

"I lied to you." He swallowed. Maybe it was because he was too tired, but words he didn't want to say spilled out of him. "I pushed him off the edge. He called me a bastard to my face, and I couldn't control myself. Before I knew it, he was gone."

"Hiero!" Her face was in utter shock. "Do you have any idea what you did?"

"I broke the Ancients' laws. I murdered. I know. I'm as horrible as the man I'm replacing." Hiero curled his arms around his knees and hugged his legs to his chest. For just a moment, he felt like a small child again, afraid of the dark. "I keep telling myself that it was a good thing to do since Gannon had no plans to remove the law against Ancient worship. He had just killed Reta himself when I came in the door, so he was a murderer too."

Hiero shut his mouth. For some reason, he didn't think this was helping his case. "I'm sorry, Joanna. The worst part is, I feel cursed now. What if this attack by Lord Fieman is the punishment of the Ancients upon my reign? What if they don't want me to reign anymore? I'm a lawbreaker."

"Look at me!" Joanna grabbed his face and forced him to look at her. "We are all lawbreakers, Hiero, in one form or another. There's not a single Faithful in Retall who has not broken a law. You cannot be guiltless because it is not possible. However, you can aspire to be more and more lawful every day."

She sighed. "That being said, murder is a truly heinous crime. If you still wish to be king over these people, you need to tell them what you've done. They need to make their decision with open eyes. That is the only just way."

Joanna put her hand on Hiero's shoulder. "Come with me. Go back to your bed. Tomorrow I'll stand beside you and help you say what needs to be said. If the people choose against you, then that is the way it should be."

He couldn't accept that. Hiero knew in his heart that if people knew, they would never trust him again. Retall needed a leader to bring back the law, no matter how dark that man's soul was.

"No, Joanna. I'm keeping this to myself. I can't risk the people rising against me. I need you to swear that you won't tell anyone."

Joanna's face darkened. "No, Hiero. This isn't the right way. If you won't tell the people, then I will. Transparency is too important."

"That's where we disagree, Joanna." Hiero grabbed Joanna's arm in a fist. "I can't let you tell anyone what you heard tonight."

"Hiero—"

Hiero got to his feet and yanked her up with him.

"Hiero, stop it! Somebody! Help!"

No one could hear them from the old palace. Hiero kept a firm grip on Joanna and pulled her after him, toward the tapestry that hid the staircase. Thankfully, he and Fritz had discovered the dungeon first.

25

FOUL VICTORY

SHELIA'S MIND WAS consumed with worry. The pounding of Beya's hooves only masked the frantic pounding of her heart. What was she doing? She needed to stop! She needed to go home! The thundering behind her seemed so close. She couldn't go home. Her father was like an enemy now. If he caught her, she would be forced to marry Sita. He would read Hiero's letter, and then he would attack Hiero. There would be war.

The man behind her gained another foot as Beya tired. Shelia squeezed tears from her eyes. She was going to be caught! The image of Hiero's body bubbled up in her mind, and she sobbed out loud.

For a moment, Shelia's attention wavered from the road, and a branch slapped her across her face. She jerked, and Beya jerked, and suddenly they were off the road and into the forest, and branches scratched at her from all sides.

Beya gave out a pained whinny, and a shout sounded from behind. "This way! She's gone this way!"

"No!" Shelia's teeth were pressed so tightly together that she could not feel her jaw. What was she going to do? There was no escape. They would catch her, and they would drag her back to her father. She wouldn't marry Sita!

In front of them, hidden by the brush, was a decline, and at their pace, Beya rushed headlong down it, her hooves sliding on the loose gravel. Shelia let go of the reins and threw her arms around Beya's neck, holding on for her life as they half slid, half fell down the slope. Beya let out a terrified scream that echoed through the forest and slid to a stop on her rump.

Shelia blinked. They were alive? She pulled herself upright and looked up the incline that was now dented with their passage. She couldn't see the top, and that meant it was likely the person at the top couldn't see them.

Beya pulled herself upright and snorted the dust out of her nose. Shelia patted her on the neck.

"Shh. Quiet." In the stillness, she could hear the men of her house shouting frantically for her at the top of the hill. Shelia stayed silent, her heart beating like hoofbeats until their voices faded away.

She walked Beya forward slowly, keeping her hooves from ringing on the stone until they were on dirt again. Then she kicked her into a gallop.

Shelia looked for the sun and turned them north. For several hours, they rotated between galloping and walking, for Shelia was still afraid that she would be overtaken. She stopped to let Beya drink from streams, but she did not dismount until deep into the night.

It was not until her mind was deeply tired that she realized her father had no idea where she was going. Her uncle said that he didn't know what she was planning. If he told her father all that the letter entailed, Father might believe that Shelia had gone to Hiero. It was the logical course to take. What he would do about Gannon, though, Shelia could not guess. Would there really be war between two lords of Reta?

Shelia's head nodded in tiredness, and Beya slowed to a walk. They were both exhausted. When Shelia's head bobbed so deeply that she felt herself slipping away, she stopped Beya and dismounted. They were out of the Great Forest for sure because the land had become farmland and hills. It was not cold, but Shelia shivered. She briefly thought of a farmhouse or an inn but abandoned the idea altogether. She could barely think.

Silently, she unstrapped Beya's bridle and collapsed into a ball on the grass beside her, the bridle in her hand. She would ride more in just a moment, when she was rested. In half a moment, she was deeply asleep.

It was not the sun that woke her, but Beya's soft nuzzling against her cheek. The sky was still dark.

"What?" Shelia sat up, her blood awake and pumping. Where was she? Why was she here? The memories rushed in a moment behind the panic, and she collapsed back onto the soft ground. Beya's bridle lay next to her head, and Shelia whispered a prayer of thankfulness that Beya had not walked back to her stable while Shelia slept. Next time she would remember to tie her horse.

Shelia stood and untied her basket from Beya's saddle. The meat and bread were long cold, but Shelia wolfed them down without a thought and drank deeply from the waterskin. She thought Beya would need water until she saw her head disappear down in an irrigation ditch, happily swinging her tail. She came up and ripped a mouthful of grass out of the ground. Shelia smiled. Some farmer would be missing random patches of hay in a couple months.

The sky grew gray in the east toward Stentil. Shelia replaced the basket and Beya's bridle and jumped up into the saddle. She knew it was a three-day ride to Lord Kiad's territory, so if that had been the first day, she would have at least one more night before she arrived. Shelia threw her tousled hair over her shoulder. She would need to find an inn before that. Lord Kiad might not even believe she was Shelia Teris if she looked too disheveled.

She rode north for hours. The food and water were soon gone. Shelia met a road and began to follow it. Long after the sun went down, she found an inn on the road. This was a new situation for Shelia, who'd never traveled before. It felt daunting to walk Beya into the yard, have her spirited away by unfamiliar hostlers, and then walk into the inn's lobby alone.

The door closed behind Shelia more loudly than she would have chosen, and she flinched, her heart jumping. She wanted to sink into the ground or turn around and run out the door she'd just come in.

Shelia swallowed and took a small step into the room. "Hello?" Her voice sounded weak and timid even to her.

The room was a rectangle. On Shelia's left was a staircase, in front of her was an empty counter, and to her right was the great room of the inn, completely empty, the remains of the fire smoldering in the far-off fireplace. Shelia pulled her cloak tightly around her shoulders. Was this place deserted? A moment later, Shelia heard a door shut on the second floor and hurried footsteps on the stairs. A man sporting a heavy beard clipped quickly down the stairs and slid behind the counter.

"Excuse me, my lady," he whispered. "My family is abed at this hour. Can I get you a room?" He looked over her shoulder with bleary eyes. "Are you alone?"

Shelia drew herself up and opened her eyes wide. "I am. I require a bed for the night and a bath for the morning."

The man nodded quickly and looked back to his logbook. "Will you require dinner for tonight?"

Shelia felt the hollow pit in her stomach with distaste. His family was already in bed, and she could see that he was tired too. She swallowed. "I just need water, thank you."

The man smiled at her thanks and reached below the counter for a key. "Just give me a moment, lady, and I will fetch you a pitcher." He disappeared into the kitchen for a moment and emerged with a full pitcher of water. "Please follow me."

He led her up the stairs and turned right down the first hallway, unlocking the second door and vanishing inside the blackness. A few moments later, Shelia heard the striking of flint, and a candle flared to life on the trunk beside the bed. With a sleepy smile, the man slid past her into the hall, placing the key in her hand.

"Sleep well, my lady. Don't forget to lock the door."

Shelia nodded and shut the door, locking it securely. Then, with a sigh of relief, she turned and looked over her room. It was bare and unadorned, but it had a bed and four sturdy walls. Shelia lifted the pitcher and smelled the water, and then she drank until she was satisfied.

With both hands, she tested the mattress and inspected it. It did not appear to be infested with bugs or rodents. Shelia cast one quick glance around the room and lay down on the bed, blowing out the candle behind her. She was asleep in an instant.

In the morning, a knocking on her door woke her. Shelia blinked in the soft light of the room and flew out of bed. She was away from home! She was alone! Shelia ran over to the door and laid her ear against it. The knock came again, a little louder. It wasn't as rough as the knock of a man.

Shelia reached for the key and unlocked the door, pulling it open. A slight young girl stood outside, a tub on its side beside her. Her eyes widened as she took in Shelia. Shelia glanced down at herself. She looked like a mess after two nights in the same dress.

"I will draw your bath, lady, if you are ready."

"Of course!"

A younger girl in the same gray cloth stood just behind her, and as Shelia spoke, she turned and ran down the hall. The older girl rolled the tub—which was nearly as tall as she was—into the room and set it in the space behind the door. Then she turned and sped out of the room. The girls reappeared a few moments later hauling buckets of steaming water that they poured into the tub, and then they disappeared for more.

Shelia was used to this routine. While she waited, she stripped down to her shift and dipped her soiled dress in the steaming water, wringing it out twice and laying it flat on the bed.

Time passed in this way, and the girls made as many trips as were needed to fill the tub. Shelia pulled her shift off over her head and lowered herself into the nearly too-warm water. The younger girl was shooed away, and the elder lathered Shelia's hair with soap as she soaked in the warmth of the water.

When the grime of the road had been scoured away and Shelia's dress had dried clean, she walked downstairs and had her breakfast in the great room and paid for her stay.

Shelia walked out of the inn feeling tall and powerful, as though she could take on the world. She'd done all that entirely by herself. She could barely believe it.

A young hostler cupped his hands for her to use as a step, and Shelia swung her leg over Beya's back. "It's a fine day, isn't it?"

The young man's eyes fluttered back and forth. "Yes, yes, miss, it is."

"Is this Lord Kiad's territory? He must be lucky to have nice roads and good inns."

The young man fidgeted nervously. "Yes, miss. This is Lord Kiad's land."

Shelia cocked her head. "Have you ever seen him?"

The man's head popped up, and his eyes widened. "Oh, no! He would never come down here!"

"Well, why not? He has so much land to look over."

The young man looked thoughtful. "He doesn't like seeing people. He stays locked up in his castle all the time."

Shelia leaned down. "A castle? Does he expect to be attacked?"

He shook his head furiously. "No! No one would dare attack Lord Kiad! Ever!"

Shelia bit her lip. "Can you tell me how to get there?"

Two minutes later, Beya was thundering down the road. Less than a day, the young man had said. Shelia would be there by tonight. It was both terrifying and empowering. She was going to stand up to a lord, and she was going to get Gannon back. It had been so long since she had seen him.

As she rode farther north, the sun rose in the sky, but it seemed to her that the light only grew more dim. The wind turned cold, and she pulled her cloak tighter around her shoulders. It felt as though a cold hand had descended on her back.

Shelia shivered, and her mind filled with worry. Something did not feel right deep in her chest. Should she go home? What had this all been for if Gannon was kept a prisoner? Could she marry Sita? And what would happen to Hiero when her father took over the capital? She could not let any of it happen. Despite how she felt, she had to keep riding.

Farms changed slowly to houses spaced closer together. Shelia passed markets and storefronts. Wreathed in fog, the castle of Lord Kiad suddenly materialized in front of her, looking as though it had been cut straight out of the rock. Shelia's heart bounded back and forth in her chest like a frightened animal.

Shelia swallowed. There it was. This was the moment. She would storm in there as the daughter of Lord Teris and demand her brother back. Shelia sat up straighter in her saddle and slowed Beya to a trot. Unless he wanted a war with her father, Lord Kiad would have no choice but to concede.

Shelia followed the road straight up to the base of the cliff. There was a gate blocking further access to the road, and two guards stood behind it, laughing at some joke that had just been said. Shelia reined in beside the gate.

"I demand to see Lord Kiad at once!"

The guards took in her finer clothing, and the captain tipped up his helmet to see her face.

"Under whose authority do you demand to see Lord Kiad?"

"Under the authority of House Teris!" Shelia raised her chin as high as it would go. "I am Shelia Teris, daughter of the lord!"

The foot soldier went running, leaped on the back of a horse, and took off up the steep hill. The captain bowed low. "Please forgive me for my forwardness, my lady, but I would not serve my post well if I let every traveler through the lord's gate." He raised the bar and pulled the gate open. "Please come in."

Shelia walked Beya in, and the gate clanged shut behind her.

"If you will be patient, my lady, an envoy from the castle will be down to guide you up."

Shelia nodded politely. "Thank you."

The silence seemed awkward. The captain shifted back and forth in his boots. Finally, he gave her a curious look. "Is your company coming along later?"

Shelia pressed her lips tightly together. Was it that strange for her to be traveling alone? What would Lord Kiad think? What if he did not believe who she was? She looked away from his gaze.

"I am traveling alone."

His silence pierced her full of guilt. This captain could not know what a terrible daughter she was, yet she felt as though he had accused her.

"I see," he finally said. Shelia did not look at him again. Her eyes watched the mountain path for this envoy to appear. After a long wait, she saw movement on the path, and the horsemen sped down the decline, coming to a quick stop before her.

There were four horsemen: three of the envoy and one gate guard. The front man of the envoy bowed his head to

Shelia. "Lady Teris, welcome. Lord Kiad is waiting to greet you in his parlor. Please follow us."

He turned his horse, and the other two rode around to bring up the rear as Shelia pushed Beya to a walk. The road was built as a continuous curving ramp up the side of the mountain. At a juncture, the path grew wide, and a wall sprung up between them and the cliff face. They had entered a courtyard with a stable at one end of it.

The front rider turned his head. "Lady Teris, the rest of the journey is by staircase. It can be quite treacherous for the untrained horse. Please leave your horse in our care here, and you will be provided a secure mount for the rest of the journey."

Two hostlers had already surrounded Beya, and their hands reached for her bridle, holding her head steady. Arms were held out to help her down. Shelia sighed and relented. She leaned down and hugged Beya's neck.

"Goodbye, Beya. I'll see you in a bit."

The hands lifted her out of the saddle and set her securely on the ground. A sleek gray horse was brought out of the stable, but Shelia barely noticed. She watched them lead Beya away until a hostler had to call her.

"Miss? Will you mount?"

Shelia turned to see the man with his hands cupped beside the gray mare. "Oh! I apologize." She stepped into his hands and swung her leg over the horse's side. She didn't want to go anywhere without Beya. Everything felt so wrong now. This horse's back felt different. Shelia didn't want to be here anymore.

She looked up at the castle apprehensively. It was so much bigger and closer now. She considered turning and claiming Beya before she got any farther away.

No! What was she thinking? Shelia's hand went straight to her head. She was so close to seeing Gannon! The gazes of the people around her came to the forefront of her mind. What would it look like to them if she turned around and left right now? What would Lord Kiad think of her? Shelia swallowed. What would he think of her father? She would shame him by running away for no reason.

She kicked the horse's sides softly and took steps toward the leader. As she drew closer, she saw the staircase etched into the solid rock. Shelia swallowed. It did look precarious. But the first hoof that touched the stone was true. Shelia shut her eyes and let the horse climb all on its own. Her fingers tightened on the reins until they had turned white. She closed her eyes and did not open them again until she felt the ground level out underneath her.

The castle was so close now. She couldn't even see its top. The leader dismounted in front of another short set of stairs. The other two horsemen were getting down, and Shelia swung her leg over quickly lest they try to help her down. She followed the envoy up the short stairs and into the castle.

It was cold. Shelia barely noticed the furnishings of the hall, but she felt cold cut straight through her clothes. It was a long walk before they stood at a doorway, and the envoy leader opened it, ushering Shelia inside. It was a parlor, and two chairs sat before a roaring fireplace.

As Shelia took the seat closest to the door, she heard heavy footfalls coming toward the room. The doorway opened, and Lord Kiad strode in. Shelia was taken aback. He was tall and broad, and his blond hair had streaks of gray and silver in it. His face was full of confusion.

"Shelia Teris? My men tell me you travel alone. Have you come in place of your father?"

Shelia's brow knit together. "In the place of my father? What do you mean?"

Lord Kiad crossed the room and sat in the chair across from her. His practiced speech had vanished in a moment. How could she not know the reason she'd been sent somewhere? And what madness would have convinced Lord Teris to send her alone? There were dangers on the road, not to mention his enemies swarming here.

The solution was quite simple to Lord Kiad: she hadn't been sent. She had come of her own volition. But why? What would've caused the daughter of Lord Teris to abandon her family and risk herself to come here all alone? He was dying to know.

Lord Kiad spread out in his chair and crossed his ankle over his knee, smiling at the girl sitting across from him. "Well, if you didn't know about the impending lords' council, nor of my invitation to your father, then why have you chosen to visit me? I highly doubt this is a simple social call."

He studied the lines of her body, the curve of her cheekbones. She was a well-built woman and far more attractive than most highborn ladies he had been introduced to. Lord Kiad's eyes narrowed. In fact, she seemed familiar somehow. He could have sworn he'd seen that face before, and recently.

Lady Teris smoothed her hands down the front of her bodice and seemed to be composing herself. "Lord Kiad, I have received information that you are holding my brother, Gannon Teris, hostage. I demand that you release him at once!" Her eyes flashed as they met his. "You should understand the implications if you refuse. Lord Teris is prepared to do what is necessary to see his son returned!"

Kiad's eyes narrowed. That was a lie. Lord Teris was an utter fool if he thought that sending his daughter alone would threaten him. Not only that, but Gannon was dead. Was this some sort of Teris ploy to pin his son's death on him? It didn't make any sense. Why would he send his daughter here? It was too large a risk. Wouldn't it be far more beneficial to circulate this about to the other lords first and keep him in the dark?

Lord Kiad pulled back in his chair. A new perspective sprung into his mind. If Lord Teris was working to turn the other lords against him with this misinformation, and this young, stubborn girl had heard it and gotten it in her mind that she could get her brother back herself, well!

Lord Kiad broke into a wide grin. It was always so simple. There was no information that did not unravel itself at his touch. He hadn't been informed of this new Teris plot yet, and that meant he would need a new agent at the manor, but that was of no matter. He was in a much better mood now.

"I do hate to be the one to inform you, Lady Teris, but—"

There was a knock on the study door. Lord Kiad's eyes narrowed. What was this? Didn't those fools know to leave him be? The door opened, and his captain stuck his head into the room.

"My lord, do you desire your servant at this time?"

Lord Kiad's eyes jumped to the clock on the mantel. Ah, it was that time of day, wasn't it? Lord Kiad had opened his mouth to refuse when a realization hit him right between the eyes. He looked back at Shelia's face. She did look so terribly similar. Kiad felt a rumbling deep in his belly. *Could it be?*

Slowly, he motioned with his hand. "Bring him in."

The captain bowed and pulled the doors open, leading Lord Kiad's newest slave in. The moment he saw their faces together in the same room, he knew it. Shelia grew curious and turned to look. She leaped out of her chair.

"Gannon!"

Kiad snapped forward like a cobra and grabbed her shoulder, pushing her back down into the chair. He couldn't stop smiling.

"Now I own both the spawn of Teris. This truly is my lucky day."

26

WEIGHTY ARRIVALS

LAMONT FELT RESTLESS. He paced the halls of Lord Kiad's castle without direction. It was not long before he found himself utterly lost. The carpets were faded, stained, and scarred. The bare walls seemed to stink of dirtiness and decay. Lamont felt a similar decay in his chest. He longed for his uncle, for his king, now gone. In only a few hours, the lords would be gathered, and he would be elected the throne. Was he even capable of managing it? It was now he needed to talk to his uncle, but he couldn't.

His emotions bubbled up inside his chest, and there was a cry. For a moment, Lamont thought it had come from his own throat, but then he heard the cry again. Lamont hurried down the hall toward it and opened a door. Inside was a bare room with only an empty bed frame against the wall. A man sat on his knees in the center of the room, his head in his hands. He was sobbing uncontrollably. His voice rose to a cry again; he'd not noticed that the door to his room was open. In front of him lay a dagger that gleamed in the room's faint light.

Anias Kaiden howled from the depths of his tortured mind. There was no hope left for him. He would never be free. Lord Kiad would not be done with him until he was dead or his body broken beyond repair. He would never have a wife, would never be allowed to father children. Now that the king's heir, this Lamont, had come and given his approval to Lord Kiad's dealings, things would continue as they had. Kaiden could dream that Hieronymus Purvis, who had already freed the people of Reta, would be able to free the rest of Retall as well, but it was only a dream. When the lords came together, they would never vote for Hieronymus. They would vote for Lamont, and Kaiden would be a slave forever.

He managed to compose himself and stared down at the dagger he'd been hiding for so long. How he wished he had the strength to thrust it into Lord Kiad like Hieronymus had done to the king. He'd be free. Kaiden's hands shook at the very thought. He couldn't do something like that. He was too afraid. He would rather die here, by his own hand, than ever face Lord Kiad again. He would never face Lord Kiad again.

The dagger gleamed. Kaiden took it in his hand and swallowed. The sobriety of the moment had stifled his cries. He breathed deeply and held the dagger over his heart. He had no hope for the future anyway. What else could he do? How else could he escape?

"Stop!"

Kaiden froze. His head turned toward the door. It was Lamont. It was the king's heir.

"Stop!" he said again. "Do not do this."

Kaiden was paralyzed. What could he do? Lamont would tell Lord Kiad. Kaiden watched Lamont lower himself to the floor.

"Look at me. Talk to me. Why would you take away your own life?"

Kaiden couldn't move. He couldn't speak. Lamont Reynard knelt on the carpet only a few feet away from him. Would he ever get such a chance again? His arm fell to the floor. The dagger dropped uselessly on the carpet. He lowered his eyes.

"My lord, will you not do anything for the slaves?"

Confusion flickered briefly over Lamont's face before being replaced by a smug disconnect.

"Slavery is illegal in Retall." Lamont's voice hit a monotone note. "If you have been sentenced for a crime, you must pay that sentence. To run from your own consequences is dishonorable." He looked at Kaiden's downcast face and shook his head. "Do as you wish."

Lamont pushed off the carpet to stand, and Kaiden's arm shot out, grabbing his wrist. "Please, my lord! Listen to me!" The screech in his voice echoed eerily down the hall.

Lamont's face was as cold as stone. "Release me!"

Kaiden shook his head. "No! I cannot. I beg you for my own life! I am not a criminal!"

Lamont's expression did not waver. "So says a very guilty man."

"I am not lying! I have been in Lord Kiad's service since I was sold to him as a child!"

"Sold?" The tenor of his voice had changed. He turned and shut the door with his free hand. "You intend to convince me that Lord Kiad is buying innocent citizens as slaves?"

Kaiden released Lamont's wrist. He could feel his heart slow. "I must convince you. It's true. I cannot live another day without hope that I might someday be free."

Lamont's face saddened. He looked away from Kaiden's eyes. "There is nothing I can do."

Kaiden's face snapped up, anger slashed across it. "You will be king!"

Lamont glared back. "The power of a king is only the power of those who will support him! Even once I am crowned, when all looks to be safe, it will not be." He set his hand on Kaiden's shoulder. "You cannot make such a decision based on the pain of today." He sighed. "It will pass."

The two sat in silence until Lamont spoke again. "I-I lost my uncle recently. He could have lived, but he chose to die. He had a dream—a goal—that he gave to me and asked me to complete for him. I must complete that for him. I feel his desire deep in my soul, rolling over and over like a stone. It will not leave me, awake or asleep. If I were to die without completing his work, it would haunt me even in the Isle. There must be something, something you desire so greatly that it haunts you."

Kaiden was taken aback. Who was this man? What did he want? Kaiden wanted to pull away from his grasp, but Lamont's eyes were on him, dragging out his thoughts.

"I want to have a family." He swallowed. "But that will never happen. Lord Kiad would never let me."

Lamont's eyebrows knit together. "Why not? Surely your lord would allow you to marry another of his servants?"

"No!" Kaiden could imagine his lord's face if he ever

dared ask such a thing. "No, my lord desires me for himself." He couldn't look Lamont in the eyes. He'd never felt so wretched in all his life. "My lord is a pederast."

Silence dropped like a stone between them. Kaiden pressed his hands against his head, unable to bear the silence, the thoughts that must've been boiling in Lamont's head. "I am a dog! I am worse than a dog!"

Lamont's hand tightened on his shoulder. "No! Don't think that!"

Kaiden looked up to see Lamont's jaw harden.

"When I am king, I will see what can be done." He met Kaiden's eyes again. "Do not take your life. You are young, and the lord will lose interest when you are older. If you die now, how will your desire ever be accomplished?" His eyes burned so powerfully into Kaiden that he could not look away. Lamont shook his shoulder. "You will achieve it."

The courtyard was full of noise and movement. Lord Kiad watched the cacophony from a shadowy corner of the stable. His face split into a grin as a group of horsemen rode in at top speed, banners flying. The banners were gold and split in the center by a blue river. Kiad knew it immediately. Lord Yus was here.

Lord Yus dismounted in a single motion, and his eyes flashed with anger as they darted around the courtyard.

"Why is a lord left standing here?" he roared.

A stable boy scurried across the yard, his head bowed and his shoulders hunched. The lord threw his reins at him in disgust, and Lord Kiad stepped out of his hiding place, clapping slowly.

"Lord Yus, your temperament is becoming well-known to my servants. How was the journey?"

Lord Yus scowled at him. "Your servants are slow, Kiad. A lash or two might be useful in loosening their joints!" He shook his head, and his voice lowered as he stepped in place beside Lord Kiad. "The journey was terrible. Fall is fading quickly in the west. This will not be a pleasant winter."

Lord Kiad's smirk turned grave. "Is there a chance we might be attacked?"

Lord Yus shook his head. "Not this year. The wind has been mostly driving the sand to the south during the growing season." He sighed. "But that will bring a very dry, chapped winter to the west. Next year may be a different story if the winds do not turn north before spring."

Lord Kiad nodded. "There are many things we must all consider in the days to come." He motioned to the horses that had been brought for them. "I have matters to be discussed in private. Will you join me?"

"I will."

Once in the castle, Yus threw his cloak at the nearest servant and strode into the study. "This place is as sickly as it has always been. How do you live without windows?"

Lord Kiad shut the door. "I prefer it, actually."

Lord Yus pushed off his boots and collapsed into a chair. "What is this matter you want to speak about? I'm eager to get into a warm bath."

Kiad sat down slowly. "Lord Fieman."

"You have not changed once in all these years. He is dead. Has no one informed you yet?"

"How did he die?"

Lord Yus sighed with a deep weariness. "My anger is long gone, but I ordered it done. I sent my lieutenant to see it carried out."

"Did you not think that it might be seen as a threat to the power of the other lords?"

"Perhaps it will give them cause to pay more heed to their responsibilities. Lord Fieman had long forgotten his purpose and had been testing both my patience and the crown's. A lord given reign over agriculture has no right to build an army, especially when he has been strictly ordered not to. The defense of Retall is my responsibility."

Lord Kiad shook his head. "Very well then. I do believe you acted rashly. We needed his vote, and I assume the child will not make the journey for the council."

Yus sneered. "Why would his vote be needed for the throne? There are no contenders. He'd only become a contender himself."

Kiad smirked. "That is where you are wrong. We do have a contender."

"Who? Teris's son is dead, and the prince has been lost for years!"

"The king left an heir."

"The lost prince?"

Kiad's eyes sharpened. "There is another. The king left his kingdom to him in his final hours. I have information not only from the man himself but from witnesses within the palace. They have overheard the rebel speaking with his manservant and confirming it."

Lord Yus sat forward in his chair. "Who is it then? Who is the heir?"

Lord Kiad smirked. In the end, they were all the same. "It is Lamont Reynard, the grand general of Retall."

"The king's nephew?" Lord Yus paused and sat back in his chair. His hand curled around his chin. "That could work." His eyes seemed riveted on a single cord in the carpet. "That would work beautifully."

Lord Kiad could not stop grinning. "Naturally, he will be beholden to us for electing him, a man who has no natural right to the throne."

"Yes." Lord Yus nodded. "I will vote for that." He met Lord Kiad's eyes. "You have my vote."

"Good. Then what about the others?"

Yus shrugged. "You would know better than I who is attending."

"Lord Ene is here, as is Lord Damis. They arrived last night. I have also heard that Lords Jobin and Privit are only a day away."

"Lord Teris and Lord Sita are not attending, I presume?"

"Just so. They appear to be hatching their own plan for the throne, one that involves marrying Lady Teris to Lord Sita."

Yus raised an eyebrow. "You seem remarkably nonchalant about such a development."

Lord Kiad waved his hand through the air in front of his face. "It won't be an issue."

Lord Yus's boot began to tap angrily at Kiad's flippancy. "Speak the words crawling on the inside of your mind before they burst you open, lord of tattlers!"

Kiad smirked. "You wound me. It is a badge of honor!"

Yus sighed and put his head in his hand. "Just speak already."

"Lady Teris is my prisoner."

Lord Yus's head snapped up. "What?"

"Lady Shelia Teris is—"

"I know who she is, you fool! How in Isle's name did you manage to capture her? How do you think this will affect how the lords vote? Think of how Lord Teris will react!"

"The lords will react how they did when they heard of Lord Fieman's death. Lord Ene has not ceased to ponder the implications since he arrived, and I grow weary of his endless theories of conspiracy. He has brought a sizable guard with him just in case." Lord Kiad sneered. "And I care not what Lord Teris thinks. He cannot do a thing as long as his daughter is in my hand."

"But how did you capture her? Lord Teris's woodsmen are impossible to sneak through!"

Kiad smiled. "You will not believe it. She came to me."

Yus grimaced. "If you continue to test me, Kiad—"

"I am not lying. Apparently, she was told that her brother was my prisoner here." He pulled a couple rumpled sheets of paper from his breast and tossed them lightly to Lord Yus. "Read it. It is a tale spun by a mastermind."

Lord Yus unfolded the papers, and his brow wrinkled as he read them. His gaze darkened as he finished, and he read the undersigned name out loud. "Hiero? Hieronymus Purvis? The leader of the rebels is connected to the Teris family?"

Lord Kiad's grin had turned malicious. "Lord Ene's conspiracy theories may yet find a resting place. I have not heard of Purvis before, but I suspect he may be more dangerous than Lord Teris could ever hope to be."

"Why do you say this?"

"Beyond the fact that he has the ability to manipulate people? Not just the common folk, but lords and lordlings?"

Lord Yus slapped the paper. "What reason would he have to send Lady Teris to you if he so clearly cares for her?"

"I don't believe that was his intention." Kiad reached across and pulled the papers from Yus. "From reading it several times, I have come to the conclusion that he intended to start a war between me and Lord Teris. He presumed that this information would be taken directly to Lord Teris and that he, in turn, would attack me. That is Purvis's game. He intends to make us destroy ourselves. He has already succeeded with one." Lord Kiad glared across the top of the paper. "Lord Fieman is dead."

"This peasant intends to harry out lords?"

Lord Kiad got right in Yus's reddened face. "Is he not already succeeding? Lord Reta and Lord Fieman are dead! The line of Teris has been cut short, or so some believe."

"So, Gannon Teris is actually alive? And your prisoner?"

Lord Kiad smirked. "He is."

Yus slapped a hand to his head. "Blessed Ancients! Do you not understand what has been given to you? The Teris family is in your hand!"

"I am aware." Lord Kiad's hand began to shake with restrained passion. "To have the son of Teris in my hand, to do with him what I will, is almost too much for me. Even in the last two days since I learned his identity, I have had to restrain myself lest I break him."

Surprise was replaced by disgust on Yus's face. "He is your dog then. I see." He shook his head. "So, Teris will not pose a threat any longer. How do you intend to approach the lords' council with this information? Theatrically, I presume?"

"But of course. My words will smack of fire and thunder. We must come together to destroy Purvis! He is the ultimate threat. I am sure I can convince the rest of the lords to promise men for an army."

"I see our minds are in the same place. I too was thinking an army would be necessary to dislodge Purvis. I have a thousand ready men patrolling the western border as we speak, with more in training. They will be put to good use removing this thorn from the palace."

"I have men lounging in prison who would jump at the chance of a pardon. It won't be necessary to pull our reserves from the peasantry, especially during harvest."

Lord Yus nodded. "We will see what transpires at the council, but I agree with you." He placed his hands on the arms of the chair and leaned forward. "May I take my leave then? I'm sure my bath is waiting, and I would like to relax before tomorrow."

"Yes, of course." Kiad stepped forward, and the men locked hands. "It is good to have you here again, my friend."

Even after Yus had left, Kiad sat, still deep in thought. His captain leaned into the room.

"My lord, do you desire your servant at this time?"

Kiad roused from his thoughts. "Yes, bring him in." As the door opened, Kiad softly cracked his knuckles. Why should he not relax as well?

27

CURSED DECISIONS

THE ROOM WAS full of noise. The lords sat together at a rectangular table at the front of the hall. Their entourages, courtiers, and guards sat at long perpendicular tables that stretched the hall to the back.

The lords seemed tense and rigid in their chairs. Other than Lord Kiad, they talked little and drank even less. The exception was Lord Privit, who before the third course had already drained his glass five times and was turning a cheery red.

Lord Kiad sat at the head of the table, and Lord Yus was on his right. On his left sat the young Damis, lord of mining and metalworking, his long brown hair pulled back with a string. Jobin, lord of education, sat next to him, a gaunt figure with streaks of silver already showing in his hair. Ene, lord of hunting, sat directly across from Kiad, and he acted nervous, looking all about the room as if he expected to be stabbed at any moment. Privit, lord of hospitality, infrastructure, and the roads, sat between Lord Ene and Lord Yus, talking loudly to everyone and being spoken to by none.

The lords may have been tense and silent, but their servants were not. Conversation and wine flowed freely together. A rowdy song swept the back of the room. Kaiden sat with his face in his mug, grateful for a moment away from Kiad's gaze, grateful that he could drink all he wanted and forget. There was no comfort in conversation for him.

He took another long, slow draft, and when he set his mug down, a man sat down across from him, staring at him intently. Kaiden raised an eyebrow and looked back at his mug.

"You're the man I'm looking for."

Kaiden sucked in a snootful of beer and sputtered, coughing until he could breathe again. "What?" He eyed the man across the rim of his mug. He was giant, larger than Lord Kiad, and his hair was shorn clean across the top of his head. He might have been somewhere around his thirtieth year. His gray eyes were unbelievably intense. He smiled with his lips alone.

"You are a slave, a prisoner to the old rule. Our king desires that you be free. Will you be free?"

The ringing in Kaiden's ears and throat did not come from the beer. His body was not breathing. The world seemed to turn sideways, and Kaiden felt like he should turn his head to compensate. What was this? A trick? A trap? Or a path to freedom? Kaiden studied the man's face for a moment longer, trying to discern his intention. Then he set his mug down.

"If it is possible, I would be free."

The man leaned in. "Then once the contender has been presented, you will find me near the door."

Kaiden nodded. "Very well, but who—"

"Near the door. That's all for now."

The man stood, and Kaiden pretended to be deeply interested in his mug. He couldn't let on that they had talked. Watching him leave would only bring suspicion. Kaiden suddenly wished that the meal would be finished. He'd had enough beer, probably too much. Now he wanted to be alert. The words that had already been spoken would burn in him until they could speak again.

Carefully, he looked down the table to Lamont, who sat among Lord Kiad's servants. How long until he was presented? Lamont was smiling and chatting happily to the man beside him. Kaiden had not seen him frown since yesterday, when Lamont had spoken to him. He greeted him often in passing, and always kindly. Could Kaiden hope that Lamont would free him, or was he a fool for trusting him?

The giant man had stressed the word "our" of "our king." Who could he have been speaking of but Hieronymus? Hieronymus desired that Kaiden be free? Did this mean that the man knew Hieronymus personally? Did this mean that Hieronymus knew of Anias Kaiden?

Kaiden shook his head. It was too much to process. The giant had called him the man he'd been looking for. Was it even possible? How would Hieronymus have learned about him?

Kaiden put his face in his mug to hide the tears that spilled from his eyes. Oh, the thought that the king would look at him, that the king would reach out his hand and lift Kaiden up—there was no thought like it! There was no other hope, once ignited, that could fill Kaiden's breast with fire.

How much longer? Lord Kiad drummed his fingers on the tabletop. He was running out of things to talk about, and the mood at the table was foul. It was time to move the program forward. He set his hands on the table and stood.

"Lords of Retall, it is clear to me that our bonds of brotherhood have completely disintegrated. We are not here for company, hospitality, food, or wine." He paused for a moment as Lord Privit gave a cheer for the wine. "We are only here because it is our duty. Because the solemn weight of tradition compels us to arrive and cast our votes. I feel a very great discontent at this table. Can this rebel, Hieronymus, be correct? Is it time that this tradition be removed?" He slammed his fist on the table. "Is it time that the people of Retall choose who their king will be?"

The whole hall went quiet. Every eye looked furtively from Lord Kiad to the other lords and all around the room. Lord Yus cleared his throat. Lord Jobin pushed his spectacles up his nose and glared over the top of them. Lord Privit laughed, and Lord Ene's mouth hardened into a white line. Even young Damis's eyes flashed. He had insulted them.

Lord Kiad's mouth split into a grin without mirth, cruel and cold. "My lords! Where is your fire? Are you not ashamed that this peasant, this bastard, now sits in the seat of Retall, mocking us?" He paused again, waiting for them to reply, and their silence fed his fervor. What was wrong with them? If a man had dared throw such words at Kiad, he would not have let him stand. These men were pathetic.

"Pitiful." Kiad sneered. "What fat, useless lords of Retall you are, wallowing in your own opulence! I can hear your wives crying, lords of Retall, begging for real men to fill them! Where is your pride? Has the blood of Brandon Terys grown so thin in our veins that we cannot muster the strength to roust one contemptible peasant off a stolen throne?"

Lord Yus looked around the table at the barely contained anger growing on the faces of the lords and laid his hand over his eyes. He would not stop Lord Kiad now. It was working.

The moment Yus closed his eyes, Kiad grabbed the edge of the table and shoved it forward. The lords jumped backward as cups and plates went flying. Wine splashed across the table and onto the floor.

"You are mad!" Lord Ene hissed, his shoulder curled like a cobra ready to strike.

Kiad's eyes shot daggers back. "I am distressed at the lack of passion in all of you! What do I have to do to get you men to act?"

"What's the point?" Damis's whisper was close enough to Kiad that his head whipped around.

"What was that?"

Damis quailed in the spotlight. "There's no point!" he exclaimed. "We don't even have anyone to elect! Why not let the peasant stay king? The people already love him!"

Kiad couldn't believe he had heard that properly. "You want to vote for the bastard when any one of you has a better claim to the throne than he does?"

Lord Jobin twisted his normally downward mouth into a sour smile. "Haven't you noticed, lord of tattlers, how the peasantry speak about us? They want us all dead, paying for crimes that most of us have not even committed. If we do not improve the opinion of the nobility, soon there will be angry mobs at our own gates!"

Kiad's brow furrowed as he turned to look each of them in the eye. Was there really no desire in any of them to fight? Lord Kiad shook his head. "How quickly the passion of life has fled the sons of Brandon Terys. As pointless as it may be, I have something to tell you." He set his hands on the table, suddenly weary. "And you will stay to hear it, all of you!"

He glared at them before stepping onto the dais at the front of the room. "The king, in his last moments, was strong. He did not ignore the imminent doom he was to face, and he did not ignore his duty. In his death, the king named an heir, and you would give that man's throne to a peasant! To a bastard!"

The shock on each face was clear.

Ene grabbed Jobin by the arm. "Did you know?" Jobin pulled away, and Ene reached for Lord Yus, who was trying desperately to hide his grin behind a fist. Lord Ene turned him about. "You knew! You knew that the king left an heir! You two conspired behind my back! You let him parade us around like fools! Who is it?" Lord Ene turned and raised his fist to Lord Kiad. "Who is it?" he demanded.

"Sit down, and I will tell you!" Kiad boomed.

The lords skirted puddles of wine as they pulled their chairs back around the table. Kiad pulled himself up to his greatest height. "The king's heir came to me, running for his life, because he trusted no other lord. Because the bastard knows he is the heir and is seeking his life. Here he is!" Kiad threw out his arm, and Lamont stood and walked to the front of the room, where he stood beside the dais.

Lamont was almost afraid to look the lords in the eye, expecting anger or confusion, but as he looked up, he saw quiet approval on each face. Lamont reached into his shirt and pulled out the chain on which hung the old king's signet ring.

"I am Lamont Reynard, the Grand General of Retall! I am the king's heir. In his foresight, the king granted me his ring and his power after his death. I humbly beg the lords that they would accept my words as his."

After a moment of silence, Lord Yus stood. "I call for a vote of the lords' council for Lamont Reynard, nephew of our late king."

Lord Ene held up a finger. "One moment please. Don't be so hasty, Yus. There are questions." He paused, and Lord Jobin interjected, his voice as fast and sharp as a blade.

"Young man!"

Lamont swallowed. "Yes, my lord?"

"Is it true that you are the late king's nephew?"

Lamont nodded. "Yes, my lord. My mother was the king's sister."

"I see. No direct blood claim to the throne then. Did you, at any point in our late king's reign, find yourself desiring the throne?"

Lamont's face turned anxious. "No, my lord." He looked down. "Even at the end, I begged the king to choose another."

"So, no blood claim, and no desire to rule. Why are you a contender, young man?"

"I—" Lamont's voice faltered. "It is the command of my king that I carry on with his work, that I not leave

Retall to another who would send it back to where it was thirty-two years ago." Lamont swallowed. "It was his belief that Retall back then was a land gripped by superstition and fear of mythical beings that could no longer affect our lives. He would not wish that way of life to return."

"Ah, good to know." Jobin nodded to Ene. "You may continue."

Ene scowled. "Reynard, did you witness with your own eyes the king's death?" His voice was gruff.

Lamont shook his head. "No. At the time of his death, I was being escorted out of the palace."

"So, you have no idea how the king died?"

Lamont swallowed. "That is not entirely correct. I know how the king died, at least, by whose hand he died."

"Whose?"

"By the hand of Hieronymus Purvis. He wanted to kill me as well, but a guard who worked for the rebels stepped between us and stopped him."

Lord Yus cocked his head. "Do you mean to say that there is a man to whom Hieronymus answers? Would I be correct in saying he obeys him?"

Lamont thought for a moment. Whatever he said here would change possible military strategy in the days and weeks to come. Lamont grimaced as he wondered how he would ever reign over these men once he was king. They were shrewd and suspicious. Lord Yus had picked up on a thread of thought that Lamont would not have seen by himself.

He was pulled from his thoughts by the movements of a servant boy who was quickly replacing the lords' spilled wineglasses. Lamont glanced around the hall. This was not the place for such a sensitive discussion.

"Your words are too strong, Lord Yus. We should speak more on this later, in a more private place."

Lord Kiad raised his arms and jumped from the dais. "All hail the new king of Retall!" The benches of servants beyond them cheered, and in those few moments, Kiad's shoulder brushed against Lamont's ear. "I didn't catch what you said, Reynard."

"We will speak on it later," Lamont whispered, and Kiad nodded, pulling back with a full smile on his face.

"Who can say no to such a handsome young man? Your rightful king!"

Lord Ene's arms were crossed. "Is that meant to persuade us to vote, Kiad?" Ene sighed. "Fine. I shall. In favor of Lamont Reynard!" He raised his glass, and Lord Yus did the same.

"In favor of Lamont Reynard!"

Lord Privit, Lord Damis, and Lord Jobin followed suit.

"In favor of Lamont Reynard, may we drink our oaths back on ourselves!" The lords put their glasses to their lips and drank.

"Goddess curse us if we break them," Kiad whispered into his glass.

Shelia's face was sore from wiping it again and again, and still she cried. Tears dripped off her chin and splashed on the stone floor. The edge of her dress was soiled all the way around from mopping at her eyes.

Gannon hated her. He would not speak to her. He would not look at her.

"Gannon!" she cried again. "Please! Please! Say something!"

Gannon sat on the other side of the room, separated from her by a wall of bars. He was curled up in the far corner, his chin on his drawn-up knees, his face hidden by his hands. For the past two hours since they had brought him in, he had not stirred, and he had not spoken, no matter how she pleaded with him.

He had to hate her. She was so stupid. How could he love her?

Outside the room, she could hear the noise of the lords' council. If the rest of the lords knew what Lord Kiad had done, he would be in so much trouble. Just because he was a lord didn't mean that he could hold them here against their will, not when they hadn't committed any crime. If the lords knew, she and Gannon would be freed at once.

Shelia sniffed. Her father could be out there right now. He would surely have come to the lords' council. It was his duty.

Shelia couldn't stop staring at Gannon. Didn't it mean anything to him that she'd come to rescue him? He was so cruel. Her gaze shifted to the door. There was no use banging or pushing against it. It was so heavy she couldn't even make it shake, and there was no way her shouting would be heard over the din outside.

She turned to Gannon again. Begging and pleading would not make him speak, but he couldn't stop her from talking.

"Gannon, perhaps Father is here! It is the lords' council. I'm sure he's out there right now, and Uncle read the letter I got from Hiero, so he knows that we both are here! We will be free as soon as he has a moment to reveal it to the other lords!"

She forced herself to smile. "I will be so glad to have

you home. It hasn't changed at all! Your room is just the way you left it. Uncle and I missed you so much." Shelia realized what she was saying and laughed at her own scattered mind. In the corner of her eye, she saw Gannon jerk from her sudden laugh.

"I don't know what I was thinking. Of course you aren't going to need your room anymore. You'll be living at the palace! And I'll be there, and Father, and Uncle. Oh! And Hiero!"

Gannon flinched at her voice. It bubbled over now; she couldn't stop it. Was he finally coming out of his spell?

"I have missed Hiero so much. I wanted to be married to him every day he was away. If it hadn't been for Hiero, I wouldn't have known that you were alive at all. Father thought you were dead—"

Gannon's head rose from his knees. His eyes were sunken and haunted. "Hiero." His voice sounded like gravel. "Hiero betrayed me."

Shelia could have wept for joy at the sound of his voice. She turned over and crawled up against the bars. She'd been thinking about this all wrong. He needed her to assure him that all would be well.

"No, Gannon! It was all a misunderstanding. Hiero explained everything to me. He sent a messenger to the manor, and the man knew our special letter-hiding place. Hiero said that he'd looked everywhere for you and that Lord Kiad must have taken you because you weren't anywhere to be found. Oh, and he wanted you to know that the throne is safe with him. He's going to protect it from Lamont until you get back."

Gannon's mouth opened and shut, and his head dropped back onto his knees. "Shelia, why? Why did you come here?"

Shelia looked down. He didn't need to sound so accusing. It was Kiad's fault, not hers. "I wanted to rescue you, Gannon."

"Why didn't you tell Father?" Gannon's voice was high with frustration. "He could have brought an army!"

Shelia's hands twisted together in her lap. She couldn't tell Gannon what she had heard Father say. He would be so hurt.

"I couldn't." Shelia gritted her teeth. "Father wouldn't have believed some letter from Hiero, and he was planning on marrying me to Lord Sita. I don't want to marry him!"

"Better him than Hiero!" Gannon's hands balled into fists. "Shelia, this is a terrible, terrible place. We are not going to be rescued, and we are not going to escape."

Shelia was confused. "But the lords—"

Gannon glared at her. "Shelia, Lord Kiad could strip you naked in front of those lords, and they would do nothing. He is pure evil and far too powerful. None of them would dare stand up to him." Gannon gripped his stomach like he was ill. "He is disgusting, vile, sick." His body shook. "I don't know what he plans to do with you, Shelia, but your life is over." He looked at her with eyes that were broken. "You will never marry Hiero."

Shelia gawked at him. Her mind spun. Why did he look so empty? What had Lord Kiad been doing to him? She couldn't think of anything to say.

A key turned in the lock, and her door opened. The door on Gannon's side opened at the same time. Light and sound rushed into the room, blinding her. A man entered and dragged Shelia roughly to her feet.

"Hey! Let me go!"

Lord Kiad's voice boomed through the hall. "Look and see!"

Shelia was yanked out of the room, howling in protest.

"Shelia Teris, the daughter of Lord Teris, is in my hand! Lord Teris cannot stand against us! He would not dare attack us!"

Shelia was pulled across the room and onto the dais and shoved to her knees. She looked up to see the whole hall erupt in wild cheering. Lord Kiad stood in front of her, his arms raised to the ceiling.

"This is not all! By now all of you have heard that Gannon Teris, the only man who could match Reynard's claim to the throne, is dead!" He paused. "This is a lie made up by Hieronymus. No, Gannon is not dead." Lord Kiad threw out his arm again. "Gannon Teris is my prisoner!"

There was scattered clapping, and the room turned deathly quiet as the men watched her brother be led calmly to the dais and pushed to his knees beside her. Shelia frowned. Why was everyone so quiet? They must've been judging Lord Kiad for being in the wrong. They would surely be free in moments.

Shelia felt a gaze upon her, sharp, as though it were burning her, and her head turned. Two brown eyes, dark as coal, met hers. They were set in a handsome face framed by shaggy gray-brown hair. Their intensity was almost too much for her to keep looking. Shelia felt ice go down her spine.

"With these two our prisoners, Lord Teris will not threaten us, and there is no one else to lay claim to Reynard's throne." Lord Kiad threw his fist into the air. "We will march on Reta! We will drag Hieronymus from his stolen throne, and Lamont Reynard will be crowned king of Retall!"

The cheering was real. Hats were thrown in the air, and men beat the tables with their hands. Lord Kiad took a step back, breathing heavily. The doors opened in the back, and more food was brought in, and the feast seemed to resume right where it had left off.

The intense man stepped up on the dais, and Kiad gave him a quick bow, still grinning. "My king."

He did not look pleased. He gestured to Shelia and Gannon. "What is this? Why did you not tell me that the children of Teris were here?" Those dark eyes pierced into Kiad's. "I would not have approved of you parading them like animals!"

Kiad's smile had frozen on his face. "The children of Teris? They are a new occurrence, I assure you. They only appeared a few hours ago."

The man grabbed Kiad's arm in a vice grip. A vein bulged in his neck. "If they only appeared a few hours ago, then why have I seen this slave by your side for the past week?"

Shelia felt Gannon stiffen beside her. She was becoming more convinced that Kiad had tortured him in some way.

Kiad's smile became a snarl, and he wrenched his arm away. "You promised me that things would stay as they were! I will keep slaves as I wish, Reynard!"

Shelia swallowed. This was Lamont Reynard? She'd never seen Hiero's half brother before. He didn't look anything like she'd imagined.

Lamont shook his head. "This is entirely unrelated to that." He glanced at the crowded room before them. "We need to speak privately. Now."

Lord Kiad grabbed Lamont's shoulder, and his face twisted in pain as Kiad's fingers dug in. His voice dropped to a lethal hiss. "You would truly speak to me about freeing a man who has a claim against you? Are you a fool? You may make such demands, but remember who you make them to." Kiad shook his head. "You aren't king yet."

Lamont's eyes were ice-cold. "You will release me at once."

Lord Kiad leaned in. "You'll remember in whose castle you stand."

Lord Yus watched the exchange curiously from his seat, and Lord Kiad straightened with a wicked grin on his face. "Lords of Retall, I have a new proposal for you! Our king-to-be has no lady by his side, and just now, as he saw Lady Teris, his heart was tender toward her! What better way for the long feud between the house of Reta and the house of Teris to end than to join these two in marriage?"

Lamont jerked away from Lord Kiad. "What?" He leaned in. "That's not going to happen!"

But the words had been spoken, and now the people were cheering. Lamont glanced at her, and Shelia blinked. *No.*

"No!" she yelled, and she was jerked to her feet, struggling, and pulled out of the room.

Lamont couldn't believe what he had just heard. Uncle was surely rolling over in his grave right now.

"Escort him please." Kiad's grin was evil. "Make sure he doesn't try to get away." Another servant came up beside Lamont, and his face burned with anger as he strode after them. Every eye in the room was on him. He probably looked like a child. Kiad would pay for this. He was an arrogant fool if he thought he could tell Lamont what to do.

"What a lucky man!" Kiad crooned as Lamont got farther away. "Enjoy your beautiful bride!"

No, Shelia was not his bride, and she never would be. Lamont had been ordered by the king to destroy the Teris family, and he had given his word that he would complete it. Both Shelia and Gannon had to die. Lamont gritted his teeth. It couldn't be done now though—not while they were needed as leverage.

Farther down the hall, he could hear Lady Teris wailing. Did she honestly think that would change her situation? Lamont's impression of her was dropping by the second. He slowed his pace. He needed to figure out what to do.

Marriage? Lamont put his hand to his head. Lord Kiad could not declare him married by a simple round of applause. In all his years, Lamont had never given marriage much thought. It wasn't important to him.

Why not Lady Teris?

The thought ran through his mind before he could strangle it. How could he think something like that? His king had ordered him to destroy the Teris family. When Lamont was king, he would order Kiad to hand Gannon over to him as well.

He must've been lonely. Strange thoughts arose in men who didn't have anyone alive they could call family. He would have to find himself a wife eventually, but there was much more that needed doing before then.

What was he to do tonight? Lamont heard a door slam farther down the hall, muffling the lady's cries. The man behind him and the man standing in front of the door would see to it that he slept in that room tonight. Lamont took a deep breath, bracing himself for the emotional battle to come.

28

GROWING TERROR

IN THE MAIN hall, the party continued. Kaiden stood and made his way to the double doors in the back, acting as he would were he going to the privy. At the end of the table, he looked slowly to the right and the left, stretching his neck and yawning, but he did not see the giant. Where was he?

Kaiden continued walking toward the door, intending to look for him again once he got back, but as Kaiden reached for the doorknob, an arm slung over his shoulder from behind. Kaiden's heart hit the ceiling.

"My brother! Ah! How many years has it been? I've missed you!" A man with a cocky grin and sleek orange hair the color of a carrot hung off him. His words slurred together at the end. Kaiden hadn't had time to remove the fear from his face, and the man noticed. He winked openly at Kaiden once, twice. "I did not expect to meet you here like this! Come, you must say hello to our fellows. They haven't seen you in so long!"

Orange Hair steered Kaiden along the back of the room and into a corner where there was a little round table with two men already sitting at it. The great hall's shape naturally shaded this area. The table was nothing more than a wheel frame set on top of a barrel. Kaiden knew that hadn't been there this morning.

The giant man sat in the corner and smiled as he saw Kaiden's face. "You are late. The contender was announced several minutes ago. Glad to see you found us."

Orange Hair removed his arm from Kaiden's shoulder and sat down. Kaiden looked around nervously and followed suit. "I had to wait until my lord was occupied." He hunched in his chair, afraid he'd be looking for him now. "And I wouldn't have thought to look for you here."

The giant in the corner placed his hand on his chest. "It is of no matter now. I am Hollis Larkon, bodyguard to our king. You are all here because you face the same terrible predicament. You are not free."

Kaiden looked over his shoulder again. "Are we safe speaking here?"

The young man on Kaiden's left ran his fingers across eyebrows as black and bushy as the hair on his head. "We will be far safer if you stop drawing attention to yourself."

Kaiden turned back around, his ears burning. These men didn't understand. Lord Kiad's ears were everywhere. Hollis placed his hand on the man's shoulder.

"We are all comrades here, not competitors. All three of you are afraid, but you cannot let it separate you. Speak your name."

The young man sighed. "I am Noch Ennis, Lord Ene's manservant."

The man on the opposite side of the table leaned in. "Leon Yusir, Lord Yus's personal assistant. Please call me Leon."

Kaiden swallowed. "I am Anias Kaiden, Lord Kiad's—" His mind scrambled for an appropriate word. "Attendant."

He looked around the table. Leon gave him a sad smile, but Ennis was still fussing with the hair on his face. Kaiden wondered if they had any idea what he was referring to. What did they suffer at the hands of their lords?

"Very well. You know your lord better than any other. You know who they truly are. You suffer the brunt of their anger and the result of every frustration."

"But we are not free to leave." Leon's orange hair was chopped short just below his ears. Orange freckles dusted his cheeks. He fingered the hilt of the sword by his side. "I have no chance of a future, of any life beyond my service." He met Kaiden and Ennis in the eyes. "I did not think there were others in my position."

"Our king does not desire this to be so. He has freed the citizens of Reta, and he desires to free you as well." Hollis's easy smile turned sad, just for a moment. "Unfortunately, he is only one man. His arm is not yet long enough to reach the lords and sweep them down. But your arms"—Hollis pointed to each of them slowly—"are always near your lords." Kaiden felt his heart drop in his chest as Hollis smiled. "You have heard of what happened to Lord Fieman, yes?"

"Yes," Leon said. "Lord Yus had him executed. I was there when he signed the order. Lord Yus raged about his actions for days."

"I was referring to what brought him to that point. It was the common people who destroyed Lord Fieman's army." His finger tapped on the tabletop. "One by one."

Kaiden was becoming more and more uncomfortable with the way Hollis stared him down. "Our king calls on you to fight for your freedom."

Something poked Kaiden in the knee. He grabbed it, and his heart shuddered. The hilt of a dagger was in his hand. Leon and Ennis leaned down in their seats, and Kaiden watched them each hide a dagger in their boots.

This wasn't happening. He couldn't do this. His hand shook just touching it. Suddenly, the hilt was still. Hollis was still looking him directly in the eye. His eyes were neither hard nor cold but full of a strange look. Kaiden felt like there was a line of power traveling from Hollis's eyes into his mind.

"When our king calls us to action, we must be ready. It will not be until the last moment, until you see the fire and taste the blood, that you will strike." His eyes bored into Kaiden. "And then you will be free."

Hollis released the end of the dagger, and the weight was in Kaiden's hand again. Kaiden's throat was as dry as a desert, and he couldn't wet it even by swallowing. This was not what he wanted. He wanted to be free now. He didn't want to face Lord Kiad again, and he certainly did not want the task of assassinating him by himself.

The others were staring at him, confused, and Kaiden slid the dagger into his boot as he had seen them do. He could not do this. He knew he couldn't.

Hollis laid his hand on the table. "Remember, you are the hands of the king. Without you, he cannot strike. Do not forget."

What was he going to do now?

Lamont opened the door and slipped softly into the bedroom. The lighting was dim. Some lamps around the door had been blown out, likely by the vehement shutting of a door. His eyes snapped back and forth quickly, but he did not see Shelia. His back stiffened; he expected an attack. The door clicked shut behind him. He waited for another moment and heard a sniffling cry from the far corner of the room, behind the bed.

Lamont turned and walked to a stuffed armchair against the wall. The less he had to deal with her, the better. If he had to see her executed, he didn't want to get attached to her. He settled into the chair slowly and sighed.

Minutes later, the crying continued. Lamont had wavered in and out of sleep several times and was beginning to get annoyed. "Lady Teris, I'm not going to touch you. I give you my word. You can stop crying now."

There was a loud sniff. "I don't trust you!"

Lamont raised an eyebrow. "I don't care. You're disturbing my sleep, and I'm tired."

There was a small explosion from behind the bed. "You're a liar and an evil man! I won't marry you!"

Lamont sighed and ran his fingers through his hair. "That is something we can agree on. I am not going to marry you."

The crying stopped abruptly. Her voice quivered from behind the bed. "You're a monster."

Lamont sighed again. Was he really entertaining this conversation? "I'm not a monster. I'm a man who stays loyal to his king."

Shelia pulled herself to her feet behind the bed. "You are a monster. All his life you've treated your brother with cruelty and hatred. You'll pay for that. Hiero will have his revenge."

Lamont's eyes narrowed, and his heartbeat grew audible in his ears. How did she know anything about the bastard? "Hiero is a bastard and a murderer who will face a just execution for his crimes. As for the past, he overstepped his station in life and was punished for it."

Shelia shook her head. "Hiero is going to destroy you. He'll rescue me, and we'll be married."

Lamont felt a white-hot spike of anger sear down his spine, and he lurched to his feet. A flicker of uncertainty darted across Shelia's face as she backed up against the drapes.

"You?" Lamont could barely handle the emotion that was bubbling inside of him. "You are Hiero's beloved? The woman he wanted to marry?"

He could not imagine a viler combination: the man who had murdered his king with the family that his king had abhorred. Lamont's fingers went to the sword at his hip, and he stepped toward her. *I should kill her now, before—*

No. Lamont took a step back. He knew how badly she was needed. If she was truly Hiero's beloved, she would only be more useful to the lords.

Lamont glanced back at her. She had pressed herself against the drapes, and her white-knuckled fists were held stubbornly at her sides. Her face should have been a mask of fear, but instead her eyes shot a red-hot glare. Her twisted mouth taunted him to run her through.

Lamont turned and marched to the door, banging on it with a fist. "I've finished! I need to speak to Lord Kiad now!" Lamont's jaw tightened. He wasn't going to stay here with her. He wouldn't be safe. She had the fire of Teris blood in her, and he'd seen it.

Hollis Larkon twisted the wide brim of his hat as he walked quickly down the passage from Lord Kiad's great hall.

This news needed to reach Hiero at once.

He turned down another passage, feeling the hot touch of the torches on his face as he passed them. There were certain disadvantages to being so tall.

His boots were soft on the stone, but he could hear the approach of a guard ringing farther down the passage. Hollis turned immediately down another hall and followed it to its first turn, hiding behind it. He waited at the turn until the guard had passed. To be found down here was to be found out.

As he went on, the passages took on a decidedly diagonal tilt. They grew narrower and shorter until Hollis felt a breeze ruffle his hair and flip up the brim of his hat. He leaned down and crawled out of a small circular opening cut into the rock under the castle. He stood on a small ledge above the town below. He stooped to pick up the small circular grate and slid it back into place. It was as if he had never been here.

Etched into the rock face below were steps. Hollis began to climb down, and the ground slowly came up to meet him. In the darkness, he heard his horse whinny. Hiero would hear of all that had happened tonight just as fast as Hollis could reach him.

Once the guard let him out, Lamont flew down the hall toward the great room. The party was still active; the men offered up increasingly drunken cheers, but the lords were nowhere to be seen. Lamont grabbed the nearest elbow he saw and pulled it.

"Where are the lords?"

The man gave him a dim-witted stare. "They've all gone to bed!"

"Even Kiad?"

The man blinked slowly. "The lord has left his larders open! We will drink him out of house and home!"

Lamont grimaced. "I see. I'll find him myself."

He stepped away from the raucous noises and back out into the hall. Kiad couldn't have gotten to bed that quickly. He'd look for him in his study.

A few minutes later, Lamont stood in front of Kiad's study door. The presence of two guards outside indicated that the lord was there.

Lamont strode forward. "I need to see Lord Kiad."

The guards barred his way. "The lord is indisposed. You cannot see him at this time."

Lamont wanted to growl. He ran his hand through his hair, taking control of himself.

"Look, I'm about to be your king. The lords have elected me. For you to be more loyal to him than to me . . ." He paused. "That's treasonous."

The men gave each other a look. One of them sighed. "Sir, if we let you past us, we'll be punished. I don't want that. My partner doesn't want that. Please understand us."

Lamont glared. He was growing to detest Lord Kiad. He nodded. "I'll speak to him about that. Let me through."

The guard's face twisted in pain as he stood to the side. Lamont grabbed the doorknob and pushed the door open.

Kiad had just elicited a gut-wrenching scream from Gannon, and Lamont froze in the doorway. How had he not heard that from the hall?

Lamont's adrenaline spiked, and his heart raced as he looked across the room at the two men, the one restrained, the other working his member between his fingers.

Kiad's face first registered anger before he realized who it was. "Lamont, what a surprise! Care to join us?"

Lamont's stomach rolled, and he almost ran out. "Kiad, cover yourself. I need to speak to you."

Kiad laughed out loud. "I'm busy! Are you blind, Lamont? Or envious?"

Lamont slammed the door shut behind him. The only language Kiad understood was strength and force.

"That is enough!" He took a step forward. "I don't want to hear another word about your perversion!" He glanced at Gannon, who was up against the bookshelf, hanging limp in the shackles around his wrists. His torso was lacerated in many places, presumably by the knife resting within Kiad's reach. The man had to die, but he didn't need to be tortured. This was vile. "Release Teris and send him to bed."

Kiad raised an eyebrow. "You will hear about it, Lamont. You will hear the screams rise from your own throat if you test me further. Gannon is my slave, and I will do what I want with him."

Lamont stepped as close to Kiad as he dared, keeping the knife in his peripheral vision. "All citizens of Retall are the charges of the king. It is the king who gives responsibility to the lords. You have overstepped your authority."

Lord Kiad cracked his neck audibly. "Do you not remember, Lamont, the agreement we made? All things will remain as they are? If you mean to threaten me—"

"That and this are two separate issues. You have laid claim to a man our king has declared must die."

Kiad glanced back at Gannon. "The hatred between Reta and Teris cannot be overstated, but to wipe out the line?"

"Not only him," Lamont continued, "but also Lady Teris, Lord Teris, and the lord's invalid brother."

Kiad's head snapped back. "Have you killed her?"

"Do you take me for a fool? I know she is needed. For now. But I will not allow you to marry us, and I will not sleep in the same room as her."

Kiad's smile tugged at the corners of his mouth. "Ah, but you must. We must maintain the facade with the other lords."

Lamont's brow furrowed. "Why?"

Kiad lifted his robe from the back of a chair and threw it around his shoulders. "Hieronymus has made it clear that his plan involves wiping out the institution of the lords. If you declare your intention to wipe out the family of Teris, our frightened lords may think you might someday want to wipe them out as well."

Kiad took a step toward him, and Lamont pulled back. Kiad seemed taller the closer he got.

"And once you wipe out the Teris family, who will take over? Will you leave all of Retall's lumber production in the hands of unskilled, uneducated peasants? Or perhaps you would attempt to take that domain for yourself. Of course, if one lord takes over the domain of another, why should they stop there? Ene, Jobin, or any other lord might be next. All of a sudden, in the eyes of the other lords, you are just as much of a threat as your half-brother. But you certainly aren't like him, are you?"

Lamont nodded grudgingly. "Very well. I understand your point."

Lord Kiad put up a hand. "And one more thing." He pointed to Gannon. "The son of Teris belongs to me. I will not give him up."

Lamont shook his head. "You must."

"No." Kiad turned to the fireplace and grabbed the long thin poker from the stand, sticking the tip into the flames.

Lamont took a nervous step back as Kiad lifted the smoking tip up. He stepped over to the bookshelf and grabbed Gannon's jaw, pushing the side of his head against the wood so that his ear was crushed out where he could see it. Gannon's eyes were still closed; he was unconscious or seriously dazed. Kiad thrust the end of the poker through Gannon's earlobe into the wood.

Gannon's eyes jerked open, and a strangled howl gurgled in his throat. Lamont winced. This was old law, hundreds of years old, from before the Teris family had declared slavery illegal. A man with a hole through his ear was property until the day he died. He had no soul any longer.

Kiad pulled back with a husky, satisfied sigh and threw the poker against the fireplace. "Gannon Teris is dead. This man is my slave." He held up Gannon's head and stared into his bloodshot eyes. "You are mine, every day, until you die."

Lamont took a step back and turned to the door. There was no reasoning with Kiad. He would have to find another way to meet his king's final command.

29

PAINFUL NEWS

HIERO HAD JUST taken an enormous bite of bread when the door to the dining room burst open. Fritz stumbled in, looking like he'd seen a ghost. His eyes were wide, and his coat was hanging open as if he'd just been in a scuffle.

"Hiero—" he gasped before Hollis grabbed him by the back of his coat, hauled him backward out of the room, and strode in himself. Hiero was halfway out of his chair, scrabbling for a weapon, before Hollis bent to one knee on the carpet.

"My king, I have an urgent report."

Hiero tried to chew and swallow the food in his mouth. He'd been worried for a moment there. Before he could reply, Fritz had rebounded off the hallway walls and bumped his way through the doorframe behind Hollis.

"Hiero, it's Shelia."

Hiero's throat contracted, and everything went down at once. He coughed. "Tell me."

Hollis stood, and Fritz came around him, laying his hand on Hiero's shoulder. "Hiero, you should sit down."

Hiero's heart fluttered in his chest. He pulled the chair back underneath him, and Fritz sat in the chair to his left. Hiero nodded.

"All right, go ahead."

Hollis's face was impassive. "The mission to the lords' council was successful, but other things took place there that you should know about." Hollis paused. "The king's heir, Lamont Reynard, was elected king just as you predicted. He does indeed have the king's signet ring."

Hiero clenched his fist. He didn't care about that right now. "What of Shelia?"

Hollis raised his chin. "Lady Teris was at the lords' council. She has been taken prisoner by Lord Kiad. The lordling Teris is his prisoner as well."

Hiero did not say a word. For several minutes, it was all he could do to breathe deeply.

Hollis laid his hand on the table. "My king, there is more."

Hiero shook his head. "This was all my doing. How could I be such a fool?" His knee bounced under the table. "Why didn't I send the letter to Lord Teris? Shelia, no, Shelia had no idea what to do with it!"

"Hiero." Fritz's voice was insistent. "You must hear the rest of it. You should know what happened."

Hiero stood to pace. "I already know that Lord Teris was not there. I know what he plans behind closed doors with Lord Sita. Without his attack on Lord Kiad, we will have to deal with the full force of whatever troops they muster, and it will be more than what we faced from Lord Fieman."

Fritz only looked more and more nervous. "Hiero, there is more to this."

Hiero threw his arms out. "I know, Fritz! I know! There is no way that Lord Teris or Lord Sita will attack a coalition of the lords while they hold the children of Teris." He yanked a handful of his hair in a fist. "And I would not want them to." He rested his hands on the back of his chair, leaning with a deep weariness in his chest. "Our chances of surviving have suddenly grown very slim. I don't know if it's even possible against such odds, even with our assassins in place."

Hollis sighed. "I did not wish to spring the news on you, my king, but you have not given me space to answer. While I spied on the lords' council, Lord Kiad made a declaration regarding Lady Shelia."

Hiero's eyes were suddenly focused on Hollis's face.

"She has been given in marriage to Lamont Reynard, the lords' choice for the throne."

A mighty wind rushed in his ears. "What did you say?"

"Lady Teris, my king. Lord Kiad gave her to Lamont Reynard."

Hiero's knees went weak. His hands tightened on the back of his chair, strangling it. "No!"

"My king, if it is any consolation, she fought the men who held her all the way to the bedroom."

Fritz gave him a lethal stare, and Hollis dipped his head. "I apologize."

Hiero sank to his knees. "Shelia," he whispered. "Gone?" There was a pain inside of him, a hard rock lodged in the very center of his chest. Water rushed across his vision, outside of his control. His throat tightened. Shelia was gone? The plans he had made with her beside him crumbled into dust. Shelia was married. Why did anything matter? He would be alone.

Fritz watched Hiero's face, his own darkening. "Hiero, I think we should retire to your room. This is not the place—"

"There is no place for me." Hiero's voice cracked. "There is no place in this world for a bastard."

A few moments of silence passed. Hiero composed himself. Silently, he rose. "Fritz, we should go. We don't belong here. The palace is no place for a bastard."

Fritz's eyes narrowed. "And where will we go?"

"North, to find your sisters, just as you wanted to do weeks ago."

Fritz gawked at him. "Hiero, what?"

Hiero rubbed his hand across his face and chuckled hollowly. "We'll have to get our things moved back to Joanna's shop. I don't know why I thought I could be king."

Neither of them noticed the change that took place in Hollis until he crossed the room with a roar and pounded his fist into the table. His extra head of height on Hiero cast a dangerous shadow. He grabbed Hiero by the shirt front and pulled him off the ground.

"You pitiful, cowardly dog! How dare you leave us now!"

There was a frightened squeak from the open doorway as the serving girls ran away. Fritz stood as Hollis backed Hiero up against the wall. "Where is the man who fought for the people? For the Ancients' law? For justice? Is that all you were fighting for? For a wife?"

Hiero's mouth closed, and his jaw tightened. He found footing on his tiptoes and shoved Hollis's grip away. "No, that's not it. I was fighting for myself." He looked down at his shaking fist. "I thought if I worked hard enough, if I was principled, more righteous, I could reverse the fate of a bastard. But in the end, there is nothing I can do. At every step I take, my trueborn brother is already one step ahead! I can't win! I am enslaved to the system Reta lives under, and I can't change it! He has taken away my inheritance, my chance at the throne, and the only woman I have ever desired! What can I do?" Hiero glared at Hollis. "The Ancients' laws mean nothing to him. How can I fight back?"

Silence followed. Hollis's eyes burned into Hiero. "You're wrong. You have more recourse than any other fated life in Retall. You sit in the seat of power, a common man with a chance to change the fortunes of every life in Retall!" Hollis rested his fist on the wall beside Hiero's head. "You are my hope; you are the hope of the people of Reta; you are the hope of thousands scattered across all of Retall! How can you betray us when we have put our bodies and our souls behind you?" Hollis's arm shook. He let it drop and turned away. "I cannot stop you. If you choose to go, I won't stop you, but—" He grimaced in pain. "I would have thought you to be braver than this."

Hiero stepped away from Hollis, and his eyes jumped to Fritz. "Fritz?"

Fritz blinked, and tears rushed down his cheeks. "Hiero . . ." His voice was so tight it rasped. "My sisters."

Hiero's face softened. There were so many thoughts in his head fighting to get out that he couldn't make his throat speak. Hiero shook his head and closed his eyes, trying to focus on one thing. Immediately, Fritz shrieked like he'd been stabbed in the side.

"Hiero! You promised! You promised we would free them!" He swallowed, and his voice found its proper octave. "I should have let you kill him! If he were dead, he wouldn't be stealing from you any longer. And Shelia—"

He gasped as Hiero placed a hand on his shoulder. "No. What happened with Shelia was my fault. I made an error in judgment."

There was a smolder in Hiero's breast, small but insistent. Was this fire? Was this what Lord Teris had been talking about? A small smile crept onto his face. "I'm going to fight. I cannot believe that I will win, but I will fight. Reta will be our fortress. Hollis, close the door."

Hollis's smile had returned, and he turned to close the door. Then he moved around the table to sit on Hiero's other side. Hiero's barely touched breakfast lay between the three, and they huddled around it like eager children.

"Fritz was right," Hiero stated. "The problem is Lamont Reynard. If he could be removed, the issue of succession would cease. He has already stolen so much from me, and I don't intend to let him keep it. I know that the resolve in me is weak, but I promise you both, I will not give up. The last time I faced Lamont, I let my revenge be lax. Never again. He will suffer by my hand until he screams for death itself, and I will grant it to him."

Hollis lifted an eyebrow. "My lord, in the next two or three weeks, the army of the lords will be assembled and begin its march on Reta. What is your plan?"

Hiero's hand tapped anxiously on his thigh. "They will not make the mistakes that Lord Fieman's force did. They will certainly subdue the peasantry. And we cannot rely on Lord Teris to stand with us or engage the enemy while his children are held prisoner." Hiero sighed. "We have no other recourse. The Ancients' laws forbid it, but we have no other option. We must build a force of our own. Hollis Larkon."

Hollis leaped out of his chair and knelt at Hiero's side. "Yes, my king."

"I must send you out again. How long will you need to rest?"

"I am rested, my king."

Hiero was taken aback. "When did you sleep? Have you eaten anything?"

"No, my king, you misunderstand me—"

Hiero put up a hand. "Then sleep and eat. I command it. I won't let you leave until you've done so. Once you've rested, I will send you out to every city and town surrounding Reta. Go as far north and west as you dare. Time is of the essence. You will find every man, woman, and child loyal to me, and you will lead them to Reta. In these walls, I will protect my people from the lords." Hiero turned. "Fritzgerald Damian?"

"Yes, Hiero?"

"Your task will be to mold the men we have into a defensive army. You will prepare Reta for siege. Store food and water and see that the armory is stocked. Have as many crossbows and bolts made as the armorer can bear. Hopefully we will receive more smiths from the cities around Reta." Hiero paused. "Is there anything I've forgotten?"

Fritz smiled. "If there is, it can't be put into words." He stood. "I'll start immediately, Hiero. Today."

"And I will take my rest," Hollis said. "My king."

The two bowed and exited together, and the door shut hollowly behind them. Hiero sat in the silence for a few moments, staring blankly at his food, before the pain rolled over him again, crushing his soul into a dark corner. Hiero doubled over in his chair, sucking in a ragged breath.

"Shelia! Oh, Shelia! I will rescue you!" His teeth gritted together. "And I will kill Lamont Reynard!"

Lord Teris sat in his parlor. His head was in his hands, where it had stayed for most of the past week. The house was too quiet. The only sounds came from the servants, and they moved slower and more softly as the days passed by. It was so quiet Lord Teris could hear the creak of swinging doors as his brother wheeled out of his room and across the foyer to the parlor. There was a moment of stillness, and then he knocked.

"Renald, may I come in?"

Lord Teris sighed and lifted his head. "What is it, Beni?"

"You haven't eaten."

"I have no desire to."

Beni wheeled into the room. "That isn't healthy. You shouldn't let yourself waste away."

Lord Teris's fingers traced the sheet of paper sitting in front of him. "There is no point in staying strong."

Beni wheeled around him to get a better look. "What is this?"

Teris sniffed. "An ultimatum from Lord Kiad. A rider brought it in the night." Lord Teris sighed. "Lord Kiad has her."

Beni grimaced. "I was afraid of that."

Lord Teris shook his head. "That isn't all." His fist shook. "Hiero was telling the truth. Kiad has Gannon."

Beni shook his head. "How is that even possible? How could a man fall from the pinnacle of Reta and survive?"

Lord Teris shook his head. "I don't know. I don't know what I was thinking. I was so close to giving his kingdom to another man! And now Shelia will be married to Lamont Reynard, her pure blood mingled with his pitiful line! The nephew of my enemy!" He shook his head. "How can the lines be reconciled? How can a tree be married to a wave? I will not accept it! I cannot!" He paused. "Lord Kiad has ordered me to remove my servants from the path of the lords' army. I must do so if I desire my children to live."

Beni closed his eyes. "Then you must."

"But I will never accept Lamont Reynard as my king. I will work for his death until mine."

30

SPREADING EMPTINESS

THE DREAM WAS full of fire. Gannon woke from his sleep in a cold sweat. In the dim light of the creaking wagon, the fire he had seen and felt still danced before his eyes. Fear squeezed his heart like a vice. An arm lay across his chest.

Gannon turned his head slowly. Lord Kiad lay next to him, fast asleep, his breath in Gannon's face. His blond hair was loose and flung about his face like a halo. Gannon felt a surge of nausea. Lord Kiad must've come in during the night.

Gannon wanted to escape. His heart pounded in his ears, but he could not move. His fear of waking Lord Kiad was so terrible that his consciousness felt trapped in the nether portions of his brain, where he could not logically form a movement or stop his terror from escalating.

Gannon was not sure how long he wavered in that predicament, but the light outside the wagon changed, and

Gannon grew tired. His adrenaline failed him, and his eyes slipped shut. Then Lord Kiad shifted. Gannon snapped back to wakefulness with such ferocity that it caused him to jerk back.

Lord Kiad's eyes were open, watching him. Gannon lay frozen as Lord Kiad pushed himself up on his elbows.

"Cursed wagon." He groaned. "I hate traveling." He ran his hand across his face and smoothed back his hair. "Everything rattles." He stretched forward on the bed and pounded on the front wall of the wagon with a fist. The wagon rumbled to a stop, and Lord Kiad yawned. "Much better."

Gannon could hear the shouts from outside as the rest of the column came to a halt and the order to stop was passed backward. He grimaced. Lord Kiad was stopping an entire army because he disliked the noise of a wagon. Kiad's mind was juvenile.

Lord Kiad reached over and grabbed his jaw, holding it with his thumb and forefinger, and turned him slowly to inspect the cauterized hole in his earlobe. His eyes lacked their normal manipulative sparkle.

"It's strange," he whispered. "You look like your grandfather in almost every way, yet I never saw it. It never occurred to me that you might have been noble." Kiad shook his head. "It was so obvious! I wonder if I was blinded by my security, by the monotony of routine."

He ran his thumb across Gannon's chin, and Gannon's skin prickled all the way down to his toes. Lord Kiad chuckled and continued to trace his cheekbone.

"I only saw King Teris once. I was just a youth at the time, and he was already an older man. I can see the lines of his face in yours." He sighed. "It's so beautiful. The

lines, the form, the structure. The blood of Teris is strong!"
There was a hush of awe in Kiad's voice. "When this is over,
I will breed you with another of excellent blood. I would
like to see what beautiful children can be created."

Gannon's eyes must have given away his horror because
the look on Kiad's face shifted, and the cruel light returned.

"You look pained, son of Teris. Do my words disturb
you?" Kiad's hand rested heavy on Gannon's neck, and his
rough thumb slowly grazed Gannon's cheekbones. "You
look afraid," he hissed. "Seeing such fear in Teris eyes is"—
he smiled—"intoxicating."

Lord Kiad's chuckle seemed to reverberate in the hard
ball at the base of Gannon's back. It was so heavy he could
not move. His arms and legs had been disconnected.

"You didn't think that I would let you go while you
still rival Reynard?" Lord Kiad lifted himself up and leered
down at Gannon. "You belong to me. For the rest of your
life."

Gannon's stomach tightened. He was going to be sick.

The sun was two fingers above the horizon when Lord
Yus strode up to the door of Kiad's wagon and pounded
on it. His nose scrunched into his face at the breathing and
moaning coming from within.

"Lord Kiad! I demand you get out here this instant!"

There was a scream from inside, and then Lord Kiad's
heavy tread shook the wagon all the way to the door. The
bolt clanged into its place, and the door creaked open,
almost lazily. Lord Kiad's nakedness shone in the bright
sunlight. Lord Yus's eyes narrowed to slits.

"I've been informed that this little rest stop of ours
was on your command! Please tell me you didn't stop our
whole column simply so you could relieve yourself."

Lord Kiad grinned as he lounged against the door-frame. "Lord Yus, I did not take you for the kind of man who wants to be lied to."

Lord Yus groaned in disgust. He turned, and the snap of his fingers was brittle in the air. "Leon, take my order to the front! We are moving now!"

The young man holding Lord Yus's horse nodded and leaped into the saddle, spurring to a gallop. When Lord Yus turned back, the door was shut, and the bolt slammed into place.

Several hours later, Kiad emerged. Kaiden had been enjoying his horse's easy pace, the bright sunlight, and the soft breeze. He hadn't even realized that the door to his lord's wagon was opening. Then Kiad's eyes latched on to Kaiden.

"Kaiden, I have need of you."

His spine stiffened. The room beyond Kiad yawned like the opening of a dark cave. But Lord Kiad's manner was strange. He seemed disinterested, distracted. Kaiden dismounted quickly and crossed the space to the wagon. Kiad stepped aside for him to enter, and the cold metal in Kaiden's boot seemed to grow heavy.

The young Lord Teris was collapsed in Kiad's bed, sweaty and shaking. The room reeked of semen and sweat.

Kiad gave an impassive nod in his direction. "See that he is cleaned and dressed." He strode out of the wagon and mounted Kaiden's horse. "Then bring him to me."

Kaiden felt the wagon jerk back into motion as he turned back to Teris. Clean air rushed in from the door-way and whirled around the cabin, making it bearable.

Kaiden knelt beside the bed. He didn't want to see this. He swallowed.

"Are you injured?"

Gannon's back stiffened at the sound.

"Do you need to see a physician?"

Gannon shook his head.

"All right then. I am going to help you get cleaned—"

"Help me?" Gannon wheezed. "You are the one who hurt me! You put me here!"

Kaiden's heart was caught in his throat. "I—"

Gannon curled up even tighter. "If you want to help me, free me!" His voice sounded on the verge of tears. "I don't belong here! Help me leave!"

Kaiden had a mental image of them escaping the army on the back of a single horse. But he could also see them being pursued and overtaken, and he knew the punishment would be far worse than it was worth. He had angered Lord Kiad before.

The dagger in his boot called him back to reality. To escape would be blessed, but the words Hollis had spoken would not stop echoing in his head. Kaiden was the arm of his king. If he did not strike, there would not be a strike.

Kaiden felt like the inside of his mind was boiling over with thought. He couldn't strike Lord Kiad; he was too afraid! He didn't even have the courage to run. Why was he telling himself that he had to kill him? And if he did not kill Lord Kiad, who would?

His throat was so dry it rasped. "I can't help you," he whispered. "I have to stay by Lord Kiad's side. If I were to let you go, I would suffer a punishment far worse than death." Memories swarmed him, and Kaiden felt faint.

He remembered Kiad's black chest full of metal implements. Some were for cutting, some for piercing, but most were made to enter from below with the greatest of pain. Kaiden gripped the edge of the bed as he rotated between waves of dizziness.

Gannon looked over his shoulder, and his haunted eyes bored into Kaiden's. Did he see the pain in his face? Did he have any idea what surged through his mind? Kaiden swallowed. He had to get back under control. He had to finish his job—both of his jobs.

He took a few deep breaths, and his face cleared.

Several hours later, Gannon's hands were secured to the pommel of his saddle as his mount lazily followed the back end of Lord Kiad's horse. Kaiden rode on Lord Kiad's left, and most of the ride passed in silence.

Gannon relished the sun on his skin. It had been so long since he had felt it. Early autumn was on the breeze, a spicy yellow smell, and the fields he could see from the road were ready to be harvested. The road they traveled was well-made, flat and smooth.

Gannon searched either side of the road for people— normal villages and towns—and tears welled up in his eyes. The common people would greet him with a smile. They would wave. They would not know who he was or that he was a slave.

The breeze was snatching away Lord Kiad's conversation, but it sounded like he was talking about a town nearby. Gannon's head swiveled. Could they be passing through it? How much farther?

And then Gannon smelled smoke. A burnt mast stuck out of the ground at a stark diagonal angle. A charred, blackened signpost dangled off it. There was a solid thunk as Gannon's heart dropped into his stomach. What had they done?

The burnt abandoned village slowly passed by them on either side. Gannon could feel himself sinking lower and lower in the saddle. He did not see any people, but thankfully, he did not see any bodies either. Could the lords really do this, wipe a town completely from existence, and no one would stop them?

As the village faded into the miles behind him, Gannon could not help but think of the road ahead. How many more towns would be on their path? Gannon felt a growl rise in his throat, and he gritted his teeth to keep it in. This was Lamont's fault. He could not let Lamont become king.

This was a new thought process for Gannon. It seemed to wash over him like a cold waterfall. He'd never thought of the throne as a place from which he could help Retall; it was his birthright. But Hiero had seen the throne that way, and he'd won the hearts of the people because of it.

Gannon straightened in his saddle. Had the world around him changed? The crystal blue sky above him was suddenly clearer, and Gannon's eyes narrowed in on a flock of birds as they disappeared across the horizon line. Something inside of him had been freed.

Farther ahead in the caravan, Lamont ran his fingers through his hair, distracted. The beaters had done their work and cleared out the inhabitants of the town long before the line of torchbearers had reached it. It had been Lord Yus's idea, to prevent the losses that Lord Fieman's army had incurred. They must have been more than a day ahead of them because Lamont couldn't see a single ember still alight.

But the road was not on Lamont's mind. The king's voice echoed in his ears. *The house of Teris must be destroyed.* That meant both Shelia and Gannon.

Lamont kept fiddling with his hair. What he heard was the king's voice over and over, but what he saw was Shelia's face, her eyes wide and terrified as Lord Kiad's servants pulled her up to the dais. There had been no malice in that face. And then she'd heard his name. The shift he'd seen was almost indescribable. Anger, hate, pride, power: all of these had shone from her emerald eyes as she threw out her chin at him.

Lamont had once struggled to understand his uncle's rabid hate for the Teris family and why, even though they had been stripped of all power, he feared them so much. But he understood it now. A Teris was power—pure, un-controlled power. Lamont would cut off that power at its root, just as his king had commanded him.

A sigh bubbled out of him, so impassioned that the cart driver seated next to him glanced over nervously. Lamont had promised Lord Kiad that things would remain as they were, but clearly, they could not. If Kiad wouldn't give up Gannon peacefully, Lamont would have to persuade him. Beyond that, he would have to put a stop to the practice of innocents being enslaved, and Lamont was certain Lord Kiad wasn't the only lord who had been overstepping his bounds.

As the miles slipped by, the lines only deepened on Lamont's forehead. Was he ready to become king? He had no idea how to control these powerful men or how to hold back the people now that they had tasted rebellion. It was a hard time for anyone to rule Retall.

Lamont stretched out his arm and flexed it. It wasn't just for Retall though. The king's work needed to continue. He remembered when he had first learned of the king's experiments and how that power had felt the first time something had worked.

Now he did not have to fear wounds that would be lethal to the normal man. Now his life would be lengthened, if not to the lifespan of an Ancient, then somewhere close. What if the Teris family were to get ahold of that knowledge? The king had been right in looking after the welfare of his legacy.

It was his king and the experiments that had made sure the Ancients would not return to this world, at least during his reign. Lamont had helped the king see to it that any Ancient they found wandering about disappeared without a trace. But that vision . . .

Lamont had taken most of his education in Jasberan, and he remembered reciting the laws of the Ancients every morning before class began. The memory made him shudder. The law of the Ancients was a law of blood. The Ancients had tyrannized humanity for thousands of years before humanity had been strong enough to fight back. As long as Lamont lived, he would continue to fight back.

The Ancients would not return, no matter what the king had seen. Lamont did not know how long he had before the king's final prophecy was made sure, before Hieronymus discovered what lay under Reta. He had to be destroyed immediately. That was Lamont's priority.

31

High Ground

IT HAD BEEN two weeks of traveling for the army of the lords. To Kaiden it felt like a lifetime as his mind waffled back and forth from one option to the other. Finally, he concluded that he only had one option: kill Lord Kiad or die. And he did not want to die.

The road had wound its way through many towns, all of them deserted and burned-out, but Kaiden had barely noticed. His mind was consumed.

Thankfully, he was no longer Kiad's favorite. After a couple days riding with them, Gannon had been locked inside Kiad's wagon, where he'd remain for the rest of the trip. As they passed through the Great Forest, Lord Kiad kept himself confined as well, with the threat of attack high. But Lord Teris had been properly cowed. They saw no woodsmen on the entire forest road.

As the Great Forest waned around him, Kaiden tried to decide when would be best for him to strike. Hollis had told them to wait until they saw the fire and tasted the blood, but Kaiden was at a loss as to what that meant. He mulled over Hollis's words until he began to hear them in his dreams. One night he even dreamed that he heard Hieronymus calling him from Reta, and he woke weeping, wishing he could be within Reta, safe from what he had to do.

On the second day out of the Great Forest, the cliff of Reta rose up in the distance, a pale pink. At first Kaiden thought it was a trick of the light, but after several hours of travel, he realized it wasn't.

The cliff of Reta had been painted with a giant bloodred sword pointing straight down, the symbol of the Ancients.

Both the groups of beaters met the main convoy several miles from Reta and reported that they had found the entire countryside around Reta deserted. As they'd approached the gates, they had been fired upon, and several men had been lost.

The army of the lords was led by Yus, Ene, and Kiad. The others had committed troops, but they had not personally come to the battle. Yus, Ene, and Kiad met in a large tent erected in the middle of Kiad's camp. The dry grass crunched underfoot as they dismounted and walked inside.

"Hmm." Lord Ene surveyed the ground. "It's been many years since I've been this far south during harvest, but is it normally this dry?"

Yus chuckled. "I live on the edge of a desert, so this feels humid to me!"

Ene's eyes bored into the ground with pensive fierceness. "Something about this does not bode well with me."

At this, Kiad, too, burst into laughter. "Come now, Ene! What evil has Hieronymus wrought that could squelch the very water from the air? He's a man, not an Ancient!"

Ene growled. "Not the air, you fools, the ground! Look at it! Has there been a drought here? Why else would grass wilt like this?" He turned back to the tent flap and pulled it open. "Ennis! Go see that the men find fresh water before they put down another spike! Quickly!"

Ennis leaped to untie his horse and threw himself onto her back, taking off. Kiad lounged back in a chair and propped his boots up on the table.

"Come now, Ene! This is southern Retall! There's water everywhere!"

Ene glowered as he took his seat across from him. "Have your men found water yet? I wouldn't want to be the one facing an angry crowd of thirsty men!"

Kiad shrugged. "If we go thirsty, so do those inside the city. They are trapped. We are not. We'll be fine."

Yus gave them both a cool look. "Yes, well, onto the matter at hand. Hieronymus has clearly pulled all the outlying peoples in with him."

"It must be terribly crowded in there."

Yus shot another cold look at Kiad. "Yes, I'm sure. But what does this mean for our attack? How can we take the city without the loss of many citizens?"

Kiad sniffed. "It isn't an issue. They have closed their gates; they have attacked our forward party; they have arrayed for battle. When the gates come down, we can't waste time trying to identify who is a soldier and who is not. Every person who fights against us dies, whether it be man, woman, or child." Kiad's smile was cruel. "Painfully simple, no?"

Yus's and Ene's eyes were critical.

Finally, Yus sighed. "I suppose that will be adequate."

"Yes, the true problem we have is a lack of knowledge," Ene said. "What is Hieronymus's plan? I'm sure it has something to do with breaking our resolve."

Kiad sighed. "What other plan could he have but survival?" He leaned forward in his chair. "He's trapped, Ene, like a rat!"

"Don't underestimate the man! He's not a fool, and he wouldn't trap himself without an escape!" Ene shook his head. "There is an ominous feeling in the air here. Something terrible is about to happen."

Yus nodded. "A great terror. The streets of Reta running with blood. I'll admit I don't have the stomach for slaughter, but how else can we reach Hieronymus?"

"There isn't any other way unless we starve the city out."

"That would lead to a greater loss of life."

"I agree. We must attack the city head-on."

Yus smiled sadly. "So, nothing's changed then. Tomorrow morning, our forward parties will be in position before the gates. Bowmen will lay a stream of cover while the horsemen ride in, leading the weapons of siege. We will batter the gates until they fall. Once they have fallen, it will be the task of the far camps around the base to waylay those who would attempt to flee down the sides of Reta."

Kiad sat back with a sigh. "We should all stay a safe distance from the fighting. Knowing that the bastard plans to wipe out the lords of Retall, we would be fools to put ourselves at risk."

"Clearly. What of Reynard?"

"He will stay on this side, with me. It is the safest place he could be."

I will not." Lamont stepped into the tent. He twisted his face in disapproval that they would have such a discussion without him. "I will not stay back here during the fighting." He'd spent weeks with Shelia in that small wagon, and she was driving him mad. She rolled back and forth in her sleep, and during the day she cried, whined, and hurled insults like a petulant toddler. He would not stay with her a single night longer than he had to.

The lords' eyes were wide with surprise. Yus stood.

"Your Majesty, it would be far safer for you to stay outside the battle. If you were to be lost, our entire campaign—"

Lamont stepped up to the table. "I must go into battle. Hiero murdered my king with his own hands, and I have sworn to avenge him. When the gate falls, I will be in the forward party. I will be the first in the palace lest any other man take my vengeance."

Kiad's face sobered as he nodded. "I understand. Your wishes will be honored."

Lamont felt a little surge in his spirit. He'd gained a measure of approval from the man. He pulled back from the table with a satisfied smile. "I am grateful."

Kaiden couldn't stay in the camp. He felt like every eye was on him, like every man knew of the dagger in his boot. It seemed to burn him.

He untied his horse from her post and threw his leg over her back. Off he went. The camp of the lords was not just one camp. There were several camps spread around the base of Reta. With snipers on the gates and the threat of something being dropped from the plateau, it would've been foolish to place the camps right against the rock face, so the camps had been placed around the radius about half a mile away.

Kaiden rode into the slums. This had been his haunt while he'd searched for Kiad's perfect slave—or while he had pretended to anyway. His beaters had brought Gannon to him only weeks later, torn up and weak but still innocent and delicate.

Kaiden rode up to that very inn. Silently, he walked inside. The stillness was almost creepy. Dust floated in the air, and every surface was covered in a thin layer of it. He swallowed. It really hadn't changed a bit. He walked to the counter and stared at the stacked rows of corked bottles. If Kiad knew he was here, he'd be in real trouble. The men had been charged not to leave the camp.

What was he thinking? How could he drink now? Kaiden turned away from the counter and strode right back out. If he decided to face Lord Kiad, he was going to do it with a clear mind. He would need to focus.

Kaiden jumped back on his horse, ready to return to the camp before he was missed. When he looked toward Reta, a strange curiosity took hold of his heart. He was on the dark side of the city, where he could not see the sword, but he remembered it, and without thinking, he turned his horse north toward the base of the cliff. Perhaps there he would find the answer to Hollis's riddle.

As he grew closer, he could see that the paint still shone like fresh blood. Kaiden swallowed. The Ancients' law was a law of blood. He hoped that wasn't really blood.

The trail grew rocky as he neared the face, and Kaiden dismounted, leaving his horse tied. Carefully, he picked his way up the broken land. The field below him looked like it might have been farmland at one time, but now it was dead, a field of dry grass and brush.

Kaiden labored up half the thin trail before realizing he was on an outcropping and the tip of the sword lay below him, pierced right in the middle of the field. He huffed and sighed and finally sat down, looking over the field and up at the sword. Even from his limited perspective, it was spectacular. The hilt of the sword may even have reached the wall of the palace, it was so high. He wondered how they had managed to paint it.

Kaiden took a deep breath, and his nose wrinkled. There was an odor of tar and oil on the wind. Kaiden cast a glance at the rock face. That much paint was bound to cause a stench, but this was something different. The hair in his nose seemed to stand on end. Kaiden covered his mouth and nose with his sleeve.

He didn't know what he'd expected to find here. His name and instructions chipped into the rock? He chuckled despite his disappointment, and his eyes traveled up the length of the sword to the palace. A small dark semicircle indicated the presence of the king's balcony. Kaiden felt a deep longing throb from his heart. Was Hieronymus there now? Oh, what Kaiden would do to be up there by his side!

He looked back at the rock face and wondered briefly if he might be able to climb it. Perhaps if he stuffed his nose with cloth and breathed through a handkerchief. Kaiden shook his head. He didn't even have any equipment, and he wasn't a fit man. His arms would give away before he was halfway up.

Kaiden's gaze fell to the ground, and he sighed. After one more wistful look up at the palace, he turned away. He rode back into the camp just as the lords were leaving the meeting tent.

Kiad gave him a dangerous look as he tied his horse back to her post. "Where have you been?"

Kaiden swallowed and nodded back to the rock face. "I wanted to get a closer look."

Lord Kiad sneered. "Disgusting, isn't it? A bloody sword. The fools have declared their desire to be slaughtered. They will be."

Kaiden winced at the thought of Reta burning. He would not taste blood until he was in battle, and from where the camp was, far from the cliff, there would be no battle. The only fires he saw as the afternoon dragged on were those of the cooking fires of the lord's entourage as they settled down for the night.

They were too peaceful, too at ease. Every man here knew that the victory of the lords was sure. Kaiden swallowed. The time for his action seemed to be farther away than ever, yet he was afraid. Could he not assassinate Lord Kiad now? Wouldn't the other lords be alerted if he did? Then Leon and Ennis would be in danger.

Slowly, Kaiden paced in the direction of Lord Kiad's wagon. He only had to wait until Lord Kiad was distracted, and then he could slide his dagger between his ribs. No one dared to enter Kiad's wagon. Perhaps no one would discover his body until the other two lords were assassinated too.

Kaiden's heartbeat quickened. He had no desire to get so close to Lord Kiad. He knew what would be necessary to distract him. Kaiden's breath turned urgent. He couldn't do this. His hand flew out to steady him on a tent post.

This was impossible. He could barely settle his thoughts now when he only saw the wagon in the distance!

Kaiden looked back at the cliff, stark black against the fading purple sky. He could see lights in the palace far above him, and he knew Hieronymus was there. Hieronymus needed his arm to be strong. If he were here instead of Kaiden, would he not destroy Kiad now, before any more lives were lost?

Kaiden stepped tentatively toward the wagon. Yes, that made sense. Kiad would die tonight, and then he and Gannon could escape to Reta while it was still dark, before anyone could stop them. Kaiden balled his hands into fists. He was doing this.

Kaiden half walked, half shuffled across the empty space and stopped before the wagon door. He lifted his arm and a moment later it fell back to his side. He couldn't just stride in there and stab Lord Kiad. He needed an approach. Kaiden closed his eyes and tried to calm his heart. Kiad was going to have to touch him. There was no other way to thoroughly distract him.

Kaiden hadn't been touched since the night he had delivered Gannon. He didn't want this. He didn't want to be here. Kaiden ran from the wagon about ten paces and bent over to breathe. He was too afraid. He needed to relieve himself first.

Fifteen minutes later, Kaiden again stood at the door. His hand wavered just above it. His heart fluttered, and his hand shook. He had to do this. Why couldn't he control himself? Finally, his hand sprung forward and struck the door, one clear knock. Kaiden was bathed in cold sweat. His legs turned to jelly at the sound of Kiad's tread across the floor.

The bolt inside was drawn, and the door creaked open. Kiad blinked down at him in the dim torchlight.

"Kaiden, what happened?" He turned to reach for his coat.

"No!" Kaiden snapped before he thought.

Kiad turned back. "What?"

Kaiden's whole body trembled. He could not meet Kiad in the eyes and instead stared solidly at his boots. *What should I say?*

"I'm afraid," he whispered. Kaiden squeezed his eyes shut with embarrassment. What was he thinking? "I need . . . I-I need to be safe."

Lord Kiad's boots slowly stepped aside. "Come inside." His voice had changed. It was deep now.

Kaiden had to calm down. His heart was going wild. He stumbled past Kiad. Gannon lay on the bed, propped up on one elbow, his face concerned.

What is going on? Gannon's eyes screamed.

The door shut with a solid click. Kaiden wanted to run so badly. He was trapped. Lord Kiad was right behind him.

And he passed right by him. Kaiden's eyes widened as he watched Lord Kiad sit down on his bed. He hadn't touched him. Kaiden needed him to be distracted, but there he was, focused intently on Kaiden's face.

Lord Kiad patted the bed next to him. "Will you join us?"

What was Kiad doing? What was he planning? Kaiden had no point of reference to deal with this situation.

Lord Kiad raised an eyebrow. "Don't worry. You're safe here even if we do get attacked."

Kaiden swallowed. A thought ran back and forth inside his skull, and he tried to push it away.

Seduce him, it whispered.

The spit in Kaiden's mouth went sour. No, he couldn't do that. That was disgusting. He would wait for Lord Kiad to fall asleep. That was much safer.

He took a step back and raised his arms. "No, I'll just—" He turned his head, searching for the corner. "I'll just sleep here." He looked back, and his heart thumped. Lord Kiad's eyes had narrowed.

"Hold on just a moment. You said you were afraid." Kiad beckoned with his hand. "You will sleep here."

Kaiden was already sitting in the corner, his legs drawn up protectively in front of his chest. "I'm not afraid," he whispered. His voice sounded unconvincing even to him.

Lord Kiad tilted his head. "What do you want from me, Kaiden? You come to me, claiming to be afraid, and now you say that you are not?" Kiad smirked. "You've never come to me of your own volition before. That by itself is suspicious."

Kaiden recognized the tone in Kiad's voice. It was coming.

"Don't be afraid of your desires."

Kaiden gritted his teeth. It was definitely coming.

Lord Kiad held out his hand. "Come over here, Kaiden."

Kaiden closed his eyes and hugged his legs. It would all be over soon. Just one more time. Then he would be free.

Lord Kiad stood. "All right, Kaiden, since you want to do this the hard way." He strode across the room and hauled Kaiden to his feet by his shoulder. He pulled him across the room and threw him down on the bed, front first. Kaiden gasped for air. Lord Kiad's hand pushed him firmly back down. He had very little patience tonight. Kaiden's fingers fumbled in the open air. He couldn't reach his boot!

Lord Kiad ignored Kaiden's flailing and set his knee on Kaiden's back, leaning into it. "Hush," he commanded.

Kaiden stilled. He needed to calm down. He would never get anywhere by struggling. He needed to wait for the perfect moment.

"Yes, you're safe. Don't be afraid. I'm protecting you." He lifted his knee from Kaiden's back and turned him over. Gently, he sat across Kaiden's hips. His thumb stroked Kaiden's face, wiping away an errant tear. "You came to me," he whispered. "I always knew it would happen. You've finally grown up."

Kaiden wanted to scream. Oh, Ancients, what had he gotten himself into? His heart was beginning to pound again. Kiad's fingers quickly undid the buttons of Kaiden's jacket. He pulled the cloth over Kaiden's shoulders and halfway down his arms. Kaiden tried to twist his arm free, but his own jacket held him like a chain. There was no way he could reach his dagger in this position. Kiad pulled Kaiden's shirt out of his belt and, with no warning, leaned down.

"Aagh!" Lord Kiad ran his tongue over Kaiden's chest, and Kaiden stretched away from the touch in every direction. His eyes rolled back, and he caught a glimpse of Gannon, pressed into the corner, as far away from them as he could get. He had never seen it happen to someone else, had he?

Kaiden closed his eyes and twisted his arms against his jacket. Shivers ran up and down his body from Kiad's touch. He had to free himself or he could never strike.

"Ah, Kaiden, you always were so sensitive. So innocent."

He couldn't reach it! Kaiden was going to go mad before he ever got ahold of his infernal boot! Kaiden's fingers stretched as far as they could, and he tried to bring his knee up. Kiad noticed immediately.

"Kaiden, don't be so eager! I'll take it off for you!" He stepped back a pace so that one foot was secure on the floor, and he lifted Kaiden up, pushing him farther onto the bed so that his legs would not dangle. Kaiden's head pushed up against the pillow, and his shoulder brushed Gannon's leg.

Gannon jerked away, ready to leap entirely off the bed. Kiad put up a hand.

"You stay right where you are!" Kiad growled. Gannon crouched back down, shaking. "I'll have need of you later."

Gannon was already backed into the corner of the bed, his eyes darting from Kiad to Kaiden. Kaiden's eyes were on Gannon, but his fingers were tracing the lip of his boot, stretching, stretching to reach inside.

Kiad grabbed Kaiden's boot in one hand and yanked it off. He flung it across the wagon, followed by the other. Fear spiked up Kaiden's back. What was he going to do now?

Kiad crawled over him, his eyes alight with mischief. "You've been holding yourself back, Kaiden." His fingers pulled at the laces of Kaiden's breeches.

Kaiden gritted his teeth. No. This was over.

Kaiden sat up. He pulled at the edges of his jacket, and it fell onto the bed. He reached down and grabbed Kiad's wrist to pull his hand away.

"Kaiden." Kiad's voice held a dangerous edge. "What do you think you're doing?"

Kaiden's heart fluttered, but he forced himself to meet Kiad's eyes. "I won't stay. I don't want this."

Kiad's eyebrow rose. "One strange thing after another. First you come to me, then you dare speak back to me?" Kaiden's grip on Kiad's wrist suddenly went weak, and Kiad wound his fingers around Kaiden's wrist, his fingers digging into soft veins. "I think I made a mistake with you. You need to be put back in your place!"

Kaiden felt the wind rush past his ears. He would be punished. The look in Kiad's eyes made it clear. He wasn't going to get away. He was going to suffer.

Kaiden jerked his wrist, attempting to pull it away, and Kiad wrenched it cruelly, twisting it behind Kaiden's back and flipping him over onto his stomach. He kneed Kaiden hard in the buttocks, shoving him forward and smashing his face into the wall of the wagon.

Dazed, Kaiden heard the click of a shackle closing around his left wrist, and he felt warmth running down his face and into his mouth. It was his own blood.

Hiero stood on his balcony, on the very tile where he had claimed the throne and thrust Gannon off its edge. His chest rose as he watched the camps of his enemies surrounding his city on every side. They were exactly where he wanted them. Not a single soldier of the lords would escape tonight.

32

FATED BATTLES

HIERO STARED DOWN at the valley filled with tiny dots of light. He breathed in until his chest rose high and proud. Hollis stepped up behind him, holding a small light, little more than a brand. Hiero turned and grabbed the end from him. "This is it."

The light glinted strangely off Hollis's eyes. "Yes, my king."

Hiero felt no reassurance from those eyes. He turned away from him, stepping up to the balcony's edge. "Are the men in place?"

"They left over an hour ago. By now they should be."

"Good." Hiero gripped the brand a little tighter. "Can I confide in you, Hollis? I'm afraid."

"Afraid of what, my king?"

Hiero swallowed. "I am afraid that I will find her charred body when the smoke has lifted."

Hollis shook his head. "That is unlikely. Reynard has been spotted at the gates, and she would likely be—"

"Yes, Hollis, I know." Hiero took a deep breath and let it out slowly. He pushed Shelia out of his mind and remembered the words he had prepared. "In accordance with the laws of the Ancients, for the crime of building an army for the purpose of war, I sentence you to be burned." His voice dropped to a whisper. "Ancients have mercy on you all."

He lowered the brand to the marble railing, where a thin line of red paint had been dripped along it and down the side. The paint caught on fire before the brand even touched it and flashed like nuts thrown in a flame as it flew along the edge and down the side of the balcony.

"Back! Back!" Hiero shouted, jumping backward, his hand flying up to protect his face. He tossed the brand away and ran inside the balcony doors. Hollis slammed them shut and locked them tight just as the smoke began to rise from below. Hiero grabbed the handful of rags set aside inside the doorway and began stuffing them into the crevice between the doors. The smoke billowed up in a gigantic dark cloud that blocked out the light of the night sky. Hiero coughed as he stood, watching it with open eyes.

"It's so big. It's so much more powerful than I imagined!"

Hollis had to place his hand on Hiero's shoulder. "My king, we must go."

Hiero sucked in a ragged breath, coughing at the smell of smoke that still leaked in.

"Of course." He turned away. "Let's go."

Something was wrong. Shelia knew it. She could feel it in her veins, in every pulse of her blood. Something was not right.

She had rolled to and fro for hours until she was thoroughly frustrated. For weeks she'd been unable to sleep peacefully with Lamont on the other side of the wagon, and now he was finally gone. Why could she still not sleep?

Shelia threw off her covers and sat up. If she couldn't sleep, she wasn't going to try. She crossed the wagon to the window and hooked the shade up. With Lamont gone, the wagon door had been latched from the outside, and there wasn't a guard. Shelia could see the campfire in the distance and men milling about it, but she would have to call for them to hear her.

Shelia curled her hand around the thick slat that divided the window in half. If it hadn't been there, she could've conceivably slipped out. Shelia gave the slat an experimental tug. It was sturdily built, but she could feel it shift slightly in its setting. If only there were some way she could crack it, then she could get out and run to the cliff. She had read about the Slum Road on the outskirts of the city. She would find it and climb it before the fighting started. She pulled on the slat a little harder, hoping it would crack.

Suddenly, there was a hissing roar. Shelia had never heard anything like it. The men around the campfire leaped to their feet and shouted, their flailing arms pointing to something on the other side of the wagon, outside of Shelia's view. Somebody shouted, "Fire!"

Lord Kiad smashed Kaiden's face into the wood, and Gannon watched as Kaiden crumpled like wet paper. He crouched even farther into the corner as Kiad clapped the shackle around Kaiden's wrist. His hands went immediately to Kaiden's waist, ready to yank his breeches down. Gannon closed his eyes.

Then there was a shout and furious banging on the wagon door. Kiad was already angry, and he drew himself up, roaring like an angry bear, and ripped the door open.

"What?" His voice fell away, and his arms fell limp at his sides as he stared out into the night. "Great Goddess," he whispered.

He seemed to suddenly forget about Gannon and Kaiden. Kiad stepped out of the wagon as if hypnotized. Gannon climbed over Kaiden's unconscious form and stepped onto the floor where he could see what Kiad was seeing.

The cliff came into view, and Gannon's breath failed him too. The cliff of Reta was on fire. The fire burned in the shape of a sword. It was the sign of the Ancients.

Gannon's knees gave out, and he fell with a crack. Was this Hiero's doing? Had the Ancients truly returned? Kiad seemed to be lost in the same sort of fear.

Suddenly, the fire flashed and flew the gap between the sword and the ground, and the ground exploded.

Gannon's heart leaped into his throat as the ground below the cliff sprang into the air. It was the Ancients. No human was capable of this. They were here.

The stories he had been told in his childhood rushed into the forefront of his mind.

All those who would dare commit the crime of war would be punished. Gannon's mind was flying, racing for a way to escape. As the flaming chunks of ground came back down, the dry grass in the field between them and the cliff caught fire and burned toward them. Gannon's mind blanked into autopilot. He had to get away from Reta.

He stood and lunged for the door, stumbling out into the night. Kiad was gone, off somewhere waving his arms and screaming at his fleeing men. Gannon's head swiveled back and forth as he searched for a landmark. The fire was burning everywhere, and he could not see where to go.

Shelia heard the shouts before she saw men running past her wagon. It must have been a terrible blaze because the men weren't running to fight it; they were running away.

Shelia stumbled off the bed and grabbed her shoes from the floor. She looked back and forth for something she could use as a lever. She grabbed her hairbrush from the saddlebag. She didn't know if it was strong enough to keep from bending, but the tip was thin enough to slip under the wooden bar.

Shelia jumped back onto the bed, yanking her skirts out of her way. She pushed the handle into the hollow, shoving it, trying to make it slip under the wood.

Shelia heard the ground explode under the cliff. It sounded like the whole cliff was falling apart. Her heart leaped into her throat, and her hands jerked, and the wood that the comb was forcing against broke. A chunk splintered up, and Shelia used the handle like a sander, ripping more chunks away and gouging into the wood. She grabbed the bar, and this time it wiggled easily in its setting. She yanked at it, hoping it would spring free, but it was still too thick.

There was a sense of urgency in the air now. Shelia

could smell the smoke. She attacked the broken part of the wood with all the strength she had. She was afraid. She heard screaming.

During a particularly strong attack, the edge of the brush slipped, cutting into her hand. Shelia dropped the brush and squeezed her hand, letting out a single high-pitched wail. In the dim light, she could see dark liquid pooling in her palm. That wasn't just a tiny cut. Shelia collapsed on her knees, moaning.

"Somebody! Please help me!"

"Shelia?"

She heard her name outside the wagon and sat up immediately. "Gannon?"

"Shelia! Oh, thank goodness. I found you! I've got to get you out!" He stood under the window.

Shelia blinked the tears from her eyes. "Gannon, the door's locked! I can't get out!"

Gannon looked terrified. "It can't be! It must only be latched. Come around!"

He disappeared from view, and the pain in her hand grew worse. It throbbed with heat. Shelia shook as she stepped off the bed. She didn't want to move anymore. It hurt! She heard Gannon fumbling at the door. There was a loud crack, and the door swung open. Heat and smoke streamed in.

Gannon threw out his hand. "Hurry, Shelia! We need to get away from the city!"

Shelia stumbled toward him, whimpering. "Get away from it? Gannon, Hiero will protect us!"

Gannon grasped her arm a little tighter than was needed. "Shelia, by this time, Hiero and everyone inside Reta is dead."

Shelia gave him a blank look. "What?"

Gannon cast a fervent look around. "The Ancients are attacking Reta! The cliffside was just destroyed! They are raining down fire on the city!"

Shelia shook her head. She was coughing. The smoke was everywhere. He was lying. He had to be lying to her. The Ancients had come back? Why here? Why now?

"Shelia!" Gannon gripped her even tighter. "We have to leave now, or we'll all be slaughtered!"

"No . . ." Shelia couldn't breathe. She could barely hear him. Her hand and her heart burned together, pulsing together. The air she sucked in was as hot as her chest, and the world spun madly. She sank to her knees. "I can't . . ."

Gannon grabbed at her hand, intending to pull her up, and his hand slid against her blood.

"Shelia! What is this? You're bleeding! Cursed Isle! Why didn't you say anything?"

He dropped to his knees and slipped his hand around her shoulders, pushing her skirts aside so that he could wrap his arm under her knees. He strained for just a moment, and then he was standing, Shelia in his arms, crying into his chest.

"Gannon, don't. Hiero is . . . he's not your enemy."

Gannon ignored her and stumbled away from the wagon. He had to get them both to safety.

Hiero sat in the saddle of a tall stallion at the head of Trader's Square. All about him, pressing in on every side, were other horses, chomping and stamping as their riders kept their eyes skyward. They wanted to get out. The whole square was tense with energy.

Thirty minutes ago, Hiero had stood on the palace balcony, condemning the army of the lords. Now was the moment to bring an end of that justice. Outside the gates of Reta, the forward party had set up their tents, prepared to take Reta in the morning. Hiero was going to destroy them and take back Shelia.

The image of his sword slicing through Lamont's belly, ending the man who'd unceasingly brought him pain, seared through Hiero's mind. He tasted the metal in his mouth, and he swallowed.

No. He couldn't allow himself to lose control and kill Lamont suddenly. Lamont needed to die slowly, suffering intense pain like he had caused Hiero.

From the ramparts, the sentries pulled out their yellow flags and waved them in the air. Other than the sound of the animals, the square was deathly silent. Hiero ticked off seconds in his mind. It had already been half an hour. Surely the news had reached the forward party by now. Why weren't they panicking?

A drop of nervous sweat rolled down his spine. What if they did not panic? What would he do then? Were his forces really prepared to face a focused, deliberate enemy?

"Ancients defend us," he whispered, forgetting for a moment that they were striving to be utterly silent. The men nearby who'd heard him nodded, whispering the blessing back and forth through the ranks. The Ancients would defend them, for they were the dispensers of justice.

The sentries reached for their red flags and lifted them cautiously over their heads. There was a pause. Hiero held his breath. What was going on out there?

Suddenly, the sentries' arms came down, flapping wildly. Hiero's breath was sucked out of him. It was time. The men standing above the ballast weight brought their swords slamming down on the ropes. The bags of stones fell, and the gate flew up. The riders in the front dug their heels into their horses the moment those swords hit the ropes, and they thundered out as the gate was still rising, Hiero in the lead. The enemy camp was several hundred yards away, just outside bow range.

It took them less than a minute to cross the field. They did not come with a battle cry or a roar, but with silence. Hiero felt the silence in his soul like a rushing emptiness. He felt like he had only just blinked and then the camp was before him.

The army of the lords was in the middle of waking, throwing on their breastplates and stumbling out of their tents with bleary eyes, hearing that the Ancients were attacking. Hiero came upon the first man at the edge of the camp, where he had been standing guard all night.

The man had seen their white uniforms reflecting the light as they flew across the field, and he stood ready to face him. And then Hiero was over him. The red sword in the center of his chest and the red kerchief that was tied over his nose and mouth gave him an unearthly quality, and the young soldier's eyes widened in shock.

He was distracted as Hiero's sword cut him down, and Hiero kept riding. Adrenaline made his heart shake in his chest, but his sword arm was steady. He'd just killed a man for the first time. There was an instinct inside him that flared with joy, just like it had been when he'd bested Lamont and Gannon.

His plan was working! They flew through the camp, swords coming down again and again. The army of the lords was powerless against them. They could not stand against legends coming to life, mowing down their comrades on every side. Screams punctuated the night, and everywhere Hiero looked, men fled the battleground.

The kills blurred together in Hiero's mind. They were winning. And then Hiero saw Lamont. The rest of the battle slipped away. He pulled his kerchief completely off his face. His vision narrowed to a single point. He and Lamont were the only soldiers on the field.

Lamont saw him at the same time, and the hurried, stressed look on his face disappeared. Hiero dismounted. They walked toward each other slowly.

"Reynard." Hiero's voice felt husky in his throat. With Lamont standing before him, it was much easier to imagine him defiling Shelia. Hiero had to calm the pounding in his chest, or he would kill Lamont right here.

"Purvis!" Lamont's voice came out with a hiss and a bite, sharp as a sword. It was typical of a pompous well-bred true son to look down at a filthy bastard. Hiero had dealt with it all his life. But it still made his blood boil. "How dare you try to play as the arm of the Ancients! You have no idea what you're dealing with!"

"How dare I? How dare you!" Hiero choked. "How dare you steal what is rightfully mine!" He couldn't stop his heart; he couldn't control it. His chest burned like fire. "It was my inheritance! Father left it to me! Shelia loved me, and you stole her! You took her against her will! And finally, you want to take my throne, the throne the people of Retall gave to me! By the laws of the Ancients, I am the rightful king of Retall! And you"—he lifted his sword—"are nothing more than a thief! A thief who will meet his end by my hand!"

Through all of Hiero's rage, Lamont did not sneer or chuckle. His heart was as cold as stone. He had to kill Hiero today. If he didn't win this fight, Retall would be destroyed. The king had seen it.

"How dare I? How dare you, Purvis, attempt to re-instate the Law of Blood, the law of the Ancients, upon the backs of humans? Those creatures were not worthy of honor, and they never will be. They were heartless, uncaring taskmasters that bound humanity by their law, keeping them trapped in primitive life. There was no freedom. How could you want that to return?"

Hiero's face registered only disgust. "How can any man love this present situation? You speak of freedom for humanity, but you would force them to have you as their king! You would force them to follow the whims of tyrannical lords, such as Kiad!" Hiero shook his head. "True freedom lies under the Ancients' laws, where man can choose his own leaders, where he can be safe from violence. You're not capable of granting them the freedom they deserve!"

Lamont gritted his teeth. He understood what Hiero was saying. He was mocking his king for leaving the lords to their devices. Lamont wouldn't make that mistake now that he understood what they had been doing in the shadows. All the people really wanted was the former balance restored, and they would never know of all the old king had done to keep them safe from the Ancients. When Lamont was on the throne, his king's work would continue.

"If you can't comprehend the dangers that the Ancients pose to humanity, you aren't fit to be king!" Lamont raised his sword. "I will exact vengeance for my uncle's death!"

Hiero sneered. "If you can."

Lamont ran at him, calmly smashing Hiero's blow away. He was ready for Hiero's trick, the rush followed by the left-handed feint, but Hiero didn't use it. Instead, he circled around Lamont, backing up, forcing him to chase. What was he doing? Where was his ferocious anger from the last fight?

Hiero controlled himself for the time being. He couldn't let himself mortally wound Lamont. He parried and blocked Lamont's blows, constantly circling. He would wait for Lamont to grow tired. He had been training for this physical exertion months before Gannon had ever arrived. Then he would strike Lamont unconscious.

"So, Lamont, if you are truly as honorable as you claim to be, how did you find it within yourself to forcefully deflower Lady Teris?"

Lamont glared at him, backing up a bit to have a moment to breathe.

"You're vile!" He spit. "I didn't touch her, and I would never. She disgusts me, not only a spawn of the Teris family, but blindly devoted to you!"

Hiero blinked, for a moment forgetting that he had to block Lamont's strike. It came too fast and slid across the edge of his blade with a shriek, slamming against his shoulder pad. Hiero winced.

"You lie! Where is Shelia? Where is your tent?"

Lamont forced him back even farther. Suddenly his blows came so quickly, Hiero could barely block them. "She isn't here, you dolt! I left her behind in Kiad's camp because I couldn't stand to be near her!"

The world under Hiero's feet spun. He'd sent fire at Shelia. The image of his nightmare became reality. Shelia was burning!

Something snapped inside Hiero's skull. He didn't have time to wear Lamont out. He had to get to Shelia immediately.

Hiero jogged backwards, away from Lamont, his eyes searching for his horse. The fight had let them probably a hundred yards from the rest of the camp. There wasn't anyone he could call to help him. Hiero swallowed. He was on his own here, but so was Lamont.

Lamont came running at him, his hair and his eyes wild. Hiero pictured the movement in his mind once, twice, before he reached him. He could do this.

Hiero stayed still until Lamont's blade was inches from his chest, and then he smashed the sword away as hard as he could. Lamont was off balance for a half second, just long enough for Hiero to drop to his knees and shove his free elbow into Lamont's groin. The weight of Hiero's blow sent Lamont jumping away, wheezing through gritted teeth.

"You—dirty—monster!"

Now Hiero had to chase him. Lamont kept jumping back, wheezing, covering his stomach with his arm.

Hiero cursed the Isle under his breath. He needed to immobilize Lamont now, or he would never reach Shelia in time!

It was an all-or-nothing move. Hiero sprinted forward and leaped into the air above Lamont, bringing his sword crashing down on Lamont's head with such force the hilt nearly dented his skull. Hiero stood over his twisted form for just a moment, gasping for breath.

"You're the monster." He wheezed.

Lamont didn't matter anymore. Hiero slammed his sword back in its sheath and ran for his horse. They flew for the other side of Reta, Hiero praying he would make it there in time.

The smoke was everywhere, and the flames seemed to be too. Kiad felt like he was the only one trying to organize this mess. His men were running for the hills, screaming about the Ancients attacking. Kiad's jaw tightened. There were no Ancients. This had to be some trick of Hieronymus.

Suddenly, figures loomed up in front of him, emerging from the smoke. Kiad whipped out his sword.

"Who are you?"

The figures made no challenge, offered no explanation; the red sword emblazoned on their chests made it for them. Kiad's eyes widened. This couldn't be real.

"You're no gods," he whispered.

With his arm raised, he charged them, slicing one across the chest and spearing the other through the abdomen. They staggered and fell. Kiad reached down and ripped the red kerchief off one face.

"Nothing but a human."

Rage spiked through his temples. Kiad threw his head back and glared at the smoky sky. Hieronymus had done this. Hieronymus had destroyed his grand army through nothing but trickery.

"Curse you!" he hissed at the sky. "I curse you to the Isle. I curse you by the Goddess. I curse you by your own people. I curse you to die by your own hand!"

He spat on the ground. This was disgusting. All he could do was curse the man? Kiad turned around in a circle. His military strength was broken. What else could he do?

The idea had taken him before it was even fully formed. He needed Shelia Teris. She was loved by Hieronymus. With her he could hold Hieronymus captive. What a stroke of luck that Lamont had left her behind. Kiad turned about quickly. He knew the direction where Lamont's wagon lay, and the girl should've still been inside.

Kaiden opened his eyes to pain sharp as a needle poking through his head. The blood from his forehead had dried down his face, and the wagon was full of smoke.

Kaiden jerked himself fully awake. Why was the wagon full of smoke? He tried to jump out of bed, but the shackle was still about his wrist. Kaiden pulled the clasp open and rolled off the bed.

Fire burned its way across the dry field toward Kiad's camp. Kaiden's heart caught in his throat. He saw fire, and he tasted blood. It was time. New resolve grabbed him. He ran to the corner of the room and pulled the dagger from his boot. Without putting them on, he leaped out of the door into the night. He was the arm of Hieronymus. He must kill Lord Kiad.

But where was Lord Kiad? Kaiden turned in a full circle. There was no seeing anything in this smoke. Then he heard it, Kiad's voice rising above the fire.

"I curse you to die by your own hand!"

Kaiden zeroed in on the voice, and he ran at it like a hound. A few minutes later, his bare foot stepped into wetness, and he slid, stumbling onto something soft.

Kaiden drew back in revulsion. His knee rested on the body of a man. His uniform bore the red sword of the Ancients, and he'd been sliced clean across the chest.

"One of Hieronymus's soldiers," Kaiden whispered. So, the battle had already started then. How long had he slept? What if the time for his strike had already passed?

Kaiden stood shakily. He needed to take Kiad out quickly, or Hieronymus might think he was still loyal to

Kiad. He stilled his breath and listened. Through the roar of the flames, he heard Kiad muttering. He followed it.

"Where is that cursed wagon?"

Kaiden was getting closer to him now. It was easier to make out what he was saying. Kaiden felt a large drop hit him in the center of his head. Was that rain? No, not now! Rain would only obscure his vision further! There was a plop, then another. The skies were breaking.

Kaiden hurried forward. Where was Kiad? He sounded so close! Kaiden needed to do this now! His resolve was weakening. Fear was coming back to the corners of his mind.

Kiad cursed, and Kaiden's spine quavered. He was already afraid.

"Gone! How?"

Kaiden's heart dropped like a stone. He couldn't do this! Kiad would hear him coming. He would hold him off with his longsword.

But he had to do this! He had to! What other choice did he have?

Kaiden forged forward, searching. The rain was falling softly, and the smoke was clearing. Finally, he spotted Kiad, and Kiad spotted Gannon, weighed down with Shelia, who seemed to be faint.

"Stop!" Kiad roared, running at them.

Kaiden almost wet his pants. That was Teris and his sister. Was Kiad going to kill them? Kaiden forced himself into a weak-legged run. Everything in him screamed at him to run the opposite way.

Kiad grabbed Gannon's shoulder and whirled him around. Shelia screamed as he grabbed the back of her dress and hauled her out of Gannon's arms. Unencumbered,

Gannon grabbed Kiad's sword and tried to wrench it out of his hand.

"Get out of my way, boy!"

Kiad twisted his sword out of Gannon's hands, and the tip of his sword caught Gannon in the side, gashing him. Blood sprayed onto Shelia's dress. Gannon collapsed in the mud, groaning.

"No! Gannon! Gannon!" Shelia's shrill voice cut through the air. Her hands pounded against Kiad's side, and she twisted her body, trying to wrench her dress out of his grasp.

Kaiden was so close. He slipped in the mud and fell on his face. Only two steps more! Kiad's open back beckoned to him. He was completely distracted. Kaiden imagined his dagger buried to the hilt in that back. He crawled forward. Kiad had to die. He had to die now. Only one more step.

"Silence, you stupid girl! You'll bring every dog of Hieronymus down on us!"

Kaiden pulled himself to his knees. His body quivered in the rain. He must! He must!

Kaiden lunged forward and slammed his dagger into Kiad's side, between two ribs. Kiad shrieked, and Shelia fell into the dirt. He turned his head.

"*You!*"

Kaiden's mind seemed to be frozen. Kiad's eyes looked into his. But somewhere in his subconscious, the imagination took over. The dagger was only halfway into Kiad's back. It had to go in to the hilt. Kaiden pushed into it harder, and it plunged past the obstruction.

Kiad's mouth opened to say more, but he was silenced. His sword fell from his hand. He clawed at his chest as it heaved furiously for air. Kaiden closed his eyes and held on as Kiad fell to his knees and slumped face-first into the mud.

Even then Kaiden's hands stayed curled around the dagger, and he followed him to the ground. His eyes clouded, and rivers of tears slid down his face. Kaiden couldn't stop his body from shaking. His chest heaved for air, and his body curled over his lord. It was over. It was done.

Two feet away, Shelia had her arms around Gannon, crying and shaking him with no response. Hoofbeats echoed through the ground and came to a stop nearby.

Kaiden raised his head weakly. A tall man in the red sword uniform stared down at Shelia from his horse. His leg was already coming up over the side of the horse, and he jumped to the ground.

"Shelia? Shelia, you're safe! Thank the Ancients!"

Lady Teris raised her head, wiping the tears and grime from her eyes.

"Hiero?"

Hiero? As in Hieronymus Purvis? The king of Retall?

Shelia threw herself into his arms, shuddering and weeping. "Hiero! Gannon won't open his eyes! Why won't he open his eyes?" She buried her face in his chest, sobbing.

Hieronymus curled his arms around her and stroked her hair. Calmly he looked over the silent form of Gannon Teris.

"Let me see him, Shelia, please?" Hieronymus managed to disentangle her fingers from his clothes and kneeled beside Gannon. He lifted the man's head to examine him. Kaiden watched his eyes widen as he took in the bruises, the scarring, and the hole in his ear. Hieronymus shook his head. "He's gone, Shelia." There was a hint of awe in his voice. "I can barely believe it this time." Carefully he shrugged off his cloak and laid it over Gannon's body. Goodbye, brother."

Shelia only sobbed louder.

Hieronymus finally glanced across the charred stubble at Kaiden, and Kaiden released the dagger's hilt. Slowly he bowed his head.

"My name is Anias Kaiden, my king. I was recruited by a man named Hollis to be your arm against Lord Kiad."

Hieronymus nodded. He pushed himself up out of the mud and slapped the dirt from his knees. "I know who you are. I sent Hollis to find you." His voice grew husky. "Thank you for doing what you did. You saved Reta from the clutches of Lord Kiad. And you saved your future queen from his hand."

"Yes, my king."

Hieronymus beckoned with his hand. "Please stand. You don't have to be afraid of me. You're free now. And I owe you a great debt."

Kaiden stood slowly, barefoot and shivering from the wet ground and emotional trauma.

Hieronymus wrapped his arms around Shelia again. "I think all three of us need to go home."

33

EMERGENT LINE

SHELIA WOKE UP in a big four-poster bed, staring at the ceiling. Her eyes were red and swollen. Her hands slowly kneaded the puffy covers. It felt so strange. She'd never slept in a bed so soft before. She'd never woken up staring at intricate gilded ceiling tiles.

Light filtered into the room through heavy curtains that blocked off the balcony. The room smelled of smoke. Shelia didn't know if she would ever get that smell out of her nose. Her eyes welled up with tears again, and she rolled over, burying her face in a pillow to smother her sobs.

Later they would knock on the door and offer her food or another bath. Disgust welled up in her throat. She didn't want to eat. Nothing tasted good anymore. She'd only make herself ill. Was she really grieving? Did grief come with so much self-loathing and apathy? She didn't want to see Hiero. She didn't want to see anyone.

Oh, why had she fought Gannon? Why hadn't Hiero come a moment sooner? Why had that soldier struck Kiad so late?

Shelia pounded the pillow with her fist. Why hadn't she just told her father that Gannon was still alive? It was all her fault. Gannon had died because of her decisions. Shelia squeezed tears from between her lids. She was such a fool!

"Gannon!" she wept. "Gannon, where are you?"

Hiero stood in front of the mayors of Reta. It felt almost nostalgic. Like last time, he had barely slept, but his clothes were clean, and he had washed himself of the battle's grime. He stood straight and proud.

"Mayors of Reta, the attacking army has been vanquished. The lords who sought to remove me and the contenders against me are dead. Reta is victorious."

The mayors looked at one another. He knew all their names now, and he could see their thoughts on their faces. The apprentice, Grailess, who now wore the sash as the mayor of trade, nodded.

"You did it. You protected us." His eyes were wet. "I wish that my father could have seen this day."

Hiero took a small step forward. His heart pounded with excitement.

"Mayors of Reta, will you accept me as the new lord of Reta?"

The mayors stepped out of their seats and knelt on the throne room marble.

"The throne is yours, Hieronymus Purvis. You are our king."

How could he describe the rush and the sudden power that coursed through his veins? He was king. A bastard had become king of Retall.

Grailess raised his head. "We would ask of you one thing, Lord Reta: that the battlefield around Reta be cleansed before your coronation."

Hiero nodded, still giddy with excitement. "That is most reasonable. I will make that my first priority." He turned and strode quickly out of the throne room.

It was still only early morning. Mere hours had passed since he'd ridden back into Reta with Shelia and Kaiden. Both should've still been asleep. He'd been able to tell they were utterly exhausted. Shelia had nodded off against his breast as they'd ridden. She'd been shattered by the ordeal.

Hiero's gaze darkened. Lying to her was cruel, but it was necessary. Gannon had to be dead to her. He had to be dead to everyone.

Hiero met Fritz right outside the doors. He leaned stiffly against the wall.

"Well?"

Hiero spread out his arms. "I am officially the king of Reta, and if the rest of the people will have me, king of Retall."

Fritz smiled. "You did it. I didn't believe you could. One city against the might of the lords?"

Hiero shook his head. "It wasn't just me. It was the Ancients. They blessed our just cause."

Fritz looked a little dazed. "The Ancients. When I'm with you, I can almost feel them watching."

Hiero grabbed Fritz's shoulder. "We have to convince them to do more than watch! I still have the book of the Ancients' designs. We can build their weapon—their machines," he said, correcting himself. "The fire powder was only the first of the Ancients' substances achieved by men! I can lead Retall, and the whole known world, into a new future, a future of machines!" His eyes were bright. "Think of it, Fritz! Someday we might even rise into the sky and bring the Ancients back to us! Can you imagine it?"

Fritz's lips parted. His eyes took on the gaze of a spellbound child. "I will follow you, Hiero. I can't say I believe in your future yet, but I will follow you to it."

Hiero embraced him. "Thank you, my friend." Suddenly, he shook his head. "Already I'm getting distracted!"

"What do you mean?"

"The mayors of Reta asked that I withhold my coronation until the battlefield around Reta is cleaned." He gave Fritz a strong pat. "Gather men and sweep the area around Reta. All the dead must be burned. It is the Ancients' command. All those who still live but will not accept my rule must be rounded up and sent away, perhaps to one of Kiad's prisons. I haven't had a chance to think about it. They can't be allowed to threaten the throne I just earned."

Fritz nodded. He grabbed Hiero's elbow, and his voice dropped to a whisper. "What of Lamont?"

Hiero's eyes widened. "Ancients! I almost forgot him! Get a search party. He should still be unconscious near the gates." He rubbed his chin thoughtfully. "When you find him, bring him to the dungeon." Hiero gave him a look. "*Our* dungeon."

"Of course." Fritz nodded. "I'll start right away."

Kaiden fidgeted in his stiff new uniform, trying to stretch out the neck hole with a finger. He shot a nervous look at Leon and Ennis, who seemed perfectly comfortable in theirs. The royal red of Teris met the gold of House Reta across their chests, and the downward-pointing sword was embroidered upon the cloth. Hiero smiled down at the three of them from his throne as they approached. He could not have been prouder to see the uniforms finally worn. They were the symbol of a new kingdom.

The three men kneeled before reaching his throne. The room was silent for just a moment.

"Anias Kaiden, Leon Yusir, and Noch Ennis, you have my gratitude. Without your help, our victory against the armies of the lords would not have been so easily won."

Kaiden felt his face burn hot. "I was proud to be your arm, my king, and now I'm free." Kaiden flexed the muscles in his hand. He was free. For two days he had slept without fear. He had no more reason to be afraid. "I am indebted to you."

Hiero smiled. "All of you can do me no greater service than to protect those I hold most dear."

Kaiden nodded, trying not to cry. "I am honored."

"I am honored."

"I am honored." The other two repeated after him.

Kaiden closed his eyes. He finally had his freedom. This was his dream come true.

For the next five days, fires burned continuously around Reta. Unbeknownst to the people of Reta, a steady stream of wagons was heading northeast toward the Allege

Mountains. Anyone who would not give their loyalty to Hiero had to go, and the Ancients' laws would not allow him to execute them.

Hiero playfully called the prisoners "colonists." They were off to start a new city in northern Retall, but they wouldn't be coming back. Many of the lords' soldiers refused to give their loyalty to Hieronymus. The count came to several hundred.

Then, at the end of the week, Fritz stood before the door to Hiero's office. Shelia had taken up residence in Hiero's bedroom, and he'd moved his work elsewhere. Fritz took a deep breath, then rapped softly on the door.

"Come in."

Fritz turned the doorknob and stepped inside, shutting the door behind him.

"Well?"

"Hiero, we can't find him. Lamont is missing."

Hiero's jaw tightened as he looked out his window over Reta. "He escaped then."

Fritz winced. "He must have regained consciousness before we got to him."

Hiero turned around slowly. "Fritz, I know how you feel. For me, this just means he's escaped me again. He will only continue to fight against me."

Fritz gripped the cloth just above his heart. "What should we do about him?"

Hiero slapped the desk. "We have a chance. This time he has no one to turn to. His allies are gone. Find him. Follow his trail, wherever he chooses to run to, and bring him back."

Fritz snapped to attention. "Yes, my king! Right away! I'll put together another team and—"

"No." Hiero shook his head.

"No?"

"Only one man is needed to track one man. And only one man is needed to bring him to me. This needs to remain undercover. If people find out that Lamont is still alive, it could turn them against me. Go as a private citizen. No one should know that you work for me."

Fritz nodded. "I understand." He smiled a cruel smile. "I'll bring him back."

"In one piece."

"If I must."

The coronation of Hieronymus Purvis was set to take place on the ninth day of Borouse, fifty-three days after the night of destruction and the death of the old king. So much had taken place in only fifty-two days. Hiero almost didn't feel himself. Everything had changed, not only for him, but for the whole of Retall. He felt certain that nothing would ever be able to return it to the way it had been. Like in the days of the plague, the minds of men had been shifted forever.

Hiero stood at the door to his bedchamber. He had only entered it once or twice in the two weeks since Shelia had gone in. She hadn't wanted him there. She hadn't wanted his comfort.

He knocked on the door softly, then opened it, slipping inside.

"Leave me alone!" Shelia moaned, not even turning her head.

"Shelia, it's me."

Shelia curled into the corner of the bed. "Please," she whispered, "just leave me alone."

Hiero stepped farther into the room and closed the door behind him. "I won't, Shelia. I can't."

He crossed the room in three swift strides and grabbed her shoulder to turn her around. What he felt sent a shudder straight down his spine. He felt nothing but bone. Spurred by fear, he grabbed the edge of the blankets and yanked them off of her.

She had changed. Hiero's heart caught in his throat.

"Haven't you . . . haven't you been eating?"

Shelia wouldn't meet his eyes. "I wasn't hungry."

Hiero closed his eyes. He felt ill and dizzy. Shelia's arms and legs were that of an old woman, wasted away. She curled around a pillow like a little child. Hiero took a deep breath and swallowed. This was all his doing. He had to repair it. He could blame no one else.

Hiero came around the bed and knelt on the floor beside her.

"Shelia, tomorrow is coronation day. Tomorrow I'll be crowned king."

She wouldn't look at him. She squeezed her eyes shut.

"And," he continued, "your father is here. He wants to see you, and he wants to take you home."

"No!" she croaked. "I can't go home. Anywhere but there! Please just leave me alone!"

Hiero wanted to cry. There was a dryness in the back of his throat, choking him.

"I can't, Shelia. I'm sorry. I'm sending you home. I should never have dragged you into this. You don't belong here, and I'm clearly not capable of helping you through your grief. You need to be with your family."

Shelia sat up. Her eyes burned as she glared at him. "No! I won't go home! That place is a prison. If I go back there, I'll never get out! Father will force me to marry Sita!"

Hiero's fingers left little indents in the bed. "You must, Shelia. If you stay here, you'll die! Can you not see that you're starving to death?"

Shelia looked down at her hand. "I'm just not hungry," she whispered.

"You are going home. Once you are well again, if you ever wish it, we can be married, but I cannot bear the sight of you wasting away right before my eyes."

Something snapped inside Shelia's head. "I'll eat!" she shouted, her eyes wide. "If I eat, I can stay, right? Can we be married?"

Hiero's eyes narrowed. "I-I . . ." He swallowed. "Yes, if you will eat, you can stay." His hand curled around hers. "You're grieving right now. Don't think about the wedding. It can wait."

Shelia's eyes wandered over the room to the covered tray sitting on the table. "I'll eat."

Hiero bit his lip. At least she was trying. This was a good sign. He nodded to himself.

"I'll send in the serving girls to help you get ready to meet your father."

Her eyes grew fearful again, and Hiero's grip tightened on her hand.

"He just wants to see you. It's been hard for him too." Hiero stood. "I'll leave you to prepare."

Hiero sat on the very edge of the throne. His left leg bounced nervously on the marble. After all he had been through, Lord Teris still terrified him. The last memory of their time together flashed through his mind. He'd been strong. He'd told Lord Teris to leave his palace. But this was different. Hiero had never stood between Teris and his daughter before.

The door at the end of the hall opened slowly, and Hollis appeared.

"My king, Lord Teris has demanded an audience."

Hiero nodded. It was just as he'd expected. "Let him in."

Hollis stepped aside, and Teris pushed by him, striding quickly down the carpet. Hiero forced himself to stay seated. This was his throne, and he would relinquish nothing to Lord Teris.

"Good afternoon, Lord Teris." He kept his voice level and polite. "So good to see that you accepted my invitation."

Lord Teris reached the bottom of the steps before the throne and came to an abrupt stop. His arms kept swinging, as if he weren't fully in control of them.

"Was there anyone else left to accept it?"

Lord Teris's words slapped Hiero in the face. Teris wasn't angry, not really. Instead, he sounded discouraged. Was that even possible for him? Lord Teris had always had the world in his hand. The chess pieces had always been right where he wanted them. What had happened to that confidence?

He glared blankly into Hiero's face, as if he didn't even know him. "Where is my daughter?"

Hiero straightened his shoulders. To business it was.

"She has been informed of your arrival. Shelia has been in mourning—"

Teris glared. "You aren't allowed to call her so informally!" he sneered. "Dirty bastard."

Hiero bit deep into his tongue, feeling the pain shoot into his jaw. Of all the disrespectful things Teris could have said, that was the worst. He breathed out in a long, slow sigh.

"Lord Teris, I believe I must have misheard you. I am the king-to-be of Retall."

There were footsteps on the marble behind him. Slowly, Teris raised his eyes, and his lips narrowed. Behind Hiero's throne stood two men.

Leon gave a small bow. "My king, Lady Teris requests an entrance."

Hiero sat up even straighter. She had come so quickly. Lord Teris looked so relieved by the news that his shoulders drooped forward. His eyes searched the door that Ennis stood in front of.

"Let her in."

The door was opened, and in Shelia walked, a serving girl on her left, supporting her. Hiero bit the inside of his cheek this time. Before this was over, he was sure his mouth would be full of blood. In the light, Shelia looked even more pale and worn. He couldn't look at Lord Teris. He was afraid that his guilt would be written on his face.

A choked sound gurgled from Lord Teris. He took a sudden half step forward. "Shelia!"

The serving girl led her toward him, but Teris darted across the room and threw his arms around her.

"Oh, Shelia!"

The panicked look on her face melted, and Shelia curled her arm around him. "Father, I've missed you."

Teris drew back and ran his thumb across her cheekbone. "Shelia, you've been starved. Has he kept you in a dungeon?"

Shelia's eyes widened. "What? No—"

Teris whirled around before she could finish. "You

monster! You lie to my daughter for years about your love for her, you plot and scheme behind my back to murder my son, and then once you finally have what you want, you starve her like an animal!" His hand fumbled around his sword hilt as he marched toward him. "You'll pay for everything you've done to my children!"

Kaiden was the closest guard, and he jumped forward, wrapping his hand around Teris's wrist.

"I-I won't allow you." His voice was unsteady, and Teris's eyes narrowed in confusion. He twisted easily out of Kaiden's grasp.

"Your hands are soft, boy. Were you—"

"I'm a free man." Kaiden's eyes were sharp. "I won't allow you to touch my king."

Teris took a step back, chuckling. "You poor fool. You can't see that he's used you?"

Kaiden would not answer.

Teris's eyes jumped back to Hiero. "Where is my son then? Why have you not brought out my son?"

Hiero swallowed. "Did you not receive the notification of his death?"

Teris shook his head. "You told me he was dead once before. Where is he?"

Shelia's eyes were on him too. Hiero felt the burning in his chest, a sickly flame. He was burning away his guilt.

"I made a mistake last time. I believed that no man could survive a fall from the height of Reta. I was wrong. But this time he is truly dead. I saw him die."

Teris growled. "You murderer!"

Hiero hardened his face. "I would not murder my own brother!"

"He didn't do it, Father!" Shelia cringed as all eyes

turned to her. "I saw him die too. It was—" Her face twisted. "It was my fault!"

Teris's eyes bulged out of his head. "What are you talking about? You couldn't have—"

"I fought him." Shelia stared at the floor, fighting to keep in her tears. "When I got Hiero's letter, I should have gone to you. I knew what was right. I knew that you would fix it, but I was selfish! I only thought of myself." She paused. "I heard you talking to Lord Sita, and I didn't want to marry him! I convinced myself that made everything all right."

Hiero felt his heart flutter. She really believed it. Had she starved herself on purpose?

Lord Teris wrapped his arms around her again. "I accept your apology. Lord Sita is still preparing for your wedding. We can take care of that quickly, and—"

"*No!*" Shelia jerked away from his grip. "I won't marry Sita!"

Teris turned to stone. His feet were rooted to the floor, and his eyes blinked rapidly. "Wh-what?"

Shelia was surprised at her own boldness. She'd never spoken to her father like that.

"I will not be marrying Lord Sita, and I will not be going back with you. The future king of Retall, Hieronymus Purvis, has asked for my hand in marriage, and I have accepted." Her eyes flashed, and for just a moment, her weakness disappeared. Shelia felt like every scattered thought that had been crowding through her mind these two weeks suddenly came together in a rushing wave. "I will be queen of Retall. A Teris will sit on the throne of Retall again. My children will be Terises after me, and they will never be usurped." She clenched her jaw. "The Teris family will take back the throne for all time."

Lord Teris's face turned angry. "I won't allow this marriage. You're my daughter, and I know what's best for you! You're coming home."

Hiero stood from the throne. "She is Lady Shelia Teris, and she makes her own decisions. Guards, take Lord Teris to his apartment. I want him out of my city as soon as the coronation ends."

Guards around the room's perimeter jumped to obey. They placed their hands on his shoulders and led him out of the room. Hiero did not respond to his protests, and the doors slammed solidly shut behind him.

Kaiden's energy seemed to deflate right off him. Standing up to a lord like that had been difficult. Lady Shelia, on the other hand, seemed to stand taller. She gave Kaiden a curious look as he bowed.

"My lady, I am so glad to see you feeling better."

"You were one of Kiad's men."

Kaiden swallowed, expecting trouble. "Yes, I was."

Shelia's smile was sad. "Thank you for stopping that evil man. You have my gratitude."

Kaiden nodded, unsure of the proper protocol. Hiero stepped up behind him and placed his much larger hand on Kaiden's shoulder.

"Can you give us a moment?"

Kaiden nearly tripped over himself to get out of the room. "Yes, my king!"

Hiero held out his hand to hold Shelia up, and the serving girl left the room. "Shelia."

They stood there for a few moments, just looking into each other's eyes.

"Do you . . . did you . . ."

"Yes, Hiero. I want to marry you. It all makes sense now. Without Gannon, the line of the Teris family falls to me. I have to live. I have to—"

There was a rush in Hiero's ears. He hadn't thought it would be possible to actually be part of someone's house. In his mind, he had accepted that he would always be a bastard king, but with Shelia's declaration, he could be a Teris too.

Hiero hugged her so tightly that her voice cut short. "Thank you, Shelia! All I've ever wanted is to be a part of the Teris family, and now, now I can be a part of that line! I'm overwhelmed."

Hiero could feel her heart pounding through his clothes. The symbology of his flag and uniform was perfect now. The Ancients' sword wasn't just a symbol of justice; it was the symbol of the Ancients, in the red of the Teris name. The heritage of the Ancients would now be melded to the royal family of Teris.

"Hiero," she whispered, "we can make this happen. We can bring the Ancients back to Retall."

"Yes, I know! I have so much to show you now that you're here. There's this book I found, a journal, from the time of the Ancients. Well, not exactly the time of the Ancients. It was after the plague. It has detailed diagrams and—"

"Hiero, can we get married?"

"Well, of course!"

"Soon," she clarified. "Tomorrow?"

Hiero pulled back, lifting Shelia's chin. "Is that all right with you? You just came out of mourning today."

Shelia sighed. "I know. I'm ready. I want to show my father my resolve."

Hiero nodded slowly. "All right. I would love to have you by my side tomorrow. It will be special for us both then." And then he grinned, lighting up the whole room with his smile. "This means the preparation for tomorrow will have to be completely redone. The servants won't get any rest."

Shelia chuckled. "The servants? The whole of Reta will be wide-awake. You're just making excuses."

"No." Hiero grabbed her hand and placed it on his shoulder as he knelt to the floor. "Shelia Teris, I want you to be my wife and the queen of Retall. Will you join with me and bring the law and freedom back to Retall?"

Shelia smiled. "Yes. I will."

The coronation of Hieronymus Purvis and his wedding to Shelia Teris took place on the same balmy day. As predicted, when the wedding was announced, half of Reta didn't sleep through the night. In the morning, energy sparked throughout the city. Hiero and Shelia rode from the palace through the whole of Reta, coming to rest at the city council hall. The citizens of Reta lined the streets to cheer as they passed, throwing ribbons into the air. The mayors' council met them at the steps and handed Hieronymus the documents needed to surrender their power.

They passed into the hall, where the lords of Reta were waiting. All living lords of Retall were in attendance, even the child lord Fieman. But instead of following tradition and being crowned by the lords, Hieronymus was crowned by the mayors' council, showing the world that the power of choice in Retall had passed to the people.

The wedding took place in the palace courtyard directly following, with the people of Reta from every quarter crowding in to catch a glimpse. Lord Teris's eyes burned with hatred through both ceremonies, and he was shown to his carriage as soon as the streets were clear enough.

The city of Reta and the people of Retall rejoiced in their new freedom.

34

UNDESIRED JOURNEYS

WAILING CUT THROUGH the fog inside Gannon's head. It was maddening. He wanted to scream at it, but his throat felt like it was sealed shut.

With the screaming child as an anchor, he slowly pulled himself out of the mire until he could feel the shaking of the wagon underneath him. He was lying on hard wood with only a thin rag under his head. His lips opened for a low moan to escape.

His eyes opened just a sliver. The first thing he saw was red hair, as red as Hiero's. The woman it was attached to was looking away from him, and seemed to be speaking, but she could barely be heard above the cacophony. Gannon tried to block out the rest of the noise to focus on her.

"Leave him alone, Gatlin! He's sick!"

"He's dead, Joanna! It's been a whole week, and he hasn't even woken up once!"

Joanna? The same Joanna who housed Hiero? Gannon felt a hand against his side, and his eyes squeezed shut as searing pain shot through his body.

"Look at this! You think this is getting better? It hasn't changed at all."

"Gatlin, I'm warning you! If you don't stop it, you'll tear him open again!"

Gannon tried to find his voice to tell them he was alive, but his mouth was so dry his tongue wouldn't move.

"I'm putting him by the door. They can throw him out when we stop next."

"Gatlin! Gatlin, don't you dare!"

He was being lifted now. His limbs hung limp like noodles. Gannon struggled weakly. "Hey!" he croaked. "Hey!" A moment later, he was dropped back against the floor.

"Gannon! Blessed Ancients! He's awake. Look at his eyes, Gatlin!"

Another face moved into his vision, a man, a little older than himself, with a face like raw meat.

"Blessed Isle! What a lucky moment that was for you! I almost took your boots, friend!"

Joanna glared at him. "You idiot! Move aside! Gannon, it's good to see you awake. How do you feel?"

Gannon ignored her. "Where am I?"

The two looked at each other. Gatlin frowned. "We don't know where we are. We're prisoners of the bastard. That's all we know." The wagon hit a bump. "And his soldiers are taking us somewhere."

The sheer cliffs of the Allege rose up on either side of the small pass known as Sentriss. All travel and trade between Retall and Stentil took place through that pass. It was the law.

Lamont Reynard hid in a crevice, watching the two lanes of traffic pass through the guarded checkpoint. There was no way he was getting through there. He'd be captured and hauled back to Hiero in chains.

The king's signet ring brushed against his chest as he shifted positions, and Lamont grabbed it tightly in his fist. He would take back the throne of Retall. The queen of Stentil would side with him, he was sure. He just had to get to the capital.

Lamont looked up at the sheer cliffs. It wasn't just illegal to cross the Allege Mountains another way; it was dangerous. Dragons lived in these mountains.

Slowly, Lamont crawled backward on hands and knees until he was out of sight of the checkpoint. He had no other choice.